FERRARA

T L SWAN

Copyright © 2022 by T L Swan

This book is a work of fiction. Any references to real events, real people, and real places are used fictitiously. Other names, characters, places, and incidents are products of the Author's imagination and any resemblance to persons, living or dead, actual events, organizations or places is entirely coincidental.

All rights are reserved. This book is intended for the purchaser of this e-book/print book ONLY. No part of this book may be reproduced or transmitted in any form or by any means, graphic, electronic, or mechanical, including photocopying, recording, taping, or by any information storage retrieval system, without the express written permission of the Author. All songs, song titles and lyrics contained in this book are the property of the respective songwriters and copyright holders.

ACKNOWLEDGMENTS

There are a million people I need to thank, there is never enough room on the page.
To my beautiful mum, thank you for reading everything I write a million times. You are the best beta reader, the best mum and the very best friend.

To Kellie, the most wonderful PA who runs SWAN HQ, thank you for everything you do to make everything run so smoothly. I love you!

To my amazing beta team and friends, Lisa, Rena, Nadia, Rachel, Nicole and Amanda, thank you for putting up with me, I adore you all.

To my incredible editing team, Lindsey Faber, Imogen Howson and Proof reading by Kats Literary Service. Italian Translations by Alice Arcoleo.

Hang Lee my soul sister cover queen.
Thank you for making me better.

To Amazon for providing such a wonderful platform for me to publish on.

To my amazing girl gang, The Swan Squad, thank you for giving me a safe place to hang out and have fun in internet land. You really are the best friends.

To my Cygnet girls, you are a blessing that keeps on giving, you amaze me every day.

To my family, thanks for putting up with my workaholic ways, one day we will sit on a beach for longer than two hours, I promise.
I love you all so much,
Xoxoxo

And to you!
My amazing readers.
You make my dreams come true, there aren't enough words to express my gratitude to you for picking up my books.
With all of my heart,

THANK YOU
XOX

ALSO BY T L SWAN

Stanton Adore

Stanton Unconditional

Stanton Completely

Stanton Bliss

Stanton Box Set (all 4 books)

Marx Girl

Gym Junkie

Dr Stanton

Dr Stanton's Epilogue

Mr. Masters

Mr. Spencer

Mr. Garcia

The Italian

Our Way

Play Along

Find Me Alastar

The Stopover

The Takeover

The Casanova

GRATITUDE

The quality of being thankful;
readiness to show appreciation for, and to return kindness.

DEDICATION

*I would like to dedicate this book to the alphabet.
For those twenty-six letters have changed my life.
Within those twenty-six letters, I found myself
and live my dream.
Next time you say the alphabet, remember its power.
I do every day.*

FERRARA

PROLOGUE

Giuliano, aged 13.

I KICK hard and the ball goes careering into the sky, my father stops it with his foot. The afternoon sun is setting and the distant sound of an engine drones in the background. Dad lines it up and kicks it back and I in turn, stop it with my foot.

We've done this for hours most days of my thirteen years, play football in our backyard. The engine gets closer and we both turn to look out over the lake to see a luxury yacht sail past.

We read the name on the side of the boat:

Moments

"Nice," my father says. We both stand still as we watch it, there's a woman in a big fancy hat lying on the deck, she has a glass of champagne in her hand and a man is standing on the edge looking out into the water.

No matter how many times you see a luxury yacht, which is a lot on Lake Como, you never can't watch it sail past. It's tradition.

"It would have been nicer in black," I announce as I picture the yacht in another color.

Dad nods. "Or navy blue."

"Yes." I kick the ball back. "With a better name, written in gold."

My father smirks as he returns the ball with a swift kick. "What's wrong with the name, *Moments*?"

I shrug. "Bit stupid if you ask me."

He chuckles as he kicks the ball again.

"Dinner is ready," my mom calls as she walks out onto the back deck.

"Okay," my father replies, he picks up the ball and we walk toward the house, he puts his arm over my shoulder as we walk. It's Christmas Day in our house, only it isn't.

"Why do we celebrate Christmas a day early?" I ask.

His brow furrows as he looks down at me. "I have to work tomorrow, you know that."

"Every year?"

He exhales heavily. "I can't help it, son, I'm sorry." He messes up my hair and continues up the steps. "We've had a nice day today, haven't we?" He pokes me in the ribs. "And you are the most spoiled son in all of Italy."

I shrug, I could care less about the presents, I hate that he works away for half of the week. This big old house is lonely with just me and Mom here.

"I'll be back first thing on the twenty-sixth," he reassures me. "I promise."

"Can I come with you?" I ask. "I'll be quiet while you work."

Dad's eyes meet my mother's. "No, son. I don't want your mother left here alone."

I exhale heavily and continue to trudge up the stairs.

Dad takes Mom into his arms and kisses her and I roll my eyes.

These two, always kissing and cuddling. They don't leave each other alone.

"Me and Mom can both come to Milan." I smile excitedly at the idea. "Yes, can't we, Mom?" I put my arms around my mother. "That way we could all be together for Christmas tomorrow."

"Darling...." She sighs.

"Giuliano, enough," my father snaps. "Your Christmas was today. You know that. We will not have this conversation again."

My shoulders slump in disappointment and Mom gives me a sympathetic smile. All my friends celebrate Christmas tomorrow...why do we have to have it today?

Why do we have to do everything different?

We sit at the dinner table. "This looks incredible, my love." Dad smiles as he leans over and kisses my mother, he takes her hand in his and she smiles all adoringly back over at him.

He drops his head. "Father, we thank you for this food."

I watch him as he says our prayers, he will eat with us and then after we've spent time together, we'll all go to bed and somewhere in the middle of the night he will leave. Like he always does.... I hate his job, it takes him away from us so much.

I just want him to stay home.

Giuliano, aged 18.

"Pick you up in an hour," Valentino says.

"Okay." I hold the phone to my ear and glance at my watch. "I should be back by then." I walk into my wardrobe and take a pair of jeans on a hanger and throw them onto the bed.

"Where are you going, again?"

"My mom is trying to get me a job with some guy she knows."

"Yeah well, try not to get it, at least until after summer break. Fuck working all vacation, we've got plans."

I smirk in agreement. "As if he's going to hire me anyway."

"Giuliano." My mom's voice echoes up the stairs. "Lorenzo is here."

"I've got to go. See you soon." I hang up and throw on my jeans and a shirt. My mom appears at the door, she looks me up and down.

"You're wearing that?"

I look down at myself. "Yeah, why?"

"I told you to wear something nice." She brushes past me and walks into my walk-in wardrobe. "

"This *is* nice," I scoff.

She throws a pair of black pants and a collared shirt onto the bed. "Not nice enough."

"I'm not going to a funeral. I'm not wearing that." I walk into my bathroom and do my hair.

She appears at the door. "Giulio, please. For me, will you just try to be nice this afternoon. Enrico Ferrara is not someone you mess with and I really want this to work out."

I roll my eyes, unimpressed. "What makes you think I want to work for him anyway?"

"Because this is an amazing opportunity." She straightens my collar. "And...." She pauses as if choosing her words carefully. "Your father would have wanted you to work for him."

"Stop using Dad to get me to do what *you* want."

"Please?" She smiles hopefully.

I twist my lips.

"Best behavior, promise me?"

I exhale heavily. "Fine, but we are only staying for ten minutes, the boys are picking me up in an hour."

"When are you going to stop gallivanting around with your friends? It's time to take some responsibility. Today is important."

"Mom, seriously." I brush past her out into the hall. "Stop nagging me. I'm not five, I'll get my own job."

"I want you to work for Ferrara," she calls after me as I take the stairs.

Fucking hell, what is it with her and this guy?

"Let's go," I call back. "I have to be back early, I have a party on tonight."

"You always have a party on."

I widen my eyes. "Exactly my point."

We walk out and get into the back of the waiting car.

"Hi."

"Hello Giuliano, Angelina."

Lorenzo smiles happily, he was my dad's best friend. A constant in our lives since my father's death three years ago.

"It's a good day, yes?" He smiles.

"Let's hope," Mom replies. I frown over at her, why is she so wound up about this?

Lorenzo is a good friend, he stepped up and looked after my mom and me. I'm not quite sure what we would have done without him, the last few years have been hard.

He and Mom chat away as we drive and fifteen minutes later, we pull into a grand driveway. I peer in at the expansive property. Huge stone fences with a waterfront mansion in the distance.

Nice….

We pull up at a checkpoint and a man comes to the window, he dips his head and opens the oversized metal gates.

As we drive through, I look back out the rear window at the gates slowly sliding closed behind us and the guards all standing around.

Fuck, I thought our house had hard-core security, but this place is next-level. The car pulls into a circular driveway area, another group of men stand around.

What are they all doing? Do they work here, or is some kind of meeting going on? Maybe this is a group interview thing?

"Just act natural," my mother whispers.

Huh?

The door opens and a man steps back and nods. "Angelina, lovely to see you."

"Thank you, Mario." My mother smiles softly as she climbs out of the car.

His eyes find mine.

"Giuliano, it's a privilege to meet you, sir." He dips his head.

I frown, how does he know my name?

"Hello."

"This is a great day." He smiles to my mother and holds his hand toward the front door. "This way."

We walk up the huge sandstone steps and my mother

knocks on the door, I glance back to see everyone standing around watching us.

What are they all doing?

This is fucking weird.

The door opens in a rush. Large brown eyes meet mine and not the friendly kind.

I instantly feel uneasy.

"Enrico," my mother says softly.

"Hello," he says coldly as his eyes stay fixed on me.

How rude.

Who the fuck does this guy think he is?

"This is my son, Giuliano. Giuliano, this is Enrico Ferrara."

He glares at me and then puts his hand out. "Hello."

I reluctantly shake it. He's tall with dark hair, olive skin and brown eyes. He has this aura around him of power.

Animosity swims between us like a tangible force.

I get the feeling he doesn't like me and that suits me fine, because I already know that the feeling is mutual.

Rich, spoilt prick.

Like fuck I'm ever working for him.

"Please, come in." He turns and walks up the hallway and I give a subtle shake of my head to my mother, she hits my leg.

"Giulio, please," she whispers. "You promised."

I may be a lot of things, but a good actor isn't one of them. My father always said that my honesty was my greatest strength and yet, my greatest weakness.

We walk out into the kitchen area, and I lock eyes with a girl. She's around my age and has long dark hair and porcelain skin, with the most unusual eyes I've ever seen.

We stare at each other and my heart somersaults in my chest.

Who is she?

"This is Olivia." He points to a hot blond woman. "And this is Francesca, my sister."

Francesca.

My eyes flick to him, his sister...fuck it.

They all continue to talk, but Francesca and I just stare at each other as the air swirls, the physical attraction between us is palpable.

I feel hot and flustered, excited, very unlike me.

An awkward silence falls over the room.

"Francesca, why don't you show Giuliano around the property?" Enrico asks her.

She gives me a shy smile and I feel it all the way to my toes. "Okay." She gestures to the door and I follow her. We go out onto a large patio area and down some steps, then we walk out across the lawn toward the lake.

She stays silent and seems nervous, while I can't take my eyes off her.

Seriously, she's the hottest girl I've ever seen in my life. She makes me feel nervous and I'm never fucking nervous.

"Hello," I force myself to say.

"Hi."

I try to hide my delighted smile and fail miserably. "And to think I didn't want to come today."

Her brow furrows. "Why do you say that?"

"Well." Before I can stop myself, I whisper, "If I didn't come, I wouldn't have got to meet you and.... You're just so—" I shrug as words fail me, "—beautiful."

Her eyes widen as we walk down to the water's edge, we look out over the lake. "It's beautiful here." I say.

She smiles, "It is." She points to a house we can see in the distance, "I'm going to live in that pink house one day." She announces proudly. "It's my favorite house in Lake Como."

I smile as I look at the house across the lake. "It's gorgeous."

Like you.

We walk around the side of the house.

"Do you have a boyfriend?"

She gives a nervous shake of her head.

"Enrico is your brother?"

"Yes."

How have I never seen her before? "Do you live here?" I ask.

"No, I live in Milan."

We walk up the back staircase and arrive into a grand hallway. I look up and down. "How many bedrooms are there?"

"Eight."

"Where's the bathroom?"

A frown crosses her face, why did I ask that?

Where's the bathroom, is that the best you can do...seriously?

Fuck, ace it up.

"It's in here." We walk in and I look around, it's super modern and all white. A large stone bath is in the center of the room. Being alone with her in a small, confined space changes the mood between us and something comes over me as I instinctively close the door and step toward her.

"What are you doing?" She frowns.

I have no idea, but I can't fucking stop myself. The pull to her is next-level, like nothing I've ever felt before.

"I want you to kiss me."

Her eyes search mine. "I've never kissed anyone."

Fuck yeah...*she's untouched.*

I lose control of my head and cup her face in my hand. "I'm a good teacher." Before she can reply I kiss her softly. My lips brush against hers and she doesn't seem to mind, I kiss her again.

She's soft and sweet and....

Oh....

Every hair on my body stands to attention.

Fuck.

She smiles softly against me and parts her lips ever so slightly.

"That's it," I whisper. I trail my fingertips down her arms and feel the scatter of goose bumps on her skin. I take her hands, and she closes her fingers around mine.

She likes it.

We kiss again and again. "Open your lips," I whisper.

She does as she's told, and my tongue gently swipes against hers. "Oh," she murmurs as if surprised.

I smile against her. "You're a very good kisser, Francesca." I hold my forearm out. "Look, goose bumps to match yours."

She bites her bottom lip to stifle her smile. "Do you always kiss strangers in bathrooms?"

"No." I lean forward and kiss her again. "You're the first." I snake my arms around her, and we move closer together.

The blood is rushing around my body at high speed and pooling right between my legs. Her eyes widen when she feels it.

Shit, she's not this kind of girl.

What am I doing?

"I'm sorry," I apologize as I take a step back from her. "I don't know what's come over me. I can't help myself, you're just so beautiful."

She steps toward me, closing the distance. "You think I'm beautiful?"

"My God, yes." I kiss her again as I hold her tight. This time she kisses me back immediately, her hands trail up over my shoulders and I...my eyes close.

Fuck.

For someone who's never kissed before, she's doing a damn good job of it.

"Can I see you again?" I murmur against her lips.

"I'm not allowed to date."

I pull back to look at her and frown. "Says who?"

"Everyone."

"Can I call you?"

"I don't have a phone."

"What?" I screw up my face. "What do you mean?"

"I'm not allowed to have a phone." She seems embarrassed.

I stare at her in confusion. "Are you brushing me off?"

"No." She goes up onto her toes and kisses me. "I promise, I'm not allowed."

I stare at her, everyone has a phone. Is she lying?

"You have to believe me."

"Why can't you have a phone?"

"Because I have a guard with me at all times and—" She cuts herself off with a shrug.

"All the time?" I gasp.

She nods.

"Well, how am I going to see you again if you aren't allowed to date and you're always guarded?" I demand, indignant.

"Maybe you can come back and visit," she says hopefully as if a plan is taking place in her mind. "Yes. Do that. Come back over and visit my brother." She looks toward the door. "We have to go, he'll be suspicious."

I clench my jaw as I search for an answer.

Well. This sucks.

I meet the most beautiful girl in the world and I have no way of contacting her.

Just my fucking luck.

"Will you still be here if I come back tomorrow?"

"Yes."

We kiss again, it's sweet and unexpected and man…it does things to me.

I'm a hot mess down there.

I've kissed a lot of girls, none have ever affected me like this.

With one last look she walks out of the bathroom and downstairs as if totally unfazed.

I stare after her with my heart nearly beating out of my chest.

Huh?

I stand on the spot and deep breathe as I try to contain myself, I pull my shirt out of my pants to cover my hardened dick.

The fuck was that?

With shaky legs I walk down the stairs and out onto the patio where they are now sitting. Everyone turns their attention to me, and my mom glances up and smiles, I fake a smile and go up onto my toes.

This is awkward.

"Are you studying?" Enrico asks me.

"I start university in the new year."

"What are you studying?"

"Double degree, commerce and law."

"That's incredible," Olivia gushes. She turns to my mother. "You must be so proud."

"I am." Mom smiles.

Enrico's eyes hold mine and he tilts his chin to the sky as if annoyed.

What *is* this dickhead's problem?

Francesca bites her bottom lip to hide her smile and I get the feeling that she liked my answer.

"Are you still at school, Francesca?" my mother asks her.

"Yes, hoping to study interior design when I finish," she replies shyly.

I catch myself smiling goofily over at her and I snap my eyes away.

Keep it together, fool.

"We should get going, Giulio," my mother says as she stands.

So soon?

My eyes flick back to Francesca, but...I don't want to go yet. I want to get down and dirty with Francesca on the bathroom floor.

I can still taste her on my lips.

Enrico stands. "Yes, okay, I have to go into the village and pick up a few things now anyway."

We all walk out onto the front porch and Olivia bends and kisses my cheek and then my mother's. "It was so lovely to meet you both."

I like her, she's nice.

Enrico glares at me and then shakes my hand. "Goodbye." He turns his attention to my mother. "Goodbye."

So dismissive, that was an *I'm never seeing you again* kind of goodbye.

This guy is fucking weird.

My eyes find Francesca's and she smiles softly over at me, as I stand in her light, time stands still and I swear I can hear the angels singing.

She's breathtaking and not just in looks. She has this aura around her.

"Goodbye," she murmurs.

My heart hammers in my chest. "Goodbye."

We stare at each other and damn it, why is she *his* sister?

With a last wave she turns and heads back inside and I get into the car, Lorenzo gets behind the wheel and we drive away as I peer through the rear window.

The guards are all standing around as if it's a prison, perhaps it is.

As the house disappears into the distance, I feel my elation deflate.

How the hell do I contact her?

She doesn't have a phone and she isn't allowed to date.

I glance over to my mom and she smiles awkwardly. "They seem nice."

"The girls were," I reply.

Lorenzo's eyes meet mine in the rearview mirror and he gives me a stifled smile. "Enrico Ferrara is an acquired taste, you'll warm up to each other in time," he says casually.

My gaze drifts back out the window. "I seriously doubt that."

Ten minutes later we arrive home and I trudge upstairs to my bedroom and flop onto my bed in disgust. I remember Francesca and the way she kissed me and I smile up at the ceiling.

So hot.

My mind is wandering to places it shouldn't, of stealing kisses, forbidden meetings and rolling around under blankets. And if I'm completely honest, I'd be happy with a simple conversation.

But how do you contact someone who doesn't have a phone?

I sit up with urgency, yes that's it. I go to my drawers and look through, where is it? Rummaging through, I keep looking, I open another drawer and another. I know I have an old phone here somewhere, but where did I put it?

I wouldn't have thrown it out, I always keep them for a backup in case. I go to my wardrobe and, standing on a chair, I pull a box down from the top shelf. There are cords and old electrical bits and pieces and I smile as I see the target in the bottom of the box.

Bingo, a phone.

I dig the cord out and quickly roll it up and stuff both into my pocket, I grab my keys from my side table and I run down the stairs two at a time. "Mom, I have to go out and get something quickly," I call as I head for the front door.

"Are your friends here already?" she calls back.

Oh shit, I forgot they were picking me up. "Tell them I'll be five minutes if they turn up, I'll be back before they get here anyway."

"Oh, okay. What's so urgent?"

"I forgot to get some drinks for tonight," I lie.

I run out to my car and plug the phone into my car charger, and I speed down the street and pull up at the shops and run in.

"Hello, can I help you?"

"I would like to buy a new sim card and some credit for this phone please."

She types into her cash register. "How much credit do you want?"

All of it.

"Umm, fifty euros please." I glance at my watch, shit, my friends will be at my house right about now.

After some more typing on her computer, she hands over a card. "This is your sim card here." She points to a number. "This is the new phone number." She prints out a receipt. "And here is your credit, the number you type in is right here." She points to another code on the receipt.

"Okay, thanks." I pay her and run back to my car and then carefully put the new sim card into the phone and type in the credit and save the number into my phone.

Right. Ready to go.

Now to get it to Francesca...hmm, how the hell do I do that? Enrico said he was going into town, let's just hope that's true. I drive back to the house and park out on the street, I sit in my car for a moment as I stare through the large metal gates at all the security guards standing around.

This could go bad, real fucking bad.

With a deep steeling breath, I get out of my car and walk up to the gates.

"Hello," the guard says.

"Hi, I was just here and I left my phone inside the house," I lie.

The guard looks to his colleague and the second man nods. "Yes. This is Giuliano. Let him in."

The man opens the gates. "My apologies, Mr. Linden."

"That's okay." How do they all know my name?

Stay calm.

I walk up the long driveway and past at least fifteen men and up to the front door, I knock as my heart hammers in my chest.

The door opens and I come face-to-face with Olivia. "Giuliano." She smiles in surprise.

"Sorry to bother you."

"Enrico isn't here, he's gone into town."

"That's okay, I think I left my phone here."

"Oh." She stands back, granting me access. "Come in." She looks up the stairs. "Francesca," she calls.

Francesca comes to the top of the stairs and her face falls as she sees me.

I stare up at her in awe, seriously, this girl is ridiculously hot.

"Giuliano left his phone here; did you see it?" Olivia asks.

Francesca's eyes widen. "Umm."

"I think I left it on the table upstairs," I say.

Francesca opens her mouth to say something, but no words come out.

She can't lie...oh, I like that about her.

"Help him look, will you?" Olivia asks.

"Yes, of course," Francesca mumbles.

I take the stairs two at a time and Francesca turns and follows me up the hall. "What are you doing?" she whispers.

I dig the phone and charger out of my pocket and hold it out to her.

She stares at it in my hand. "What's this?"

"It's a phone."

Her eyes widen.

"This way I can text you, you just need to charge it up. I've got you a new number and there is credit on it, my number is already saved."

She bites her lip as if not sure what to do and I hold it out to her again. "Do you want to speak to me or not?" I prompt.

Her eyes rise to mine. "Of course, I do."

"Then take it, don't show anyone. Keep it hidden."

She quickly takes it from me, and we hear Olivia coming up the stairs. Francesca stuffs the phone and charger underneath a cushion on the armchair and stands up guiltily.

"Found it," I call as I walk back toward the stairs just as Olivia reaches the top, I hold my phone up. "Sorry for the inconvenience."

"No problem." Olivia smiles. "Glad you found it."

I walk back down the stairs and to the front door.

"Goodbye, Giuliano," Olivia says.

"Goodbye." I glance up to the top of the stairs and lock eyes with Francesca, an unspoken message passes between us and she gives me a soft smile. Feeling proud of myself, I bounce down the front steps.

Nobody gets to tell her who she can and can't talk to.

Nobody.

The party music echoes from inside and I take my phone out of my pocket and check it.

Two a.m., no texts, no missed calls.

Unimpressed, I roll my lips and put it away.

A loud laugh sounds over near the bar and I glance over, beautiful, scantily dressed girls are everywhere, along with every doe-eyed man in town.

But I don't want to be here.

Not in the least, I would rather be at home talking on the phone to her.

If she would just fucking call me already.

"Mia is looking exceptionally hot today," Alex whispers.

I glance up and my eyes sweep up and down the girl he talks about. "I guess."

"There's no guessing," Valentino chimes in.

Right on cue, Mia looks up and smiles over at us. As if feeling suddenly brave, she walks toward us.

"Ugh," I mutter under my breath as I sip my beer.

Val bumps me with his shoulder. "The fuck is wrong with you?"

"Hi, Giuliano," she breathes.

"Hello." I force a smile.

"I didn't see you last weekend, Giuliano. I thought you would have been at Pria's party for sure."

"I had something on," I lie. Well, it's not technically a lie. I *was* on a date with another girl.

"What a shame," she replies. "I only went to that party in hope to see you."

"Sorry to disappoint." I smirk. "You'll have to make it up to me."

"I'll see what I can do." I lift my beer to her in a silent salute.

She bites her bottom lip with a sexy smile. "Do you want to dance?"

I glance inside to the dance floor. "No. Not yet, maybe later. I want to hang with my friends for a while."

"Oh." Her eyes flick to my two friends.

I grab her hand and lift it. I kiss her fingertips. "I'll come and find you later, hey?"

"Um, okay." She smiles sexily before sauntering off through the crowd.

Alex and Valentino stare after her and I continue to drink my beer. Their attention comes back to me.

"What?"

"How the fuck do you get all the hottest girls?"

I shrug.

"Seriously, I mean. You're not even nice to them." Val rolls his eyes.

I shrug again as I pull my phone out and check it again. *Call me, fuck it.*

"Did you see her?" Alex sighs. "Fucking hell, that body." He pretends to wipe his forehead.

I glance around at my surroundings, same people, same girls. Nothing exciting or new. "I'm going to get going." I announce.

"What?" Val frowns. "It's only early."

I shrug. "I'm bored."

"What about Mia?" Alex gasps.

"Meh." I shrug. "Zero interest." I drain my beer. "You should go for it."

They both stare at me as if I'm stupid and I put my beer bottle onto the counter. "Catch you both later."

"Are you serious?"

"Completely, bye." I make my way around the side of the house.

"Giuliano." I hear a voice from behind me. I turn to see Maria and I inwardly wince. "Hi."

"Where are you going?"

"To get some more drinks from my car."

"You didn't call me."

"I...." I pause as I try to think of an excuse. "I lost your number, sorry."

"Oh." She smiles hopefully. "Well.... Thankfully, I can give it to you again."

"Thankfully." I fake a smile and look out onto the street. "I'm just getting some drinks for my friends, back soon."

"I can't wait."

I widen my eyes. "Me too." I walk toward the street as fast as I can. I hear another girl call my name. "Giuliano." I roll my eyes in disgust.

Fuck.

I put my phone to my ear and pretend I'm speaking to someone and ignore the voice. I keep walking up the road and into the darkness.

As the music and laughter echoes in the distance from behind, I feel a strange detachment. Everything I should want is at that party, and yet nothing there interests me in the slightest.

I don't know what I want, but I do know it isn't here.

I dig out my phone and check it again.

Francesca Ferrara.

Call me, fuck it.

1

Francesca

I STARE at the phone in my hand, "Just call him already," Anna says from her place on my bed. "I can't believe you haven't called him yet, it's been five days. He's not going to wait forever, you know?"

"Exactly my point." I slip the top off my empty shampoo bottle that I'm now using as a secret phone safe and put the phone back in its hidey spot. I screw on the lid and put it back in my bathroom cabinet.

"And what stupid point would that be?" she scoffs.

"He's a player, Anna, what's the point of starting something up with a heartbreaker who we both know isn't going to wait for me to be allowed to date."

"You don't know he's a player."

"What kind of guy kisses a girl in the bathroom of a house tour and then sneaks her in a burner phone?"

"The hot kind."

"I already know how this will go."

She rolls her eyes. "And how is that?"

"I'll fall for him and he will be out partying with every girl in town while I stay at home, for which he will have the perfect excuse because I'm not allowed out. And to be honest, I wouldn't even blame him. Who wants to see a girl that you can't even see?"

"Seriously, your brothers need to lighten up. You're seventeen for fuck's sake."

"I know." I flop onto the bed beside her and we both stare up at the grand ornate ceiling, lost in our own thoughts. Anna and I've been best friends since the first grade, she knows me better than anyone. Her parents knew my parents from when they were young so there have never been any issues with me going to her place, I stay there often and she stays at mine. She's an only child and with my brothers being so much older, I may as well be. We have bedrooms at each other's places.

She's allowed to do a lot more than I am and yet, never once, has she made me feel left out.

"You should call him." She sighs.

"Maybe."

"I mean, if even just to return his phone. It's probably worth a lot of money."

"But if he wanted to talk to me, why hasn't he called or text me?"

"Because for all he knows, the phone may have been found by Enrico or something. He has no idea what's going on over here."

"True. Hmm, I hadn't thought of that." We fall silent for a while.

"Are you going to call him?"

"I'll text him."

She sits up in excitement. "Do it now."

Nerves hammer in my chest. "No, later."

"No, now."

"Tomorrow night, that way I know he'll be home."

"How do you know he'll be home?"

"Well, it's Monday night and nobody does much on a Monday night, do they?"

"True." Anna takes my hand in hers. "What are you going to say?"

Fear overwhelms me, I get the feeling that a lot of girls would message him every day. "God knows."

It's late on Monday night, I'm home alone, my mother has gone to my grandmother's with Lorenzo, I want to do it, but I don't want to do it. Unfortunately, I know that there is no way around this, I close my eyes and hit send.

Hi

A reply bounces straight back.

Can I call you?

My eyes widen. Oh fuck…umm. Shit, shit, shit. I think for a moment.

Nobody is home, I guess this is the perfect time. I type.

Okay

The phone instantly vibrates, and I jump out of bed and begin to pace, oh my God.

What do I do?

Answer it, you idiot. I go to answer it and fumble and drop the phone.

Ahhhh...

"Hello," I answer, my voice sounds high pitched and nervous, I scrunch my eyes shut.

Act cool.

"Hi." His voice is deep and raspy and it instantly makes my stomach flutter, how is he so hot? "Took your time," he says.

Huh?

I open my mouth to say something.

"What the hell, Francesca, I've been waiting for seven fucking days for you to call. Talk about making me sweat."

I smile, surprised by his lecture. "I've been busy."

"Doing what?"

Thinking about you.

"Schoolwork," I lie. I screw up my face, why did I say that? Now I sound boring.

"Not a good enough excuse."

I feel my cheeks heat as I blush, just the sound of his voice sends me giddy. "What have you been doing?" I ask.

"Thinking about you."

What?

I begin to pace back and forth in my bedroom. "What about me?"

"The way you kiss."

I smile goofily at my reflection in my mirror. *Is this really happening?*

"What about it?" I try to act casual. "I'm sure you've kissed a million girls."

"None like you."

Silence hangs on the line between us as I try to think of something to say.

"Have you thought about me?" he asks.

"No."

"Tell me the truth."

"Maybe," I snap way too fast.

"Good."

"Why is that good?" I whisper.

"Because it's only fair, I think about you all day and I dream about you all night." My eyes widen. "What do you dream about?" I whisper.

"Kissing you."

I smile goofily.

"Among other things," he adds.

"What other things?"

"I don't think you could handle my thoughts at this stage."

I bite my bottom lip as nerves dance. "What is this stage?" I ask.

"The getting-to-know-each-other stage."

I smile shyly and I don't know what else to say without sounding geeky. "I should get going, it's late."

"So soon?"

The line falls silent.

"Can I call you tomorrow night?" he asks.

"Umm." I shrug, surely that wouldn't hurt. It is just talking. "If you want."

"Text me when you get into bed and I'll call you to say good night."

"Okay."

We fall quiet again.

"Good night, sweet Cheska," he whispers.

I smile an over-the-top smile, he called me by my childhood nickname, everything with him just feels so natural. "Good night, Giuliano."

"You can dream about me tonight if you want."

I giggle and he laughs too.

"I'll think about it." I smile.

I hang up the phone and twirl in excitement and flop down onto my bed. No need to think about it, I already know I will.

The last six weeks have been a whirlwind of flutters and blushing and goose bumps in the dark.

Is it really possible to fall in love with someone over the phone?

I would have thought not, but now.... Maybe.

Giuliano and I text all day and whisper to each other for most of the night, every day now for six weeks.

He's never not called me, not even on weekends when he's out. And while he's out living his best life, he's explaining things to me as he does them.

A running commentary of his life.

He's unlike anyone I have ever known, funny, sweet and intelligent and open. So unlike the men in my family.

I've been thinking about this a lot and I think that perhaps it's because his mother is English, he's been brought up very differently to me. He doesn't live the stereotypical Italian lifestyle.

In my house, the men have always been treated differently. They have their freedom, they have the power, and the women are seen as fragile things of beauty that need protecting.

But in Giuliano's house, his mom was the boss. She ruled

the house, unfortunately his father has passed, but apparently when he was alive, he was sweet and kind and hopelessly in love with his mother.

Just like my Giuliano.

I think back to when my father was alive, I don't remember much but I do know that he was absent a lot. He worked away, but even when he was home, he and my mother hardly spoke. I don't ever remember them kissing or showing any affection for each other. They were nice to each other, sure, and they didn't fight. And the weird thing is, I never even realized it was like this, I thought this was normal until I hear Giuliano talk about his parents and the grand love that they had for each other.

One day I want that life, a heart filled with love and laughter. Deep and meaningful friendship that will last a lifetime.

I don't care about the Ferrara money and power, and the more my darling Giuliano educates me on another way of life, the more I'm determined to have it.

It's funny the things that stick with you, Giuliano once told me how his father loved his mother the most when she had no makeup on and was wearing a tracksuit. They would lie around on the couch and watch movies together.

I can't stop thinking about that weird piece of information, it seems so bizarre, my mother is dressed to the nines and wearing sky-high stilettos every day, I don't know if I've ever seen her in a tracksuit—in fact, I know I haven't.

The only thing my parents did together was go to church and family gatherings.

I get a particular vision of the two of them arriving at a gala ball one night, I was in the car in front of them, Dad was in a black dinner suit and was holding the car door open for her as she climbed out in her beautiful cocktail dress.

All eyes were on her, but his eyes were on me and my brothers, as if he didn't even notice her. Bianca Ferrara is a beautiful woman, everyone knows it.

But did my father?

Thinking back, I really don't think so, and it makes me sad that she never got that with her husband.

I'm glad my mother has now found happiness. Lorenzo was my father's closest friend, a widower. When my father and grandfather were killed in the car accident, Lorenzo came to stay at our house to care for us, he never left. Over time, he and my mother's friendship grew and blossomed into something deeper.

I already loved him, he was like a second father to me and my brothers. I like seeing my mother finally happy and I'm glad it's with an honorable man like Lorenzo. I know my father would approve, how could he not?

My phone vibrates in my hand and I smile into the darkness. "Hi."

"How's my girl?"

"Still yours."

"She better be," he whispers.

Just the sound of his voice makes me feel happy. "Do you know what day it is?" I ask him.

"Monday," he replies and I can tell he's smiling.

"It's six weeks today since we first spoke."

"Feels like six years."

"It does, doesn't it." I'm not joking, it really does. I can't even remember what I used to do before we spoke.

"I need to see you," he says softly.

My heart drops, because I know that it's not a possibility. The problem with having money is that your family is a target. I'm guarded at all times, never left alone even for a minute.

"Did you ask your mother?" he asks.

"Yes."

"And?"

"She said I'm too young to date."

"You're seventeen, Francesca." He exhales heavily.

"I know."

He stays silent and my heart constricts. I don't want to lose him, and yet, I know that I will if I can't find a way for us to meet up. What nineteen-year-old boy wants a pen pal for a girlfriend.

"I'm just going to man up and come and knock on your front door in Milan."

"Don't."

"What would happen? What's the worst that could happen?"

"My brother will kill you."

"Who, Enrico? He doesn't scare me."

"He should."

"You're overthinking this."

"No, Giuliano, trust me, you are underthinking this. If they get suspicious that I'm seeing someone they will tighten the noose around my neck even more."

"You haven't seen me."

We fall silent.

Eventually I whisper, "Are you angry?"

"Disappointed."

"I know, baby," I whisper. "Me too."

"I'm tired, I'm going to go." He sighs. "I'll call you tomorrow."

My eyes well with tears, this is the first time he's ever wanted to get off the phone. "Okay," I whisper.

"Good night, Chesk."

"Good night, Jules."

We stay silent on the line, waiting for the other to say something to fix it, but there is no fix to this.

He will move on, and how could I blame him?

Six weeks is a long time to invest in someone who he will never get the chance to meet up with.

"Dream of me," I whisper hopefully.

"Always do."

The phone clicks as he hangs up and deflated, I stare at it in my hand for a while.

I shower and sadly climb into bed. I've met the man of my dreams and now I'm going to have to endure him slowly withdraw from me.

If only my family just knew what an amazing person he is, I'm sure they would grow to love him.

I need to fix this, if we can't meet in the open, what about…? We could meet in secret? But how?

I'm only allowed to a few places: Anna's, the library…my eyes widen. Of course, why didn't I think of that before?

The library.

I dial his number, he answers first ring. "What's wrong?"

"Can you come to Milan?"

"What?"

"I'm allowed to go to the library, if you get there before me and hide while my security do their checks, I can see you."

"They don't stay in the library with you?"

"No, they do their check and then wait outside. Could you hide for ten minutes in the bathroom or something. I mean, I don't know how it would work but…."

"I could."

"When?" I ask.

"Tomorrow."

So soon. "It's risky, Jules, what if they catch us?" I whisper.

Ferrara

"Five minutes together will be worth it."

The car pulls into the parking lot of the Milan public library and I close my eyes.

Shit.

My two guards climb out of the front seat and Antonio opens my car door. I peer out with trepidation.

Oh hell.

What am I doing?

They're going to catch us and then they're going to beat Giuliano to a pulp and he will get the blame, when really, this was all my fault.

I glance up at the building in front of us, is he in there? I couldn't even bring my phone in case it's found. I stalled at home as long as I could to give him enough time.

What if he hasn't hidden yet?

Fuck.

"Everything alright, Miss Ferrara?"

"Uh-huh." I fake a smile and climb out. "Thank you, Antonio."

We walk up the grand steps and through the double doors and into the main hall and study area and I see Anna sitting in the corner at one of the long tables. I made her come as a decoy, she has textbooks open and looks the studious part. My eyes dart around in search.

No sign. Thank God, he's hidden.

I wave and make my way over and sit down. "Hello." I smile, I open my textbook and get out my pens and notebooks. My heart is hammering hard in my chest, and this is undoubtedly the scariest thing I have ever done.

Antonio walks around the library as he does his check while Hugo goes back to wait out the front.

"Is he gone?" I whisper to Anna.

She watches Antonio over my shoulder. "Not yet." Her eyes widen.

"What?" I stammer.

"Oh shit." She puts her hand over her heart. "I thought he was going into the men's bathroom."

That's where Giulio is hiding. "Did he?"

"No, he's heading toward the door."

I hold my forehead and slump into my chair. "Fuck, I'm so nervous."

"About seeing him or getting caught?"

"Both."

Anna giggles as she looks toward the door. "I'm going to go and check that the coast is clear."

My scared eyes hold hers.

"Will you relax, you look like you saw a ghost," she whispers as she walks over to one of the big windows looking out over the street, she peers out and then returns to the table.

"What's happening?" I whisper. "What are they doing?"

"Antonio is on his phone and Hugo is leaning up against the car having a cigarette."

I nod, feeling a little better. "Okay."

Anna takes out her phone, she texts.

The coast is clear

I feel my underarms begin to heat as nausea rolls my stomach. "What if he doesn't like me?" I whisper.

"There's no chance of that, have you seen yourself?" she says as she watches the men's bathroom door.

"I can't even look," I whisper as I stare straight ahead. "I swear to God, I'm about to throw up."

Her eyes widen and she gasps.

"What?"

"Is that him?"

I nervously look over my shoulder and see Giuliano walking toward us, he's wearing blue jeans and a black T-shirt with a navy cap pulled down to cover his face.

He's tall, broad and muscular.

I don't remember him being this hot. "Yes," I squeak.

"Holy fuck, he's gorgeous." She swoons.

My heart hammers so hard it's about to escape from my chest. "This is a bad idea."

"This is a great idea." She smiles at him as he approaches. "Drag him into an office and have your wicked way with him."

I hit her leg. "Will you be serious?"

"I am."

"Francesca," a deep voice says from behind me. I look up into the most beautiful brown eyes I have ever seen.

Oh....

We stare at each other for a moment. "Hi," I whisper.

The air crackles between us and he gives me a slow sexy smile.

Anna interrupts our moment. "Hello, I'm Anna."

His gaze shoots up as if remembering his manners. "Hello, I'm Giuliano." He shakes her hand. "Piacere di conoscerti." (Translation: Nice to meet you.)

Anna smiles goofily up at him.

Italian.

He spoke to her in Italian.

We only ever speak in English.

He pulls out the chair beside me and sits down, he unpacks

books onto the table to look the part. I can feel the warmth coming from his close proximity and I hear my pulse in my ears. I've never been this nervous in my entire life.

"Hello," a voice says, we look up to see another boy, he has brown hair that has a bit of a curl to it and big lips and holy shit...*who is this?*

"This is Valentino, my best friend," Giuliano says.

"I'm the wingman." He smiles. "Call me Val."

Anna's eyes widen as she and he stare at each other, he gives her a slow sexy smile as he holds his hand out to shake hers.

I smirk as I watch the blood drain from Anna's face, she nervously drags her hand through her hair. "Hello, I'm Anna."

"Nice to meet you."

Giuliano takes my hand in his and pulls it over onto his leg under the table, his quad muscle is large and hard. His hand sits over mine and is big, warm and soft, it exudes power. Anna glances down, her eyes widen with excitement and I swallow the lump in my throat.

Jeez.

Let's get right to it then.

I feel faint.

"Let's leave them to it," Val says as he gestures to another table. "Shall we, Anna?"

Anna's eyes flick to mine and I try to hide my smile. *Who's nervous now, bitch?*

"That would be great," Giuliano replies. "Behave, Val."

My eyes widen. Huh? Where are they going? Are they just going to leave me here with him all alone?

Oh hell.

What if I mess this up? Which is completely possible because I have literally no idea what on earth to say.

Anna picks up her books and moves her things to another

table in the far corner and I watch as she and Val sit down and start talking as if they've known each other for ages.

Why am I so awkward?

I bite my lip as I feel the blood drain from my face.

"Don't be nervous," he whispers.

My eyes meet his, how does he know?

"Your hand is shaking," he replies as if reading my mind.

"Oh." God, I inwardly kick myself. "Sorry."

Giuliano smiles over at me and I feel my cheeks heat, he's just so....

"You know—" he tucks a piece of my hair behind my ear, "—I remembered that you were good looking. But I didn't realize you were this beautiful."

Same.

I stay silent, unsure what to say. We stare at each other for a moment and there's this otherworldly energy between us. It's like he's magic or something, every cell in my body is drawn to him.

"Where's my Francesca that talks my ear off every night?" he asks.

I break into an embarrassed smile. "Not feeling so brave now, I'm afraid."

"It's only me," he whispers.

My heart swells, *only him* is incredible.

He goes to lift my hand above the table and I push it against him. "Someone will see us."

He twists his lips, unimpressed.

"I'm sorry, it's just that...."

"I get it." He cuts me off.

Damn, I've ruined it already.

"Come find me," he whispers.

"Huh?"

He gets out of his chair and walks over to the rear of the library and goes up the spiral staircase that leads to the upper level. I watch him disappear up the stairs with my heart in my throat and I know that I have two options.

Follow him, or stop seeing him altogether, because this is ridiculous. I can't ask him to meet me and then play hard to get. I look over to Anna, she gives me her best evil eye and points to the stairs. "Go," she mouths across the room.

Crap.

She thinks I should go too.

Okay, *you can do this.*

With my heart hammering so hard in my chest that I can hear it, I wait a few minutes and after looking left and right, I slowly make my way up the winding stairs. Every step, I feel a little more nervous. A little closer to being caught.

I arrive at the top floor, shelving and books are everywhere, there are tables and chairs and lounges, much similar to downstairs only a little darker, the lighting is dimmer. It's deserted and actually quite nice, it feels cozy and intimate. I've never been up here before.

Maybe we should sit up here next time.

Next time.

If you fuck this up, Francesca, there won't be a next time.

My eyes roam through the shelves and around the level, I can't see him. I walk to the front windows and peer out onto the street below, Antonio's car is just out of sight.

Damn it.

Making my way through the shelving, I arrive in a back corner and then I feel my hair being swept to the side from behind, I stop still and feel his breath on my neck.

"Cheska," he whispers.

I close my eyes and his lips dust my ear, goose bumps scatter all over my skin.

"We're finally alone, baby."

I force myself to turn and he smiles down at me, his eyes are big and brown, his jaw is square, and he is undoubtedly the most handsome boy I've ever seen, my heart stops.

Oh....

"It's your turn to kiss me this time," he breathes.

I don't even know what I'm doing.

"Remember how I taught you?"

Not really.

He takes my hands in his and leans in, we stand cheek to cheek.

"Do you even want to?" he asks.

I nod, and before he can reply I stand up on my toes and kiss his lips, he smiles against me. "That's it." I take his face in my hands as my lips linger over his.

His hands slide down to my waist and we kiss again, longer this time.

With a little suction...and so much want.

His tongue slowly slides into my parted lips, and I smile against him. "You like that, angel?"

I nod shyly.

"Do you like this?" He kisses me deeper, my eyes close as his tongue dances seductively against mine, it does things to me as I begin to feel my pulse between my legs.

My hands slide up over his muscular back and shoulders as we really kiss and damn my security guards. This is worth the risk of being caught, I don't even care anymore.

I don't want to be the little girl my family demands of me anymore.

I want to be a woman for him.

Suddenly, I'm desperate, I push him up against the wall and kiss him harder.

"Fuck yeah." He smiles against me and I can feel his erection as it pushes up against my stomach.

Euphoria runs through me, excited that he's excited. I love the feel of his hardened body up against mine, I love that I've done this to him. I slide my hand down over it in his jeans, I can feel the outline, it's big.

I want to know more.

Our kiss turns frantic, it's like our lives depend on it, because at this moment this is all we have.

We stumble to the side and he pulls back, panting. And if I'm not mistaken, shocked.

"What are you doing?" he whispers.

"Kissing my boyfriend, what does it look like?"

"You want.... You.... Want." He swallows a lump in his throat as he trips over his words. "You want me to be your boyfriend?"

Oh crap, now I've done it. What did I say that for?

Unable to stop myself, I nod as I rub my hand up over his dick. Who even am I? He's turned me into a sex-starved animal.

"Jesus, Chesk," he whispers.

"Yes. Or no?"

He takes my face in his hands and stares down at me. "Then it's a fucking yes."

We kiss as we smile against each other, and he looks around and then takes my hand and pulls me into the bathroom.

He locks the door behind us and suddenly in the small space the air between us crackles. There's a bench seat he sits down on and straddles my legs over him.

We stare at each other as our most private parts touch.

"Teach me more," I whisper.

He looks up at me in awe and slides his hand up under my dress and grabs my behind, he begins to rock me over his dick.

Back and forth. Back and forth...and the feeling begins to grow between us.

Closeness, tenderness, but more than anything.

Desire.

Then he slides his finger under the leg of my panties, we stare at each other as his fingers explore me there.

"You're so wet," he murmurs.

Oh no.

"Is that bad?" I whisper.

He smiles, amused by my innocence. "No, baby. That's good." His lips softly take mine as his finger slowly slides inside of me and I whimper into his mouth.

"Oh...."

He begins to slowly work me and I shudder as I hold my breath.

For the love of all things holy....

I see stars.

He puts his lips to my ear. "You're not as innocent as you make out." He bites my neck and I smile bashfully, maybe he's right? I sure don't feel innocent right at this moment.

"Only for you."

He pumps me hard as if losing control. "That's right, only for me."

Knock, knock, sounds abruptly on the door. "Francesca," the voice snaps.

Our eyes widen in horror, Antonio.

2

Francesca

I jump off his lap and Giuliano pulls my dress down and smooths it.

"Yes," I call.

"Is everything alright?" Antonio asks.

Giuliano puts his finger to his lips to signify silence.

I wave my hands around in a panic. "I'm not feeling well."

"Can I...."

"I'll be out in a moment." I cut him off. "I would like some privacy, please. I'll meet you out the front, we should go home."

"Okay."

I put my head into my hands in dismay, my body is still pumping with arousal.

"It's okay, just go out there and act natural," Giuliano whispers as he straightens my hair and kisses me softly. "Call me when you get home."

I nod sadly as my eyes fill with tears.

His face falls. "What's wrong?"

"I just wanted ten minutes alone with you," I whisper.

"I know." He kisses me softly. "Me too." He turns me toward the door. "But now, you need to go." He stands behind the door and I steel myself. I walk out and close the door behind me and I hear him flick the lock. I storm down the stairs and glance over at Anna who is now back sitting at our original table, she looks like she is about to pass out. I walk over and kiss her cheek. "I have to go."

"Did you get caught?" she whispers.

"No."

She puts her hand over her chest. "Thank God."

"I wish I did," I whisper angrily as I pack up my books. "I just wanted to be alone with him, is that too much to fucking ask. I'm running away."

"What?"

"You heard me. I'm running away."

"You can't run away, what are you talking about?"

"Well, I can't live like this. Prisoners get more freedom than I do."

"I'm sorry," she says sadly. "This is so crap."

"Where's Valentino?" I ask as I look around the library.

"He's gone up the other set of stairs in case Giuliano needed him." She smiles goofily and widens her eyes. "Ahh, forget to mention how hot his fucking friend is, didn't you?"

"I didn't even know he was coming," I gasp. "What were you two talking about, anyway?"

"I don't remember, he was talking and I was too busy staring at him to reply."

I smirk. "Can you wait for Giuliano and see if he's, okay?" I whisper, "He's locked in the bathroom upstairs."

"Okay."

"Thanks." I bend and hug her and then make my way to the front door, Antonio is waiting and I glare at him and storm past toward the car. "Is everything alright?" he asks as he follows me.

"I would just like two minutes' peace, Antonio, without you following me everywhere. I was in the bathroom, for Christ's sake," I snap.

"Just doing my job, Miss Ferrara."

I turn toward him, infuriated. "Do not enter this library again. Do you hear me? Unless you hear me scream, I don't want to see you."

He steps back, surprised by my venom. "It has never bothered you having security before."

"Well, it bothers me now." I open the car door and get into the back seat and slam the door hard.

The two guards get into the front seat and drive off into the night. Through tears I stare out the window as the scenery flies by.

I'm not joking…I am running away.

I want to be with him.

It's late at night and I lie in bed with tears running into my ears.

I'm embarrassed.

Ashamed that my own family don't trust me enough to date. I'm not asking for the world, I just want to be normal.

I'm seventeen.

I think of my beautiful Giuliano and how understanding he's been and how he deserves so much better. I picture his face when I left him, flushed with arousal.

Hiding in a fucking library bathroom while we make out… it's pathetic.

My body is still throbbing from his touch.
I need more. More of everything, but most of all, him.
A text comes in, the tenth one tonight.

Call me

And say what?
I'm sorry I left you in the bathroom? I'm sorry you're dating a child.
Another text.

**I'm getting worried, Chesk
Call me please.**

I exhale heavily and dial his number.
"Hey," he answers softly.
Hearing his voice instantly brings tears to my eyes and I angrily wipe them away. "I'm sorry," I whisper.
"What's wrong, are you crying?" he whispers.
"I hate this." I sob.
"It's okay, baby. Don't cry."
"How can I not, Giuliano, I'm so embarrassed."
"About what?"
"You know what."
"About what we did?"
"No, not that," I scoff.
"What are you talking about?"
"What must you think of me being treated like a child?"
"Francesca." He sighs. "It's okay."
"I'm running away."
"No. You're not."
"Yes. I am."

He stays silent for a moment. "I can't run away yet, I need my university degree to support us."

My mouth falls open in surprise. "You would come with me?" I whisper.

"Well, you aren't going without me."

I smile through tears.

"Anna and I have come up with a plan," he says.

"A plan?" I frown.

"I'm going to sneak into Anna's house on the weekend."

"What?"

"You're staying there, right?"

"Yes."

"And her parents are away."

"But her grandmother is staying, my guards sit outside all night, there's no way in," I stammer.

"If Anna keeps her grandmother busy and I get there before you do, I could hide in your bedroom."

My eyes widen, a whole night with him would be a dream. "But...what if we get caught?"

"It will be worth it."

I bite my bottom lip as I listen to his plan unfold.

"I'd do anything to be alone with you," he whispers.

"Me too."

We fall silent for a while.

"Giuliano," I whisper.

"Yes."

"Do you think it's possible to fall in love with someone you hardly know?"

"I wouldn't have thought so before...but now...maybe I do."

I smile hopefully.

"Good night, my beautiful Cheska," he whispers. "Dream of me."

Always do.

My eyes well with happy tears. "Good night."

Saturday night, I glance over my shoulder to my guards, I give them a wave and walk up the front steps of Anna's house, she opens the door in a rush. "Hi."

I force a smile. "Is he here?" I whisper.

"Uh-huh," Anna smiles as she pulls me inside. "Safe and sound waiting for you upstairs. He's been here for over an hour."

My God....

"Where's Grandma?" I ask.

"Watching a movie downstairs."

"Do you think she suspects anything?" I whisper as I take off my coat and hang it up.

"Nope, I left a key out for him and then she and I took the dog for a walk and he snuck in while we were gone. I've disarmed the cameras, so we are all good," Anna whispers in a rush.

Butterflies dance in my stomach. "Thank you." I hug her, sneaking my boyfriend into her house so that I can spend some time with him really is next-level friendship. "What would I do without you?"

"Shrivel up and die I expect."

"No doubt." I smirk as we walk through the house and down to the basement where Grandma has her little apartment for when she stays. "Hi, Grandma," I say.

Violet smiles over at me. "Hello, Francesca, how are you, dear?"

"Good, thanks." I kiss her cheek and glance up at the television. "What are you watching?"

"*Atonement*. Have you seen it?"

"No."

"It's great, you should watch it."

"Maybe we will later tonight." I look up to Anna for some guidance. "Should we get started on our assignment?"

"Yes, okay, we have so much work to do, going to be at it all night."

"You girls run along, dinner is in an hour," Grandma replies.

"I've already eaten," I reply, half panicked, I can't leave Giuliano upstairs alone while I eat dinner.

"That's okay, you keep working on our homework. I'll eat with Grandma down here," Anna replies.

My scared eyes hold hers. "Okay."

Oh jeez, this plan could go to hell on a broomstick. If we get caught, I know that death is near.

I'm not even joking, Enrico my brother will go batshit crazy.

Anna leaves the room and I follow her up the stairs, we walk through to the grand foyer and Anna takes my hand in hers. "What the hell do I do now?" I whisper in a panic, this plan seemed genius when we planned it, now it's plain stupid.

"Just talk to him, you two are crazy about each other."

"Yes." I nod. "You're right. This is fine, totally fine."

"And you're not going to get caught," she reminds me. "I'll text his number if there's any sign of trouble."

"Okay." I nod nervously. "Make sure you do." I think for a moment. "What are you going to do all night?"

"I'll be doing homework with my headphones in."

"What are you talking about?" I whisper. "You need to listen for trouble, you can't wear headphones. What are you going to hear over headphones?"

"Oh shit, that's right. Okay, I'm on it."

I begin to sweat, please don't let this go wrong, I really need this night.

We take the stairs up to the top floor, there's a large living room and two double bedrooms, each with their ensuite bathroom. One bedroom is Anna's and the other is mine. Not one to brag, but my room has a really cute boy waiting in it for me right now, my heart just might not be able to take it.

Anna pulls me into a hug. "I can't believe he went to all this trouble...just to see me," I whisper.

She smiles broadly. "I can."

I grab the door handle and turn back to look back at my dear friend and give her a grateful smile.

"Good luck," she whispers. "He's in the bathroom, knock gently three times and he'll know that it's you."

"Okay." I screw up my face, walk in and close the door behind me and I flick the lock as I glance around the quiet bedroom. I've stayed in here so many times before and never seemed to notice anything about it. I look around to try to see with new eyes, imagining what Giuliano would be seeing for the first time.

There's a queen bed with a plush navy velvet quilt, a television mounted on the wall and two armchairs with ottomans by the window. Thankfully, the drapes are closed, effectively blocking us out from the world...and my guards.

On the side table that sits under the television, there's a basket of snacks and a few bottles of soft drink and water. God, I love Anna, she's thought of everything.

I look over to the closed bathroom door.

He's just in there.

Okay, let's do this, I knock softly three times. "Giulio," I whisper.

No answer.

I knock three times again. "It's me."

The door opens and big brown beautiful eyes come into view and my heart somersaults in my chest, my smile nearly beams from my face. "Hi."

"Hello."

He pulls me in for a hug and we stay in each other's arms for an extended time. Connected by closeness.

He's big and warm and he makes me feel so safe.

He's just so....

He takes my hand in his and leads me over to the armchairs, he tentatively sits down on one. I frown, it seems like an awkward place to sit, I nervously sit down in the chair beside him.

"Hi." He smiles as he picks up my hand and kisses my fingertips.

I watch him in a detached state and his face falls. "I'm sorry." He instantly releasees my hand.

"For what?" I ask.

He puffs air into his cheeks. "I don't know what happens to my brain when you're around."

"Why?"

"I can't not touch you."

"What do you mean?"

"It's like...." He pauses as if searching for the right words. "I'm so drawn to you, I don't mean to be so forward every time I see you, but I honestly can't help it." He shrugs. "It feels unnatural *not* to touch you."

I get up and sit on his lap, I brush his black hair back from his face and smile down at his beautiful face. "I don't want you to help it," I whisper.

"What must you think of me?"

"How so?"

"Last time we saw each other and I dragged you into the bathroom...." His voice trails off as if disgusted with himself. "I'm sorry, I didn't mean for that to happen."

I frown. "You wish that didn't happen?"

"I didn't say that?"

"Giuliano, what *are* you saying? Stop talking in riddles, I don't understand."

"I'm saying that I know that you're not that kind of girl and I'm sorry that I treated you as if you are. I lost my head for a moment."

I stare at him, confused.

"Like tonight, for instance." He pulls his fingertips through my long dark hair as he articulates his words. "I haven't snuck into your bedroom for the normal reason a guy would sneak into a girl's bedroom, I'm here because...." He pauses. "It's the only place I can see you alone, and I know how this looks and I don't want you to think that I'm here to take advantage of you."

Oh....

"I don't."

"And...."

I put my fingertip over his lips. "I like that you've snuck into my bedroom to see me and I liked that you dragged me into the bathroom the other night, and I like what we did."

His eyes search mine.

"And I like the way you make me feel and I don't care how it looks because this is between me and you and only us."

We kiss softly, our lips lingering over each other's.

"I just don't want you to feel rushed," he murmurs.

"I don't."

He gives me a crooked smile as if mollified, has he been worried about this?

He picks up my diamond necklace and rearranges it on my neck. "This is beautiful."

I hold it in my hand, "Enrico bought it for me when my father died, it's so special. I never take it off."

"I'd never take you off." He whispers as his eyes drop to my lips.

"Well...." I stand, unsure of what this means. "What do you want to do, then?"

He looks around the room and shrugs. "We could watch a movie."

"Okay." I pick up the remote and pass it to him.

"You don't want to choose?"

"No."

He smiles as if amused and points the remote to the television on the wall, he begins to flick through the channels.

"What?"

"I thought you would want to pick."

"Why?"

"Because that's more like you."

"You think I'm bossy?" I ask, affronted.

He holds his hands up playfully.

"I am *not* bossy, Giuliano," I reply. "I just happen to know that I won't be watching the movie because I won't be able to concentrate, so you may as well pick what you want to watch. The word you are searching for is thoughtful."

He chuckles and flicks through the channels. "If you say so."

"That's not being bossy." I smirk.

"Okay," he mouths.

"Have you seen this?" he asks, it's an Avengers movie, I've seen it a hundred times.

"No," I lie.

He hits play and stands and pulls back the covers on the bed, I glance down at what he's doing and then back up at him.

"It's cold, we should probably…."

"Get under the covers?" I finish his sentence.

"Does make sense to stay warm." A trace of a smile crosses his face.

"I guess." I try to hold my smile, this all feels so naughty.

Sneaking a boy into my room, getting into bed and under the covers…who even am I?

He climbs onto the bed and stares up at me, a thrill runs through me. I climb in beside him and he covers us over with the blankets. Instantly, the heat from his body warms my blood, he pulls me close and puts his arm around me…this is so nice.

He kisses my temple and I snuggle in closer. We watch the television for a while, his fingers trail up and down my arm as if he's itching to touch me. A thought crosses my mind and I look up at him. "How many girlfriends have you had?"

"A few."

I frown, what does that mean? "What happened with them?"

"Didn't work out." He kisses my temple as if dismissing the subject.

Hmm, I need more information as my mind begins to go into overdrive. "How many people have you slept with?"

A frown crosses his face. "Does it matter?"

I stare at him. "No."

"So why do you want to know?"

"Because I would like to know who you've had sex with."

"Why? So you can break up with me?"

"No." I suddenly feel stupidly insecure. "I just…."

"You just what?"

"Well." I pause *Just shut up, right now*. "I don't know what I'm doing, so when we...." I cut myself off.

He rolls me over onto my back and holds my hands above my head as he stares down at me. "When we what?" His knee spreads my legs.

I open my mouth to reply but his proximity steals my words. *When we fuck.*

He gently kisses me, his tongue swipes over my lips and I feel it to my toes. "Trust me, you do know what you're doing. Nobody has ever affected me the way you do. I get hard just thinking about touching you."

Suddenly I feel brave. "I want you to be my first."

"I want that too."

"But you'll need to teach me what to do."

He kisses me again and this time it's different, I can feel a sense of urgency, a hunger that I haven't felt from him before. He rolls over on top of me and nestles his body between my legs as we kiss deeply, I can feel his erection as it grows.

Good lord.

For a long time, we kiss as our bodies rock together, my hands are roaming up over his back and down to his tight behind and he winces.

"What?"

"These jeans." He rearranges his crotch. "Tight."

I stare up at him and I know that this is it, the time I need to decide.

Do I want this to happen tonight, or do I want to wait until another time? But what if we don't get another time? What if tonight is all we have?

I glance at the locked door, we've already jumped through so many hoops just to be alone.

"Take them off," I whisper.

His eyes hold mine. "Are you sure?"

"Uh-huh."

"I told you I wasn't here for this."

"And I told you to take your jeans off, so shut up."

"See, you *are* bossy," he whispers as he stands.

I giggle, and with his eyes locked on mine he slowly unzips his jeans, I watch on with my heart hammering in my throat. He's wearing tight black Calvin Klein boxers and his hard erection is pressed up against his stomach and peeking over the waistband. My insides begin to melt into a puddle. He is the most beautiful specimen of man I have ever seen...I mean, not that I've seen any, but still.

Holy wow.

"Everything," I say.

He raises an eyebrow and then in slow motion he lifts his T-shirt off over his head and throws it to the side, his skin is olive, his chest is broad and scattered with dark hair, his stomach is ripped and has that V of muscles that disappear into his boxer shorts, and he slowly slides them down and kicks them to the side.

Jeez.

Okay...that's a bit more man than I was expecting, I swallow the nervous lump in my throat, not feeling so brave now.

He climbs back in under the covers and pulls them over the two of us. Leaning up on one elbow, he kisses me softly, and after a few minutes my nerves subside to the sound of arousal pumping through my veins. For the first time since we met, I have him alone and all to myself. My hands roam all over his torso, and I tentatively reach down and touch him there, I run my fingers through his pubic hair.

This feels so...*intimate.*

He's hard and soft and damn enticing, he puts his hand over

mine. "Like this," he whispers as he strokes himself; I do as he shows me and he smiles softly down at me. "That's it."

I smile goofily up at him as we stroke him together, I like this game. It's kind of like show and tell, except I get to touch too.

Unable to help it, my legs begin to fall open by themselves and his fingers trail over my panties, and with his lips locked on mine he slides them down and takes them off.

His fingers trail through my swollen lips and I whimper as my toes curl. *Oh God.*

He sits and pulls me up by the hand and lifts my dress over my head and then reaches around and undoes my bra behind my back. It unlatches first go.

He's done that before.

Stop it.

I push the distressing thought from my mind and lie back down as he pulls the blankets back up, protecting us from the world.

His hand trails up and over my breasts and down between my legs. "So beautiful."

"Do you know how much I think about you?" he murmurs against my lips. "Every day, all day. Every night I touch myself imagining that it's you." He slides his finger deep into my sex, my mouth falls open as we stare at each other.

His thumb dusts my clitoris as he adds another finger and I feel something building deep inside. "Oh," I whimper as my hand goes to his forearm. I can feel the muscles in it flexing as he works me.

"You like that, baby?"

I nod as my legs fall wider. If I could answer him, I would. But I can't. I'm too preoccupied with having the best time of my life.

His fingers get deeper, stronger and my body begins to writhe beneath him. "Giuliano," I whimper, I need. "Oh...God."

"Fuck," he whispers. "You feel so *fucking* good." Our kiss turns frantic as he rolls me onto my back, his head drops and he takes my nipple into his mouth.

My hands go to his hair...*oh*.

He sucks and nips at me and then his mouth trails lower. "Giuliano...no."

"It's okay," he reassures me.

"I don't know...." I stop myself because I really want to do what he wants to do, but this is all so full on.

"I've got you." He kisses my lower stomach. "I need this."

Why would anyone need to do this?

Men are fucking weird.

Oh God, I scrunch my eyes shut as he goes lower and kisses me there.

I hold my breath as my heart thumps hard in my chest.

He kisses me again as he spreads my legs around his body, he gently licks me there and I nearly bounce off the bed.

Fuck.

Fuck.

He licks me again and my legs curl up around his head and he smiles into me. "Relax."

"How the hell am I supposed to relax with you doing that?" I whisper.

"Lie back and enjoy it." He sits up and rearranges me and puts my hands above my head and then with his eyes locked on mine, his tongue swipes through my open sex, his eyes close in ecstasy and as I watch him I float into a subspace.

Trust rolls over me and I feel a sense of calm.

This is nothing like what I ever imagined, he takes his time worshipping me, my back arches off the bed as he brings me closer and closer.

I begin to shudder hard and deep and I reach for him. "I need...."

"I know." He slides up over me and we kiss, a tangled mess of tongues and arms and my taste on his lips and *fucking hell*.

"Condom," he says as if reminding himself out loud, he climbs out of bed and shuffles through his jeans. He rolls on a condom and crawls back over me and lifts my legs around his waist, his hard cock slides through my sex as we stare at each other. "I've been waiting for you," he whispers.

I smile up at him in awe.

"To feel like this." He kisses me softly.

I take his face in my hands as I smile against him. "I've been waiting for you."

He slides deep into my sex, he meets resistance and I whimper. "Ow...." My grip on his shoulders tightens. "Jules."

"Are you alright?"

He's big.

I nod, but I really don't know. Ouch, that smarts.

"Nearly there, sweetheart." He circles his hips to loosen me up as I close my eyes to block out the burn. "Look at me," he pleads.

I open my eyes, he kisses me softly with such beautiful tenderness.

"Do you know how perfect you are to me?"

My eyes well with emotion, this is fairy tale love, the kind you read about in storybooks

"Relax," he pleads with another soft kiss.

I let my guard down a little and he pushes forward and in a sharp movement slides in deep. "Oh...," I whimper.

He smiles as his lips drop to my neck,

"You seem pretty pleased with yourself," I whisper.

"I am." He pulls out and slides in deep and we stare at each other as we do it again and again and this doesn't feel sleazy or dirty. It feels natural, like I was born to do this with him.

He's mine.

Then we begin to build, both lost to our own arousal, and pretty soon we are hard at it, he holds himself up on straightened arms as his body rides mine with force. His knees are wide and perspiration dusts our skin and oh my God, this is perfection.

The bed begins to thump. "Sshh," I remind him.

He drops down to lie close and kisses me tenderly as we fall silent.

"Promise me that it will always be like this between us," I whisper as we kiss and I shudder hard as something happens deep inside and then he holds my two legs back and I feel him jerk deep inside of me.

"I promise."

We kiss again.

"I love you, Francesca," he whispers.

I smile as I'm overcome with emotion. "I love you too."

Giuliano

Laughter echoes around through the forest, the group I sit with loud and jovial. I sit to the side, slightly detached, completely alone.

Six days feels like a lifetime.

It's Friday night, late. Two a.m. We've been to a party, and now a group of us are drinking by the lake at one of the girls' holiday house.

I haven't seen Francesca for six days and six long nights, I didn't call her tonight, as bad as I wanted to. It only makes me miss her more.

I know it's not her fault and I know that I knew the conditions before we started. But when I'm out at a party and my friends are all with their girls, I want to be with mine.

"You're quiet tonight," a voice says as I feel someone sit down on the grass beside me.

I glance up to see Mary, we used to be a thing. "Am I?"

"Anything I can help with?" She gives me a sexy smile and raises an eyebrow and I instantly know what she wants to help me with.

"No." I sip my beer and stare straight ahead. "I'm good."

She rubs her hand up my thigh. "I miss us."

I puff air into my cheeks and instantly hate myself. Francesca opened a can of worms last week, or should I say *the* worm. I'm suddenly a sexual deviant, walking around hard and dreaming of her beneath me. Everywhere I look, everything I feel, everything I want, revolves around ejaculating. I've watched that much porn this week that it's a wonder I've got any skin left on my dick.

"Do you want to go for a walk?" she whispers as she rubs her fingers over my crotch. My cock twitches under her touch.

Fuck, this isn't good.

I instantly stand. "I've got to go."

"Where to?" She frowns. "The night has just begun."

"Home." I can't stay here with her touching me, I don't want.... "I have to go." I turn to the rest of the group as they all chatter between themselves. "Catch you all later."

"Where you going?" they all call.

"I've got to go." I turn and walk off into the darkness.

"What's wrong with him?" I hear Mary ask.

Ferrara

"He's got a new girl," I hear Alex say.

"Don't worry, he'll snap out of it," a male voice says. "You know what he's like." The group all laugh and as I disappear into the darkness I feel like shit. They're right, I don't have a great track record with girls, I lose interest before we even begin.

She's different.

I take out my phone and scroll through to my favorite name.

Francesca

I hit call, she answers first ring. "Hello."

"Hi," I sigh sadly.

"Are you okay?" she says softly.

"Can I come over?"

"What?"

"I need to see you."

"Jules, you know you can't."

Deflation fills me.

This is fucked.

"I love you," she whispers.

I stay silent. *What good is it if I can't even fucking see you?*

"Where are you?" she asks.

"Walking home from a party?"

"Alone?"

"Yep."

"That's dangerous, I don't want you walking home alone."

"Well, the alternative was stay and get hit on by girls all night, so this was the only option."

"Oh...."

She falls silent and I feel like shit.

"I shouldn't have said that, I'm sorry."

"Five months."

"Until what?" I ask.

"Until they can't stop us, after I'm eighteen they have no say."

"What will happen then?" I ask.

"Whatever you want."

Hope fills me as I walk in the darkness.

"I miss you," she whispers.

"Me too."

"Anna's parents are away on Tuesday, can you come over and stay?"

I get to see her.

A broad smile crosses my face. "Try and stop me."

"I can't wait."

"Me too. I should let you go back to sleep," I say. "I'm being selfish calling this late."

"No. I'm staying on the phone until you get home safely."

I smile, it makes me happy that she worries about me. "How was your night?" I ask.

"Crap without you."

"Climb out your window and come and stay at my house," I reply.

"Where would I stay if I did come to your house? Where would I stay?"

"In my bed with me."

"What would your mother say?"

"Hello, it's nice to meet you, I expect."

"Will you be serious?" she scoffs.

"I am, she wouldn't mind if you stayed over. I know for a fact that she would love you, she wants me happy."

"She sounds nice."

"The most selfless person on earth."

"She's lucky to have a son like you."

"I'm the lucky one. What's your mother like?" I ask as I turn the corner and continue in the darkness.

"Hmm." She thinks for a moment. "Glamorous."

"That's a weird word choice to describe your mother."

"Well, that's what she is."

"Is she sweet, loving?"

"Hmm."

I frown. "You're not close to her?"

"I am, but I'm not…if that makes sense."

"How so?"

"Well." She pauses as if choosing her words correctly. "I live with her, and we talk about random things, she cares for me, but in reality, she doesn't really know anything about me. I would never tell her about you or anything personal like that."

"But she's your mother."

"I don't know." She exhales heavily. "It's hard to explain, she's not easy to talk to. She's so wrapped up in keeping up appearances that she wouldn't have a clue what is going on in my brothers' lives and mine, as long as we toe the line to family tradition is all that matters to her."

"Oh," I mutter, unsure what to say. I can't even imagine what it must be like, my mother is the polar opposite.

We stay silent as I continue to walk, both lost in our own thoughts.

"I can't stop thinking about the way you sucked me the other morning," I whisper to change the subject.

"Oh really," she says and I can tell she's smiling. "What about it?"

"Seriously, Francesca. So, fucking good, it's all I can think about."

"I'll do it again on Tuesday if you be nice to me."

"Ha," I scoff. "When am I ever not nice to you, I'm like your fucking puppy."

"A very naughty puppy," she whispers darkly.

I feel the blood begin to pump through my body. "What's your favorite thing that we did?"

"Everything."

"One thing."

"The way you kiss me."

I stop walking and stand still. "Kiss you?"

"Yeah." She sighs dreamily. "I love kissing you, I get to hold you in my arms and be close."

My heart swells as I turn into my street. "I love kissing you too."

"Three days."

"That's a long time."

"I'd wait forever to kiss you."

I smile. "Luckily you don't have to."

She giggles and I press in my code and walk through the security gates. "I'm home."

"I love you," she whispers.

"I love you too, good night, angel."

"Good night, baby."

Tuesday afternoon

I sit in the back seat of Alex's car. His eyes flick up to meet mine in the rearview mirror, "You know, you're going to get yourself killed."

Val turns to face me in the back seat. "What do you think

that big brother would say if he knew you were sneaking in and giving his baby sister the dick?"

I roll my eyes.

"Did you bring more condoms this time?" he asks.

"Yep."

"Did you bring lube? I feel sorry for the poor bitch dealing with your monster cock."

"Will you shut up?" I cut him off. "She seems to like it."

"*Seems to* being the operative word." The boys smirk as they exchange looks.

"I'm not here for sex," I spit.

"Oh...but you *will* fuck her all night, won't you?" Val mutters.

"Because I like her, you fucking idiots," I snap. "Stop pissing me off."

And anyway...I more than like her.

I'm going to marry her.

———

Knock, knock, knock.

I wait in the bathroom with the door locked.

Knock, knock, knock.

"It's me," I hear Francesca whisper through the door.

I open it in a rush, her beautiful face comes into view and she smiles broadly and jumps into my arms, I laugh as I hold her tight and her legs lift off the floor. We stay like this for a while and then she kisses me as she steps down and flicks the lock on the bathroom.

Without hesitation she lifts my T-shirt over my head and unzips my jeans. I smile against her lips, she's getting braver every time I see her.

"Is my girl hungry for it?"

"Hmm," she moans as she kisses me harder. Her eyes close as she takes my cock into her hand.

She strokes me hard and, losing control, I slam her up against the wall and lift her leg around my waist.

Yes....

Fucking starving.

Anna

"I know what you're doing?" Valentino says as he stands beside me at the drinks table.

"What's that?" I ask.

Giuliano's friend is annoyingly handsome, and he knows it.

Ever since I met him in the Library with Francesca, he keeps popping up everywhere I go.

"Wishing you were here with me instead of him." He gives me a slow sexy smile.

"I don't think so." I lie.

That's exactly what I was thinking. Damn it, why *do* I have a boyfriend?

I know Valentino's type, the player kind. There's no way I'm letting myself break up with a nice guy to chase a heart breaker...as tempting as it is.

"You know...." His eyes drop to my lips, "We could just get out of here."

"Where would we go?" I ask as I act uninterested.

"The question is...where wouldn't we go?" He raises his eyebrow in a sexy playful way.

I swallow the lump in my throat, damn it. That's a great answer.

I pick up my drinks, "Goodbye Valentino."

"Say hi to Mr. Boring for me." He teases.

"No." I walk off toward Mr. Boring, damn it...running away with Valentino sounds so much more fun.

Giuliano

Francesca's beautiful smile beams across the table at me.

"Do you know how beautiful you are?" I ask her.

We are in the library, sitting in the back corner. One month today that Francesca and I first slept together, one perfect month of stolen nights in each other's arms.

Francesca goes to Paris tomorrow with her mother and I can hardly stand the thought of it. There will be too much distance between us.

"You're biased." She giggles. "Tell me again."

I pick up her hand and kiss her fingertips as we smile at each other.

From the corner of my eye I glance up and see something coming at me fast, Enrico Ferrara storming toward us like the Hulk. "You," he growls.

"Oh no," Francesca cries.

Before I have time to respond he has me by the arm dragging me toward the door, I struggle to break free and we burst out the front doors and he hurls me down the stairs, I crash to the ground on the grass.

"No, no," Francesca cries as she runs behind us. "Leave him alone, I love him."

Enrico stands over me, his eyes are bulging from their sockets, I've never seen someone so angry.

Lorenzo grabs his arms. "Leave it, Enrico. Leave it," he pleads.

I climb to my feet. "You can't keep her from me. I love her."

"You what?" he screams. "You cannot fucking love her." He grabs me by the throat as he loses control. "How dare you go behind my back." He pushes me hard and I go flying into the bushes.

He grabs Francesca by the arm and pulls her toward the car, she kicks and screams to get away from him.

"You don't fucking touch her," I scream as I run after them and shove him in the back.

He turns like the devil himself and steps toward me, contempt dripping from his every pore. His fists are clenched by his sides and I step back, unsure of his intentions.

Francesca's face falls. "Just go, Giuliano," she pleads. "Leave it. Please."

"Enrico," Lorenzo whispers. "He's just a boy."

Enrico pushes Francesca into the back of the waiting car.

I step forward. "You cannot keep her from me," I demand.

"You go near her again…and I *will* kill you," he sneers, with a long filthy glare he turns and gets into the car and it takes off with speed.

I pant as I struggle for air, furious as I watch the car pull into the distance. Adrenaline is pumping through my veins as I try to calm myself.

No.

He can't keep her from me, I won't stand for it.

I hear the car tires screech in the distance and I close my eyes, my every worst nightmare just came true.

Fuck.

Ferrara

It's one a.m. and I lie in the darkness, Francesca hasn't called me and I'm beside myself.

I have to know if she's okay.

I dial her number, it rings once. "You were warned," Enrico growls.

My eyes widen in horror, oh no. He found the phone.

"Prepare to die, fucker." The line goes dead.

3

Giuliano

I KICK the soccer ball and it flies high in the air, Alex and I are practicing at the fields.

"Where is that dickhead?" Damn it, why is Val always late?

"I don't know, did he call?"

I pat my pockets. "My phone's in the car, I'll check."

I jog to the car and grab my phone from charge.

9 missed calls - Mom

Huh?

I listen to my messages.

"Giuliano, you need to come home urgently," Mom's panicked voice says.

That's weird. I listen to her next message.

"Oh my God, Giuliano, please answer your phone, sweetheart. This is an emergency."

Shit, what's happened? I dial her number. "Giuliano, thank God," she stammers, she sounds panicked.

"What's wrong? Are you okay?"

"Yes, but I need you here now."

"What's happened?"

"Just come home, I'll explain when you get here."

"I don't...."

"Giuliano," she cries. "Just get here immediately as a matter of urgency."

The fuck?

"Okay, fine. I'm on my way." I hang up the call, what the hell is wrong with her? I look up at Alex. "I've got to go," I call.

"What do you mean?"

"I don't know, my mom's going batshit crazy about something, needs me home urgently."

"You think Enrico Ferrara is at your house?"

My eyes widen. "Oh fuck. I hadn't thought of that."

"Well, why else would she need you home urgently."

"Shit...." I think for a moment. "True."

Valentino's car pulls into the parking lot and finally he gets out.

"Took your time," Alex spits.

"I'm busy, alright? Stop busting my fucking balls."

"I've got to go. Mom is losing her shit."

"About what?"

"I don't know."

"Any money Enrico Ferrara is at his house." Alex smirks, "It was nice knowing you."

"Are you serious." Val's eyes widen as he looks between

us. "He's at your house right now, oh fucking hell, this can't be good." Val opens my car door and throws the ball in. "Come on, then."

"What are you doing?" I frown.

"You don't think we're going to let you get your ass kicked alone, do you?"

"And what are you two going to do?"

"Kick some ass...or maybe just die alongside you, I guess." Alex gets into the front seat and Val gets into the back.

I get into the driver's seat and look back to them. "You don't have to come."

"Yes. We do."

"If he touches you—" Val punches his fist, "—I'm literally smashing his face in."

"I'd like to see that." Alex rolls his eyes.

"If you're going down, we're coming with you." Val slaps me on the back in reassurance. "Don't worry, bud, we've got you."

I frown. "Thanks...I guess."

I pull out of the parking lot filled with the knowledge that I have the two best friends in the world. "You know, we're all going to die, right?" I mutter.

"One hundred percent."

We pull into the driveway of my house to see a cavalcade of black cars parked inside. There are a group of men in black suits standing around on the porch. I've seen them before, they're Enrico's guards, the ones I saw at his house the day I was there, they all turn and watch our car pull in and our eyes all widen in horror.

"Fucking hell," I whisper.

"He brought backup."

"Of course, he did."

"Oh crap," Alex whispers. "It was nice knowing you, boys."

"What the fuck am I going to say?" I whisper as I turn the car off.

"Make it quick and painless," Alex whispers.

Val chuckles in the back seat. "Right?" He slaps me on the back. "Hope she was worth it."

For the first time my mind goes to my Francesca and I smile. "Totally." With a return of my bravado, I climb out of the car and walk up toward the front door.

The men all dip their heads in a greeting.

What the fuck is this about?

The boys and I exchange looks as we walk into the house.

"Giuliano," my mother whispers as she pulls me in for a hug, she's been crying. "Thank God, you're home."

I turn to see Lorenzo standing in the hall, his face is solemn.

"What's going on?" I ask.

Lorenzo's eyes hold mine. "I need to talk to you, son."

My eyes flick between him and my mother. "What about? Where's Enrico?"

My mother's eyes well with tears and she gives a sad shake of her head.

Lorenzo drops his head.

"Has something happened?"

"I need to take you to the office to discuss it."

Panic runs through me. "Where's Francesca? Is she okay?"

"She's fine."

Thank God.

Lorenzo takes my arm. "Let's go."

I snatch it out of his grip. "I'm not going anywhere until you tell me what's going on."

They both stare at me.

"Mom?"

"Enrico and his fiancée Olivia have been killed," she whispers.

"Killed." My eyes flick between them. "How?"

"They were murdered, the yacht they were on was bombed."

I turn to see my two friends are wide eyed and as white as a ghost. What the fuck?

"Murdered."

Francesca.

Oh my God...

"It's a very dark day for Ferrara," Lorenzo whispers as he grabs my arm. "We need to go now."

"Go where?"

"To the office."

"Why, what does this have to do with me?" I stammer.

My mother breaks into full-blown sobs.

"Your life will never be the same, my boy," Lorenzo replies.

My eyes widen. "I didn't do it, I know nothing about his death. I promise," I splutter.

"He didn't, I swear," Alex says. "We wouldn't even know how to make a bomb."

"This is the first we heard of it," Val splutters.

"I know, I know." He pulls me into a hug and kisses both of my cheeks. "You are safe, we know it had nothing to do with you. But now, there are things we need to discuss."

I look to my mother for reassurance and she forces a smile. "It's okay, Giuliano, I promise."

"We're coming," Valentino demands. "We go where he goes."

I look back to my two loyal friends. "Can they come?" I ask.

"This is a private matter."

"I tell them everything, we have no secrets," I snap. "I'm not going without them."

"Very well." Lorenzo nods. "As you wish."

I nod, feeling a little better. My mother pulls me in and hugs me tight, she holds my face in her hands and looks lovingly up at me. "Giuliano, I love you so much," she whispers.

"I know."

"Promise me that nothing will ever change between us?"

I frown in confusion, what the hell is she talking about now, why would anything ever change between us?

"We need to go," Lorenzo urges. He takes my arm and leads me out to the waiting black Mercedes wagon, he opens the back door and the boys and I climb in.

The car pulls out and the cavalcade of cars trail behind us. The boys and I exchange scared looks.

I don't know what the fuck is going on, but it can't be good.

Two hours later we have arrived in Milan. We travel to the top floor of the Ferrara building; my mind is a clusterfuck of confusion. We have six men with us, all big and burly and I have no idea what the hell is going on.

Once we arrive at the top floor, we walk through a grand foyer and into a large office reception and waiting area. "You boys wait here," Lorenzo instructs my two friends.

"But..." Val objects, one of the men pushes him into the chair abruptly and he falls back. "Sit," he growls.

Alex tentatively sits down too, scared for his life.

Fuck.

I'm led into a large office and the door closes behind us, I turn to see two men. "As you know, I am a longtime friend of your parents and you can trust me."

I nod.

"This is Andrea and Matteo."

"Hello."

Lorenzo exhales heavily. "There are some things that you don't know, son. You have been protected up until now, but with the passing of Enrico Ferrara, you must be told of your heritage.

I frown.

"Your father...."

"Leave my father out of this," I snap.

He glares at me, unimpressed that I interrupted him. "Your father's name wasn't Linden. His real name was Giuliano Ferrara."

"What?"

Lorenzo and the other men exchange worried looks.

"It's a very complicated story." He pauses as if searching for the right wording. "Giuliano, your father lived a double life—one with your mother and you and one with his wife and their four children."

I frown as his words sink in.

How could that be?

"What? That's ridiculous!" I scoff. "He wasn't married to someone else. You have the wrong man; he and my mother were married."

"We don't. These are your two brothers, Giuliano." He

gestures to the two men and they nod in a sad acknowledgement. "Andrea and Matteo, I'm sorry that you had to meet under these circumstances."

My eyes flicker between the three of them. "You're lying." I stand abruptly.

Lorenzo stands too, he pushes me back into the chair. "Your oldest brother was murdered; his name was Enrico Ferrara."

My eyes widen as I begin to hear my heartbeat in my ears.

The floor moves beneath me.

"You have been left in your father's will to take over management of the Ferrara family empire."

My face falls.

"It's okay," Andrea says softly. "You won't be alone, Giuliano."

"We will be here every step of the way to train you and to help you with the transition," Lorenzo says.

I stare at him as the walls close in.

She's my sister.

I drop my head as the sound of my heartbeat rings loud and hard in my chest.

No....

Through my daze I see that Lorenzo leaves the room and then returns with a man. "This is Mario," he introduces him. "He is our lawyer, he will explain things in greater detail."

Huh?

I'm so confused.

"Hello, Giuliano," Mario says as he puts his hand out to shake mine. "It's an honor to meet you, sir."

I shake his hand as my manners take over. "I don't understand."

"You will." Mario takes out a large leather box and opens

it, it has a folder inside. "Your father has left a very specific and detailed will, in the event of his and then...Enrico's death."

I stare at him.

"You have been left the entirety of the Ferrara businesses."

"I don't understand."

"You own everything now."

"Like what?" I screw up my face. "What *are* the Ferrara businesses?"

Mario begins to read from the folder, "Ferrara Sports Cars valued at nine billion euros. The Flamingo Bell Football League side and the four football stadiums."

What?

"Seventy-six million euros worth of real estate." He slides his finger over the assets as he reads them out loud. "Five hundred and eighty-three high-class brothels. One hundred and twenty-six VIP strip clubs. Nine casinos worldwide, valued at an estimated fourteen billion euros."

I slump back in my chair. "I don't understand. How in the fuck did my father own all this without me knowing?"

Mario exhales and takes his glasses off. "Son...." He pauses as if choosing his words. "You have been kept out of the family business on purpose, but in the event of Enrico's death, it has been decided that you will take over and lead."

My eyes flick to the two men sitting in the room listening.

"I don't.... I mean." I gesture to them. "Why...what do you mean?" I'm tripping over my words as I try to make sense of all of this.

"Enrico was to tell you this when you turned twenty-one, he was going to train you up and have you working alongside of him. As it turns out our hand has been forced to bring that forward."

I blink, shocked. "Did he know about me?"

"Yes."

"How long for?"

"He found out about you when his father died."

"He wasn't happy..." I mutter under my breath, of course he wasn't.

"Why hasn't it gone to either of you?" I ask the boys.

"Your father wanted it to go straight to you," Andrea replies.

"And you're okay with this?" I snap.

They both give a shrug. "It was his wishes."

I stare at them, and they're just going to take that sitting down?

Wimps.

"Your father always said that only his oldest and youngest son were born for this role. Enrico...and now, you."

I drop my head as the room spins once more, I stay silent as I try to process everything.

I can't even begin to, it's impossible.

"You have four thousand staff and another twelve hundred personal staff."

"What for?" I spit. "What on earth would anyone need twelve hundred personal staff for?"

Mario and Lorenzo exchange looks.

I snap as I lose my patience. "Explain this to me, now."

Mario exhales heavily. "The Ferrara family has run Italy, the good and the bad, for many generations."

Criminals.

The hairs on the back of my neck stand to attention.

"Not all Ferrara businesses are reputable. Stefano, your grandfather...."

Grandfather.

I had a grandfather? I was told he died before I was born.

Everything is a lie, my stomach rolls with nausea.

"Stefano built an empire, and because he died on the same day as your father, Enrico learned of the business this way too."

"He didn't know?" I gasp.

"No, he and his brothers, like you, were kept in the dark. Your father wanted you all to have a normal childhood, a privilege he wasn't offered."

"How the fuck could I have a normal childhood when he had another wife and family?" I spit. "I don't want anything to do with this. You're lying and none of this is true and if it is, I hate him." I look around the room and stand abruptly. "And I hate all of you." Adrenaline is pumping hard through my veins. "I'm going home. Stay the fuck away from me."

Lorenzo stands and pushes me back into my chair, I fall hard back into my seat. "I know this is a lot to take in, Giuliano and with your personality it won't be easy to conform with family tradition."

"Because it isn't my family," I yell. "Stop fucking lying!"

"We are all here, at your service. You have your brothers' full support and in time, you will learn to lead as your father wanted."

I stand and march from the office, Alex and Valentino immediately stand. "We're leaving," I snap as I storm past them.

"Not without security," Lorenzo calls from behind me.

I turn toward him, infuriated. "Fuck your security."

"Who do you think murdered your brother, Giuliano?" Lorenzo bellows.

I struggle for air as adrenaline courses through my veins, I've never been so angry.

"You are now a marked man," he cries. "You have two choices. Learn to lead us into the next generation. Or be the next murdered Ferrara, because trust me, they will come for you."

4

Giuliano

NIGHTFALL, the bringer of evil.

At the going down of the sun, dark thoughts have rolled in. And as the whole world peacefully sleeps, mine has come crashing to a devastating halt.

The lines have been blurred between a nightmare and reality.

I lie in the dark and stare up at the ceiling, my mind a clusterfuck of confusion.

Why is this happening?

I'm on the trundle bed in Alex's bedroom, next to him. His regulated breathing calms me, a peaceful reminder that I *can* depend on someone.

My friends are all I have now.

I can't go home, because then, I'll have to see her.

I can't bear it.

My mother's words of wanting nothing to change between us are now crystal clear in meaning. She knew how I would feel.

My entire life has been a lie, her betrayal runs deep. I am the child of a mistress.

My heart broken beyond repair.

The only thing that I know for certain is that I didn't know my father at all.

I'm not who I....

He was married to another woman.

My beloved father is nothing more than an adultering criminal. Head of the Mafia.

And I...I don't even know who I fucking am anymore.

Unable to lie still for a moment more, I get up and go to the window and stare out through the darkness at the cars parked on the street.

The guards who now watch over me.

It all makes sense now; the reason Enrico treated me with such contempt. How must they have felt when they learned of me? His father's mistress's child.

The betrayal, to them too.

This is why I felt that he hated me before we even met. I didn't imagine it.

She's, my sister.

Francesca and I can never be together, no matter how much we care for each other.

There is no answer, this can't be fixed.

I imagine us together, kissing in the darkness, the closeness we felt.

The love.

Oh....

My chest constricts with sadness and as I sit in the darkness, I feel so betrayed.

So alone.

The salty tears run down my face. I thought the day my father died was a bad day.

I was wrong, at least then I knew who I was.

This is the worst day of my life.

Incompetence, is there a worse feeling in the world?

I don't think so.

I sit and stare at the computer screen, determined to try to understand the information before me. Books are strewn all over the desk in front of me. I've studied and studied this week, so much to learn.

It's been seven days since I learned my fate.

Ten long days since I've spoken to her.

I exhale heavily and pick up my father's handwritten letter. I skim through it. I must have read it over five hundred times.

Every time it hurts more than the last.

Knock, knock sounds on the door.

"Come in," I call.

Lorenzo puts his head around the door. "The tailor is here with your suits, Giuliano."

I nod once. "Thanks."

I've had people fussing around me all week; apparently, I have to look the part now.

"Have you got a minute?" he asks.

I exhale and put my letter down. "Yes, come in."

Lorenzo walks in and sits down at the desk. He stays silent and I know he has something on his mind.

"What is it?"

"I don't...." He cuts himself off.

I raise my eyebrow impatiently. "What?"

"With all due respect, sir, I really don't think it's a good idea that you employ your two best friends."

"Why not?"

"This is a family business."

The audacity.

I smirk, annoyed. "I trust nobody here and my two right-hand men will be loyal to me and only me. They are my only family now."

"You can trust me," he whispers.

"I couldn't even trust my own fucking parents, Lorenzo, what makes you think I would trust you?"

"How long are you going to hold such contempt for us all?"

I stare at him flatly. "Until you die."

His brow furrows. "You say that like it's a promise."

"Maybe it is."

We stare at each other.

"That is all," I eventually sigh.

"Yes, sir." He stands and makes for the door. "The penthouse is ready in Milan for you."

"Thank you."

"When will you be moving in?"

I turn back to my computer. "Tonight."

"So soon?"

I stay silent.

"Your mother...."

I clench my jaw, I haven't spoken to my mother since this all went down. I have nothing to say, my heart wouldn't take it. I need to be stronger before we have this conversation.

"Is none of your business," I snap.

"I don't think...."

I look up at him, annoyed. "Lorenzo, do not question my decisions. They are mine to make."

"Yes, sir."

"Close the door."

The door clicks quietly and I pick up my father's letter and reread the last few lines.

Look after your beautiful mother.
 I miss her dearly.

I love you, my son. More than anything, I love you.
 Be brave, be strong, and try to understand my life and why I haven't always been honest with you. My only goal was to protect your sense of self.
 I pray that I have.

All my love,

Papa.
 x

I get a lump in my throat.

My mother loved him with all of her heart, she gave up her family, her country, all of her friends, everything...to be with him...and to think of how he treated her.

An insignificant mistress.

He took her dignity.

I imagine her alone all those nights, knowing that he was in bed with his wife.

The guards that went between the houses, everyone knew and like a fool, she was forced to face them.

Every time he left us and returned to his family, how must she have felt? How did she feel when he returned?

Betrayal washes over me like a toxic wave.

She had no one to share this burden with, she was all alone with a little baby.

His baby.

And he let her be.

The letter blurs as the tears steal my vision.

Contempt pumps through my blood like a poison.

I hate him, with all of my soul.

I fucking hate him.

I pull the car in through the grand gates and I'm stopped by security, the guard's face falls as he sees me. "Hello, Mr. Ferrara."

"Hello."

His eyes flick to the cars behind and Lorenzo runs up to my window. "No, no, no. What are we doing here?" he stammers. "Giuliano, no."

"Are you going to open the gates or shall I drive through them?" I snap.

He wrings his hands together as if praying. "Please, I beg of you. Leave them out of it. This has nothing to do with them, they do not need to be involved."

I glare at him.

"I beg of you."

"Open the fucking gates," I scream as I lose my patience. "Do. Not. Make. Me. Ask. Again," I warn them.

The guards and Lorenzo exchange worried looks and the gates slowly open.

I drive up the long driveway with my heart in my throat.

Francesca

I lie on my side and stare at the wall. It feels like the end of the world; perhaps it is.

Enrico, my beloved brother and Olivia are gone.

And so is my love....

Where has Giuliano been? Why can't I reach him? I'm heartbroken and he is nowhere to be seen, this isn't like him at all, has something happened to him too?

My door opens in a rush, Anna bursts in. "Giuliano is here."

I sit up. "What?"

"He's out the front fighting with Lorenzo."

Without a thought I run out of the room and down the stairs and burst out the front door, just as Anna said, Giuliano is standing near the procession of cars having a stand-up argument with Lorenzo.

"Giuliano," I call.

He looks up and my heart skips a beat as I smile.

He's here.

Screw this, I'm not playing this game anymore. "Let him in," I call.

"I don't think...." Lorenzo says.

Giuliano brushes past him and rushes up the steps toward me, he takes my hand and pulls me into the house and slams the door. "Where is your bedroom?"

"Huh?"

"Your bedroom?" he demands.

"Upstairs."

Pulling me by the hand, he leads me up the stairs, we pass Anna on our way.

"Hello, Anna," he says.

Her eyes widen. "Hi."

My mother comes out of her bedroom on the second floor and she gasps when she sees him. "What are you doing?" she cries.

Giuliano stops still and glares at her. "Whatever I fucking like," he sneers.

My eyes widen in horror.

Oh no, this is bad, nobody speaks to my mother like that and lives to tell the tale.

"Where is your bedroom, Francesca?" he barks as he continues to lead me up the stairs.

My shocked eyes look back at my mother and Anna who have been rendered speechless. Why the hell is he being so rude?

"Top floor."

We arrive at the top floor and I gesture to my room and he walks in and closes the door behind us and locks it.

"What are you doing?" I stammer, I glance down to see him dressed in a charcoal suit and tie, trendy shoes and all businesslike. "Why do you look like this?"

He puts his hands on his hips and stares at me.

"And why haven't you returned my calls?" I whisper angrily. "It's been a nightmare, my brother Enrico was killed, I've been distraught, I needed you."

"I know." His eyes search mine. "That's why I'm here." He takes my shoulders in his hands and sits me on the bed. "Francesca, baby. You need to listen."

"What's wrong with you, why are you acting so weird?"

"Do you know who I am?"

"What?"

"Do you know who I really am?"

I screw up my face in confusion. "What the hell's gotten into you? You're my boyfriend."

He holds his hands out wide. "Is that all I am?"

"What are you talking about?" I whisper angrily.

"When your father died, did he leave you a letter?"

I shake my head. "No."

"Do you know anything about your brothers' letters?"

"What letters?"

His face drops and he sits beside me, he cups my face in his hands and leans in and gently kisses me. "I love you," he whispers.

I smile through tears. "I so desperately needed to hear that. I love you too."

He takes my hands in his as if steeling himself. "This week...." His voice trails off as if lost for words.

"What is it?"

"I've learned something." He swallows the lump in his throat. "About myself...and you."

"Like what?"

He stares at me. "It's not great."

I smile up at my beautiful man. "It's okay, whatever it is, we can handle it together."

He opens his suit jacket and pulls out an envelope from an inside pocket and passes it to me.

I stare at it.

Enrico

"What's this?"

"It's the letter that your father left for your brother Enrico when he died. You will understand this letter better than the one I got." He kisses my fingertips. "I thought you may have gotten one too."

I frown, it is my father's handwriting. "How did you get this?"

"Read it."

"How did you get this?" I snap as fear begins to run through my veins.

"Read it." He stands and walks to the window and looks out the window, his two hands go into his suit pockets.

With shaky hands I slowly take the letter out of the envelope and open it. It's a few pages long and handwritten.

Dad's writing.

My darling Enrico,

If you are reading this, my son, I have left this world.

I want to start this letter by telling you how proud I am of the man you have become.

Emotion overwhelms me and I blink through my tears.
I miss him.
God, how I miss him.

Hopefully, you will never read this and we will have had this conversation face-to-face. But, in the tragic event that both my father and I go together, I needed to leave this letter for you.

I'm guessing that you are reading this letter in the days after my death...perhaps weeks.

I didn't want this handed to you until you were searching for answers. I know you would have had enough to deal with at the time of my sudden passing.

I'm so sorry, son. I wish we had more time together.

I can almost hear his voice.

I have no idea how to write this or what to say, so the beginning seems like a good place to start.

I don't understand.

You may ask why I kept the Ferrara business from you, Enrico—why I didn't prepare you better.

It was my greatest dream that, by the time you learned of this, I would have held the helm for a good period of time and the violence would have been a distant memory for our family. I knew that one day you'd find out who your ancestors really were, and I wanted you to be prepared.

Violence?
I don't understand...I read on.

Although I didn't train you for our business, I did prepare you in my own way. The day you became a policeman, Enrico, was the proudest day of my life. You learning that side of the law will help Ferrara greatly in future generations.

I'm guessing that you are searching for this because you have found out about Angelina.

I'm sorry I disappointed you, son. I felt this burden every day of my life.

Your mother and I were promised to each other on your mother's birth, when I was only three years old. We met a few times over our lives, and we were to marry when I was twenty-two.

When I was seventeen and visiting an aunt, I met an English girl in Lake Como who was an exchange student. Her name was Angelina Linden, and she was the most beautiful woman I had ever seen. We talked, and I convinced her to let me take her on a date. One turned into two, two turned into three.

I fell hopelessly in love with her. We spent two wonderful years together in Lake Como, and when she had to return to England, I ran away to go to her. I couldn't stand the thought of a life without her in it.

My family were appalled. I was promised to another. Many financial deals had been negotiated from this arranged marriage. Stefano, my father, came to London and made me return to Italy without my beloved Angelina.

    It broke my heart. I never thought I would recover.

"Is this...your mother?" I screw up my face. "I'm so confused."

"Keep reading," he snaps.

I focus back on the letter.

Your mother and I began the courting process and I told her that I loved another. We spoke often of Angelina. There were no secrets between us. She was a dear friend who helped me through the process. In fear that I would run away again, the marriage was brought forward and your mother and I exchanged our wedding vows. By this time, we were close friends and I began to have feelings for her. Not the same as my feelings for Angelina, but feelings all the same.

Your mother is the most beautiful, selfless person I have ever met. I adore her with every sense of my being. Over the next four years, we had three beautiful sons together. We traveled along and I was comfortable...but there was a part of me missing.

I close my eyes.
Oh God.
I don't think I can read on. After a moment, I force myself to.

I went to France for business. You can imagine my shock to run into my Angelina, who was there for business also.

In the ultimate act of betrayal, I spent a week in Angelina's arms and fell deeply in love with her again.

This time, there was no end in sight. I knew I couldn't live without her.

I returned home and told your mother everything. I asked her for a divorce, which she declined. She wanted me to be with her for our children's sake. She wanted the security of having me at home. Your mother didn't want me to leave her completely. She put forward the idea of Angelina moving to Lake Como, and that I live between the two houses. At first, I declined. It wasn't fair to either woman. But my heart was with Angelina, and I couldn't leave your mother with three small children alone.

Finally, it was agreed on. I would become your mother's companion. I moved into the spare room of our family home. Your mother and I became just friends, and Angelina became my partner.

For many, many years, the three of us were happy with this arrangement. Your mother had my support and devotion, and I got to live with my sons as they grew. Angelina always had my full heart. But Angelina was missing a part of her life. At the age of thirty-two and running out of time, she wanted a child.

I begin to hear my heartbeat in my ears as I read on.

My haunted eyes rise to meet Giuliano, a tear rolls down my face and then drops onto the letter in front of me, I blink to try to focus on the familiar handwriting.

No.

I wanted to give Angelina a family of her own. She had given up her whole life and family to be with me. To have half of me.

Angelina's family disowned her when they found out she had moved to Italy to be a married man's mistress. When I wasn't with her in Lake Como, she was completely alone.

It was a heavy burden to carry for her, and yet her devotion to me never wavered...not once.

She paid the ultimate price for my love: her dignity.

I loved her desperately, Enrico, please understand that this was not something that was created out of lust. I am a bigger man than that. I couldn't fight my love for her.

I tried. For six years, I tried.

It only got worse with time, not better.

I agreed that she could have a child, and a year later, Angelina became pregnant. For the first time in my marriage, your mother was furious—crazy like I had never seen her before. She wanted to have my only children and she didn't speak to me for three months. We fought. She showed me a side of her I hadn't seen before. Heartbroken, I worked desperately hard to get my best friend back. I missed her. I missed your mother's love, and then the unthinkable happened. For the first time ever, I fell in love with your mother. It was a different love to what I had with Angelina, but love, nonetheless.

She deserved better than I gave her.

I don't know how my life turned out the way it did. I was in love with two women.

My beloved wife and my devoted soul mate.

The three of us suffered, but Angelina ultimately sacrificed the most.

How could fate be so cruel?

The day Giuliano was born, my heart sang with happiness.

The joy that he brought to my Angelina was indescribable.

I gasp as my hand flies over my mouth, Giuliano's haunted eyes hold mine.

My biggest regret in all of this is that he didn't get to grow up with his brothers. Enrico, when I look at him, I see you.

Brave, strong, and loyal.

I love you, son...more than you could ever know.

I drop my head as the tears roll down my face.

No.

You may ask why I didn't tell you any of this, Enrico.

The answer is simple: it changes you. It changes every part of who you think you are. Knowing that your family's money comes from crime, knowing that your father has committed adultery for all of your life...it's soul destroying. Trust me, I know first-hand.

I was eleven years old when I found out about the family business. I was eleven years old when I witnessed my first murder. I was eleven years old when Stefano brought his mistresses into my life and paraded them in front of me as if I should be proud. There were multiple women—too many to remember. Sometimes three or four at once. This was his normal. This was how he was brought up. This was how he was going to bring me up.

He had no respect for my mother or me. It changed who I was, and for a long time, I hated him for it.

I vowed that I would never let my sons be tainted and bitter the way I was.

I wanted my sons to be proud of who I was.

I'm not perfect.

I know I loved two women, Enrico. The three of us were victims of circumstance. I know that I am still a Ferrara.

But I hope you remember the good in me, and how much I loved you.

I begin to hear my heartbeat in my ears.
This can't be happening.

Please listen to what I am about to tell you. I know you will be angry, but I have my reasoning.

Giuliano does not know anything about my other life. Like you, I have tried to protect him. He knows me as Papa—his father who worked away for a few days a week. The one who idolized his mother.

My eyes rise to see Giuliano staring at the ground.
Clearly devastated.
Oh...dear God.

Enrico, I need you to be the strong man I raised and step up and look after my beloved Angelina and Giuliano.

They are all alone.
  I have taken precautions and they have been guarded up until you find this letter, but they are now in your care.

I have thought long and hard about this, Enrico, and I have made my decision based on personality alone. I have four sons, but only two are strong enough to be leaders. Giuliano is to be your successor, Enrico.
  He will one day follow in your footsteps and lead Ferrara.

My eyes widen as the floor spins beneath me.
This can't be happening.

When Giuliano Ferrara Linden is twenty-one, and not a day before, he will receive a letter similar to the one you are reading now, and he will learn of everything. He will be publicly claimed as my son, and his name will be legally changed to Giuliano Ferrara. He will then hate me, I have no doubt.

I screw up my face in tears and put my hand over my mouth.

I need you to take him under your wing and remind him of how much he was wanted and loved.

My love for his mother has not waned in death, he was my gift to her. Love personified.

Care for him, love him, and teach him what I have had the time to teach you.

Look after my beloved Angelina, and your beautiful mother.
　　I miss them both dearly.

I love you, my son. More than anything, I love you.
　　Be brave, be strong, and try to understand my life and why I haven't always been honest with you. My only goal was to protect your sense of self.
　　I pray that I have.

All my love,

Papa.
　　x

The room is silent, tears stream down my face and I drag my eyes up to meet his.

We stare at each other for an extended time and then he

comes to me and cups my face in his hand. "I've come to say goodbye," he whispers.

My face distorts as I shake my head. "No." I push him in the chest. "Don't you dare say that to me." I begin to slap him away as I lose control. Don't touch me, I'm outraged at this terrible lie he's telling me.

"Baby." He wrestles me and then takes me into his arms and holds me tight as I cry against his chest. "I'm sorry. I'm so, so sorry," he whispers against my forehead. "I need you to go to Paris."

I pull out of his arms. "No, I'm not leaving you."

"You are not safe here. The person who killed Enrico is still here in Italy. I need you to go live with your brother, Andrea."

"No. I'm not leaving you. Ever."

He screws up his face and this time it is him fighting tears. "We can never be together, Francesca."

"Don't say that."

"I'm your brother."

I step back from him, I need to get away from this hurt.

"Stop it," I spit. "Stop lying." I grab the letter and scrunch it in a ball and throw it at him. "I don't want your stupid fucking letter. Take it away. I hate it," I cry.

My chest is shaking as I struggle for air and he just stares at me in a detached state.

"I have to go," he says calmly.

"No." I reach for him. "Don't you leave me."

He kisses my forehead. "Goodbye." He pulls out of my arms and walks toward the door.

I cry, howl-to-the-moon sobs, this can't be happening.

He opens the door and Anna is standing there, her face falls as she sees me so upset.

"Francesca," she whispers.

He brushes past her and walks down the steps, I sob out loud.

"What have you done to her?" my mother yells after him.

"Stay out of my way," he growls.

"You are not welcome in this house again; do you hear me?" she yells.

Oh no. I run to the top of the stairs.

Giuliano turns back toward her and lifts his chin, as if infuriated. "I believe *I* own this house, Bianca," he sneers.

My mother frowns.

He steps toward her, contempt dripping from his every pore. "I *was* going to give you a grieving period. But now...." He gives her a sarcastic smile. "Now, I'm not. You have twenty-one days to get out of my house."

"What are you talking about, this is my house?"

"And yet, everything is in my name." He smiles sarcastically. "I wonder why that is?"

"You've gone crazy," she whispers.

He steps toward her and she steps back. "You have cuckolded the last Ferrara man."

Her mouth falls open in shock.

"Do you think I don't know what you did to my mother," he whispers darkly.

Her face falls.

"You are going to pay for every fucking tear she has cried."

"Giuliano, no," Lorenzo says. "Don't do this."

"Stay out of my way, Lorenzo, or I will kill you myself," he bellows.

What the hell?

"You will not get one more fucking cent of Ferrara money, you conniving bitch!" he screams.

"What am I supposed to do with no money?" she cries. "You cannot throw me out on the street."

He stares at her, cold as ice. "Watch me."

He turns and walks out the door, it slams shut behind him.

My mouth falls open in horror.

Dear God.

5

Francesca

THE CAFÉ IS busy and bustling, Anna holds her newspaper open to show me a pic on the social pages. "Look who it is?"

"Who?" I narrow my eyes and peer across the table, coffee in hand. "I can't even see it, I swear to God, I need glasses?"

"I told you to get your eyes checked ages ago. Guess who Amber Lopez is dating?"

I roll my eyes; Amber Lopez is an insanely beautiful supermodel. The current it girl, she's everywhere. "Ugh...who?" I sip my coffee.

"Giuliano Ferrara."

"What?" I snatch the paper out of her hands. "Let me see." I speed-read the heading.

Amber Lopez off the market

The half-page picture is of Amber and Giuliano walking

hand in hand down the street. He's in a black dinner suit and she's in a skimpy pink evening gown. "What the hell?" I scoff as I stare at it. "Where was this taken?"

"Brazil. The wedding of Fabio Grimaldi the soccer player," Anna replies.

I stare at the photo, Giuliano and she are holding hands as they walk toward a yacht. He's smiling as he talks, his dark hair is messed to perfection and she's looking up at him all doe-eyed. Amber is beautiful, a body to die for, coffee-brown colored, shoulder-length hair with blond sun-kissed highlights around her face. Big lips and green eyes. She's absolutely stunning. I flick the paper back to Anna in disgust.

"That's a blast from the past, hey?" Anna reads the story. "Imagine how good-looking their kids would be?"

"I'd rather not," I reply deadpan. "And I wouldn't get too excited, it won't last."

"It's Amber Lopez." Anna smirks. "No guy on earth would dump her."

"It is Giuliano, remember." I roll my eyes. "He probably fucked the bride in the bathroom at her pre-wedding dinner," I mutter into my coffee.

Anna giggles. "Probably."

It's been ten years since I last laid eyes on Giuliano Ferrara and to this very day, it annoys me that women love him, it annoys me even more that he loves them back. I still have a twinge of ownership over him, even though I know I never did.

Sometimes, when I'm alone, I let myself think of him.

Of what happened between us all those years ago when we were kids.

I wonder what our father would make of his choices and who he's become.

Unlike my father and the generations before him who

worked in the shadows, unnoticed and unobtrusive, polite in company and secretive until the very end.

Giuliano Ferrara runs Italy with an iron fist, he does things differently.

He makes his own rules, the ultimate enigma.

He doesn't get chauffeured around in the back of a black Mercedes, he drives himself in his black Ferrari. He doesn't have secret mistresses hidden in Lake Como, he dates models and film stars, and flaunts them to the world.

He doesn't have guards, he *is* the guard. He looks after his men, not the other way around. Known for his intelligence and cold calculation, nobody messes with him.

Ferrara Industries now own the biggest cocaine market in the world.

And I only know this because I have to listen to my mother vent to my brothers about how his father would be rolling in his grave at raising such a violent criminal.

But if I'm completely honest, and I can be with you...I'm happy he's doing things his way.

Being a criminal is not the life I would want for him, but I'm proud that he's done it his way and not conformed to what was expected. In the beginning there was a major backlash by his men, but in the end, he won their respect and is now revered by all.

I also know that in reality, if he didn't step up to the plate and become the leader that my father thought he was, he wouldn't have survived, he has a huge target on his back and I'm glad he's good at dodging bullets.

I just wish he didn't shoot them…. But, unfortunately, that is who he is now.

It is what it is.

I should probably have regrets that I lost my virginity to my brother.

But, the truth is, I don't. Not one single regret.

How could I regret falling in love with such a beautiful boy?

Of course, I know that same boy doesn't exist anymore. But our secret is safe. That short period of time in our life was sacred. We both know what happened, and while it's never been discussed or touched on, we both know we were just a stepping-stone in each other's lives.

He's never tried to contact me, nor have I contacted him. It was like the world as we knew it stopped on the day he found out that I was his sister.

They say time heals all wounds, and I guess in some ways that's true.

I've watched from the sidelines as he's brought my mother to her knees.

Just as he promised, she has never received another cent from the Ferrara dynasty. Not that she needed it, my father paid her a salary of millions of dollars every month that they were married, she's a very wealthy woman in her own right.

It's just that now, she spends her money and not Ferrara's. He won't even pay for her security, she's completely cut off.

Surprisingly, a month after he took over, Giuliano transferred the real estate portfolio into my, Matteo and Andrea's names. He broke rank and instead of the assets staying together in the collective Ferrara pool, he gave us our equal share. Something that has never been done in all of our family history over the generations.

In return, he won my brothers' respect, infuriated my mother and gave me the freedom to live my life as I want to.

I'm no longer controlled, my every move monitored.

As Giuliano asked, I relocated to France in the month after

Enrico's death, I felt safer there. And if the truth be told, Italy didn't have the same sparkle to it for me anymore. Knowing that your family's money comes from generations of crime is shameful. The day I found out was soul destroying.

And while I'm not stupid, I appreciate the luxury I'm afforded. I understand my ancestors and what they have passed down, I don't think it will ever sit with me well. How could it?

A mutual respect hangs silently between us.

We don't need to say anything to each other, we don't need closure, we both know where we sit in the world.

Giuliano Ferrara's place, a leader in the dark world.

My place, an interior designer with the biggest design house in France.

I'm happily in love with a wonderful man who I've been dating for three years.

Marcel is a blond-haired, blue-eyed French diplomat. We met at university and he is kind and loving and all that is good. We don't live together, although he would like to. I live with Anna, she was always visiting me and eventually met a French man too. We have a great time together and unlike me, Anna wants to return to live in Italy one day. I'm happy here.

My future with Marcel is bright, and refreshingly normal.

I'm not trailed by huge amounts of security all the time, although four Ferrara men who live in Paris are at my beck and call. They are around but never in my way, I hardly know they are there. And when I visit my mother in Milan, I do fly home in one of the Ferrara jets. Lorenzo won't allow me to catch a commercial flight, some things will never be completely normal, but that I can live with.

"Amber is twenty-four," Anna reads.

"So?" I mutter into my coffee.

"Giuliano is twenty-nine, that's a big age difference, don't you think?"

"Have you seen her?" I mutter dryly.

"I can just imagine her lying all over his yachts in her skimpy bikinis," she continues. "God, she would be loving herself sick."

"Ugh." I roll my eyes in disgust as I imagine it. "Don't even."

My buzzer sounds on my desk. "Francesca, Pierre would like to see you in his office."

"Thanks, Inga. On my way."

I close down my email and make my way up to the top floor, Pierre Moran is my boss. One of the most well-respected interior designers in the world. He has been the most amazing mentor possible and I owe him so much.

"Knock, knock." I stand at his door.

"Francesca." He smiles. "Take a seat, darling."

I smile and walk in and sit down at his desk. "Did we get it?" I put my hands together as if praying. "Tell me we got it."

He smiles broadly. "We got it."

"Yes." I jump from my seat in excitement. "I knew it. Yes. We got it!" I screech in excitement.

We just got the Remington job, the most luxurious hotel chain in the world has just hired us to do their entire refurbishment.

Pierre swings on his chair and laughs out loud. "It's incredible, isn't it?"

"Oh my God." The magnitude of this begins to hit me and I put my hands over my mouth. "Can you believe this?"

"One hundred and eighty-eight hotels around the world are going to be redesigned by us." He smiles. "And we have you to thank for it. Your tender was incredible. Take a bow, my dear, you deserved this."

I laugh out loud, I worked for months on this tender. "Thank God it paid off." I smile. "Can you imagine if we did all this work and we didn't get it?"

"But we did." He laughs. "But we did."

"I'm so excited."

"Now comes the work." He smiles. "You know that it will mean a lot of international travel."

"I know."

"And long days and even longer nights."

"I know."

"I want you to head the design team."

What?

My eyes widen, I put my hand on my chest. "Me," I gasp.

"Why not? It's your pitch that won us the account."

I open my mouth to object, I'm not experienced enough for this. No way in hell.

He holds his two hands up. "Now, now, I'm not taking no for an answer. You are the right person for this job."

"Are you sure? I don't mind working under someone on this, it's a big responsibility, Pierre."

"One that you can handle."

"Thank you." Oh my God, this is incredible. "Thank you so much."

Pierre smiles. "We start in two weeks, I'm unsure of the first hotel they want to start on. I'll get more details shortly, I'll keep you posted."

"Thanks." I beam as I stand.

"Congratulations, Francesca, this is an amazing coup for our company. Take next week off, you won't be getting a break for a while."

"Okay, that sounds great, thank you so much." I bounce out the door and float back to my desk, I immediately dial Marcel's number.

"Hi."

"We got the account," I splutter.

"Are you serious?"

"Yes," I whisper in excitement.

"Congratulations, well done."

"Can you believe it?"

"I can. Are we celebrating tonight?"

"You bet we are." I laugh.

"Cordoni's for dinner?"

"Yes." I laugh. Cordoni's is my favorite Italian restaurant, there are a few things from Italy I can't live without.

"Do you want Anna and Frank to come?"

"Is that okay?"

"Of course."

"Okay, I'll call Anna now." I laugh. "I'm just so excited."

"Congratulations."

"I have next week off so I might go home and see Mom for a few days, maybe you could meet me in Milan for the weekend?" I offer. "If I go Tuesday, you could meet me there on Friday and we'll fly home together on Sunday night or something?"

"Yeah, okay, that sounds fun."

I smile, excited. "See you tonight?"

"Goodbye."

Cordoni's is bustling and busy, the restaurant is semi-lit with a tantric beat being pumped through speakers, it has a trendy European vibe.

There's a cocktail bar and a dance floor and the restaurant spans over three stories. Frank and Marcel are friends, they met through Anna and me but are happy to hang out together, which makes life a lot easier for us.

They are at the bar getting our next drinks and Anna and I are sitting at the table, we are on our fifth margarita.

Liquid gold.

"Oh my God, I feel drunk." Anna hiccups.

"Right?" I whisper. "I'm seriously a lightweight now."

"Wow." Anna's eyes widen. "Look at that guy over there."

"Where?"

"At the table over there." She gestures with her glass and I casually look over.

A tall, dark and handsome man has just sat down. "Yum." I smile as I watch him.

"So hot."

"He is." I swoon. "You have to admit it; Italian men are the hottest race in the world," I whisper.

"Undoubtedly." We both watch him for a moment. "Do you reckon that's his wife?" she asks.

"Well, if he's Italian, it's probably his mistress," I murmur into my drink.

Anna laughs, we have a constant running joke about mistresses, my father scarred us both for life. In my family no man has ever been faithful to his wife, it's pushed me to lose faith in Italian men.

My phone vibrates on the table and the name *Mom* lights up the screen.

"I'll quickly take this," I say as I answer. "Hi, Mom."

"Hello, darling." She smiles. "Where are you, sounds noisy."

"In a restaurant," I reply, there's no point telling her about the account we won today, she doesn't care about my work. "What are you up to?"

"Angelina Linden died today."

My face falls. "What?"

Suddenly the restaurant is way too loud and I need to hear what she has to say. I hold my finger up to Anna, "Back in a minute," I mouth, I stand and rush from the restaurant and out onto the street. "What do you mean?" I reply.

"Angelina Linden died."

"When?"

"Today."

"How?"

"She had a cerebral hemorrhage, collapsed on the spot. It was sudden with no warning signs at all."

"Oh no." My heart sinks. "Was she alone?"

"She had her two guards with her, she was rushed to hospital by ambulance, but unfortunately she died a few hours later."

"She was so young."

"Only sixty-one."

I stay silent on the line as I try to process the information. God....

"I just thought you should know."

"How's Lorenzo?" I ask, "He and she were always so close."

"Distraught. There are men crying everywhere here."

Giuliano.

I stay silent, unsure what to say, my mind is running a million miles per minute.

"When's the funeral?" I ask.

"No idea. I'll let you go sweetie."

"Okay, thanks for letting me know." I hang up and stand still on the pavement in shock. It's dark and people are rushing past on the busy street but my mind is a jumble of confusion, sadness and shock.

What the hell?

She was so full of life, why would she be taken so young? It's just not fair.

Life can be so cruel.

I stay outside alone for a few minutes, for some reason, I feel like I need to show my respect for a woman who changed my father's life.

He loved her and she loved him.

And now, she's gone too.

Giuliano.

My heart sinks in sadness, he'd be so devastated.

I trudge back into the restaurant and sit back at the table, Marcel and Frank are back at the table now.

"Everything alright?" Marcel asks.

"Oh...." I frown as I try to collect my thoughts. "Angelina Linden died."

"Oh my God," Anna gasps.

"Who's that?" Marcel asks.

"My half-brother's mother."

Frank frowns, confused.

"Long story." I roll my eyes as I sip my drink. Marcel doesn't know about my family's roots, I've kept them from him. It hasn't been easy.

The table all carry on with their conversation and I sit and stare into space, my thoughts are in Lake Como in Italy. I imagine Angelina's house and what must be going on there now.

Her friends, the guards, the crying. The broken hearts.

Giuliano.

Bianca Ferrara is a beautiful woman; my mother turns heads wherever she goes. We sit in her favorite restaurant in Milan.

"This caviar is to die for." She smiles. "You should have some, dear."

I wince. "It's not my thing." I sip my champagne and steel myself for the oncoming onslaught. "I'm going to go to Angelina Linden's funeral tomorrow."

She drops her knife with a clang. "You will do no such thing."

Here we go.

"I'm not asking for your permission, I'm just telling you that because I'm already in Italy and out of respect for Lorenzo and Giuliano…and my father. I'm going."

"And what about respect for me?" she whispers angrily.

"I'm just going to go to the service. I'll be there half an hour…tops."

"No. You *are* not." She looks around guiltily. "How will it look if my only daughter goes to my late husband's mistress's funeral?"

I stare at her, infuriated but not surprised. "I don't care how it looks."

"I do."

"Seriously?" My annoyance begins to bubble. "Please don't act the innocent one here mother. You encouraged him to have that mistress, I've read the letters, it was your idea. Stop playing the victim," I whisper. "It's getting very old."

"Giuliano had no right giving you that letter to Enrico," she snaps. "If your father wanted you to know these things, he would have written a letter for you. You are not going," she chastises me.

I sip my drink, honestly, why did I even tell her? "Fine."

"You won't go?"

It's not worth the trouble.

"I have a lot on tomorrow anyway," I lie.

She reaches over and rubs the back of my hand and smiles triumphantly. "Thank you. I appreciate it, I don't want you mixing with that crowd, they're bad to the bone."

I exhale heavily. "It's a funeral, Mother, what do you think is going to happen, strippers dancing on the tables or something?"

"If Giuliano organized it, nothing would surprise me." She mutters in disgust, her hand rises up to the waiter with a smile. "Two more martinis, please."

I stare at my reflection in the mirror, my long dark hair is out and full, my makeup is natural and I'm wearing a Valentino fitted black dress with long sleeves with the sheer black stockings and patent sky-high stilettos. The dress is stylish without being too much, it laces up with a black satin ribbon down the front.

I'm nervous about going to Angelina's funeral today, I really have no idea if it's the right thing to do, but it feels wrong not to go.

At the very least, the woman who loved my father so deeply deserves my respect.

My phone beeps a text.

Your car is here

I take one last look at myself and reapply my lipstick, I grab my purse and jacket and I make my way downstairs. I stay at my penthouse whenever I'm in Milan, it feels so weird having my own places.

Good weird.

Like my brothers, I'm grateful that Giuliano has set us all up financially for life.

He didn't have to do that, the fact that he did means a lot.

The elevator opens to the grand foyer and a doorman dressed in a gray suit opens the front door for me. "Good morning, Miss Ferrara," he says with a kind nod.

"Good morning Steven." I smile. The staff are all so nice in my building, my visits home always leave me feeling welcome. I walk out the huge glass doors to see that it's raining, Antonio is waiting by the door with an oversized umbrella.

"Good morning, Miss Ferrara." He holds the umbrella over my head as he leads me to the black Mercedes that is waiting by the curb.

"Good morning, Antonio." I smile. "Thank you." I climb into the back seat and the car door closes behind me. The car pulls out into the heavy traffic and we head toward Lake Como.

I have no idea what awaits me, but the thought of the oncoming event makes me nervous.

Maybe my mother is right and I shouldn't have come.

I pull my jacket around my shoulders and sit back into the leather seat, I guess we'll soon see.

The car pulls up out the front of the Catholic church as the rain pours down.

As if the day isn't depressing enough as it is.

Antonio opens my door as he protects me with the umbrella, I am ushered inside and led to the fourth row of the already packed church. I sit at the end near the aisle. I look up to the dark wood casket sitting in front, covered in pink roses of every shade. A large photo of Angelina sits on a gold easel. I stare at her face as she looks out over the church, she was such a gorgeous looking woman, her face oozes kindness.

"Francesca Ferrara is here," I hear someone gasp from behind me as I sit down. "Oh my God," whispers someone else.

Fuck.

Mother was right, this doesn't look good.

With my back ramrod straight, I clasp my hands on my lap and wait.

The front row is empty and I know it's reserved for the family, they mustn't be here yet. I let myself look around and see so many familiar faces, my stomach drops.

So many friends of my father.

He really did live a double life; all his friends knew Angelina. I wonder did they socialize as a couple with people that my mother knew.

Lorenzo walks up the aisle and sits in the second row, he's visibly upset and I watch him as he stares at Angelina's photo. There are a lot of men in that row and I'm assuming they are Giuliano's closest friends.

What must Lorenzo have seen in his lifetime? As my father's best friend, work colleague and confidant, he adored Angelina. He and she were strong friends until the very end. He has been there for her and Giuliano all along.

He is also now dating my mother, talk about a confusing conflict of interests. One thing I do know for sure is that my mother would never have been able to stop him from supporting Angelina, even if she had wanted to. His loyalty to her has never been questioned. I guess Lorenzo was strong friends with her long before he and my mother became a thing.

Another group of people walk up the aisle, they are crying and look very different to the rest of the church. Blond.

English.

They must be her family.

Trailing behind them is a lone figure in a black suit.

Giuliano.

My eyes instantly well with tears as I see him.

He's broken, I can feel it.

They all take their seats, he sits down at the end, there is a spare seat next on the left of him.

A seat for my father.

His eyes rise to the coffin and he stares at it blankly.

I get a lump in my throat as I watch him, he looks so sad and forlorn.

Utterly broken.

The minister takes his place at the podium. "Thank you all for coming. Today we are here to celebrate the life of Angelina Linden. Beloved partner of Giuliano and adored mother to Giuliano."

My heart drops.

The service begins and the English relatives all hug and console each other.

Giuliano sits alone, staring at the coffin.

Why is he alone?

People are crying all around me, the sad sobs are deafening.

Giuliano sits alone, completely composed and straight faced.

Why isn't anyone comforting him?

I begin to look around, what the hell is going on here? Where are all his support people?

Then it dawns on me, he doesn't know the English relatives.

He really *is* all alone.

He doesn't have any family left.

My heart breaks as I watch him, a lone tear rolls down my face and I look at my father's empty chair beside him.

I can't stand it.

I know that I'm not my father, but at this moment I'm the closest thing to it.

I stand and walk up the aisle to the sound of gasps behind me and I sit beside Giuliano.

He looks over at me and a frown crosses his brow.

"Hi." I smile softly and take his hand in mine and hold it on my lap.

He squeezes my hand in a silent thank-you and I squeeze it back.

With his eyes fixed on the coffin, he swallows the lump in his throat as his jaw clenches and I know that my act of kindness has perhaps weakened his defenses.

As the service goes on, I lean my head on Giuliano's shoulder and after a while, he puts his arm around me.

Leaning against each other, we watch the service in silence and it may as well be just me and him in the room. I don't care what anyone else thinks, I'm here to support my brother in his time of need.

And he needs me, I can feel it in my bones. The sadness seeping out of him is overwhelming.

The service comes to an end and Giuliano stands and puts a pink rose on her coffin and then Lorenzo and a group of young men, I'm guessing Giuliano's friends, take their place at the side of the coffin.

Giuliano's eyes well with tears as he drops his head.

Oh no.

I just want to comfort him.

"One, two, three," they whisper.

The men all lift together and carry Angelina's coffin to the hearse waiting outside.

Everyone gets up and slowly leaves but I stay seated in the church and stare into space. A little shell shocked and a whole lot of devastated.

I haven't been to a funeral since Enrico's and Olivia's. Only two years before that I went to my grandfather's and father's. And now, this.

There have been too many deaths in my family, too much heartbreak.

I hear the cries as the funeral car pulls away outside and I close my eyes to try to block out the sobs.

I stay seated for a long time, I'll wait until everyone leaves before I go out there. I don't want to see or talk to anyone.

"Thank you," a deep voice says softly from behind me.

I turn to see Giuliano standing in the aisle.

"It means a lot that you came." His voice is deep and raspy.

"That's okay." I stand. "I hope I didn't intrude."

"Not at all."

He's different now, older. Taller and broader. He seems a lot harder and has a few scars on his face around his eyes.

How did he get those...was it from fighting?

"I should get going," I say.

"Will you come to the wake at my mother's house?" he asks.

I open my mouth to say no. "Yes," comes out.

What?

"Thank you."

We stare at each other and I don't know what to say. "I'll see you there?"

"Okay."

We walk out of the church together and a lot of the crowd are now gone, my car is waiting and Giuliano walks across the road and gets into the back of another car that has a few men in it.

"To Milan?" Antonio asks.

Shit.

I know what I should say, but the words won't come out. "To Angelina's house, the wake, please."

Twenty minutes later, the car pulls up out the front of the house and I close my eyes, *what the hell am I doing here?*

"We will only stay half an hour," I tell Antonio.

"Of course." He drives into the circular driveway and stops the car and opens my door and lets me out. Thankfully, it's stopped raining now, there are people everywhere, a lot more than were at the funeral. Clutching my bag with white-knuckle force, I walk in the front door, look up, and my step falters.

A huge oil painting of my father and Angelina with a small boy hangs on the wall.

They are in a field, they all look so happy and in love.

My eyes instantly well with tears as I stare at it.

Oh....

I weave through the crowd as I walk through the house, there are photos of my father and Angelina with Giuliano everywhere. It's like a shrine to their family.

This house is such a vast contrast to my mother's house, with not one photo of anyone anywhere. Especially not of my father.

I walk through to the backyard, it's full of people and waiters are circulating with silver trays of food and champagne. I catch sight of Giuliano talking to Lorenzo and a few people in the corner of the backyard.

I walk back into the house and look at the photos on one of

the side tables, there's one photo of my father and Giuliano at a football game. Giuliano looks to be about five or six, he's hugging my father and has a football under his arm. They are both laughing.

Betrayal washes over me.

I don't remember doing anything fun with my father, he was so absent with us. No wonder…he was always with them.

Suddenly, I need to get out of here.

For the first time, I feel resentful. Mother was right, I shouldn't have come. No good can come of this, I don't need to know about his other life.

The one that didn't involve me.

I walk back to the front door and glance up the stairs, I wonder what's up there?

I look around guiltily and before I can stop myself, I go up the stairs, I get to the top floor and look around. The house is decorated in Hamptons beach style, warm and friendly, such a contrast to my mother's Versace decorating style.

I tentatively walk down the hall until I get to Angelina's bedroom.

I glance up the hall to check nobody is around and I walk in. The air leaves my lungs, a giant black-and-white photo of Angelina and my father hangs above the bed, they are lying on the floor in what looks like a log cabin. They are young and in front of an open fire, naked, strategically covered in blankets, their hair is tousled and they look so in love. My eyes scan the room as a realization sets in.

I can feel him here; his presence is so strong.

This is where he is.

I stare at the photo as tears roll down my face and, overcome with emotion, I sob out loud.

"They're together now," a voice says from behind me.

I spin to see Giuliano standing behind me, his eyes are also on the photo, his two hands in his suit pockets.

I wipe my tears, embarrassed that I'm crying and even more embarrassed that I've been caught in his mother's bedroom. "I'm sorry, I was looking for the bathroom."

He nods as his eyes hold mine, we stare at each other as a weird familiarity runs between us.

"It's good to see you," he says softly.

"It is."

He steps toward me, only centimeters away, his close proximity causes the air to leave my lungs as we stare at each other.

There's a pull, a yearning to be in his arms.

"Your memory lingers," he whispers.

The air crackles between us as a wildfire ignites in my memory bank.

If I could say something, I would. But I've been rendered speechless. In slow motion, his thumb lifts and he trails it over my bottom lip.

My heart races out of control as we stare at each other. He picks up the ribbon that laces down the front of my dress and holds it between his fingers, his eyes follow his fingers as he pulls it and it slowly undoes.

His dark eyes rise to mine as electricity bounces between us.

Kiss me.

A sound comes from up the hall and we step back from each other guiltily. "Do you know where the bathroom is?" a woman's voice asks.

"Down the hall to the left," he replies calmly.

My heart is racing as I stare at the floor.

"Thank you," she calls.

My eyes rise to meet his and we stare at each other.

"You need to leave," he says, devoid of emotion. "Now."

6

Francesca

W*HAT?*

Did I hear that right?

That wasn't my fault, he undid my ribbon, not the other way around.

"Just go." He turns and leaves the room and with my heart hammering loud in my ears I stare after him, I hear him take the stairs two at a time.

Did we just have a moment?

Shit.

I need to get out of here.

I shouldn't have come, what was I thinking?

I glance up at the huge photo of my father, suddenly infuriated with the situation I find myself in. "Are you happy with the mess you left behind?" I whisper under my breath.

I head toward the door and look back at what may just be the most romantic bedroom I have ever seen.

Only it's not, because it's tainted with lies.

My father wasn't a hero…he was a married man.

And for the first time since I learned the truth, I see things as my mother does. In black and white, there are no blurred lines.

You are either married or you aren't.

He should have divorced my mother and he most definitely shouldn't have had two women pregnant at nearly the same time.

Giuliano would have only been one when my mother was pregnant with me.

My stomach rolls.

Panic sets in and I need to get out of here. I take the stairs two at a time,

I imagine him leaving a woman here with a small baby to go home to his pregnant wife.

Making love to both of them.

One lover nursing his infant, another lover carrying his unborn child.

My eyes well with tears and I burst out the front door and march to the car with urgency.

Antonio's face falls when he sees me. "Are you alright, Miss Ferrara?"

"I'm fine." I open the back door before he gets the chance to. "I would like to go home, please," I say as I get into the back seat, he stares down at me. "Now," I demand.

"Yes, of course." He closes the door and gets into the driver's seat, I glance up at the house as we pull away. Everything appears so sweet, filled with love and memories and photos.

I never really knew my father at all, but I do know one thing.

He was selfish.

Giuliano

The phone rings and I answer it. "Giuliano," my mother's soft voice says.

"Hi, Mom."

"Honey, can you come over and fix the tap."

I look over to the end of my bed and the naked woman lying there. "I can't, I'm busy," *I reply.*

"What am I going to do about the leaky tap?" *Mom asks.*

The girl spreads her legs for me and I tear my shirt over my shoulder as urgency to get off the phone fills me. "Call the plumber, Mom. I know nothing about pipes," *I snap, frustrated.*

"Oh..." *she whispers, disappointed.*

Damn it, why does she always call at the most inconvenient time? "I've got to go," *I say.*

"I love you, Giuliano" *she says.*

I hang up in a rush and as if hovering up above, I watch myself kiss the girl and then, in the background, I can hear my mother crying.

She's heartbroken from a selfish son who never had time for her.

Suddenly I'm standing at my mother's kitchen window, I can see her, she's sitting on her couch, still crying.

Oh no.

"I'm here, Mom," *I call.*

She cries and cries.

I try to open the door but it's locked.

She's still crying. "I'm here, Mom," *I call louder, but she can't hear me.*

I feel panic rise within me.

"I'm here, Mom," *I call as I bang hard on the window.* "I'll fix the tap, I'll do it now. I promise."

She stands and then holds her head as if in pain.

"I'm here," I cry.

She holds her temples and her face contorts.

No.

I bang hard on the window as I try to get to her.

She collapses.

"Mom," I cry, I bang hard on the window, but she can't hear me.

It's like I'm hovering and watching from above.

"Angelina," I hear one of her guards cry, two of them run in the front door and they begin working on her, someone else calls an ambulance.

I need to get to her, quick, hurry.

I run around to the front of her house. I try to open the doorknob.

Locked.

I can't get in, I begin to kick the front door in as I yell for them to let me to her.

"Stay with us, Angelina," her guard yells as they begin to perform CPR.

I'm banging on the glass, yelling, crying. Desperate to get to my dying mother.

Panic fills my every cell.

"Mom," I cry. "Don't go, I'm here. I'll fix the pipes, I'll visit more, I promise."

I jump awake with a start; my heart is beating fast and hard and I pant as I try to control my breathing.

I look around my bedroom, it's dark and still.

Normal.

As if my whole world hasn't just ended.

I stare at the ceiling, as if I don't have enough to deal with without having fucking nightmares.

There are a lot of feelings rushing through me, sadness, despair, hopelessness...but the overwhelming one is guilt.

I never truly forgave my mother for lying to me as I grew up. For the last few years, I avoided seeing her, visiting only occasionally.

And now that I've finally worked it out, it's too late.

She's gone.

I drag myself out of bed and go to the bathroom, I get a glass of water from the kitchen and drink it at the sink. My skin is wet with perspiration, I've never felt so unhinged. I'm like a time bomb waiting to explode.

Alone.

I stare into space as I imagine what I would say to my father if I saw him now. If I could just have the chance..., what would I say? I see his face and without a doubt, I know what I would do.

I'd kill him.

Without a single regret, I would kill him. I've never hated someone so much in my entire life.

My mother was too good for him...too good for me.

I get a lump in my throat, if only I could turn back time.

I'm sorry, Mom, I failed you.

It's Wednesday and I pull my car to park curbside, I turn off the ignition as the traffic whirls by. I look across the road at the apartment block and up to the top floor, her apartment.

The afternoon sun shines through my windscreen and I

don't know why I'm here, or what I'm going to say, but I need to see her.

Francesca.

The woman who so kindly offered support and friendship to me at the funeral.

I can't stop thinking about her.

And I know that if I were a better man I would, but it's already established that I'm not.

Tap, tap, sounds on the window and I glance up, startled. "Everything okay, boss?" Antonio asks.

"Yes." I run my hand through my hair in frustration. *Fuck off and mind your own business.* "Is she home?"

"Who?" Antonio's face falls. "Francesca?"

"Who else would I be talking about?" I snap.

"She's about to go out." He looks across the street at the apartments. "We're waiting for her to come down now."

"Where is she going?" I ask.

"Shopping with her mother, I believe."

"Right." I roll my lips, annoyed.

Antonio looks at me for a beat longer than needed and I raise an eyebrow.

"Shall I get her?" he offers.

"No. Nothing important."

The front doors of the building open and Francesca walks out, she's wearing a tight, fitted, cream knitted dress and sky-high stilettos, her long dark hair is swept up into a high ponytail. I can see her big red lips and chiseled cheekbones from here, impeccable posture, innately feminine, Italian to the bone.

Perfect in every way.

"Will that be all, sir?" Antonio asks interrupting my thoughts.

"Yes, I'll call her later," I reply as my eyes stay glued to her.

"I've got to go." Antonio runs across the street and opens the back door of her car.

She's talking to the doorman, he and she laugh out loud and I stare over at her in awe.

In slow motion, I watch her walk out, she says something to Antonio as she gets into the car and he smiles and says something back.

He closes the door behind her and I watch as their car pulls out into the traffic and drives away.

I lean my head back onto the headrest and exhale heavily.

She's gone.

Francesca

"Good lord, these are delicious." My mother holds her glass up to inspect it.

"I know." I sip the last of my margarita and smile. "How is it, though, that every time we go shopping together, we end up at this restaurant drinking cocktails?"

"This is how you do it, darling." She holds her glass up in a silent salute and I giggle.

My phone rings, it's Anna. "I'm just going to take this."

"Hi," I answer.

"Oh. My. God." She splutters excitedly, "Can you talk?"

"Yes, I'm just having dinner with my mother."

"Can she hear me?"

My eyes rise to see if Mom's listening, "Possibly."

"Go for a walk."

"But...."

"Trust me, go for a fucking walk," she cuts me off.

Weird.

I fake a smile. "Just going to go to the bathroom, Mom."

She nods, preoccupied with her drink.

With my phone to my ear, I weave through the tables and go to the corridor for the bathroom. "What?" I whisper.

"So, I found some porn on Frank's computer."

I frown, I wasn't expecting this. "Okay."

"He'd downloaded it from a website called Pornhub."

"And?"

"I logged in through his computer to see if he had an account."

"Did he?"

"Fucking Platinum Membership."

My eyebrows rise by themselves. "Oh." I shrug. "Well, that's okay I guess, isn't it? No harm in looking."

"I know, but guess what else I stumbled across," she replies.

"What?"

"Giuliano Ferrara is on there."

"On where?"

"Pornhub."

I screw up my face. "What?"

"He's in a threesome with two girls."

My eyes widen and someone walks past me and I push the phone into my ear so that nobody can hear the horrifying things that I'm hearing, I don't want to hear them myself. "What do you mean?" I whisper. "Are you sure it's him?"

"Positive. He's in a pool and they're oiled up and he's fucking two girls."

My eyes bulge from their sockets. "What…like…full fucking."

"Like fully fucking, full frontal, hard oily cock, dick sucking, huge dick porno."

My mouth falls open. "Can't be him," I gasp. "He would never do that?"

"Have a look for yourself, I'm sending you the link now."

I look around, guilty. "Fucking hell," I whisper, suddenly desperate to get off the phone.

"Call me back when you've watched it," she says.

"Okay." I hang up and march back to the table on a mission.

"One more?" Mom asks.

"I can't, I have to go," I say. "I have so much to do."

She rolls her eyes. "What could you possibly have to do? You're on vacation."

"I still have to work, Mom." I put my hand up for the bill, "Come on, let's go."

"What's the rush?"

Oh, nothing important, just my ex first love who also happens to be my brother in a fucking orgy on an international porn network.

I pinch the bridge of my nose, this is un-fucking believable.

We pay the bill and walk outside and I see Antonio waiting for me across the road.

"Bye darling." My mother kisses my cheek.

"Bye."

"Come by tomorrow for a swim?"

"Okay." I wave her off and cross the road, Antonio opens the door for me.

"Hello, Miss Ferrara."

"Hello." I smile as I get into the car, we pull out into the traffic and Antonio's eyes flick up to meet mine in the mirror. His eyes go back to the road and then flick up to me again. Back to the road and then back up to me in the mirror, he looks like he wants to say something.

"What is it?" I ask.

He opens his mouth to speak and then swiftly shuts it again. "I wouldn't want to speak out of turn, Miss Ferrara."

Huh?

"What is it?" I ask. "You couldn't possibly speak out of turn, Antonio. We are friends."

"I was just wondering...." His voice trails off.

"What?"

"What did Mr. Ferrara want?"

"Who?"

"Giuliano came to your house today to see you earlier, he said he was going to call you. What did he want?"

"What?" I sit forward, suddenly interested. "When was he at my house?"

"He was sitting outside in his car when you left to go shopping."

"Where?"

"Across the road, in his Ferrari."

What?

"What did he say?" I ask.

"Nothing." He hesitates and his eyes rise to meet mine once more and I know he wants to elaborate.

"Tell me."

"He's a very dangerous man, Francesca."

"Not to me."

"To you...more than anyone."

I frown, confused.

"I was at that library all those years ago. I remember him declaring his undying love for you. Enrico had warned us all to keep him away from you at all costs."

Oh...I think for a moment.

"It's different now, that was before we found out that we were brother and sister."

"Do you really think that would stop him?"

Our eyes lock in the mirror.

"If he wanted you. He would have you."

"Antonio." I give a subtle shake of my head. "I don't think so."

"I know so."

"What makes you say this, anyway?"

"Because I see them all fall at his feet, I know the caliber of women he attracts, they can't resist him. Nobody is off limits, he has no moral compass, he fucks nuns, Francesca."

My mouth falls open in horror.

Nuns...what the ever-loving fuck?

"Why are you telling me this?" I snap, horrified.

"To warn you." He pulls into the underground parking lot of my building. "If he's turning up at your building, he has an agenda."

"You don't need to worry," I say. "Thank you for your concern, but it's not like that between us anymore, it's really not. And besides the point, we are both in relationships with other people."

Antonio's eyes hold mine in the rearview mirror and I can read his mind as clear as day.

Liar.

The elevator door opens and I rush into my apartment on a mission, I grab my laptop, I drop to my couch and click on the link.

Sinita

"Sinita?" What's a Sinita?

The screen opens up and I put my hand over my mouth in horror.

It's Giuliano, naked and rock hard. He's lying back onto his elbows and covered in oil on the side of a pool.

"What the fuck?" I whisper, horrified. A song starts playing, I've never heard it before but it has a very distinctive piece of music, it's been added after, like dubbed in over the top of the footage.

It looks like it's late at night, perhaps early morning. It's dark, the area seems to be lit up by the pool lights. Giuliano is covered in oil, his broad body rippled with muscle.

His dick is hard...and big...and oh God.

A blond girl bends and takes his hard cock into her mouth, he smiles darkly and then turns to a woman with dark hair and tongue kisses her, I see their tongues dance together as his eyes flutter closed.

I can hardly breathe as I watch on.

The dark-haired woman bends and starts to suck him too, they take turns as he lies back on his elbows watching them take their turns. They are both drop-dead gorgeous, both covered in oil.

My God....

Giuliano's legs are spread, the muscles on his stomach ripple with oil in the light as he moves, his cock is huge and engorged and just.... *Oh.*

I feel myself flutter with arousal.

The music gets louder and he reaches up and slides his fingers deep into one of the girls, my sex contracts as I shudder.

I can almost feel it.

"There's my girl," Marcel's voice says.

Huh?

I look up to see Marcel is standing in the doorway.

What the fuck?

I slam my computer shut. "Hi," I squeak. "Wha.... Wha... what...what are you doing here?" I splutter nervously. "I thought you were getting here tomorrow."

"Surprising you." He holds his hands out wide, "Surprise."

"Great." I fake a smile.

Damn it...I was kind of in the middle of something here.

Marcel takes me into his arms and hugs me, I'm hot and flustered and sickly aroused.

I look over his shoulder at the computer as it sits on the couch and a sense of dread fills me.

I want to know what's going on inside that computer...and worst still, more than anything.

I want to watch him come.

I lie in the darkness and stare at the ceiling.

Antonio's words come back to me. *"If he wanted you. He would have you."*

In the darkest corner of my depravity, I wish that were true.

I close my eyes in disgust...God.

I'm the worst form of human.

Marcel and I made love tonight, only...when I closed my eyes, I wasn't here in this room with him.

I was poolside with Giuliano.

It was his body that I saw, it was his body that I sucked. His hands that rubbed the oil into me.

And I was so hot for it, like never before with Marcel. I hit a new level of arousal.

Ferrara

It was Giuliano who made me come so hard…and he wasn't even here.

A hot tear of regret rolls down my face.

I hate myself.

———

I lie on the deckchair by my mother's pool, I'm being eaten alive by questions. I want to know about Angelina and Giuliano. "I know that we've never talked about Dad."

She exhales heavily.

"I want to understand how…." I frown. "The dynamics of how it went down back then."

"Why would you want to talk about that?"

"I don't know, I guess I'm at an age where I want to understand it from your point of view. If you will just be honest with me today, I promise to never bring it up with you again."

She exhales heavily. "What do you want to know?"

"Did you know about Angelina?"

"I knew that he fell in love with her before we met, but she lived in London and he married me."

I frown as I listen.

"Just as he said in the letter, he went away for work and spent a week with her."

"He told you when he got back?" I ask.

"No."

I frown.

"He saw us both for years, she knew about me but I didn't know about her. He had her set up in Lake Como in her own house, she was his official mistress. The whole of Milan knew about her, he paraded her around while I was at home looking after his children."

My heart drops.

"He told her that he was only with me because of our children and that as soon as they were old enough he was leaving me for her."

"Was that true?"

She shrugs. "Perhaps."

"Were you sleeping with him?"

"All the time, we were closer than we had ever been."

"How did you find out about her?"

"She came to see me."

I sit up in my deckchair, surprised. "What?"

"She was fed up and wanted more from him." She glances over. "She told me everything and I appreciated her honesty, she wasn't the villain in this story, she loved him and was promised the world."

"What happened then?" I ask.

"I was devastated, demanded a divorce which he declined."

Was the letter all lies?

"He said he loved me and that he would never go to her again." She smiles sadly. "But we both know that he couldn't stay away."

I frown as I stare at her. "So, you just accepted it?"

She exhales heavily as if disappointed. "I know it sounds pathetic...."

I reach over and take her hand in mine.

"I loved him, the thought of living without him broke my heart."

I get a lump in my throat.

"When he was home, he was so...attentive to me."

"You were still having sex?" I gasp.

"The best sex, we were...." She frowns as if the memory pains her. "When he was home with us, he was perfect. I conceded that he loved the both of us and both relationships had their place in his life. You must remember at this time; your father was a very powerful man. Most Italian men of his stance had a harem of women, I somehow convinced myself that one woman who I knew about was better than the many that his friends took."

I puff air into my cheeks, I hate this story.

"And then he did something unforgiveable."

"What?"

"He got Angelina pregnant."

My face falls.

"He swore it was an accident, but I don't think it was."

I watch her as I listen.

"Then the boy was born," she says sadly.

"What happened then?"

"Your father loved him so much."

I smile softly. *He's easy to love.* I think for a moment, "But how...."

"How were you conceived?"

"Yes?"

"I told your father that I had met someone else and was going to pursue a sexual relationship with him. He flipped out. Threatened to kill him and then beat him to a pulp if he didn't stay away from me."

"What?"

"He was home for three months straight and begged me night and day for another chance, and slowly but surely, made me fall back in love with him. We spent a wonderful six months in each other's arms."

"Where was Angelina at this time?"

"I was told that they were over."

I frown. "But?"

"Turns out that she was just in England because her father was terminally ill."

She falls serious and stares straight ahead.

"What happened then?" I ask.

"I still remember the day she returned. I was seven months pregnant with you."

My heart drops.

"He was so excited and had hardly slept the night before. He left early one morning and said he wouldn't be back for a week as he was going away for work. In my gut, I just knew that something was amiss and I was sure it had to do with her. This woman had become the death of me, every one of my nightmares and insecurities revolved around her. I knew that he loved her and that no matter how hard he tried, he just couldn't stay away. I found out that Angelina had been in London because her father was terminally ill and that she was to return to Lake Como. I found myself heavily pregnant to a man who was a stranger. That was the day my marriage ended. There and then, I wouldn't even let him come into the delivery room with me."

"You went in alone?" I whisper.

"No." She smiles sadly. "I had a girlfriend."

I sit and stare into space as I process everything. Wow... information overload.

"I wasn't the only victim in this story. Poor Angelina, she loved him so much. Gave up her family and her country for a man who was married and still happily sleeping with his wife. She too, suffered years of emotional insecurity."

"He wasn't a very nice man, was he?"

She smiles sadly. "That's the contradicting thing, he was a wonderful man. Even after everything, I adored him until the very end.

I exhale in disgust. "You're a better woman than I am."

"One day, you'll meet someone special and will understand."

"Understand what?" *That all men are douche bags?*

"That deep true love isn't something that can be turned off when you want to. If you love someone, you love them for life. Love isn't a choice, Francesca. Love chooses you, not the other way around."

My mind goes to the image of Giuliano in the movie.

Like a sick and twisted stalker, I've watched it over and over this morning. The sheen on his skin, the lust in his eyes. The expression on his face as she bares her teeth as he reaches climax.

The deep ache to have him come inside of me.

Just once….

Stop it.

Just fucking stop it.

Why am I thinking such destructive thoughts?

I'll have a perfectly wonderful life with Marcel, we will be happy and I'll be fulfilled, and everything will be okay…except for one small detail.

He'll never be him.

I sip my wine as I stare into space, miles away.

There's one thing I know for sure.

Secrets are hard to keep.

Anna has asked me if I watched the Pornhub video, I told her it wasn't Giuliano.

So that's not actually a secret, it's an outright lie.

And every time over the last two days that Marcel has asked me what's wrong, I tell him that I'm thinking about work.

Not picturing my own brother naked.

I'm disgusting.

I need to get over this, I will not allow myself to think of Giuliano Ferrara one more time.

He's no good...and I'm no good when I...I get a lump in my throat as emotion overtakes me.

Just once.

No.

"Surprise," Anna's voice calls.

My eyes dart to the foyer as I see Anna dance in. "What are you doing here?" I frown.

"I asked her to come to dinner with us tonight," Marcel says as he steps forward. "Actually, I asked everyone to come." I look around to my two brothers, my mother and Anna who are all standing around, actually, why *is* everyone in town tonight? My eyes go back to Marcel to see him down on one knee.

Oh no.

He opens a ring box. "Francesca, will you marry me?"

The air leaves my lungs.

"Well?" He smiles hopefully. "Don't keep me waiting."

Confusion washes over me like a wave, but I can't...I can't deny him in front of everyone.

I need to move on, I can't keep thinking about that damn Giuliano Ferrara.

Maybe this is how it's supposed to be?

Why wouldn't he do this in private?

My eyes flick to my mother and she smiles sadly as if reading my mind.

"Well?" He smiles up at me.

He's a wonderful man, who loves me, and who, up until five days ago when I went to that stupid funeral, I was happy with.

Even if I was going to say no, I wouldn't do it in front of others.

I owe him that much respect.

I nod and force a smile, I watch on as he slides the ring on my finger and I stare at my hand.

My heart sinks, my life is one big colossal fuckup.

This can't be happening.

The restaurant is busy and bustling. My family are laughing and celebrating.

I want to crawl under the table and die.

The waiter brings a bottle of the best champagne and we watch as he pops the cork. He pours six glasses and passes them out.

"A toast," Andrea says.

We all hold our glasses together. "To a lifetime of happiness."

"Giuliano," Anna says.

We all turn to see Giuliano has just arrived, he's wearing a black shirt and jeans. My heart constricts just from seeing him.

Oh no.

"Hello," he says politely.

"Hello," everyone replies, my mother tilts her chin to the sky, annoyed to be sharing air with him.

"I'm so sorry about your mother," Andrea says.

"My deepest condolences," Matteo says, they both stand and shake his hand.

Giuliano nods. "Thank you."

Anna stands and kisses his cheek and he gives her a genuine smile. "Hi, Anna."

Seeing him so broken and vulnerable at the funeral has opened a part of my heart to him that I thought was closed forever.

I sit, glued to the chair, desperately wishing that I could stand and kiss his cheek too.

Not being able to touch him is a torture of epic proportions.

"Join us, we're celebrating," Matteo, my brother, says. "Francesca and Marcel just got engaged tonight."

Giuliano's eyes flick to me.

Dear God.

7

Francesca

GIULIANO'S EYES meet mine and I want to deny it.

Only we did, and I can't.

His eyes turn to Marcel. "Congratulations."

Marcel smiles broadly. "Thank you." He puts his hand over mine on the table, "We're very excited." He kisses my cheek. "Aren't we, darling?"

Giuliano's eyes drift between us as he watches our interaction.

My heart drops and I want to die.

This is not how I would want him to find out...but then the reality is that he is nothing to me, and it shouldn't matter anyway. My eyes flick to Anna and as if reading my mind, she gives me a sad smile and a reassuring nod.

"I'll leave you to your celebrations, enjoy your night," Giuliano says.

"Goodbye," everyone calls as they sip their champagne.

His eyes hold mine for a beat longer than they should and then he turns and walks out of the restaurant.

Hang on, he only just walked in.

Isn't he going to go and see whoever it was that he was meeting?

A tray of exotic-looking cocktails arrives and the boys and Mom all fall into conversation about them, laughing and betting on which is which.

My eyes flick to the door that Giuliano just left through.

"I'm just going to the bathroom." I stand and pretend to walk to the bathroom and then I quickly dart out the front of the restaurant and burst out the front doors, I look left and right up the busy street, there's no sign of him.

He's gone.

I stare out into the darkness and my phone rings in my pocket, I glance at it to see the name *Antonio*.

Damn it, stop watching me.

My eyes roam over the road to where his car is parked and I give him a wave and go back inside and into the bathroom.

I sit on the toilet with my head in my hands, where did he go?

I have to see him…no you don't.

Stop it.

I just got engaged, this is supposed to be the happiest night of my life.

Then why the fuck does it feel so wrong?

I take my time and try to get myself together and eventually, I weave back through the tables back to my family, even if I caught up with Giuliano, what would I have said?

Probably for the best that I didn't get the chance to talk to him. Marcel hands me over a fancy red cocktail. "Here you are, we saved the best one for you."

The table erupts into laughter and I know its code for this is the worst one. I force a smile and take a sip.

Ugg, I wince. "Tastes like poison."

They laugh some more.

I take another sip, good. I deserve it.

I'm an asshole.

The sound of Marcel's regulated breathing is calming. Like the sound of the ocean, a comforting background noise.

The sound of my heart, not so much. A million horses galloping through the forest, lost and angry.

I can't sleep.

And what does it mean when you make love to your fiancé, but feel guilty to another man for doing it?

I have a huge lump in my throat and I don't know if I want to cry, throw up or simply howl to the moon.

Ever since the funeral I have a monkey on my back, the grim reaper in my soul.

Taunting me toward the darkness, wanting something I know that I shouldn't.

I keep seeing Giuliano's face fall when Marcel told him about our engagement, the way his eyes searched mine as if he didn't believe it.

I feel bad, but I shouldn't, because he isn't the man I once loved anymore. He's a gangbanging criminal, and if the truth be known we would never work out even if we were able to be together. We're two different people now, our lives in different universes.

He probably doesn't even care.

I remember the way he used to love me, the way he held me

in his arms after we made love as if I was the most precious thing in the world.

The feelings of closeness between us.

My eyes fill with tears because I know that time is gone forever.

The reality is, that maybe the memory is so special simply because he was my first love, everything is so exaggerated in my mind. Everyone talks about their first love as being special. I know it's just that, but damn it, I wish I would hurry up and forget. Why do I compare everything and everyone to him?

Why does it always come back to him?

I snuggle into Marcel's back and my mind goes to Giuliano again, I get a vivid memory of him going down on me, I let myself sink into a happy feeling of home as I rewatch Giuliano's tongue lick me up. His eyes on mine, my hand tenderly in his.

The way he loved me so completely.

Stop it.

What in the hell is wrong with me? I have a wonderful man sleeping beside me and I need to get my act together or I am going to lose him too…and then what?

Somewhere down the track I realize that I can never have Giuliano anyway and I live my entire life alone without children. I would be forced to watch him take a wife and give her the family that I desperately wanted. Watch him bring up his children as their aunt, always secretly in love with their father from the sideline.

No.

I need to cut this out, I can't let myself go down this path. It's destructive and damn well toxic. I already feel the heartache before it happens and I need to snap myself out of it, this is bad for both of us. Giuliano is better off…*I am better off without him.*

What I need to do is go back to France and concentrate on Marcel and my work and my life there. I have a wedding to plan.

I need to forget all about Giuliano Ferrara.

I roll over and nestle into the blankets to try to get into a good sleeping position, I close my eyes and once again I see Giuliano's hauntingly beautiful face.

If only it were that easy.

"Are you ready, darling?" Marcel asks.

We are just about to go out to breakfast, we fly back to France tonight. "Yes, hang on, I'll grab my phone off charge." I walk into the bedroom and pick up my phone to notice I have an email from my boss.

Hi Francesca,

Sorry to interrupt your weekend, I hope it's a great one.

Great news.

I've just had confirmation that the first hotel we are working on will be in Rome.

The perfect setting!

They want to have a meeting on Wednesday this week to go over the plans and timeframes. Feel free to work from home on Monday and Tuesday to prepare the spreadsheets if you like.

Looking forward to Wednesday,

Safe travels,

Pierre

Shit.

I exhale heavily.

Don't give me extra time to get home, I need to get out of Italy ASAP. I click out of my phone in disgust.

"Are you coming?" Marcel calls.

"On my way." I grab my coat and purse and make my way out. "Let's go eat, I'm starving."

The thing about the human mind is that it reconciles your bad choices. Musters up some kind of excuse for you to justify your upcoming mistakes.

I know I should leave it, there are words between Giuliano and me that need to be left unsaid. I sip my coffee and stare into space, if I stayed here for another day. I could go see him.

Just...to see if he's okay.

I mean, his mother just died and he did come around to see me the other day but I was going out. He probably had to tell me something urgent and then I didn't call back. It would be rude not to check in on him.

Masochist.

But honestly, I really should at least tell him about the porn on that website, he would be horrified if he knew it was up there. One of those stupid girls uploaded it without his permission, I'm sure of it.

He needs to know, the very least I can do is to tell him, that way, he can get it taken down and then he will know what kind of girls they are.

Yes, I should do that, and not as an ex-girlfriend but just as a friend.

Masochist.

"So, I got an email from my boss this morning." I say to Marcel casually.

"What did he have to say?"

"The first hotel is Rome."

"Ah." He raises his coffee cup in a cheers symbol. "Oh la la, beautiful."

I smile. "Pretty exciting." I sip my coffee. "I have to be there on Tuesday, my boss thinks I should just fly there tomorrow straight from here so I can prepare," I lie.

What am I doing?

His forehead crinkles. "Oh."

"Would you be alright flying home...by yourself?"

"Yeah, I guess."

"I'll get the plane," I offer.

"No, no. I'll catch commercial. No bother."

"Are you sure?" I frown.

"Of course." He smiles warmly. "This contract is a big deal for you." He takes out his phone and gets online to book a flight as I watch on.

I'm a terrible person.

Just go with him to France...do not go and see Giuliano.

He goes through the motions, "Done. I'm on the four p.m. flight." He smiles up at me. "See, easily done."

I take his hand over the table. "Sorry."

I really am sorry...*about everything.*

"That's okay, darling, you can make it up to me when you get home. I think we should move in together, it's a natural step in our relationship now that we are getting married, and we have a big wedding to plan." He winks playfully.

My face falls before I catch it and quickly fake a smile. "Talk about it when we get home, hey?"

God.

This is the nightmare that keeps on giving.

———

The car pulls up at the Ferrara Building and I look through the window at the huge glass tower. Antonio gets out and opens the car door for me.

"Thank you." I give him a soft smile and he raises an unimpressed eyebrow back at me. "I'll be right here."

"Okay."

Antonio isn't impressed we are here and refuses to hide it.

I walk in through reception and up to the counter. "I'm here to see Giuliano Ferrara."

The receptionist subtly looks me up and down. "Do you have an appointment?"

"No. Tell him his sister, Francesca, is here."

Her mouth falls open. "Yes, of course. My apologies." She picks up the phone with urgency. "Mr. Ferrara, Francesca, your sister, is here." She listens as her eyes flick up to me and her brow furrows as if surprised. "Mr. Ferrara is very busy today," she replies.

What?

"Tell him I'll wait," I snap.

"She said she'll wait," she whispers uncomfortably, she nods as she listens and then her eyes flick to the front doors. "Three that I can see, sir."

I frown and my eyes flick to the front door, he just asked her how many guards I have with me.

Why?

I lose the last of my patience, I didn't have to come here. I'm being nice, for fuck's sake. I hold my hand out for the phone and she frowns. "Give me the phone."

She tentatively hands it over.

"Giuliano," I snap. "I'm coming up. Now."

"Fine," he growls.

I hand the phone back to her and she listens and nods. "Yes, sir." She gestures for a security guard and he comes over and runs a gun scanner over me and then leads me through a metal detector. I am then taken to the elevator and the guard gets in with me.

I stare at the doors as we ride to the top and I realize that I have never been in this building, not even once when my father was alive.

That's weird, isn't it? That a child was never brought to their father's work.

I guess it all makes sense now, it's crystal clear why daddy didn't bring his little girl to the crime capital of Italy...ugh, makes me sick to my stomach.

We get to the top floor and the doors open to another swanky reception area and an office door opens in a rush. Giuliano stands there, in a black shirt and gray suit, looking every bit the crime boss that he is. He raises an impatient eyebrow and I see red, I storm past him into his office and he closes the door behind me.

"What are you doing here?" he snaps.

"I'm asking myself the same question."

"I'm very busy today, I don't have time for you."

"Make time," I growl.

I have no idea why we're fighting but bring it on because I am ready to rumble. "What is your problem?" I put my hands onto my hips, outraged.

"*You* are my fucking problem."

"Me," I gasp.

"Yes, you. Do not come to my fucking office and demand to be let in. I won't have it."

I step toward him. "Listen here, you son of a bitch. Do not tell me where I can go. If I want to come to your stupid office then I will."

Amusement flashes across his face, and he leans his behind on the desk and crosses his feet at the ankles. He grips the desk with his two hands and my eyes drop to them. Strong, tanned and covered in veins.

Hand porn, in all its glory.

He gestures to the seat. "Sit."

For some stupid reason, my body instantly obeys his bossy demand and I find myself falling into the seat.

"What do you want?" he asks.

This was not the reception I was expecting, far from it. I grip my handbag on my lap. "I just...." I straighten my back, annoyed by his tone. "I wanted to see if you were, okay?"

"I'm fine," he says dismissively. "Why wouldn't I be?"

"On Saturday...."

"Ah yes, congratulations." He smiles sarcastically, "What a lovely couple you make." He rolls his lips as his eyes hold mine. "I'm sure you're in for an exciting life, there."

I feel my cheeks heat as fury begins to burn in my blood. "What's that supposed to mean?"

He stands and goes and sits behind his desk, he picks up his pen. "What I said."

"What is wrong with you?" I snap.

"Nothing. What's wrong with you?"

I open my mouth to say something, but words fail me. "You know, I came here as a friend to check on you and I'm met with this attitude."

"Saint Francesca." He smiles as he rocks back on his chair. "I have enough friends."

Our eyes are locked.

"So...." I shrug as I try to work out what the hell is going on here. "Fine. You don't want to be friends." I throw my hands up as I stand. "Okay then, that clears it."

"Clears what?" he snaps. "Your conscience."

"You know what? I was thinking about you losing your mother and was stupidly worried about you and now I see I shouldn't have been, because you are quite happy being an entitled asshole."

He holds the pen in his fingers and smiles as if goading me.

"Well...this is goodbye," I say.

"Goodbye."

"I'm going back to France."

"Good." He turns to his computer. "Fuck off."

I put my hand on my hips, fully pissed now. "What is your problem?"

"You." He hits the computer keyboard with force. "Taking up my time with your bullshit reason for a visit. If you have something to say, fucking say it."

"You think you're so tough, don't you? Mr. Ferrara, head of the Mafioso." I lean my two hands on his desk. "I came here to be nice and you are acting like a spoilt brat."

"How am I a spoilt brat?" he fires back. "Nothing about me is spoilt."

"What is this rudeness?" I half yell.

"Who is being rude here? You barge in, unannounced and expect a fucking greeting party. Do you have something to say or not!"

"One of your bimbos has uploaded a video of you having sex to Pornhub."

He sits back, instantly silenced.

"And I came here to tell you about it before you bring the family name into more disrepute than you already have."

He turns to his computer and types in his code. "What's the name of it?"

"Sinita."

His eyes rise to mine and amusement flashes across his face. "And may I ask, what would the angelic Francesca Ferrara be doing on Pornhub?"

Oh crap.

"I was told about it, by a friend," I stammer guiltily.

"Marso?" He raises his eyebrow.

"His name is Marcel," I snap.

"What a stupid name," he mutters under his breath as he types. He brings up Pornhub and then types the word *Sinita* into the search bar, he enlarges the screen and then leans back on his chair, the vision of him hard and oiled up with the two women comes up on the screen, his eyes flick to meet mine. "Did you watch this?"

"No," I spit way too fast.

He turns the screen toward me. "Liar."

His hard cock is right there in my face, and two women are fawning over his oiled-up naked body, I begin to feel unhinged. "You need to get this taken down immediately. It's disgusting, and morally wrong," I stammer in a fluster.

He smiles and then chuckles, before tipping his head back and laughing out loud.

"You think this is funny?" I gasp, indignant.

"Francesca, you kill me." He chuckles. "This is probably one of the most angelic things I've done."

I frown, what?

Who are you? I don't even know him anymore.

Our focus goes back to the screen and the two women are now taking turns sucking his dick, he smiles darkly as he watches and then his eyes rise to meet mine. "Did you come when you watched it?"

"No." I snap. "As if."

A million times.

"On your fingers or a dildo?"

Arousal begins to sweep through me. "Stop it."

"Hmm." His eyes stay glued to the screen. "Tell me, how many fingers does it take now? One like the good old days or do you come harder with a good fisting?" He smiles darkly as if imagining it. "I must say, there is nothing hotter than a woman fucking your whole fist."

What the hell? Who even says that? I begin to feel a slow heated throb between my legs.

"Stop it, you animal," I whisper, acting disgusted.

But I'm not, not even close.

He smiles and turns his attention back to the screen; the blond girl is now flicking her tongue over the end of him as his eyes roll back in his head. "That...tongue," he murmurs, distracted. "Tongues," he corrects himself.

Asshole.

The thought of him coming in someone else's mouth triggers me and I begin to lose control. "Stop it," I snap. "Turn it off."

"The way she bares her teeth," he murmurs.

My eyes go to the screen to see him as he tips his head back, his body glistening with oil, two women sucking his cock in unison.

"Turn it off," I demand. "Turn it off now."

Emotion overwhelms me at his pleasure in watching this. "Turn it off." I become unexpectedly emotional and my eyes well.

"No." He rubs the tips of his fingers over his thumb and smiles as he watches. "I'm quite enjoying myself." He cups his cock in his suit pants. "It's making me hard actually, I may have to catch up with the girls tonight for a rematch."

What?

"Are you trying to hurt me?" I spit.

"If I was trying to hurt you." His dark eyes hold mine. "I would marry someone else."

We stare at each other; raw emotion runs between us.

"That's not fair."

He pauses as if composing himself. "Fuck off back to France and get married Francesca, I don't want to see you again. Your vanilla lifestyle is boring to me."

My heart stops. "What?"

"I'm not interested in what you have to say."

I stare at him as I battle tears, I had heard that he had changed. I had heard that he was now cold and heartless. But I never imagined.... *Oh.* Hearing those words out loud hurt more than they should.

"Fine." I stand still on the spot, waiting for him to say something.

He unzips his fly. "Close the door on your way out."

My eyes flick to the screen just in time to see him slide into one of the women from behind in a doggy position, the lump in my throat begins to hurt.

"Unless, of course, you want to stay and watch." He turns up the volume and the sounds of the woman's moans of pleasure fill the room.

Tears well in my eyes. "You're a fucking asshole."

He fake-gasps as his eyes stay glued to the screen, he is now mounting one of the girls, his knees are wide and as he pushes into her the sides of his behind hollow out as his muscles flex. "You know, that is the first time I've ever been told that. I'm *so* upset." He mocks me as he takes his hard cock into his hands and I want to punch him in the face.

Stop watching those women...*you fucking asshole.*

Speechless, with my heart hammering hard in my chest.

Lost for words, I turn and storm out the door and down the hall and into the elevator, the doors close behind me and once alone I screw up my face in tears. I'm perspiring and completely rattled.

What the hell?

I sob out loud as I try to control my breaking heart.

I picture him in his office right now, jerking off to those girls. Relishing in hurting me.

I wipe my eyes and square my shoulders as I prepare to face my guards and the world. Once at the ground floor, I put my sunglasses on and walk out into the foyer. I give a calm smile and walk out as if nothing is wrong. I get into the back of the car and stare out the window.

And as the car hurls through the traffic, I know that that's it, I'm done.

I *am* going to France to get married and I swear on my life, I will never think of Giuliano Ferrara again.

8

Giuliano

I sip my scotch as I stare at my computer screen, it's eight p.m. and I'm working back late.

I've had a shit day, it started with Francesca coming to visit me this morning and went further downhill from there. My phone buzzes and I answer. "Hello."

"I'm just checking in with an update on Miss Ferrara."

God, please don't remind me of her. "Yes." I exhale heavily. "What is it?"

"Are you aware that she's going to Rome tomorrow?"

I frown. "What do you mean?"

"Antonio just checked in to say that she's booked the plane to go to Rome tomorrow."

I sit forward in my chair. "For how long?"

"She's there for four days, leaves on Thursday night to fly back to Paris."

"Why is she going to Rome?"

"Apparently she's working there, will be there on and off for the next few months."

"Well, she can't. We're in the middle of a fucking war in Rome, it isn't safe for her to be there."

"That's what I thought."

Six months ago, we lost our support from the local police with the superintendent being murdered. I made the decision to withdraw our operations from Rome to minimize the risk and concentrate on bigger international markets, since then the place is in anarchy.

Two large crime families, the Lombardi's and the Girardi's, are now fighting for control of the local drug market. If either organization catch sight of me or any of my men in Rome, it will be assumed we are back in the game and working with their opponent, the war against us will well and truly start.

"No." I sit back in my chair. "She can't go."

"Yes, sir."

"See her back to Paris immediately, please."

"Sure thing." The phone goes dead as he hangs up.

I stand and pour myself a glass of scotch, I walk to the window and stare out over the city below.

I hear my words from this morning, *"Fuck off back to France and get married Francesca, I don't want to see you again. Ever. Your vanilla lifestyle is fucking boring and I'm not interested in anything you have to say."*

I exhale heavily as I stare into space, I sip my drink, it's bitter and tastes a lot like regret.

My phone vibrates on my desk and I see the name *Amber* light up the screen.

I tip my head back and drain my glass, I wince as I feel the burn all the way down.

"Hi," I answer.

"Where are you?" she asks. "I thought dinner was booked for seven."

I screw up my face, fuck it, I completely forgot about dinner. "Sorry, I got held up, I didn't realize the time."

"Oh," Amber says.

"I'll be there soon."

"Okay. Shall I order something in?"

"Sounds good."

"What do you feel like?"

"Whatever." I sigh. "Surprise me."

I hang up and pour myself another glass of scotch. I sit for a moment and stare into space and for the hundredth time today, I see Francesca's face, the tears in her eyes, the hurt quiver in her voice and I feel like shit.

It's for the best.

The table chatter and laugh, happy and jovial.

Saturday night and I'm with my people, my non-blood family. They have my back, always have and always will, we look after each other through thick and thin. There's four of us now, Alex, Val, Carlo and I. There used to be five, but Maximus went and got himself killed twelve months ago in a shootout on the docks that went wrong, it broke our fucking hearts.

While Alex and Val have been with me since childhood, Carlo worked his way up through the ranks of Ferrara until six years ago when I promoted him into our management team. I depend on them; these men are the best of the best. Things change, the girls they love come and go, but one thing always stays the same, their undying loyalty to Ferrara and me.

Amber laughs out loud with Giovanna and my gaze drifts over to the two girls. Giovanna is Val's girl, beautiful and smart. He's been with her for over a year, she's Italian, a doctor, the polar opposite to the kind of women he usually dates. His women are normally like mine, beautiful...fuckable. Submissive, this one's different, she's got him by the balls and I think this may be the one for him. Now that I know her, I can't imagine him with anyone else. He's never been more grounded. Val tends to be on the wild side, for a while there I spent my days reining him in. He looks after the logistics side of the business. The pointy end of the business, he's hard and makes harder decisions. I think Valentino would have always ended up doing this job, if not with Ferrara, then with another organization. He was born for this role, he loves it, the darker the better. He has no fear, his biggest strength and his greatest weakness.

I glance over at the other two girls, the ones with Carlo and Alex, for the life of me I can't remember their names, although I should, I've met them many times before.

Amber says something and glances over and smiles softly at me and I take her hand in mine across the table. I roll my lips, disheartened by my recent feelings for her...or lack thereof. Everything always starts out so good and then it's like a switch goes off in my brain and I can't do it.

I'm ready, I want to go there, I want to fall madly in love and have the earth move when she looks at me. She's beautiful and perfect and worships the ground I walk on. Brazilian, sweet, sexy and kind with a hot as fuck accent.

She's got everything I should want.

But I just...I don't even know what the problem is, if I knew I would fix it.

I'm sick to fucking death of feeling like something is missing.

We've been together a few months and while she often declares her undying love for me, I can't even commit to monogamy. I'm broken, fucked up beyond repair.

She deserves better, they all do.

"What's up?" Val asks me quietly as the others all chat.

"Nothing."

"You're quiet."

I shrug.

"You still thinking about your sister?"

My eyes flick to Amber and I throw him a frown. "Sshh."

"Did you see Anna?" he asks softly

"No."

He smiles into his beer before lifting it to his lips. "I always had a thing for her."

"You've told me a million times. I have no idea why you didn't pursue that."

"I was too young when I met her and then her brother beat you to a pulp. Then when I finally looked her up, she's always had boyfriends." He sips his beer again. "And now...." His gaze drifts over to Giovanna. "Timing was never right, I guess."

My thoughts go to Francesca and how nothing was ever right for us.

"You shouldn't feel bad," Val whispers. "I'm sure her fiancé is kissing her better as we speak."

I clench my jaw as I imagine Francesca with that stupid fucking fiancé of hers.

"I mean..." he continues. "She'll be married soon so...."

"Shut the fuck up." I cut him off. "I don't want to hear it."

"She still fucks with your head, doesn't she?" He shrugs. "What's it been, like ten years or something?"

"She doesn't fuck with my head. I just feel bad. That's all."

"Don't."

My eyes meet his.

"Snap the fuck out of it, man." He clinks his beer with mine. "To Amber," he toasts to remind me of what I've got. He and Alex like Amber, they think she's good for me, they want this to work. My eyes roam over to the beautiful woman sitting beside me.

I want this to work too.

Amber rubs her hand up my thigh and gives me the look.

I force a smile and sip my beer, I'm just not sure how to make that happen.

Francesca

Anna opens the door. "Hello," she says to the delivery driver and gestures into the apartment. "Just put them down here."

The delivery driver unloads the boxes and Anna signs for them, I hide in the kitchen, I have my pajamas on with no bra. "Thank you," Anna says before I hear the door close. I come around the corner to see Anna standing with her hands on her hips assessing all of the packages. "Good grief, the things they would stoop to."

"Hmm." I flop onto the couch, unimpressed. "Take what you want."

Anna smirks. "Always do." She begins to load the parcels onto the dining table. "You know the whole thing kind of sucks."

"What does?"

"All of the top fashion design houses send you their new releases and a million and one pairs of shoes and handbags in hope that you will wear them just once and be photographed. And the irony is, you are the only person in fucking Italy who can actually afford to buy this crap. They don't need to give it to you for free. Are they dumb?"

I giggle. "Lucky I have you to take it off my hands, then, isn't it?"

"Exactly," she mutters dryly. "That's what I was thinking." She opens a Valentino box and pulls out a black studded leather handbag. "Oh...come to Momma." She swoons. She puts it over her shoulder and looks at herself in the mirror. "Why is everything coming all at once?"

"It's Fashion Week next week."

"Ahh," Anna sighs as she remembers. "Who are you wearing?"

"I don't know." I sigh. "Not in the mood this year, I can't even be bothered to go really." I look over the boxes, there must be at least twenty here. "It depends on what they sent me."

Anna flops on the couch beside me. "I wish I had your good taste, you throw things together and look a million dollars. I throw the same things on and look like a science experiment."

I smile. "I seriously doubt that." I look over at her. "Are you coming with me?"

"To Fashion Week?"

Uh-huh."

"Of course. Have I ever missed it yet?"

"Who are you wearing?"

"Whoever you don't."

I walk out into the living room and flick my coat open and put my hands on my hips in an overdramatic way as I pretend to be on the catwalk.

Anna's eyes widen as she looks me up and down. "Wowsers."

I smile as I look down at myself, I'm wearing pale blue thigh-high boots, a tight leather minidress in exactly the same color and a matching trench coat. "Pretty nice, huh?"

Anna circles me. "Incredible, Chanel?"

"Head to toe."

"My God."

I pick up the matching bag with the customary gold chain strap. "You like?"

"I fucking love," Anna gasps.

It's Paris Fashion Week and today we are hitting circuit.

My long dark hair is out and my makeup is understated, the gorgeous blue is the star of this outfit, I don't want to overpower it with anything. "Which sunglasses should I wear? These ones." I put a pair of gold Ray Bans on. "Or these ones." I put on a pair of chunky tortoiseshell glasses.

"Hmm." Anna twists her lips. "The gold."

"Yeah, I thought so too." I look her up and down, she's wearing a hot pink dress and matching stilettos. "Wow, you look amazing."

"I can't beat Chanel, they just get me." She puts her hands on her hips and gives a little sashay.

I giggle. "He really does."

The car pulls up and our driver gets out and opens the door for us, Anna gets out first and then me, cameras flash. "Miss

Ferrara, you look amazing, who are you wearing?" someone calls.

"Chanel," I reply with a smile, I link arms with Anna and we pose for the photographs, first with the two of us together and then alone. This is the one and only place I will have my photo taken willingly. I know what a privilege it is to be here and to able to support the insanely talented designers is an honor.

After all the things they constantly send me, I owe them this exposure.

Anna and I walk hand in hand through the concourse and into the Chanel Hall.

"Hello." The usher smiles, he's in a fitted black dinner suit and I'm sure he's an off-duty model.

Anna's eyes widen and she smiles at him.

"Hello." I hand over our invitations. "This way please." He walks off in the direction of our seats.

"Delicious," Anna whispers.

He leads us to our seats in the front row and we both sit down.

"This never gets old," Anna whispers. "Did you see David Beckham by the door?"

"No." I glance over to the door. "Where, I can't see him?"

"He's the one wearing the fuck-me T-shirt."

"Isn't he like old now?"

"No way, he's like a fine wine, gets more fuckable every year."

I giggle. "Good to know."

The music pipes through the space and the lights dim, a hushed excitement falls over the audience. I love Fashion Week, the buzz from the press, the hushed excitement of the new collections, even the gossipy paparazzi have their place here.

A funky beat comes through the speakers and I smile, I love

this song, "Give It To Me Baby" by Jarina De Marco. The room collectively holds their breath as the first model floats down the catwalk. Brunette and elflike in her appearance, the perfect show opener.

"I love that jacket," Anna whispers. "I wish they sent you that."

"Me too." I smirk as I keep watching. Model after model, gorgeous after gorgeous, and as the show continues, the evening gowns come out, my gaze floats around the room and I stop dead in my tracks.

What the?

In the darkness, on the other side of the catwalk, Giuliano is sitting in the front row, his eyes are focused on the runway and I don't think he's seen me. I snap my eyes away, how dare he come here! This is my domain.

Paris is my safe space, away from him and all things Italy.

I discreetly slip my dark sunglasses on, hoping that he doesn't see me, also they will help me to look over at him without being seen.

"What are you doing?" Anna whispers.

"The lights are hurting my eyes," I lie.

"Oh, that's fucking weird," she replies. "Maybe you're about to have an epileptic fit or something."

"Maybe." I drop my head to hide my smile, trust Anna to catch me out being weird. I keep my face looking straight ahead but turn my eyes.

He's staring right at me.

Oh no.

How dare he even look in my direction!

I square my shoulders and straighten my back. He keeps watching me…and watching…and watching…what the hell is he doing?

Is he even interested in the show at all? I mean, obviously I'm not, now that my infuriating bastard hot brother is here.

God, that sentence is so wrong that I don't even know where to start with it.

He's in jeans and a tweed jacket over a white T-shirt, the fawn colors make his dark hair and square jawline pop. They should have got him to model for them, he's the most handsome man in the whole damn arena...or planet earth.

Ugh...why is he here?

His words run through my mind for the ten thousandth time. *"Fuck off back to France and get married, Francesca, I don't want to see you again. Ever. Your vanilla lifestyle is fucking boring and I'm not interested in anything you have to say."*

Good...that's just what I am going to do.

Get married.

To a normal person, one who isn't a fucking asshole.

I drag my eyes off him and try to focus on the show. Five minutes later one of the top models struts down the runway and I watch her in awe...now *she* is beautiful.

She oozes sexiness and confidence, I smile as I watch her strut her stuff, I have to admit she's absolutely killing it.

Go girl.

She gets to the end of the runway and bends and blows a kiss to Giuliano, he smirks up at her and replies with a sexy wink.

What?

She's with him?

Ugh.... It's the model from the paper. Of course, this all makes sense now, the puzzle as to why he's here clicks into place.

Asshole.

No wonder he doesn't want to see me again, here I am

worrying about his feelings after the funeral and he's over there sleeping with the hottest woman alive.

Typical.

I clench my hands on my lap, I'm infuriated. I get overly hot and begin to perspire, I could literally stab someone right now.

Him. All him. It's all about him...stupid, womanizing, criminal, fucking asshole.

"Oh my god," Anna whispers as she sees him.

"Sshh," I cut her off. "I saw."

"They're together?"

"Who fucking cares," I snap.

"Oh God, can you imagine their babies."

I clench my jaw so hard that my teeth nearly crack. "Wouldn't want to."

The rest of the show is a blur, I can't focus, I can't enjoy myself and relax. I just want to run.

Far, far away from him and everything he represents. My father's infidelity, my family's corruption and my desire for a man who turned out to be my brother.

Ugh, I can't believe this.

All Giuliano Ferrara does is upset me, he goes and plants doubt in my mind about life and Marcel and then is so horrible that I cry myself to sleep, without a care in the world.

For what? Why would he even bother?

He has a girlfriend and not just any girlfriend, Amber fucking Lopez.

The finale starts and I can't stand it for a moment longer, I lean over to Anna. "I'll meet you outside."

"What?'

"I have to see someone."

"Who?"

I stand without another word and make my way outside, I

burst through the doors and am met with sunlight and fresh air. I tip my head back and let the sunshine beam down on my face.

"What are you doing?" a deep voice says.

I snap my eyes open to see Giuliano standing before me.

We stare at each other and damn it, it's there again. That swirl in the air that steals my breath.

Suddenly I feel unhinged, I want to punch him in the face, say something terrible, do anything to hurt him like he hurts me.

But I won't, because I'm better than that and damn well too good for him.

Without a word, I turn my back and walk to my car, my driver opens the car door and I climb in.

He doesn't deserve a reply, I owe him nothing.

Giuliano Ferrara is dead to me.

I stare at the blonde in the mirror and I readjust my wig, I pull the electric-blue cap low over my face and put on the dark-thick rimmed glasses. I'm wearing a baggy floral dress.

I'm unrecognizable, even to myself.

Giuliano told the guards that I wasn't permitted to go to Rome under any circumstance and normally I would have confronted him and argued my case.

But I don't want to see him, at all, ever. And I'll be damned if I'm giving him the satisfaction of asking for anything from him ever again. Least of all his fucking permission to go somewhere.

I cried myself to sleep last night, mourning the loss of the beautiful boy I once loved.

I don't even know why his nastiness of late has affected me

so much. It shouldn't matter and I most definitely shouldn't care.

That damn funeral is all to blame, I should never have gone, it seemed to bring up unresolved feelings I have toward him, ones that I have pushed to the side and carried deep within my heart for years.

But anyway, screw him, I have better things to do with my life than cry over hurtful words from a criminal. Who is he to judge me?

When I was young, he hated how my family treated me, how I wasn't allowed out.

It's ironic that he's one of them now and is trying to do the exact same thing.

Karma will get him; my conscience is clear.

I put my clothes into a pink backpack and I throw it over my shoulder and look at myself in the mirror, I giggle and take a photo of myself.

This outfit is the living end.

Okay, here goes nothing. If I get past the guards, I have free rein to go to Rome by myself. I've told them that I'm working from home for the next three days and I've bought a ticket on a commercial flight, a hotel and have downloaded the Uber app.

Uber...eeek! Who even am I?

I had intended to leave in the middle of the night but then I figured that at that time nobody else will be around and I might stand out more. I take the elevator and walk out into the foyer and hang around a little until a group of ladies come walking out, I strategically loiter behind them as if I am a part of their group and follow them around the corner.

I keep my face forward, but my eyes are flicking toward my guards' cars beneath my glasses. The boys are talking and laughing as they lean against one of the cars.

Please don't let me get caught. Please don't let me get caught.

Five more minutes.

We turn the corner and I roll my lips to hide my smile, I think I might actually do this. I break away from the ladies and cross the street and around another corner and call an Uber. I hold my breath as I wait for it to arrive and when it finally does, I jump into the back seat excitedly.

"Airport?" the driver says.

"Yes, please." I beam with pride, I did it.

I walk into the ballroom with a folder under my arm, nerves firmly intact.

This is it, the most important meeting of my entire life.

As promised, I'm in Rome in the hotel we are about to refurbish. Wearing a fitted black dress and high heels with my long dark hair swept up into a high ponytail. I'm wearing natural makeup with my signature deep red lipstick. I hope I look the part.

A distinguished-looking man is waiting for me, he's in his fifties and very handsome in his Armani suit. "Hello." I smile nervously as I shake his hand. "Francesca Ferrara."

"Hello, my dear." He smiles, his eyes hold mine and a trace of a frown crosses his brow. "Ferrara...where are you from?"

"Milan."

"Ah." He smiles. "God's country. I had a dear friend who lived in Milan, you aren't any relation to the late Giuliano Ferrara, are you?"

"Yes," I reply politely. "He was my father."

"Really...he's sorely missed."

"Yes, he is."

His eyes hold mine. "It's lovely to meet you, Francesca."

"I'm sorry, I didn't catch your name," I ask.

"I'm Vincenzo Carballo."

"Hello." I smile.

"Congratulations, your concepts blew your competition out of the water."

"Thank you, I'm excited to get started. It really is going to be wonderful once completed," I reply as I look around the grand ballroom, I can almost see the magazine spread already. I'm going to nail this refurb if it's the last thing I do.

He gestures to the large double doors. "Shall we continue in my office?"

"Of course." I grip my folder and follow him out, get into the elevator and the doors close.

"I thought your company was French?" he says.

"It is, I live in France."

"Really?" He frowns. "A Ferrara who doesn't live in Italy?"

"After my brother died, I went to live in Paris."

"Enrico?"

"Yes." The elevator doors open and he gestures to the corridor, we get out and walk down it. "You knew him?" I ask.

"No, I didn't have the pleasure," he replies as we get to a series of offices.

"But if.... You knew my father?" I ask, confused, they knew all the same people.

"Ah." He shrugs. "I knew your father through work, unfortunately, I didn't have the pleasure of knowing him personally." He opens a door and reveals a huge office, it's very old world. Dark green walls and walnut cabinetry. The desk in the center of the room is gigantic. It has a very dated feel in here, I need to refit this as well. Damn, this is one hell of a huge task.

"Where did you work?" I ask.

"I used to work for the football team he owned."

"Oh" I smile as I connect the dots, that makes sense, Enrico had nothing to do with the football team. "I see." I open my folder to reveal the black title page with gold letters.

Lux

"Are you ready to create the most luxurious glamorous hotels in the world, Mr. Carballo?" I ask playfully.

He leans back in his chair and smiles, seemingly impressed. "Bring it on."

Three hours later I walk through the large foyer area and can hardly wipe the huge smile from my face. The meeting went better than my wildest dreams. Mr. Carballo is intelligent, stylish and completely in tune with my vision, I just can't wait to get started. I'm working here again tomorrow as I order in materials that I need to be on-site for and then demolition work starts next week after the last of the guests check out on Sunday.

It no easy feat refurbishing a hotel, it has to be completely emptied and stripped bare. I push out through the double glass doors and look around and feel a rush of adrenaline.

Freedom.

No guards, for the first time in my life. I have no bodyguards and I love it.

I feel grown up and to be honest, I don't think I even want security anymore.

I don't need them, never once have I had an issue.

I walk down the street and peruse through the shops and

I'm just in the best mood ever. Literally walking on air, I see a gelato shop up ahead and I make my way in to celebrate in style.

"Can I help you?" the cashier asks.

I look through the choices, I put my finger on the glass above the one I want. "Can I please have a single--" I pause. "Make that a double scoop of the decadent choc gelato in a wafer cone please?"

"Sure." She grabs her scoop. "Would you like that dipped in hot chocolate?"

"Ooh, that sounds good." I widen my eyes with a smile. "Yes, please."

My phone buzzes in my bag and I take it out, the name *Marcel* lights up the screen.

"Hi."

"How did it go?"

"Great, my God. I'm so excited. This is a dream job."

"Good to hear, listen, why are your guards still parked out the front of your place?"

I wince.

"I just went over to your apartment to pick up my spare computer keyboard because mine broke and all your guards are in their cars."

I scrunch up my face, knowing full well how petulant this sounds. "I kind of snuck out."

"What?"

"I'm sick and tired of all this security, Marcel. I wanted to come to Rome unaccompanied."

"Why would you do that?" he scolds me. "How did you sneak out?"

"Easily, I told them I was working from home for a few days and then I left wearing a blond wig and hat."

"Francesca," he gasps.

"Oh please," I huff. "I'm going to terminate my security when I get home. I'm sick to death of being followed everywhere."

"Well, if they think you need it, it's obviously for a reason."

"I get as to why when I was young, but now it's just ridiculous. If something goes wrong, I call the damn police like the rest of the adult population."

"Francesca," he sighs.

I roll my eyes, annoyed that he's raining on my good mood parade. "I'll call you later."

"Why do you have to go, what are you doing?"

"Right now, I'm about to eat a chocolate gelato and then I'm going shopping and buying shoes and then tonight, I'm going to Bellocchi's for dinner."

"With who?"

"Alone," I snap back. "I'm going, my ice cream is ready.

"But...."

"Goodbye, Marcel." I cut him off and hang up the phone. Damn that man and his sensible advice, I don't need it.

"Here you are." The cashier smiles as she hands me over the hugest ice cream I've ever seen.

"Thank you." I give her a wave and walk out into the street; I lick my ice cream as a goofy smile returns to my face. I don't care what anyone says, being left alone is fun.

Bellocchi's is everything its reputation states and more. The most renowned restaurant in Rome. Thankfully I called just at the right time and someone had just canceled their booking, I've heard there's a huge waiting list so it's lucky for me the person who answered my phone call was too lazy to look it up.

I've had lobster, I've had the most incredible salad and now, I'm just about to drink my fourth margarita. I'm on a high, buzzing with excitement and it's not just about the meeting I had today, it's everything. The sneaking away from the guards, being alone in a city that I know my father and brother Enrico loved so dearly, finally coming to the realization that Giuliano and I would never have worked even if we had the chance.

Somewhere today between my gelato and the black Chanel stilettos I bought, I came to a decision, I'm going to change my life when I get back to France. No more doing what people expect. No more toeing the line.

I am a grown woman and I want to make my own choices and it's more than that, I want to make my own mistakes. I'm so wrapped in cotton wool that how can I even call this living? All through university I had bodyguards, all through my teens it was monitored who I mixed with.

I smile goofily into my margarita glass and dial Anna's number.

"Hey," she answers.

"Hi." I beam. "You'll never guess where I am."

"Where?"

"In Rome."

"Oh, I thought you were at Marcel's?"

"Nope." I smirk, I really need to stop drinking, I'm feeling tipsy. "I snuck away from my guards and flew to Rome, by myself."

"Really?" Anna laughs. "Bravo."

"And now I'm in a restaurant all alone, drinking margaritas."

"Impressive. What did Marcel say?"

"Don't care."

"Haha, I love it. Oh God, he would hate you not having your guards with you."

I smile, although that sounded like it had an alternative meaning. "What do you mean?"

"Oh, come on, Chesk, he loves you being babysat by them, that way he can play the good guy."

"You think he controls me?"

"One hundred percent."

"Oh." I frown. "Why haven't you said this before?"

"Because you like being controlled."

"No, I don't."

"Well, you're twenty-seven and this is the first time you've ever snuck away."

That's true.... Hmm.

The waiter arrives at the table with another margarita, "Thank you," I mouth.

"Well, I'm tired of living the way I do," I announce, changing the subject. "Guess where I have to go next week for work?"

"Where?"

"Ibiza."

"Ibiza?"

"Uh-huh the artist I am using for the hotel we are working on lives in Ibiza."

"Convenient."

"Yes, and my meeting with him is on Friday afternoon and then again Monday morning. So...I'm going to have to stay there all weekend."

"Now, that *is* very convenient."

I laugh. "Are you coming, or what?"

"Hell yes. I'm so off Frank it isn't funny."

"Why?" My face falls.

"My gut is telling me he's cheating on me."

"Since when?"

"I don't know, but I'm suddenly insecure and I know that if your gut is telling you something, it's usually for a reason."

"Hmm.... I guess."

My gut is telling me that Marcel isn't the man I want to marry, but I'll never admit it.

Obviously, my gut knows zero about what's good for me.

"Has there been any signs or anything?" I ask.

"He's been watching porn all the time, and different kind of porn, the girls are all blond, opposite of me. He's working late a lot. Suddenly going away on boys' weekends."

"Hmm." I twist my lips as I go over the evidence.

"Started trimming his pubic hair."

Good God, that's not good. "Well...." I shrug. "I mean...." I cut myself off before I say the wrong thing.

"Do you think I'm crazy?" she asks.

"Not at all."

"Anyway...a weekend in Ibiza sounds just what I need."

"Me too." I smile.

"Got used to the idea of marrying Marcel yet?"

"What do you mean?" I frown.

"Well, you aren't exactly thrilled about it, are you?"

I wince. "Is it obvious?"

"To me it is."

"God." I lean my face onto my hand. "Tell me to snap out of it," I whisper. "I want to want this."

"But you don't?"

I get a lump in my throat as guilt steals my happiness once more. "Have you ever felt like you were a car crash waiting to happen? That you can see into the future at the collision, but you can't stop driving toward it?"

"Every day."

I smile, grateful for her undying support. Anna would support me into hell, and she has. "I love you."

"I love you more."

"I need to snap out of this, he's such a good man and he really loves me."

"That's not enough to spend a lifetime with someone, Chesk."

She's right.

I blink through tears. "Anyway, you and me in Ibiza next weekend, baby."

"Yes," she says excitedly. "Any luck we will meet the men of our dreams there and they will be twins with big dicks."

I burst out laughing. "Twins?" She laughs too and I take another sip of my margarita. "I have no interest in twins, I've got a margarita to drink."

"Don't get too drunk, you *are* alone, remember?"

"That's right, I am." I laugh. "Feels great too."

"Okay, have fun. Love you. Bye."

I order another drink and lift my glass to my lips and stop midair, Giuliano is striding through the restaurant toward me. The look on his face is murderous. "What the fuck are you doing?" he whispers angrily as he arrives at my table.

He's wearing a perfectly fitted black suit and cream shirt, the scent of his aftershave wafts around me.

What the hell?

He towers over me, damn it, why does he have to smell so good, it doesn't help the cause at all.

"Drinking," I snap. "What are *you* doing?"

"We're going."

"I'm not going anywhere with you." I sip my drink and look

around, annoyed, I can feel the adrenaline as it surges around my system. "Leave me alone, Giuliano."

"We. Are. Leaving," he whispers in fury.

I glare up at him. "Are your ears painted on?"

His eyes bulge from their sockets. "Don't piss me off, Francesca, I am too fucking busy to have to fly here to babysit you because you skipped your guards."

"How do you know I skipped my guards?" I snap.

"Marcel Marso called me to tell on you, that's how. Turns out he is useful for something after all."

My mouth drops open in horror.

What?

That traitor, he knew I needed this. Maybe Anna *is* right about him. "Nobody asked you to babysit me." I sip my drink as I act casual; the waiter arrives with another margarita. "Thank you, I'll have another one, please."

The waiter looks to Giuliano, "What would you like, sir?"

"He's leaving," I snap. "He doesn't need a drink."

"I'll have a Blue Label scotch," Giuliano says dryly as he pulls out the chair and sits down opposite me.

"That seat's taken," I snap.

"I know. By me." He glares at me over the table, and I glare right back.

The waiter's eyes widen as he looks between us.

"What?" Giuliano snaps up at him.

"Nothing." The waiter fakes a smile and scurries to the bar.

I try to rein in my temper, it's all I can do not to throw my drink all over him.

His dark eyes hold mine. "Why the fuck would you skip your guards when I specifically told you *not* to come to Rome?" he growls.

"I don't want guards anymore."

He rearranges the serviette on the table. "Nonnegotiable."

I roll my eyes. "Go back to Milan to your girlfriend, Giuliano. Unlike me, she likes taking your orders...and her turn," I mutter under my breath.

His cold eyes hold mine. "Trust me, sitting here looking at you is the very last thing I want to be doing."

I can't believe this is the same man I used to know, he's not even on the same planet as the beautiful boy I once loved.

My sanity rubber band snaps and I can't even act cool anymore. "I come to your mother's funeral to support you as a friend and you have done nothing but be a fucking asshole to me ever since."

"I don't want you as a friend, I have enough friends," he spits. "And stop swearing, I don't like it."

"I'll say fuck as much as I want, and the term you are looking for is groupies."

"What's that supposed to mean?"

"You don't have friends, Giuliano. You have servants."

He glares at me.

"Name one friend that you have that isn't on your payroll or waiting in line to suck your dick?"

There, take that. I sip my drink triumphantly.

His eyes hold mine.

Guilt fills me.

Too far.

That was mean, I shouldn't have said that. Damn it, this man brings out the worst in me. "I just wanted to be your friend," I say in a disguised apology.

"I don't want to be yours."

My heart drops as I stare at him.

Wow...and there it is.

How does someone go from loving you so much when they

were young, to hating you with such passion? Suddenly, I feel overemotional. Ever since I saw him at the funeral, I've been second-guessing every one of my choices, most of all my relationship with a perfect man. And for him to sit there with so much hate for me, breaks my heart.

"Every time I see you.... You hurt my feelings," I whisper.

His eyes hold mine.

Stupid tears form in my eyes, damn it, why am I such a cry baby? "Please," I whisper. "Just...leave me alone."

He looks out over the people in the restaurant, he seems miles away. Or maybe it's just that he's detached from the situation and I'm not.

Either way, his silence cuts like a knife, eventually he speaks. "You think you know it all...don't you?"

"It's not hard to work out, is it?"

"You have no idea what you're dealing with, Francesca." He sits forward and lowers his voice. "Do you have any idea what a Ferrara woman's scalp is worth?"

Huh?

"The people that murdered your grandfather, the same ones who murdered your father...and your brother Enrico. They live here in Rome, they have the authorities on their side, all crimes committed by them are overlooked."

My face falls.

"I cannot protect you here," he whispers. "You are a walking target...and by bringing me and my men here, you have put us all in danger. Because unlike you, I cannot go unnoticed, everyone knows who I am."

Fear rises in my throat as my eyes search his.

"When I told you that you *cannot* be here. I *fucking* meant it," he growls furiously. "And to sit there with that smug fucking look on your face..." he continues.

"Drinks," the waiter interrupts awkwardly.

Giuliano sits back, affronted. "Thank you."

I look up to the waiter as the blood drains out of my face, speechless.

What? I've put him in danger.

Oh my God.

I glance up to the door of the restaurant, suddenly panicked. The waiter puts the drinks down and I stare at it on the table as the need to run escalates.

The waiter leaves us alone and Giuliano picks up the full glass of scotch and drains it in one go.

"Why didn't you tell me?" I whisper.

He smiles sarcastically, as if I'm an idiot and maybe he's right, because at this moment I feel completely stupid.

"I didn't want to scare you *and* I thought you had more brains than this," he replies.

With a shaky hand I pick up my drink and take a large gulp.

"Who do you think we are, Francesca?"

I stare at him, unsure of what he means.

"We are the descendants of the most vicious men in Italy's underworld history."

My stomach drops.

"Our blood is a trophy. Our death is a sport."

I think of my beloved father and brother, tears fill my eyes.

"Never...ever, has a Ferrara woman walked the streets of Rome on her own. Why do you have guards everywhere you go? Do you honestly think that it's just for fucking fun?"

"You should have told me."

"I'm telling you now," he spits.

I look around in a panic as the walls begin to close in around me. "What do we do?"

"We leave." He puts his hand up for the bill and the waiter nods and disappears to get it.

I pick up my cocktail and down it in one go. I'm flustered, I'm half drunk…okay, maybe three quarters drunk, and now, I'm scared to death.

Definitely too young to die.

"What happens if someone sees us?" I whisper.

"Then we're fucked."

"Define fucked?"

"Dead duck."

My eyes widen. "Dead duck fucked?"

He smirks, then breaks into a smile, before throwing his head back and laughing out loud.

"This isn't funny," I whisper as I kick him under the table.

"Dead duck fucked *is* pretty funny."

"Will you be serious?" I stammer.

The waiter arrives with the bill and I go to grab my purse, Giuliano holds up his hand in a stop signal and passes his card over.

My eyes flick out the front doors to the street, are they out there waiting for us?

I get a vision of men with guns and bundling us into a car trunk and driving us to a deserted place.

Would they rape me before they kill me?

God….

Adrenaline really begins to hammer hard, I can feel my pulse in my ears as fear takes me over.

"There you go." The waiter smiles as he calmly hands Giuliano's card back to him. "Have a nice night."

"Thank you." Giuliano stands and pulls out my chair and takes my hand in his. "Let's go." We walk through the restaurant. "Keep your head down," he whispers as we head out the front doors.

What?

I drop my head.

Oh no, he thinks they're here.

He leads me out into the street, the pavement is crowded with people.

"Fuck," he whispers.

"What?"

He gestures up ahead with his chin; two police are walking toward us, they're deep in conversation with each other.

"They can't see us," he says as he pulls me into an alley between two shops.

"Why not?" I stammer in a panic as he pulls me along at speed.

"Because they're on Lombardi's fucking payroll."

My eyes snap around the alley, it's dark with no way out. "What do we do?"

He looks around quickly and then pushes me up against the wall. "Sorry." His lips take mine.

"What are you doing?" I try to pull away from him.

"Kissing you so they can't see our faces."

Ahh.

He holds my face in his hands as he kisses me, his tongue taking no prisoners as he pins me to the wall.

My eyes close involuntarily and I know this isn't real.

But.... Oh.

The way he kisses.

I feel it all the way to my toes.

He kisses me again and this time I have no resistance, I kiss him back.

My hands go to his hips as goose bumps scatter up my

spine. Our kiss deepens and the air between us becomes electrified, our breathing labored as we struggle for control.

His eyes flutter closed and when they open again, I see him. The man I used to love, the one that loved me back.

He's still in there.

9

Francesca

HIS LIPS DROP to my neck and his teeth trail up to my jaw as his hands go to my behind and pull me onto his hard cock.

Oh....

Then it snaps, all control.

We kiss like our lives depend on it, hungry and wanting. A million forbidden feelings coming to fruition.

The man I can't have.

I pull out of the kiss and I drop my head.

We stand in the darkness, our foreheads touching as we pant, struggling for air.

Silence hanging between us.

Lost in regret at what we both know we can't have...at what we shouldn't have done.

I'm a bad person.

"I think they're gone," he finally says.

I nod, unable to push any words past my lips, because no matter what I say, it will be wrong.

He takes my hand and leads me back out to the street and we turn the corner to see the black Mercedes wagon waiting for us, he opens the door and I get into the back seat, he slides in behind me. The car pulls out into the traffic and I stare out the window in a state of shock.

What the hell just happened?

"We can't go back to your hotel tonight," he says, monotone.

I nod, my gaze still fixed out the window, my body still tingling from his forbidden touch.

"If you need anything I'll have someone pick it up from a store for you. It's too risky to check out of your hotel tonight, it will only bring attention," he murmurs.

"Okay," I whisper.

My phone rings in my bag and I dig it out and read the caller's name.

Marcel

My heart drops and I glance over to see Giuliano read the name on my screen too. His eyes return out to the traffic as it whizzes by, he seems angry or pensive, or...I don't even know.

Fucking hell, this is one big disaster, I switch my phone on silent and put it into my purse. I'll call Marcel back later.

This is messed up.

We drive in awkward silence and I know that we were just pretending to kiss and I know that it didn't mean anything. I run my fingers over my lips that are still tingling, my skin still burns from his dark stubble.

It felt real.

Arousal throbs where it shouldn't, and shame fills me.

He's, my brother.

Twenty minutes later we pull into an underground parking lot, the large metal gates slowly rise and I turn to look through the back window to see three cars pull in behind us, wait...we have people trailing us? I glance over at Giuliano, his steely gaze is focused out the window, I turn back to the front, of course we do.

His words from earlier come back to me. *"Our blood is a trophy. Our death is a sport."*

"Good evening, Mr. Ferrara." One of the guards nods, the men all stay quiet and on high alert, very different to how they are with me, and I get the feeling that Giuliano rules with an iron fist. Nobody would dare step a toe out of line in his presence.

We take the elevator and once at the top floor the elevator opens into a foyer area, Giuliano puts his hand over a scanner and the doors open.

"Where are we?" I ask.

"My place," he says as he stands back and lets me walk in before him. My eyes scan the huge apartment, It's super trendy with a ceiling-to-floor window view over Rome.

"Your place?" I frown as I take my scarf off and throw it over the back of the couch.

"I lived here before we moved operations out."

I nod and look around, it's very impressive.

Giuliano walks through and disappears up a large set of stairs. "The guest room is this way," he calls, he's dismissing me.

Oh....

I follow him up the stairs and down the grand hallway. "I've had your room filled with essentials but if you need anything just call."

"Thanks." I look around, the bedroom is beautiful, rich and luxurious with exotic art.

"Keep the door locked."

My face falls. "You think that someone might come to my room?"

"I know they would want to." His eyes hold mine and suddenly it becomes crystal clear who he wants to keep out of my bedroom.

Himself.

"Oh...oh...kay..." I stammer.

"Good night, Francesca." He walks out of my bedroom and begins up the hall and I follow him out.

"Giuliano."

He turns back toward me. "Yes."

"Thank you."

He nods but stays silent, we stare at each other and the pull toward him is indescribable. His eyes hold mine as he waits for me to speak, there is so much that I want to say, not one word that I can.

"Is there any way I can just finish this design job? It's a big deal for my career, a large hotel chain and this is the first one. I just have to be here a couple of times over the next few weeks and the rest of the time I can work from the Paris office. After the Rome one is refurbished, I'll never have to come back here, but if I don't finish this I can't move on to the next hotel in another country and I'm going to have to resign."

"You don't have to work, Francesca," he says, his voice is soft, cajoling. Different to how he's been speaking to me of late.

"But I want to, this is my dream job. I studied for years to get this, I don't want to throw it away." My eyes search his. "Can we find a solution…it's only a couple of weeks."

He exhales heavily. "I'll see what I can do."

I nod with a lopsided smile, "Thanks."

We stare at each other, alone in the darkened hall. The air circles between us and it's still there.

Like a tangible entity, I can feel it between us. A force to be reckoned with.

"Don't marry him," he murmurs.

"Why not?"

"Because I asked you not to."

My heart constricts as we stare at each other and then, without another word, he turns and disappears down the hall.

I walk back into my room and I lock that fucking door.

Giuliano

I rush down the stairs as fast as I can, I loosen my tie with a sharp snap.

Distance.

As a matter of urgency.

I need to create some distance before I throw her onto the bed and punish her for pissing me off.

With my heart racing I walk into my living room and straight to the bar, I fill a glass with ice and then pour the scotch in so fast that it sloshes over the sides.

I tip my head back and down it in one go.

I fill the glass again and I glance over to the staircase as it taunts me.

She's in my house.

The woman I've been fantasizing about for ten long years…is here.

And I can't have her.

Fuck.

I refill my glass and drain it again, I wince as I feel the burn all the way down my esophagus.

I close my eyes and inhale with a shaky breath as I try to will myself to a state of calm. The pulse in my cock is unrelenting and takes me back to the alleyway, reminding me of her kiss.

The softness of her lips, the feel of her in my arms. The way she makes me feel.

I close my eyes in regret.

If ever there were a fucked-up situation, this is it.

I drag my hand through my hair and I glance over at the staircase again.

Just once.

Nobody would even know.

Stop it.

I refill my glass and walk out onto the balcony and sit down. I look out over the twinkling lights of Rome and light a cigar, I sip my scotch and take a long inhale.

It's never going to happen.

I'll just…. No.

Don't go there.

An hour later I walk inside and see Francesca's cashmere scarf lying over the couch and without thought, I pick it up and lift it to my face.

It's soft and warm…it smells like her.

The blood rushes through my body at speed and I inhale deeply again, my cock thickens.

I glance to the staircase, what's she doing up there? Does

she have clothes on, are her legs open? I get a vision of her naked and on top of me, her legs spread wide, riding my cock, her large breasts bouncing as I pump her.

She'd be wet and creamy, swollen and I....

Just once.

I inhale deeply and I shudder as my cock releases a load of pre-ejaculate, fuck.... I could come just by her scent on her scarf.

Like a zombie in a trance, I walk to the bottom of the staircase and stare up it.

How does she taste? I imagine myself holding her legs wide, her feet resting on my shoulders.

I take a step up, I take another.

Her ass.... I never fucked her ass.... I bet it's taut and tight, I get a vision of myself riding her from behind, the sound of the lube slapping, her hair would be wild and she'd be so fucking hot for it. I'd break her in...again.

I'd ride her all fucking night.

I take another three steps.

I imagine myself fucking her mouth, my load dripping over her big lips. Her cunt creamy and swollen for me, my cock shudders, I'm about to blow just imagining it.

I need her.

My cock is aching and like a zombie being called home, I slowly walk up the stairs. I stop outside her door and stare at it.

Throb...throb...throb goes my pulse down below. I lift the scarf and inhale deeply and my cock shudders hard.

I'm going to come.

I unzip my suit pants, take my cock in my hand, her door millimeters from my face. I stroke my thick length hard, the tip grazing across the timber on the door and I inhale deeply as my pre-ejaculate smears where it shouldn't. The evidence of what I so desperately need.

Francesca.

I remember the way she kissed me earlier, so feminine, so hungry.

So missed.

My strokes harder and harder, I need it to hurt. Punish myself for wanting her so badly.

I inhale her scent on the scarf and losing control, I blow hard against her door.

I pant in silence, my heart is beating so hard, my skin is misted with perspiration.

Disgusted, my forehead falls forward to lean against the door. So close, but worlds apart.

I'm in a living hell.

I need you.

"You ready to go soon?" I ask.

"Uh-huh, are you sure you don't mind taking me back to my hotel? Someone else can drive me, I don't want to be an inconvenience," Francesca replies. She's wearing a white robe that was hanging in her bathroom, her long dark hair is up in a messy bun on the top of her head and she looks beautifully disheveled.

Breathtaking.

"Of course not." I stare at her for a beat longer than I should and then snap my eyes away. "I'm ready to leave when you are," I mutter as I make myself a cup of coffee.

I feel like shit, I slept all of nine minutes. The thought of her upstairs alone in bed was a new level of torture.

My balls ached all fucking night.

She gives me a soft smile. "Thanks." She turns and walks up the hallway and I stare after her as I bite my bottom lip, okay.... Stop it.

Get a hold of yourself.

Right now.

Ten minutes later she appears in the fitted black dress and high heels she was wearing last night, this is just great.

She's like fucking clickbait.

I wish she would wear a garbage bag...and a gorilla mask. A huge-ass chastity belt wouldn't hurt either.

Eye contact, look at her eyes. *Do not look down.*

"Are you ready to go?" she asks.

Am I ever!

"Uh-huh." I walk up the hall toward the front door.

She follows me out and we get into the elevator, I stare straight ahead and remain silent.

If I don't speak, I can't be an asshole.

It shouldn't piss me off that she's moved on without me, but fuck it, it does.

"What time will you be finished today?" I ask as we go down.

"About two."

"What hotel chain is it?"

"The Remington."

I frown. "I haven't heard of that before?"

"It's a small luxury boutique chain."

"Okay, what time do you want me to arrange your flight?"

"Umm, I don't know, about five?"

"To Paris?"

She looks over and her eyes hold mine.

The elevator doors open, breaking the moment. "Yes, Paris," she replies.

She's going back to *him*.

"Fine," I snap, I stride out and walk through the foyer.

Of course, she is, he *is* her fucking fiancé after all. I feel my blood begin to boil as I march out of the building. I open the car door for her and she gets in and I slam the door behind her. I can't even be near her, if I go with her now I know I'm going to explode and say things I shouldn't.

The asshole of all assholes.

This woman makes me fucking crazy.

I turn to her driver. "Take Francesca back to her hotel while she checks out and then escort her to work, please. I want a full team with her today."

"Yes, sir."

She winds her window down and looks up at me. "You're not coming?"

"No."

"Will I see you this afternoon?" she asks hopefully.

"I have things on," I lie.

"Oh...."

"Have a nice day." I tap on the roof of the car and then before I have to look at her one more time, I turn and walk back into the building.

I walk into the elevator and make a call back to my office.

"Hey, boss."

"Hi, Marcus, I need you to get some information for me, please."

"Of course."

"Can you find out anything of relevance about who owns the Remington hotel chain?"

"Okay. Where is it?"

"They're global, I'm not sure of specifics but I know they have a hotel in Rome."

"On it, boss." He hangs on the line before asking, "Is something wrong?"

"No. Francesca is currently working for them, I just need to know that she's safe."

"Good idea."

"Okay, get back to me."

"Sure thing."

The elevator doors open and I stride out and back into my apartment and straight up to the bedroom Francesca slept in. Without a thought I pick up the pillow she slept on and inhale deeply, I close my eyes as her scent rushes around my senses.

Soft and arousing, like a memory from up above.

I do it again and again…and then I realize what I'm doing, disgusted. I throw the pillow at the wall.

The hell is wrong with you…she's your sister.

You sick fuck?

I drag my hands through my hair and storm back downstairs, I make another call as I take the stairs two at a time, I need to get the fuck out of here.

"Hey boss."

"Organize the planes for this afternoon, please."

"Planes as in plural?"

"Two. One to Paris and one to Milan."

Francesca

"Can you measure the floor space for the ballroom now, please?" I ask my assistant as I scribble down the details of the last room we measured.

Mr. Carballo has kindly assigned me two assistants today, they are the hotel's full-time handymen and today are measuring up a storm for me. I know the plans have the floor space on them, but I want to triple-check every last detail.

"Sure thing."

"Miss Ferrara." I hear a deep voice from behind me.

I turn, startled to see a man. "Yes, hello."

He smiles warmly and puts his hand out to shake mine. "Dominic Russo."

"Hi." I smile, surprised, who is *this* handsome specimen?

He smiles, knowing full well how good looking he is. He would be in his early thirties and has dark hair with a curl to it. Big blue eyes and well built.

"My dear Francesca," a deep voice says, I turn to see Mr. Carballo as he walks in. "Hello, Mr. Carballo."

He holds his hand out to the man. "May I present my operations manager; this is Dominic Russo. Dominic, this is Francesca Ferrara, our head designer from Paris."

"Hello. Nice to meet you."

"Likewise," he replies, his eyes hold mine for a beat longer than they should.

Hmm....

"I wanted you two to meet, Dominic will be handling most things from here, Francesca," Mr. Carballo says.

"Oh, okay." I smile, surprised.

"He's the CEO of our hotel chain, and you will be working closely with him."

"Great." I fake a smile. Shit...do I tell him now or later that I can't come back to Rome often?

"So, I'll leave you to it." Mr. Carballo smiles between the two of us. "Dominic has been briefed on everything, and after our day together yesterday, Francesca, I have full faith in your design and concepts."

"Thank you." A thought crosses my mind, "Are your offices here, Mr. Carballo?"

"No, not on premises, but I stay upstairs in the penthouse often, I haven't left here for a few days now."

"Oh." I smile, I love that he's hard working.

"Goodbye," he says as he heads toward the doors.

"Bye."

I look back down at my sketchpad, an awkward silence falls between Dominic and me, maybe it's just because he is good looking and he knows that I know it.

"Will you be relocating to Rome for the duration of this job?" he asks.

Shit.

"No, unfortunately I can't relocate." I try to think of an excuse. "I have a few jobs going at the moment." I don't want him to think I never come to Italy. "And I'm in Milan a lot."

"That's perfect."

"What is?"

"I'm based in Milan, we could catch up there."

"Really?" I smile, oh my God, that's so much easier. I could stay at my apartment and run the job from there. "That *would* be perfect."

"So?" He throws his hands up as if happy. "That suits me too, then I don't have to travel to Rome for our meetings. We can measure up or whatever you need today and then pick up next week in Milan."

"Great." I smile, thank God. Problem solved. Giuliano won't have to worry about me now.

My car pulls onto the tarmac to see two other black cars waiting at the plane.

Is he here?

Giuliano gets out of the back seat and leans against his car as he waits for me and my stomach does a little flip.

He came.

He's wearing a dark gray suit, his dark hair is a little messed, his chiseled jaw accentuating his beautiful face. Tall, dark and forbidden.

There's no denying it, Giuliano Ferrara is a breathtakingly handsome man.

My car comes to a stop and Giuliano goes to open my door and my heart somersaults in my chest.

I've thought about him all day.

"Hello," he says in his deep voice.

"Hi." I smile softly up at him, he takes my hand and helps me out of the car.

"How was your day?" he asks.

"Good." I smile bashfully, he makes me giddy. "How was yours?"

His big brown eyes hold mine. "Good."

The sound of the airplane engine is loud, and men are standing at a distance around us, but with the wind whipping my hair around, I can only see him.

We stare at each other, and the air between us is filled with unsaid words.

There's so much to say and I know that none of it should ever hear the light of day. "I'll call you when I get there," I ask hopefully.

"Don't."

My eyes search his and I swallow the lump in my throat. I

want to talk about him asking me not to marry Marcel. "About what you said...."

"Forget it."

My face falls.

We stare at each other. "It doesn't matter anyway...does it?" he says softly.

I get a lump in my throat.

This is goodbye.

"It was really good to see you again, Jules. I've missed you."

He gives me a sad smile and nods.

"Thank you for coming to look after me." I lean up and hug him. "I really appreciate it."

He stands emotionless, his hands down by his sides.

"Hug me," I whisper in his ear. "Please."

He puts his arms around me and we hug, clinging to each other tightly.

He's so strong and tall in my arms and damn it, I don't want to let him go.

Not again.

He pulls out of my grip and steps back from me. "You need to get going."

I smile, embarrassed that I act the way I do around him. "Goodbye." I turn and walk toward my plane and up the stairs.

"Good afternoon, Miss Ferrara," the captain says.

"Good afternoon." I force a smile.

"Just this way." The stewardess smiles. I follow her in and take a seat by the window.

I look out at the black Mercedes wagon and I know he's in the back seat.

And I want to run to him and beg him to take me back to a time when we could be in love.

But I can't...because he can't.

The stewardess closes the airplane door and the sound of the airtight seal brings tears to my eyes.

It's so final.

The plane begins to drive slowly down the runway and I wipe the tears from my eyes.

Goodbye, my love.

Again.

———

I ring the doorbell.

It's been four hours since I left Giuliano.

But I know what I must do.

I know that we can never be together and I understand that this problem will never be fixed.

But in this lifetime, I want to feel an all-consuming love for my husband...and unfortunately, I just don't have that with Marcel.

I wish that I did.

Being away from him this last few days has only cemented my fears into a reality.

I didn't miss him.

Not at all.

I missed Giuliano...when he was sleeping just downstairs.

I silently wept the whole way to France because with every minute in that plane, I was farther away from him.

This isn't right and I need to let Marcel go so that he can find someone who loves him as much as he deserves to be loved.

My grand love story didn't work out, but I want Marcel's to. I want him to be happy.

I would rather be single for the rest of my life than be forced to live a lie.

I can't do it anymore.

The door opens and Marcel's face comes into view. "Hey." He smiles.

"Hi." I smile sadly. "We need to talk."

Giuliano

I stare up at the ceiling in the darkness, it's the middle of the night and the room is quiet and still.

She didn't call.

And I shouldn't care, and it shouldn't matter.

I drag myself to sit up on the side of the bed and pull my hands through my hair.

I feel like fucking shit.

"What's wrong?" Amber whispers from behind me.

I turn to see the naked woman in my bed, beautiful and adoring, everything I should want. The sleeping pill that didn't work, I run my hand up her thigh. "Nothing, angel. Go back to sleep."

10

Francesca

I WALK into the restaurant just on six and see Anna sitting at a table near the back, I give her a smile and a wave but as I get closer I can see that she's been crying.

"Hey." I smile as I slide into the bench seat beside her. "What's wrong?"

"It's over with me and Frank."

My face falls. "What? Why?"

"We were in bed last night and he got up to go to the bathroom and a text came through on his phone." Leaning her elbows on the table, she rubs her eyes.

"What kind of text?"

"It said, *Missed you last night, come over.*"

My mouth falls open in shock. "What did he say?"

"He denied it at first. I was going postal and crying, I knew something was going on."

I watch her intently.

"He wouldn't let me go home, was carrying on and saying that I was the love of his life and this was someone who fancied him, but nothing had happened."

I fill our two glasses from the bottle of wine as I listen. "Yeah, okay."

She exhales heavily. "So I stayed."

"Did you sleep with him?"

She rolls her eyes and I know that means yes.

"Anyway, overnight I just couldn't stop thinking about all the warning signs, you know?"

"You had been suspicious." I sip my wine. "And you had good reason too," I add.

"So, this morning I got up and I told him that we could stay together, but I wanted to read the messages between him and the number that sent the text. I had been with him all night and I knew he hadn't had time alone to delete anything incriminating yet."

"Good thinking."

"And I knew that if he wouldn't show me there and then on the spot, he was hiding something."

I raise my glass to her. "True."

She screws up her face in tears.

"Oh baby," I whisper as I pull her into a hug. "What happened?"

"He wouldn't show me his phone," she whispers, "And then I told him that if he could just be honest with me, we could work this out. That I couldn't go on if I don't know the truth because I will never trust him again." She wipes the sad tears from her eyes.

My eyes fill with tears too, I hate seeing her hurt. "What happened?"

"He finally admitted it, said that he met her at work and that she was so different to anyone he'd ever met, she's Scandinavian."

"Blond," I whisper through dread. "He had been watching blond porn, hadn't he?"

"And that...." She pauses as she collects herself. "He just wanted to sleep with her and that there were no feelings, that he loved me."

I narrow my eyes. *Fucking asshole.*

"How long has he been doing it?"

"He wouldn't tell me, he promised it was just once."

"One is too many fucking times," I gasp, infuriated. I tip my head back and gulp down my wine. How could anyone cheat on Anna, she's the most beautiful, sweetest woman on earth.

Fuck men, I hate them all.

She cries as I watch her. "What happened then?" I ask.

"He wouldn't show me his phone."

"Which proves he was lying, it wasn't just once, at all."

"I know." She rolls her eyes as if ashamed. "I just loved him, you know?"

"I know, sweetie." I sigh.

"I told him it was over. Never to contact me again and he was crying and shit and trying to turn this back on me, that I wasn't adventurous enough in the bedroom, and it was just a phase he was going through."

I roll my eyes. "Is it over?"

She nods, her eyes welling with tears again. "How could I possibly have a long-term future with someone who cheated on me. He called someone and went and met her and had sex, and then came back to me professing his love. How could I ever trust him again?"

I pick up her glass of wine and pass it to her. "Especially since his admission wasn't even honest."

"Precisely," she mutters dryly as she clinks her glass with mine.

"I broke up with Marcel."

"Shit." She winces. "I knew that was coming."

"You did?"

"Yeah, you weren't in the least bit excited about being engaged."

"God." I exhale heavily. "I should've been."

"I know, he's fucking beautiful."

"What the hell is wrong with me?'

She shrugs sadly.

We sit and stare into space for a while, both lost in our own depressing thoughts.

"Maybe it's time we move home to Italy," she says.

"Maybe." I think for a moment. "Thank God we've got this weekend to look forward to."

She frowns. "What do you mean?"

"Ibiza," I mouth.

"Oh." Her eyes widen. "I forgot all about that."

"You know what you should do this weekend?" I tell her.

"What?"

"You should fuck the hottest Spanish guy of all time."

She smirks.

"And his friend," I add as I clink my glass with hers. "And his other friend, for that matter. Come Monday, you won't even remember that stupid Frank he will be three lovers behind you." I sip my wine. "And...apparently Spanish guys have big dicks."

She giggles and pulls me in for a hug. "What would I do without you, Chesk?"

"You'll never have to find out."

Ferrara

"Do you come here often?" I smile over at Dominic.

"Yes, this is one of my favorite restaurants in Milan. Don't tell me you haven't been?"

"I told you I hadn't." I shrug, "Let's see if it's all it's cracked up to be."

He widens his eyes with a cheeky smile. "Trust me, it is."

All morning at work Dominic raved on how this restaurant is the bomb. Finally, I caved in and we have come here for a quick lunch.

"Can I take your order?" the waitress asks.

Dominic opens the drinks menu. "Let's get some wine."

"We're working," I remind him.

"Oh hush, one glass won't hurt."

I smile as I peruse the drink menu. "I'll have a glass of the St Henri Shiraz please."

"Hmm, that's sounds good, I'll have the same."

"Are you ready to order your meal?" she asks.

"Yes, I'll have the salad and the grilled snapper please." I smile as I hand her back my menu.

"I'll have the linguini."

The waitress smiles and disappears.

Dominic's attention comes to me. "So tell me all about you?"

I shrug. "Not much to tell."

This is weird, this casual lunch feels decidedly date-like.

"Single, married, widowed?" he jokes.

I laugh. "Not widowed...but taken," I lie, well kind of a lie but most definitely not on the market.

"Ah, who is the lucky guy?"

"Maybe he's not so lucky."

"Your drinks," the waitress says as she places the two glasses of wine down in front of us.

"Thank you," I say, I take a sip. "Hmm, that's delicious."

Dominic leans on his hand with a sexy smile. "Tell me everything."

"Umm." I frown, I wish it were that easy, how long have you got? I just broke up with a beautiful man because I'm lusting over a bad man that I shouldn't and now I am going straight to hell because we kissed and I spent all week masturbating while watching him fuck two other women on Pornhub.

Fuck...that sounds so bad...who are you kidding, it is fucking bad.

The worst.

What the hell is wrong with me? This situation is majorly fucked up.

"Umm." I pause. "I don't know, I live in Paris and...." I glance up and my face falls.

Giuliano is here, he's with two men and they look as though they have just finished and are walking out of the restaurant, he glances over and stops on the spot when he sees me. His eyes hold mine, his tongue darts out and swipes across his bottom lip as if angered, and without hesitation, he walks over. "Hello."

"Giuliano, hi," I splutter.

Shit. Shit. Shit.

"Mind if I sit down," he says, but before I can answer he has already sat down in the spare seat. He sits back and crosses his legs, he stares blankly across the table at Dominic.

Arrogance personified.

"Who are you?" Giuliano asks him.

"This is Dominic," I reply nervously. "We work...."

He puts his hand up cutting me off, his eyes still fixed on poor Dominic. "I asked *him* a question. Let him answer it."

"Ah...." A trace of a frown crosses Dominic's face, he's completely intimidated.

Giuliano has a credit card between his pointer and thumb, with the bottom of the card resting on the table, he slides his fingers down the length of it and then turns the card and does it again as he waits for an answer.

"I'm Dominic Russo."

Giuliano's eyes hold his. "Business card?"

"I don't have one on me."

"Odd...you don't have a business card in your wallet?"

Dominic smiles as if accepting the challenge. "This is a lunch date, not a job interview. What is your name?"

My eyes widen and I pick up my drink and chug it down.

Fuck.

"Giuliano Ferrara." His eyes hold Dominic's. "Lunch date, hey?"

I fake a laugh. "Haha, hardly, we're working. This is just lunch. No date. Lunch, food."

Oh help.

I start to look around for the nearest exit, this is going to end badly, and by end badly I mean Dominic is about to get killed.

Literally.

"So...you work with Francesca?"

"Yes."

"What do you do?"

"Giulio...." I try to interrupt the interrogation.

His cold eyes flick up to me in a *shut the fuck up* look.

Oh crap. I take another gulp of wine.

I look over to try to get the waitress's attention.

Bring tequila, bitch.

Stat.

All of it.

"I'm the CEO of the hotel chain that Francesca is refurbing."

"Who owns that company?" Giuliano fires back.

"Mrs. Benedict."

I frown, huh? I thought Mr. Carballo owned it, oh...he must be just a manager or something.

"I'm sorry." Dominic frowns. "Who are you, and why are you being so rude?"

Giuliano slides his fingers down the credit card as his cold eyes hold Dominic's.

His face is emotionless, I haven't seen him like this before, he's scary, even to me.

"I'm someone who'll be watching you."

"What does that mean?" Dominic frowns.

"It means...you touch her and you're a fucking dead man," he whispers darkly, his cold eyes glare at Dominic, and then without another word, he stands and walks off through the restaurant.

Oh God....

Asshole.

Dominic's eyebrows rise as he watches him walk off. "Who the hell was that?"

The sky turns red, fury and embarrassment all rolled into one.

"He's my brother."

———

There is only one thing good about lusting over an asshole... nothing, that was a blatant lie. There is nothing good about my situation whatsoever.

I'm in a world of hell.

Ever since that damn kiss in the alleyway, Giuliano Ferrara

is all I can think about. Morning, noon and night.

The way he held my face, the way he closed his eyes, the way I felt in his arms.

There's a burning question in my soul, if he can incite this much arousal inside of me when he was acting to kiss me, what would it be like if he actually wanted me for real?

I keep watching that damn porno of him and the two girls, wishing it was me, not the gangbanging bit of course. I would *never* share him.

I don't know why I'm putting myself through this. Every time I close my computer I swear I am never watching him having sex with someone else ever again…sure enough, just like a drug addict, two hours later I'm rewatching it again, wishing it were me, all while knowing it never can be.

I mean, I'm no psychologist, but I'm pretty sure this is the most self-destructive behavior of all time.

Maybe if I just called him, I scroll through my phone and my finger hovers over his name.

What would I say?

I hate you, I miss you, I'm messed up…come over and fuck me better.

Ugh.

I click out of my phone, throw it on the nightstand and roll over in disgust. I'm not calling him, he's a bastard…remember? And even if we could be together, we wouldn't work out anyway.

He's not the boy I loved any more…he's a different man now, *powerful and virile.*

I get a vision of him holding my legs over his shoulders as he fucked me, the look in his eyes as he did it, the way he kissed me. His body oiled as he rode me hard and I would love every damn minute of it.

Stop it!

I punch my pillow in disgust.

At least I have something to take my mind off him for the next few days, Anna and I are off to Ibiza.

I exhale heavily in the darkness; the harsh reality is that I know I will think of him wherever I go.

Giuliano Ferrara is not easily forgotten

Ibiza

The car pulls into the large circular driveway of the beautiful hotel, the doorman smiles and as he approaches our car and the two guards in the front seat jump out to intercept him, Bruno opens the door with a kind nod. "Miss Ferrara."

"Thank you." I climb out and Anna follows, she looks around the swanky surroundings and hunches her shoulders in excitement. "Will you look at this place?"

"Pretty nice, huh?" I smile and as the boys retrieve our luggage, we make our way into the hotel reception. "Hello, checking in for Jones, please." I slip my fake identification across the counter to her. Ferrara protocol that I have about ten identities. Anna smirks as if knowing a secret, she says she always feels like she's in a spy movie when we use a pseudonym.

I, however, am unimpressed, it gets old very quickly.

"Hello." The receptionist smiles, he types furiously into his computer, "We have you for four nights in the..." He types again. "Two rooms, the eastern penthouses."

I frown. "No, just normal executive rooms, I didn't book the penthouses.

Normally we would have stayed in the same room but I'm

hoping Anna decides to fuck a certain someone out of her system. Hell, who am I kidding, maybe I should do that too.

And I don't mean my ex-boyfriend.

The receptionist smiles as he slides the door keys across to us. "You've been upgraded, compliments on the house."

"Oh." Anna's eyes widen in excitement. "Thank you so much," she gushes.

"Thanks." I force a smile, I was more than happy in the rooms I had booked.

"Take the lift to the top floor and your room numbers are on your keys."

"Thank you."

Anna and I make our way up to the top floor and walk down the lush wide corridor.

"I had a wonderful time in case I forget to tell you." Anna smiles in wonder.

I giggle. "Me too."

Imelda's Nightclub, 2 a.m.

The deep sexy beat echoes through the club, my face is flushed, and the dance floor is alive with scantily dressed bodies, writhing and dancing together as one. This is the third club we've been to tonight; our guards are now waiting outside. With every cocktail that Anna and I drink, we lose a little more inhibition.

As we dance, a gorgeous tall man slinks up to Anna to the beat and takes her in his arms, she looks up at him in awe and he leans in and softly kisses her.

Oh.... Shit.... Alright then.

Go Anna.

I smile and keep dancing and then as I look around, I lock

eyes with a familiar face.

Giuliano.

He's standing at the bar, towering over everyone else. He dominates the space.

What the hell is he doing here?

His eyes drop down to my toes and then back up to my face and suddenly I want to be the sexiest damn woman he's ever seen. I keep dancing, moving seductively to the beat as we stare at each other, thinking a million things we shouldn't be.

His eyes are dark and he licks his lips in anticipation, I keep moving to the beat and then as if unable to help it, he puts his drink down and walks toward me, bringing us face-to-face.

"What are you doing here?" I whisper.

"You know."

The air between us crackles and I swallow the lump in my throat.

I *do* know.

"We have unfinished business," he says.

I open my mouth to speak and he puts his pointer finger over my lips. "Stop thinking."

The song changes to Britney Spears' "Give Me More," and unable to stop myself, I keep dancing to the sexy beat, he puts his lips to my ear and whispers, "You want me to give you more, baby girl?" His breath dusts my skin, and goose bumps scatter up my arms.

My brow furrows as I stare at him.

More than anything.

He begins to dance with me, his hips up against mine in the dark crowded dance floor. My eyes flick around in a panic, someone will see us.

His hands drop to my behind and he pulls me close, I feel his hard erection in his pants.

The dominance of the act makes me flutter with arousal.

This is wrong....

His lips go to my ear once again. "We need closure." He softly bites my earlobe, and I close my eyes. "Just one time," he murmurs as his hands drag me over his hard cock. A flood of moisture rushes to my sex as I begin to lose control. "Nobody will ever know," he growls in my ear as he grabs a handful of my hair.

Something snaps deep inside of me and I can't help it, I lift my face and kiss him.

Right here in public for all to see.

His tongue slides into my mouth as his eyes close.

Long, slow and erotic.

Everyone else in the room disappears. It's just me and him.

As if coming to his senses he looks up, and his eyes roam around the room, he takes my hand and pulls me off the dance floor and up toward a service hallway.

Alone in the dark, with the sound of the music, we stare at each other.

His lips take mine, our kiss is frantic, my hands are in his hair, his hands are on my behind.

His hard cock, bulging into my stomach.

I want this.

Giuliano Ferrara, naked and on top of me.

Just once.

For five minutes we kiss in the hallway, consumed with passion...taken over by the need to put out the fire.

"Go tell Anna you'll see her tomorrow."

"I'm not leaving her here alone."

"She's not alone, she's with Carlo."

"You know him?" I gasp.

"I sent him to keep her busy."

My eyes widen in horror, what the hell?

"Don't worry, she'll enjoy it." He kisses me and then turns me by my shoulders, "Go." He gives me a gentle shove toward the dance floor and I walk up the hallway back out to the main dance floor area. My mind is a foggy mess, at what I've done... what I'm about to do.

What I fucking need.

My eyes scan the dance floor and I see them, right where they were. Dirty dancing and kissing like animals.

Jeez...he's right, she *is* enjoying it, maybe a little too much.

Get a room.

I walk up and tap Anna on the shoulder. "Anna."

She pulls out of the kiss, embarrassed she tries to pull out of his grip. "Oh, I'm coming."

"No." I smile, my eyes lock with the guy she's kissing, he's utterly gorgeous.

Go Anna.

"I'm going back to our hotel, I'm tired. I'll see you tomorrow?" I lean in and give her a hug.

"No. I'll come," she says.

"I'll get her home safe," the guy offers.

I bet you will.

Anna's eyes lock with mine and we smirk at each other, this night is turning out better than expected. "Okay, thanks." I kiss her cheek and turn and walk toward the front doors and I see Giuliano waiting beside them, his dark eyes hold mine as he takes my hand and my stomach flutters with nerves.

"Let's go."

We get to the door of the club, and he drops my hand, and we walk out as if nothing has happened. Bruno and Sav are seated on a chair near the road. "Francesca is tired, I'm taking her home," he announces.

They both stand.

"You two stay here with the others."

"I'll drive you," Bruno offers.

"Okay, but come back to Anna after you drop us off, please."

"Of course."

"Good night," Sav replies.

"Night," Giuliano replies as he walks purposely toward the car, he opens the back door for me, I scoot in and he climbs in beside me. "There's Val and Alex arriving, took their time," Giuliano says to Bruno as he looks across the road.

We look over to see Valentino and another man arriving, oh I haven't seen Val for years and years.

The car pulls out and Giuliano slides his hand up my calf muscle and I flutter deep inside.

My God, what am I doing?

There's no air in my lungs, possibly on earth and I cannot breathe for the life of me.

Arousal is pumping through my body and Giuliano casually chats with Bruno as if nothing just happened.

How can he even think when all the blood from his body is in his dick?

At least, I hope it still is.

"Just drop me with Francesca, I'll crash in the spare room, Carlo is with Anna and it saves you doing two trips."

"Okay," Bruno says as he casually drives.

What?

That's it, that's how easy it is to get away with this?

Anna

The tall dark and handsome man is overexcited as he dances toward me, I slowly dance back.

Down boy.

Jeez, maybe I should have left with Chesk. This guy could be any old creep.

"Anna." I hear a deep voice.

Startled, I turn to see a familiar face, Valentino, Giuliano's friend. I haven't seen him for years.

He's big and brawny and...*oh.*

Wow.

Shocked by his beautiful face, I stumble over my words. "Valentino."

He grabs my hand. "Borrowing her," he says to the guy I'm dancing with.

"Hey," the guy calls as he grabs my hand to pull me back.

Valentino glares at him and reading the signs, the guy instantly shuts up, he then pulls me through the crowd at speed. "What are you doing?" I call over the music.

"I should like to ask you the same thing." He pulls me outside into the courtyard, once there he turns to face me and I stare up at him.

He stares right back.

It's still there.

Valentino and I have this weird thing going on, nothing has ever happened between us. But we both know that we're attracted to each other, it's a silent letter on the wall.

"You're not to go home with him," he says.

"And why not?"

"Because...." He pauses. "Carlo is not the guy for you, trust me."

"Wait." I frown, surprised. "You know him?"

"He's my friend, we came here together."

Oh...I open my mouth to reply but no words come out.

"You go back in there and tell him to take a hike," he demands.

"Excuse me?"

"You heard me, go back in there and tell him to fuck off."

He's jealous.

"And why would I do that?"

I hold my smile as I wait for his flirty answer.

"Because if you are with him...then nothing can ever...." He cuts himself off.

Huh?

"Nothing can ever what?" I stare at him, my interest piqued.

"Happen with us."

I stare at him as my brain misfires. "But...." I search for the right words. "I've known you for ten years, Valentino, and you've never once asked me out."

"What's your point?"

"I'm saying that you've had ample opportunity."

"I have not," he snaps.

"Remember that wedding where we ran into each other a few years ago and spent the entire night talking?"

"Yes." He glares at me as if he already knows what I am going to say.

"I was sure that you were going to kiss me good night."

He rolls his lips.

"And more than that, I was positive that you were going to call me the next day."

"So was I."

I frown. "So why didn't you?"

"It's obvious, isn't it?"

"Not to me."

"If you don't know the answer to that, Anna." He rolls his

eyes in a dramatic fashion. "I'm not fucking spelling it out for you."

"Cut the attitude, Valentino." I put my hands on my hips in annoyance, his arrogance is beginning to piss me off now. "Start spelling."

"You are not the kind of girl I would fuck around with."

What does that mean?

He throws his hands up as if I'm stupid and then the penny drops.

"Oh...you just wanted to fuck me." I fume.

"I wasn't ready to settle down."

Wait a minute, I'm still confused, what's he saying, that now he is? "And tonight?"

"The timing is wrong."

"What?"

He shrugs, not wanting to elaborate.

"You have a girlfriend?" I stammer.

He puts his hands on his hips as if annoyed. "Yes."

Of all the nerve.

"So...let me get this straight. You don't want me to be with your friend so I can be on hold for you in case at some point in the future you ever want to ask me out?" I shriek.

"He's not the fucking guy for you, trust me on this," he yells as he grabs my hand. "I'm taking you home."

I snatch my hand from his grip. "Don't touch me."

"I will not have his sloppy seconds, Anna, you touch him and that's it for us," he bellows.

Asshole.

"There is no us," I yell, infuriated. "You chauvinistic fucking pig. Go home to your poor girlfriend. Does she know that you've got girls on reserve all around the world?"

"Shut up," he spits through gritted teeth.

Shut up.

"I hope your wholesome little girlfriend gangbangs all your friends...up her ass."

His eyes bulge from their sockets.

I march inside, I'm beyond infuriated. I cannot believe that entitled asshole.

I storm to the bar and Carlo comes back over. "Hey you." He smiles as he dances up to me all cute like. "What's with the angry face?"

Calm, calm, keep totally calm.

He dances some more and I know it isn't his fault that his friend is a douche bag, I feel my anger begin to ease, this guy has a naughty appeal, he oozes fun.

And he doesn't want to put me on ice until it suits him... ugh, Valentino is a complete asshole.

"Are we dancing?" I ask him.

He takes me into his arms in a dramatic fashion and pulls me onto the dance floor.

I laugh out loud as he twirls me around and as I spin I notice Valentino on the side of the dance floor, his face is murderous.

Screw you.

Francesca

As we drive through the darkness, Giuliano discreetly slides his hand up my thigh. I glance over and he's looking out the window acting casual, the guards in the front seat are oblivious.

He pushes my legs apart and as the car stays silent, excitement screams through me, this is fucked up.

So wrong...so hot.

He slides his fingers through the leg of my panties and then slowly through the lips of my sex, I'm swollen and dripping wet.

His teeth catch his bottom lip as he feels me, as if trying to stop himself from saying something out loud.

Oh....

A thick finger slowly slides into my sex and his breath quivers as he inhales, he's so turned on that he can hardly contain it. I smile over at him in the darkness.

I'm going to fry your brain tonight, big boy.

I clench around his finger and his brow furrows as he inhales sharply.

Bruno turns into the street of our hotel and Giuliano pulls his hand away and rearranges my dress. I stare out the window as adrenaline pumps through my body like never before.

My thighs are shaking.

My God...I'm so turned on that I feel like I'm about to pass out.

The car pulls to a stop and Giuliano gets out and opens my door, he takes my hand to help me out.

Electricity shoots up my arm and we stare at each other, in a sudden moment of perfect clarity, an unspoken message runs between us.

Truth.

"Thank you, we're fine now, you return to the others. I'll see Francesca safely to her room."

"Yes, sir. Good night."

"Good night."

"Thank you." I smile.

We walk in through the swanky hotel lobby and into the elevator, we both stand silently and stare at the back of the door.

We can't kiss, I feel like we can't even look at each other in case someone catches on to something.

I see a movement to the side and I glance over to see Giuliano sucking his finger.

I nearly convulse on the spot and the air fills with insanity again.

Fuck.

Fever-pitch arousal.

The doors of the elevator open and he strides out into the corridor, and like the masochist I am, I follow. "Your room key?" he says.

I unlock the door, he waits patiently beside me, his two hands in his jeans pockets. Not daring to touch me in public again.

The door opens, we walk in and he flicks the lock, we stare at each other for a moment.

Then he is on me, he pushes me up against the back of the door as he holds my face. His kiss deep and filled with suction. He pulls my dress over my head in one sharp snap and then he steps back, his eyes drop down my body and he smiles darkly.

"There she is...." he murmurs as he takes my hand and kisses my fingertips. "My girl...."

Oh....

He unlatches my strapless bra and throws it to the side; his big warm hands cup my breasts as he kisses me. I grab the bottom of his T-shirt and pull it up over his head. I'm gifted with the sight of his large torso. Rippled with muscles, tanned and golden.

Hell....

When did he get this body?

I slide my hand over his abs and through the trail of dark hair that disappears into his jeans.

What's happening right now?

Am I dreaming?

He drops to his knees and kisses me through my panties, my hands are in his hair.

The sight of such a powerful man on his knees for me brings an unexpected surge of emotion and I bend to kiss him as I hold his face in my hands.

The kiss is tender and loving, long and sweet.

He pushes my panties to the side and licks me there as his eyes hold mine.

His tongue is soft and hard, just the right pressure and I shudder.

Oh...*fuck*.

He slides my panties down and then lifts one of my legs as he licks me, deeper and deeper and my head throws back. He really begins to eat me; his eyes are closed in pleasure and I've never been taken like this.

So completely.

A gorgeous man, on his knees and at my mercy.

I glance over and catch sight of us in the mirror, me completely naked and him in jeans. Still in the foyer, not even able to make it to the bedroom.

He kisses his way up my body until he gets to my lips, his stubble is wet with my arousal.

"Bed," I pant.

His dark eyes hold mine and then he leads me through to my bedroom and lays me down on the bed and spreads my legs open. "Just like this," he murmurs before standing and unzipping his jeans.

I lie on my back and hold my breath as his black briefs come into view, his cock peeking over the waistband. He slowly slides them down and his hard penis springs over the top. My breath catches, his cock is engorged and heavy, with thick veins pumping through it.

Oh....

I'm positive that I've never seen anything so beautiful.

He kisses me as his fingers swipe through my open sex, he goes to move down my body. "No, Jules," I whimper. "I need you now."

"I want to...."

"Later," I snap. "I need you *now*."

There's no way I'm coming without him inside of me, I want the full package.

Literally.

He fusses around in his wallet and takes a condom and slowly rolls it on and then crawls over the top of me and I spread my legs around his thick body, he grabs himself and swipes the tip of his cock through my parted lips. Nudging my entry.

Hmm...he's big.

When we were younger, it seemed normal, I didn't know any different.

But now, I do.

Giuliano Ferrara is genetically blessed in that region.

"I need to warm you up or I'm going to hurt you," he whispers.

"No." I shake my head. "I want to feel it all."

He slowly pushes forward, creating a delicious burn and then he moans, deep and husky. "Fucking hell...."

I grip his broad shoulders as I try to deal with him, he pushes forward again and I smile up at the ceiling. That feels so good, and he's not even moving yet.

We stare at each other as magic swirls between us, such a perfect moment in time.

His forehead furrows as if conflicted.

"It's okay, baby," I say softly. "I'm here now." I lean up and kiss him, our lips linger over each other's and I know this is supposed to just be about sex.

But it's not.

It's more. So much more.

He slides home in one deep movement and I shudder as I cling to him.

Oww...it stings.

He pulls out and slowly slides back in, again and again. Each pump deeper than the last.

He circles his hips to stretch me out, first one way and then the other. I get a rush of moisture, finally loosening me up. "Good girl," he whispers darkly. "That's it."

Our bodies fit together so well, it's as if they were made for each other.

Maybe they were.

He spreads his knees wide and begins to ride me, deep measured pumps and...oh....

He puts my legs over his forearms to hold my legs back and really begins to give it to me. The bed starts to hit the wall and I begin to moan. "So good...oh...*God.*"

"That's it, good girl," he pants. "You like that?"

I nod, unable to answer.

"Take it all...you're so fucking creamy."

My toes begin to curl...okay, what the hell? He dirty talks now?

This is too much...I'm about to break. Emotional overload. "Jules," I pant on the edge of insanity.

He keeps going and lifts my legs even higher.

"Giuliano," I demand as I try to snap him out of it. "I need you to kiss me."

He stills as his eyes hold mine.

"Please," I whisper.

He slowly drops to his elbows and kisses me softly.

And an intimacy runs between us that breaks my heart... because no matter how perfect we are together.

We aren't. We never will be.

This isn't the happily ever after that it feels like, this is a train driving toward a cliff, an impending disaster with no survivors.

As if having the same epiphany as me at the exact same time, he pulls out of the kiss and flips me over to my knees. He wraps my ponytail around his hand and slams in hard, knocking the air from my lungs. He pushes my shoulders to the mattress in a sharp movement. He grips my two hipbones in his hands and begins to fuck me, hard and fast.

Gone is the gentle tender lover from just a moment ago.

Giuliano Ferrara, the king of Italy is here, and I am a faceless woman around his dick.

He begins to moan and the sound of it sets me off, I shudder hard as I come in a rush, my face planted silently into my pillow.

He slaps me hard on the ass as he comes deep inside of me. His pumps almost painful as he slams every last drop from his body.

He rolls off me and falls onto his back, panting hard, he puts the back of his forearm over his face as if to hide from me.

We went there, we actually went there. And damn it, it was good.

Too good.

A kaleidoscope of emotions run through me, but there's only one I can make sense out of.

Shame.

11

Francesca

Our collective panting fills the silence and then he gets out of bed in a rush.

Huh?

He begins to gather his clothes.

I sit up, my nakedness on full display. "What are you doing?"

"I've got to go." He rushes from the room with his clothes in his arms.

What?

He's leaving?

I lean back onto my elbows in shock...what the hell? I hear him drop his belt and the buckle clangs as it hits the ground, then a shoe hits the ground as he drops it.

He's panicked and rushing to get out of here as fast as he can.

Is he kidding?

Something snaps deep inside of me and I storm into the living area. "Don't you dare," I growl. "Don't you *fucking* dare walk out that door and make me feel like one of your cheap gangbanging whores."

His chest rises and falls as he struggles for control.

"You." I point my finger at him. "You are the one who wanted this. You are the one who wanted closure."

His eyes hold mine and he shakes his head as if he's a caged animal, "I can't...."

"Yes. You can." I push him hard on the chest and he stumbles back. "Man up, and stop being a coward." I point to the bedroom with an outstretched arm, "You will get in that bedroom and you will give me my fucking closure, God damn it," I cry.

He struggles to catch his breath.

"I. Will. Not...go through the rest of my life thinking about you," I scream as I lose all control, my eyes well with tears. "You get in that bedroom and you fuck this demon out of me." I sob out loud. "I can't do this anymore. I need you gone from my bloodstream. Once and for all."

His shoulders slump in defeat, he steps forward and takes me into his arms and I cry against his chest.

Because he wanted to leave...and all I wanted was for him to stay.

He kisses my temple, "I just...."

"Don't." I cut him off. "Stop thinking. You promised me closure. Now give it to me." He stares down at me and tucks a piece of my hair behind me ear.

"After Monday you can leave me forever.... But, not now," I whisper with a panicked shake of my head. "Not tonight." My eyes well with tears again. "You can't leave me tonight."

He cups my face in his hands and kisses me softly and I

screw up my face against his, because I already know how this ends.

It isn't good and maybe I hate this story, because my heart already hurts and it isn't even morning yet.

Giuliano

I lie on my side and watch her as she sleeps, so peaceful and serene.

The extreme opposite of how I'm feeling right now.

Last night after I tried to leave and she had her meltdown, we showered and one kiss led to another and another, next thing we were making slow love up against the tiles.

It was wrong. I shouldn't have let it go there, it was way too...intimate.

Then we went to bed, I tried to fix it and just as she asked me, I fucked that demon out of her all night.

Hard.

But as it left her body, I felt it enter mine.

I feel sated, angry, fucked in the head, but most of all...an attachment. Something that's been missing from my life for a very long time.

And I can't...this isn't....

Her long dark hair is splayed over the pillow, her lips are flushed red with shaving rash from kissing.

I've never known a woman so beautiful.

Her eyes flutter open and as they focus on me she gives me a shy smile, my heart constricts, the way she looks at me...*is just.*

"Hi," I whisper, unable to help it, I lean over and kiss her softly.

"Hi." She smiles against my lips.

We lie on our sides and stare at each other, both lost in our own thoughts.

We shouldn't want each other the way that we do.

A million ways that I could kidnap and keep her forever are running through my mind, all the while she's probably in a world of regret.

"You know, I had the weirdest dream," I murmur.

She runs her fingers through my hair. "Funny that, me too." She rolls over and kisses my chest and then takes my nipple into her mouth, her eyes darken as she stares up at me.

It's there again, this energy shift, an exchange in power.

She's the only person who has ever done this to me, made me feel completely at her mercy.

My Francesca, the girl I've always loved.

I would give up the world, do anything, *kill anyone*...to spend one more moment in her arms.

For her...there are no bounds. None that I can control anyway.

I hold my breath as she kisses down my stomach, she goes lower and lower until she gets to my cock, it flexes beneath her and she takes it into her mouth.

I close my eyes in relief. *She doesn't regret it.*

She sucks me and cups my balls and I inhale sharply and spread my legs, granting her access.

Just like that....

Her tongue flickers over my tip and I feel an involuntary gush of pre-ejaculate. When she's got me like this, she owns me.

With my two hands, I grab her hair and hold her head still as I slide deep down her throat.

My eyes roll back in my head.

So. So. Good.

I begin to slowly fuck her mouth as I lose focus.

Stop it.

I tip my head back and stare up at the ceiling. I don't know who you're talking to conscience, but there is no chance in hell that I'm listening.

Monday....

With my cock down her throat, she takes me in her hand and begins to slowly stroke me hard and I moan.... "That's it," I whisper as I see stars.

Fuck, she's good at this.

She smiles around me and my toes curl.

"Hmm.... Just like that, baby," I coach her. "Good girl." I gently push her hair back from her forehead as I stare down at her. Watching her suck on my cock is the hottest thing I've ever seen.

It always has been.

My legs widen, my body needing a deeper connection.

Monday.

We've already crossed the line, what does it matter now while we are away?

Nobody will ever know.

Monday.... I promise.

I will turn my back and walk away.

Forever.

Francesca

It's ten a.m.

Bruno brought a bag of Giuliano's clothes over for him so that he didn't have to go back to his own place.

Do they know?

What are the guards thinking? Have they put two and two together?

I follow Giuliano down the hotel corridor, he's wearing a white linen shirt and denim shorts, his top button is undone revealing a glimpse of his tanned chiseled chest.

I've got issues, major issues. Whereas yesterday I only had distant memories. Today, I have a full-blown addiction. There's a reason Giuliano is called the king of Italy.

He fucking is.

A literal rock star in bed, experienced, hung, and hungry.

The lethal trifecta.

He knows his way around a woman's body and boy oh boy, does he use it to his advantage. He rode me hard all night long and had me begging for more.

I'm sore, not sorry and so, so sated.

We get into the elevator, the doors close and he turns to me, his eyes sweep down my body, he does up the top button on my shirt and closes the split on my wraparound skirt. "This skirt is see-through," he mutters.

"It's a sarong."

He raises an eyebrow as he inspects it. "I think you're supposed to wear something underneath it."

"I am, a bikini. We *are* going to the pool." I raise an eyebrow back.

He fakes a smile. "Witty."

"I think so."

The doors open and he strides out and through the main foyer out to the poolside restaurant. As I walk behind him I see the women all turn their heads and watch him.

He has this aura around him.

Power.

I begin to feel my pulse in my ears as that green monster shows her ugly head.

Eyes off, bitches. He's taken. Well not really…but this weekend he is.

We walk around the pool and catch sight of Anna and Carlo, they're eating breakfast together and both look up and see us at the same time and wave.

I give a weak smile and wave. "Fuck's sake," Giuliano mutters under his breath.

"We have to sit with them," I whisper.

"Why?"

"Because we're here with them." I widen my eyes. "Be nice."

He exhales heavily and we make our way over to the table. "Hello." I smile awkwardly as I slide into a seat.

Giuliano sits down and sits back in his chair as he acts casual. "Hi." His tone is clipped. and he nods to his friend. "Carlo."

Anna's eyes widen as she looks between us. "You stayed here last night?"

"In the spare room," I blurt out guiltily as I gesture to Carlo. "He was just waiting for his friend, that's all."

Carlo's eyes hold mine and he subtly raises his eyebrow.

He knows.

Shit. Shit. Shit.

I feel my cheeks flush with embarrassment. Oh hell, please earth swallow me whole.

This is the opposite of great. This is disastrous.

Giuliano opens his menu and peruses the breakfast choices and Anna widens her eyes at me in a *what's going on* gesture.

I give her a subtle shake of my head and get to reading my menu too.

"What do you want, Chesk?" Giuliano asks.

Anna points her teaspoon at me, "That is a good question. What *do* you want, Chesk?"

Giuliano glances up at her and she withers. "For breakfast, I mean. Jeez."

"Umm...." I stare at the menu, too distracted to even read the words. This is a living nightmare, they all know what we've done. I can't stand it; I am going straight to hell.

"Are you two finished your little one-night stand?" Giuliano says casually as he stares at his menu.

"Who said it was a one-night stand?" Carlo fires back.

Giuliano glances up as if surprised.

"I'm staying with Anna all weekend," he announces. "You're going to have to stay in that spare room a few more nights."

Giuliano exhales heavily as if annoyed and I bite my lip to hide my smile, I know for a fact that he's very happy in my spare room.

Anna smiles over at Carlo. "That's a bit presumptuous, isn't it?"

Carlo reaches over and squeezes her thigh, "Behave yourself, before I punish you."

Oh....

Carlo and Anna stare at each other and I can feel the spark between them.

Go Anna.

"Do you guys still want to go shopping today?" Anna asks.

Giuliano winces and I can't think of anything worse, I'm exhausted. I hardly slept all night.

"Sure." Carlo shrugs.

"I'm most definitely out," Giuliano says. "Shopping is the very last thing I want to do in Ibiza. I'm going to the beach."

I really should go shopping with the others but screw it. "That sounds good, I'm beaching too."

"What are we doing tonight?" Carlo asks.

"There's a bar down at the beach, we could maybe go there?" Anna suggests.

"Sounds good." I smile.

"Shall I book for six p.m.?" Carlo asks, he looks to Anna. "You ready to go?"

"Uh-huh," Anna swoons as she stands and takes Carlo's hand.

I look between them in shock, is it really that easy to get Giuliano to myself today?

"Great." I smile. "I'll see you both tonight."

Giuliano stays silent and I get the feeling he would rather just stay in our room, well too bad. I'm not leaving Anna...not that she looks like she minds, she's literally glowing. "Have fun shopping."

"You two try not to kill each other," Carlo says as they walk off.

Giuliano's eyes hold mine and a trace of a smile crosses his face. "Death by cock," he mouths.

I roll my lips to hide my smile and I whip him with the serviette. "Behave yourself."

The warmth of the sun dances across my skin.

Giuliano and I are lying on our backs on towels on the beach, the sound of the waves gently lapping the shore in the background. I'm wearing a black bikini and have a black straw hat over my face. It's so weird, I've always been aware of the guards around me. Today, it has a new hurdle, I'm terrified that they are going to pick up on something between Giuliano and I.

Bruno and Sav are in the café at the back of the beach, watching over us.

Spoiling my fun.

I just want to roll over and kiss him and rub the suntan oil into his back and frolic and cuddle in the water. But I can't, *we* can't.

Giuliano reaches over between our bodies and links my pinkie finger with his and I smile under my hat. Such a simple gesture that says so much.

He wishes we were alone too.

He rolls over onto his side so that he faces me and leans up onto his elbow. "Do you regret last night?" I don't answer and he reaches over and lifts my hat so that he can see my face. "Do you?"

"What if they know?" I say.

"They don't."

"What if they do?"

"They can't prove anything, it would only be speculation. We are allowed to be friends."

I nod as I stare at him.

"It's three days, Chesk. Out of a whole lifetime, it's just three days."

I stare at him as I feel my heart break. He's right, out of a whole lifetime, I only get him for three days.

I nod sadly.

"What does that mean?" He frowns.

I sit up, suddenly motivated to do all the things. "It means I want to go back to our room. Right now."

He sits up too. "To do what?"

"Earn our ticket to hell."

He chuckles and then bursts out laughing. "Pretty sure I already got mine, but happy to help you earn you yours."

. . .

We burst through the bedroom door and Giuliano takes my hand, pulls me through the apartment and throws me on the bed. "Don't move." He disappears and comes back with my beach bag and rattles through it.

What's he doing?

He produces my suntan oil and smirks. "Wouldn't want you to get burned." He pours some onto his hand.

What in the world?

"You're a deviant, you know that?"

He bends and slides my bikini bottoms off as he pours oil all over my sex and massages it in with his strong fingers, my legs widen as I stare up at him in awe.

"As if you don't love it." He whispers darkly.

He's right.... I totally do.

The room is steamy and hot, Giuliano and I are top and tail in the huge bathtub. He is massaging my feet as they rest on his chest. We're having the best time, we spent the day in bed yesterday, we went out for dinner last night and drank way too many cocktails, went clubbing and got home way too late.

Today we've spent swimming and lying in the sun, I feel so relaxed.

I stare over at the man sitting opposite me, some people get uglier the more that you get to know them.

Not him.

Giuliano Ferrara gets dreamier and dreamier.

He's hard and cold with everyone, but not with me. I see the other side, the real him, soft and loving. The kind of man you could live a lifetime or ten with.

"Can I ask you something?" I say.

"I take it..." he massages my feet, "... you're going to anyway."

"The crime."

He glances up. "What about it?"

"What is it?"

He continues his massaging. "It's not for you...." He pauses as if choosing his words correctly. "It's not for you to worry about."

"I'm not stupid, I know it's there." I shrug, I need to know what he's capable of. "Do you murder people?"

"*I* don't."

My eyes hold his. "Do your men?"

"Sometimes."

My face falls. "Oh."

"In self-defense, nothing like your dear old grandfather, put it that way."

"Stefano murdered people?" I frown.

He chuckles. "He didn't just murder people, he cut them up while they were still alive."

My eyes widen in horror and I fall silent.

Fuck.

I open my mouth to ask more.

"Chesk." He cuts me off. "Don't ask things that you don't want to know the answer to, baby." He massages the arch of my foot.

"Drugs?" My eyes search his.

"Yes."

"You sell drugs?" I frown.

"We—" he gestures to the air between us, "Sell entertainment."

"Entertainment?" I gasp.

"Cocaine."

"Drugs kill people, Giuliano."

"It's candy for rich people." He shrugs. "Nobody overdoses on fucking cocaine. You don't see kids on the street buying cocaine for $1000 a pop. We're up-market, we supply the top end of town for most of Europe, lawyers, doctors, politicians, high-caliber clients."

Hmm....

"Well...." I think for a moment. "Where do you get it?"

"I import it from Columbia."

"You import it?" I gasp. God, that sounds hardcore.

He smiles as he massages. "Don't look so shocked, you think your property portfolio and designer lifestyle comes for free?"

"How do you import cocaine?" I blurt out. Oops, that was loud. I look around the bathroom guiltily. "How do you get it into the country?" I whisper.

"Border control works for me."

My mouth falls open.

"And the police, and the judges. And anyone who wants a luxury lifestyle for their family. I pay my employees very well."

"How much do you import?"

"It depends, usually." He shrugs casually. "Three hundred kilograms."

"A year?"

"A week."

"A week?" I gasp. "What the hell? How much is that worth?" I whisper.

"Around eighty million."

My eyes bulge from their sockets. "You make eighty million dollars a week?"

"No," he scoffs. "We have a lot of costs, two thousand staff and multiple businesses. Things cost money, Francesca, a lot of fucking money. We do what's necessary to provide for our staff."

"We?"

"Alex and Val work alongside me. Carlo too."

"What if you get caught? You'll go to prison," I stammer in a panic. I get a vision of my sweet Giuliano fist fighting till the death in a prison cell.

He smiles and lifts my foot and kisses it. "Trust me, compared to our ancestors that built this business, we are legitimate. We don't bully anyone. We run an entertainment industry, nothing more, nothing less. Besides, I have protection in place."

"What protection?"

"The yachts that it comes in on are in a false name. The people who run the ships and distribute it don't know who we are. Nothing can be traced back to us. The business model is perfect and watertight."

My eyes search his. "Are you sure?"

He kisses my foot again. "I'm not stupid." He keeps massaging.

I think for a moment. "I beg to differ," I reply. "Because I've made you massage my feet for an hour now, if's that's not stupid I don't know what is."

He chuckles and dives up over top of me, water sloshes over the sides. "Time to pay."

It's our last night in Ibiza, the last three days have been the happiest of my life.

Sun, laughter and love.

So much love.

I got ready early and went down to the hotel bar to meet Anna. After not seeing Giuliano for the last two hours, I can't wait a moment longer to see him, I left my room key behind.

Knock, knock. I wait.

Silence.

Knock, knock.

The door opens in a rush and my eyes widen, Giuliano is wearing nothing but a white towel wrapped around his waist.

His eyes drop down my body, I'm wearing a tight, hot-pink minidress with sky-high hot-pink stilettos, I give a little wiggle of my hips. "Room service."

He smirks and, in one sharp movement, bends and throws me over his shoulder and slams the door behind us. "You know what I do with naughty room attendants like you?" he says as he marches through the apartment, I giggle as I hang upside down.

Bad things, I hope.

We walk through to the bedroom and into the bathroom and he puts me down on the counter. "Sit." He kisses me quickly. "I have to finish shaving."

Oh...well that's not the bad things I was hoping for. "Okay."

He turns his electric shaver on and rubs it over his face as he looks in the mirror. My eyes drop down his body, his chest is broad with a scattering of dark hair. His abs are rippled and his skin has a beautiful sun-kissed glow.

He glances over to see me staring at him. "What are you looking at?"

"You."

"What about me?"

"When did you get so hot?

He smirks as he continues shaving, I watch him for a while. "Why are you shaving again? You shaved this morning."

"Because." He rinses the blades. "If I don't shave again now, by two a.m. my stubble will be too rough for me to kiss you."

I smile, Italian men.

"Oh...." I think for a moment. "What makes you think I'm a sure thing?"

Amusement flashes across his face.

"Huh?" I prompt him.

Without a word, he grabs my thighs and pulls my behind toward him in one sharp snap. He pushes me back so that I'm leaning up against the mirror and then lifts my two legs and places them over his shoulders.

We stare at each other as the air crackles between us.

He turns his head and licks up my inner ankle and I feel it deep inside. "Because when you wear slutty little dresses like this, you will do whatever I fucking say." He pulls my panties to the side and rubs his fingertips through the lips of my sex.

I'm folded in half, up against a mirror with my legs over his shoulders.

Completely at his mercy.

"Won't you?" he says darkly as he impales me with two of his thick fingers.

"Oh." I whimper.

He jerks his fingers hard. "Won't you," he emphasizes as he waits for an answer.

"Yes."

With his eyes locked on mine he works me with his fingers, massaging that perfect G-spot that no other man could ever find.

I'm instantly wet and waiting.

"I have a thing for stilettos," he whispers as he pumps me. "Especially around my ears." He undoes his towel and his large hard dick springs free. Holding himself at his base, he rubs his tip through my lips and I get a little nervous. In this position, he could really do me some damage.

"Careful," I whisper.

He cups my face in his hand and leans in and kisses me softly, I smile against him.

This man....

Our lips meet again as he slides his cock deep inside my body and I feel myself ripple around him. He lets out a low whistle as arousal flickers in his eyes.

No condom.... Oh no.

We forgot a condom.

He straightens his arms wide on the counter and slides out and then back in.

Out...harder in.

Oh, fuck it, who cares, I'm not stopping now.

I want him to come inside of me. I want all of it, every last drop.

He gives me another slower pump and then he lets me have it. Deep thick pumps and my body begins to convulse around him. Sucking him in.

The hair hangs over his forehead and a sheen of perspiration dusts his skin. This isn't a romantic moment; he's not wooing me in a grand gesture of love. His body has taken over.

He needs to fuck.

Hard.

He wraps both arms around my thighs as he holds them together and close to his chest while he fucks me at piston pace. I look over his shoulder to see our reflection in the mirror wall opposite us. The sight nearly brings me undone, him naked and pumping me, hell for leather with no fucks to give.

Me, totally dressed and at mercy to his pleasure.

So hot.

He grabs the back of my head aggressively and drags my face to his, he kisses me. Rough and unapologetic, our teeth clash and then he bites my neck hard. Goose bumps scatter up my spine as I lose control.

Oh God....

"Come," he demands as he fucks me. "You need to come." He screws up his face. "Now."

I smile, excited, he's losing control and wants me to come before he does.

No way.

I want to win this round.

He keeps pumping me. "Chesk." He moans.

"No," I pant.

He grabs my two nipples and squeezes them. "Ahh," I cry from somewhere between pleasure and pain, for some reason, the movement contracts my vaginal muscles. I slam hard head-first into a freight train of an orgasm.

He smiles triumphantly and then pulls out and pulls me off the counter and pushes me down to my knees. "Open," he commands.

I do as I'm told and he slides his cock down my throat and I feel it thicken and shudder.

What the hell?

He comes in a rush and I gag as I struggle to take him all, hell on a cracker. That wasn't the ending I was expecting.

Dirty bastard.

He smiles down at me and smooths my hair as he pants, trying to catch his breath.

"Did you bring clean towels?" he asks.

"Huh?" I stare up at him, a mouth full of come, fucked to oblivion and totally confused.

"Aren't you from room service?" He raises his eyebrow.

I smile. Unbelievable.

He pulls me to my feet and kisses my collarbone, then he turns me away from him and slaps my behind. "Get in the shower, you smell like sex." He glances down at himself. "Your pink lipstick looks good on my dick."

"Yeah well." I shrug casually as I turn the shower on. "Your dick looks good in everything."

"Let's dance," Carlo says with an outstretched hand. Anna smiles lovingly up at him and stands. "Don't mind if I do."

I watch as he leads her to the dance floor and takes her in his arms, they chat and laugh and I can't help but feel a little jealous.

Unlike us, they can dance with each other. They can hold hands, and if they so choose to, fall in love.

I look back over the table to Giuliano, he gives me a sad smile as if reading my mind.

My eyes roam over all the people on the dance floor, every single couple here are free to love.

We are not.

Our feelings are forbidden. "Can we go?" I ask.

Giuliano nods. "Yep." He stands and, unable to hold my hand, pulls my chair out. We walk to the door together, but alone. No touching, no togetherness.

Just cold reality.

We get into the back of the car and once again I'm reminded of what can never be.

Giuliano sits on one side of the back seat, and I sit on the other. Both staring out the separate windows.

Tomorrow we part ways forever.

And I knew that this was coming and I told myself I was prepared for it. But how do you prepare for the end of the world?

He can never be mine, and just for a moment...I forgot.

The car pulls into the hotel and our driver opens the car door. "Have a nice night," he says with a kind nod.

"Thank you."

Giuliano and I walk silently through the foyer and get into the elevator, we both stare at the closed doors as we travel up to our floor.

Like flood waters rising, I can feel it coming.

The end is near.

The doors open and we walk silently down the corridor until we get to my door.

I know this is our last night together, but I really don't know if I can finish what I started.

He can tell too.

His eyes search mine. "Are you going to ask me in?"

I stare at him standing there, all handsome and gorgeous. Willing and wanting...and then there's me, feeling weaker than water.

"I didn't get to dance with my girl yet," he says softly.

He wants to dance with me?

I get a lump in my throat and I nod, I turn and open the door and he follows me in. He takes out his phone. "What do you want to dance to?" he asks hopefully as he desperately tries to save the night.

"Something romantic." I smile, forgetting the worries of the world just for a moment.

"Alright." He opens Spotify and says the words out loud as he types. "Romantic songs." He puts his phone down on the table and holds his hand out to me in a grand gesture. "Are you ready to be romanced, my love?"

I giggle and he takes me into his arms.

Silence.

He glances over to his phone. "Play, fucker."

I giggle again and the music starts.

If I, should stay,
I would only be in your way.

My heart drops.

Oh no...not this song, anything but this song.

We hold each other tight as we dance to "I Will Always Love You," by Whitney Houston.

So romantic and heartbreaking. Never a truer song has ever been sung.

To the melancholy tune, I kiss, I dance and I love him goodbye.

Giuliano

The plane touches down in Milan, and I close my eyes. The flight has been long, Francesca stared out the window while I stared at her.

In twenty minutes, this very plane leaves again to take her and Anna back to Paris. We said our goodbyes this morning, knowing that it would be the last time we would be alone. The doors are disengaged and our guards exit the plane, everyone begins to fuss around as they retrieve their luggage from the overhead.

She's leaving.

The walls start to close in as I stare at her.

No.

"Everyone off the plane," I snap.

Francesca's eyes meet mine.

"I need five minutes alone with Francesca."

Everyone looks at each other in confusion.

"Everyone off the fucking plane," I bark. "Now," I cry as I lose control, I turn to look at the captain and the stewardess. "You too."

One by one they all walk out the door and down the stairs, leaving us alone.

"Jules," she whispers as she takes my hands in hers, sensing my oncoming meltdown. "Sweetheart."

"No."

"We don't have a choice." She tries to pull her hands from mine and I hold on to them, not letting her go.

Don't leave me.

"Baby..." she whispers.

"No."

"You need to do something for me."

I remain silent.

"I want you to let yourself fall in love with someone."

I frown. *What?*

"I need to know that someone is looking after you, keeping you safe and loving you...." Her eyes well with tears. "Because...I can't."

My nostrils flare as I stare at her. "I don't want the second prize, Francesca."

Her eyes hold mine. "This is goodbye, Jules."

My vision blurs.

She reaches up and kisses me softly. "Remember me." She takes me into her arms and I drop my head to her shoulder. We hold each other for an extended time.

No.

She goes to pull out of my arms and I pull her closer. "Don't."

"Giuliano." She tries to break free.

"You can't leave me," I whisper angrily as I lose control, struggling to hold her. "I don't give a fuck who we are."

She pulls out of my grip, her eyes are welled with tears. "Don't make this harder than it already is. I'm leaving for Paris."

"When will I see you again?"

"You won't. I'm not coming back." Her haunted eyes hold mine. "It's the only way we can do this." She kisses me softly. "We need to move on."

I step back, her detached words cut like a knife.

"Goodbye, Giuliano." She turns and walks from the plane.

No.

I grab the back of a seat to hold myself up.

No.

No.

Carlo comes through the door, he tentatively walks up the plane, his eyes hold mine, and I stare at him in a daze. He doesn't say anything because there *is* nothing to say.

We stand in silence for what feels like a very long time and he waits...because he knows.

"Let's go," he says. "We have to." He turns and walks off the plane and I stand and stare at the ground.

I can't do this.

You have to.

Ferrara

Eventually, I get off the plane and walk down the stairs. Without making eye contact with Francesca, and on autopilot, I get into the back of the waiting car, it pulls away and Carlo sits silently beside me. Forever faithful.

We drive into the night...straight into hell.

12

Francesca

A MILLION TEARS cried into the sea of devastation. An emptiness that knows no bounds.

It's one thing to lose someone, to be brave enough to walk away, but to know he's hurting too…cuts that much deeper.

I keep seeing his face on the plane, the way his eyes searched mine, the way he clung to me as if his life depended on it. I keep hearing the fear in his voice.

I want to console him, hold him, protect him from the danger.

But I can't, because I *am* the enemy.

The person responsible for that broken heart. I cannot fix this, no matter how badly I want to. Nobody can, and it makes it all that much worse.

I had to be strong enough for the both of us, although I'm not so sure that I can be anymore.

I want to sink into a ditch and never get out. The worst part is that I can't talk about it with anyone, not even Anna. I know how bad this is and there is no excuse for our behavior.

The scenery flies by the car window as I stare solemnly out of it.

Has he eaten?

Is he consoling himself in someone else's arms right now?

If loving him is a sin, then maybe I don't care anymore.

The feelings are still between us, whether we act on them or not seems irrelevant.

Just feeling this way about him is a sin....

His words keep playing over and over in my head. *"I don't give a fuck who we are. We belong together. You know it, you know we do."*

And I do.

With every fiber of my being I know that he is my one grand love in this lifetime.

To walk away from it.... Just....

The lump in my throat hurts and I feel a hot tear roll down under my dark sunglasses, I discreetly swipe it away. It's been five days since I said goodbye to my Giuliano...five days of unimaginable sadness.

I've never experienced a darkness like this before where I imagine my death and the peace it would bring me.

Us.

At least then, the hurt would stop...and he could move on.

I wonder what would be the least painful way to die? Anything would be better....

Antonio's voice interrupts my thoughts. "Is everything alright, Miss Ferrara?"

"Yes," I lie, I keep looking out the window, I haven't made eye contact with him all week.

"You just don't seem yourself, did something happen in

Ibiza?" His eyes flick up to meet mine in the rearview mirror as he waits for my answer.

Everything happened.

"Not at all." I fake a smile at my ever-loyal guard. "I'm just tired, that's all."

"Because...."

"I'm fine, Antonio," I say, sterner, cutting him off.

He rolls his lips and gives a curt nod and continues to drive.

Damn it, that was rude.

This isn't his fault, but I can't go there, I don't want him digging around and trying to discuss my train wreck of a love life. I'm simply not strong enough to talk about it, I can't anyway, even if I wanted to.

I try to make amends for snapping at him. "Tell me about your sister's wedding on the weekend?"

He raises an eyebrow as his eyes stay fixed on the road in front. "Alright."

I square my shoulders, determined to hide my feelings better. "Tell me everything."

I'm okay through the day, it's bedtime, I fear.

Darkness, the dreaded bearer of sadness, and like the masochist that I am, every night I do what I swear I will never do again. I put my headphones in and I cry silently in the darkness as I listen to "I Will Always Love You" by Whitney Houston.

I picture us dancing alone in our hotel room and him smiling down at me.

The love between us.

Why do I put myself through it?

I don't know.

But I feel like I have to get it out, because how can you be so broken inside if you don't get to show it to anyone.

I pretend I'm okay.

I don't speak his name, I don't ask about him, I don't cry, and I'll never admit it, but even after four weeks, I feel like I'm getting worse, not better.

I hear Anna wind up her phone call to Carlo, to add salt to my already weeping wound, he and her are going rock steady, while my world is falling apart.

At least Ibiza resulted in someone's happiness, I only wish it was mine.

I have no one to blame but myself, I knew what I was getting into when I slept with Giuliano. But I had to do it anyway.

More fool me, I deserve every tear that I've cried. "I'm tired," I say as I stand. "I'm going to turn in."

"Good night," Anna replies as she sits on the couch, she looks me up and down. "You've lost a lot of weight."

I glance down at myself. "Have I?" I know I have, I'm skin and bone. Food turns my stomach. "I guess I've been so busy working that I haven't had time to eat." I shrug.

Anna's eyes hold mine and I know that she knows. "Are you okay?"

"Uh-huh." I smile. "Fine."

"Are you really okay?"

"Absolutely, good night." I walk into my bedroom and close the door behind me, I slide down it to sit on the floor, the dreaded lump in my throat returns.

I'm not okay.

I click onto my hundredth website for today, I can't find the damn wallpaper that I want for the hotel. I know exactly what I want and damn it, why can't I find it?

I've seen it a lot in the past and now that I finally want to order, it seems to have disappeared off the face of the earth.

Knock, knock sounds at my office door. I glance up to see my boss.

"Hi." I smile. "Come in."

"Hi, Francesca," he replies, he comes and sits down at my desk. "How's it all going? I'm hearing great things."

"Awesome." I smile proudly. "Busy."

"Francesca," Tony says from the door. "That tile that we used on the Murdoch job, do you remember the name?"

"Blackbird in matte."

"Great. I knew you'd remember it." He goes to walk out.

"It needs to be cut on the angle, remember," I call after him.

"Ah." Tony's face falls. "Does it?"

"It has to be laid in herringbone to get that look."

"I was going to do chevron."

I wince. "It will look lovely, very different, though. If you want that same look as the Murdoch job, I would go herringbone."

"Okay, thanks."

My attention returns to my boss.

"Where are we up to with the Remington project?" he asks.

"They're currently demolishing and I'm ordering materials and furnishings."

"Chesk, what carpeting did we use in Chalet Street?" Ella asks from the door.

"Um." I screw up my face as I try to place the job. "In the bedrooms or the living?"

"Bedrooms."

"It was a tufted hundred percent wool. I'm not sure of the color, it's from the Merino latest catalogue."

"Okay, thanks." She disappears.

My boss looks over at me. "Are you always interrupted every two minutes like this?"

I give an embarrassed smile. "Comes with the job, I guess."

"No. it shouldn't, not when you have your own very important job running. Why don't you work from home for a while?"

"Really?"

"That way nobody will interrupt you every five minutes, you can actually get things done."

"That would be great, thank you." I smile, although a little voice from deep inside fears what sinister thoughts the silence may bring. Keeping myself busy is the only thing keeping me sane at the moment. "I'll only need a few weeks to get everything finalized and then I'll be back in the office, I like being here."

I need to be here.

"Okay, starting tomorrow, turn your phone off and work from home. No more interruptions."

"Wonderful." I smile. Although it's not, working alone is not great for my mental health at the moment.

I'm worrying me.

Antonio pulls the car to the curb. "Just call me when you're ready," he says over his shoulder.

"I won't be long." I sigh, this is the very last place I want to be. I'm finally having dinner with Marcel. He's been begging me to see him for weeks and I know I owe him some closure. He needs to talk it all out and I need to listen.

We haven't seen each other since the day we broke up, at first, he didn't want to, and then by the time he finally did, I was so self-absorbed over my heartbreak that I haven't been able to deal with his.

Pity it's not over the same relationship.

I'm officially the worst person I know, thinking back over the last few weeks and the feelings that have re-emerged, I really don't know if I ever truly loved Marcel.

At least, not the way I do my Giuliano.

My Giuliano...what a joke.

He isn't mine, he's probably slept with fifty women since we went to Ibiza. I'm sure he's fucked me well and truly out of his system by now.

The thought is depressing.

I peer through the window and see Marcel sitting at a table at the back, he looks up and sees me and I smile and wave.

It *is* good to see him.

Giuliano

I sit in my car outside the club, the boys are waiting inside for me...but I'm struggling to go in.

I'm low.

It's not going away...in fact, it's getting worse.

Every day away from her feels like an eternity.

I should never have gone to Ibiza, I've been in a detached state from the world ever since.

Neither here nor there ... dead or alive.

I can't stop wondering where she is, what's she doing? I feel better when I know.

I dial Antonio's number; I've been keeping tabs on her movements through him.

"Hey, boss," he answers.

"Hi, the computers will be ready tonight sometime."

"Okay great."

"Can you pick them up and deliver them to the airport? The plane is scheduled to leave at eleven p.m."

"For sure."

My computer blew up and seeing it has such sensitive material on it that I need retrieved, I can only get it fixed by someone on our payroll. Unfortunately, he lives in France, so we have to literally fly our plane to him with my computer and then we fly it home. I have another two computers that need servicing as well.

One hell of an expensive computer service, but we have no other choice.

We can't risk anyone having access to our data.

"He will call you when it's ready to pick up," I reply.

"Okay."

I close my eyes, it's always so awkward when I call with my hidden agenda. "Where are you?"

"Outside a restaurant."

She's out.

I choose my words carefully. "Having dinner, is she?"

"Yes."

"Who with?" I try to act casual.

"Marcel."

I frown. "Her ex?"

"Yeah...they got back together."

What?

I'm shocked to silence as my nostrils flare.

"I'll wait for the call," Antonio replies.

"Okay," I mutter, distracted. I hang up the phone and put my head back against the headrest.

Fuck.

I mean I knew.... But.... She was always going back to him.

With my elbow resting on the steering wheel I pinch the bridge of my nose and exhale heavily. I picture the two of them together and my stomach twists in anger.

Fuck this.

My car door opens in a rush. "Hey," Alex says as he walks past my car. "What are you doing?"

I stare out at him, I'm angry, furious with her...at myself.

But mostly, I'm just fucking pathetic.

"Come on," Carlo says. "You are going in there and you're going to get some high-grade pussy and snap the fuck out of this."

My eyes meet Alex's. "He's right, man. Trust me, you'll thank us tomorrow."

She's with him.

I get out of the car with renewed determination and slam the door hard. "Let's go." We walk in through the front doors.

The bouncer nods and unlatches the red rope for us. "Good evening, Mr. Ferrara."

"Hello." I glance in through the double doors at the club, loud music and scantily dressed women.

I'm in the mood for a blonde...and fuck it, I'm going to have one.

Maybe a few.

Francesca

I make my way through the restaurant and Marcel stands as I approach, he kisses me on the cheek. "Hello."

"Hi." I smile as I sit down.

"You look beautiful."

"Oh." I try to deflect the compliment. "How are you?"

"I've been better." He forces a crooked smile.

An awkward silence falls between us.

We both go to speak at the same time and then both stop ourselves. "You go first," I offer.

"I don't know why we broke up, but I want to repair our relationship." He grabs my hand over the table. "Please tell me we can."

"Marcel." I let out a deep exhale.

Damn it.

"I have issues." I sigh. "And it's not fair to bring them into our relationship."

"Like what?"

I stare at him as I try to think of a kind way to let him down. How the hell do I do this without hurting him?

"Is it something that I did?"

"No."

"The proposal…we can wait. If you're not ready for marriage then that's okay."

My heart drops and I squeeze his hand in mine. "Sweetie, I'm so sorry." I swallow the lump in my throat. "I should never have accepted your wedding proposal…but." Oh God, this is the worst. "You asked me in a public situation. What was I supposed to do?"

"Say no."

"I would never humiliate you like that."

"You would just leave me after I had told everyone I know that we were engaged."

"I'm so sorry. I wish I could turn back time, I would've handled things so differently."

"How?" His eyes hold mine and I can tell he's holding on to his temper by a tiny thread.

"I didn't realize we were anywhere in the marriage kind of spectrum. We had never talked about it, we didn't even live together." I shrug. "We only saw each other on the weekends."

"Because we were busy," he snaps in an outrage.

"No, it wasn't that at all. We had no urgency to see each other. I know you don't see it now, but you don't love me the right way either."

"You don't love me?" He gasps out loud as if surprised. "You really don't love me?"

The people sitting at the tables around us are beginning to look over as they eavesdrop on our conversation. I have no idea why they're listening; this conversation is a complete nightmare. I don't want to hear it myself...and I'm in it.

"What I'm saying is," I say softly, "I don't want to be in a relationship anymore and I didn't realize this until you proposed to me. Instead of feeling excited, all I could feel is panic and that it was wrong. I shouldn't be like that, and you...." Words fail me. "I'm just so, so sorry." I squeeze his hand. "You deserved so much better and I will never forgive myself for treating you the way I have."

He lets out a deep sigh.

"I missed every sign, every cue that you gave me. I must have, because to be honest, I'm still shocked. You took me completely by surprise."

We hold hands over the table as he stares at me.

"I'd like it if we could be friends." I smile hopefully.

"No. I can't be friends with you. It's all or nothing."

"Okay." I nod sadly, I get it. I can't be friends with Giuliano either, it hurts too much to see him and not be able to hold him.

I wonder where he is tonight.

I get a vision of him and me making love in Ibiza. The passion, the laughter...the feeling of coming home. The love.

All the love.

Damn it, why are we related?

"So?"

Marcel's voice interrupts my thoughts. Huh? I glance up. Oh my God, I'm the worst person I know. "I'm sorry, I didn't hear you?"

"I'm taking a transfer to America."

"What?"

"I had a job offer in Chicago, I was going to turn it down, but in light of what's happened I want a new start."

I smile. "That's exciting."

"You're not going to beg me not to leave...are you?"

My smile fades as we stare at each other. "I'm so sorry," I whisper and suddenly I just need to get out of here. "I'm going to go...this isn't...helping." I stand and he stares up at me. "Good luck with your new job."

"Goodbye, Francesca."

I bend and kiss his cheek. "Goodbye, Marcel."

And I wish I could say something uplifting, something that would turn this shitty situation in his favor, but I can't, because the truth is that I'm in love with someone else.

Someone I can never be with, and I'll always be alone.

Missing him.

Reality hits home and my eyes well with tears.

I walk out of the restaurant and down around the corner, I take out my phone and call Antonio.

"Hey, what's up?"

"I'm on the corner."

"You're finished already?"

"Yep."

"On my way."

"Thanks." I hang up and stare across the road as sadness overwhelms me.

I feel like crap...and so I should.

The car pulls into the curb and I get into the back seat. "Hi."

We pull out into the traffic. "That was quick," Antonio says as he drives.

"Yeah." I stare sadly out the window, once again my mind wonders where my beloved Giuliano is now? My thoughts always come back to him.

I hope he's ok.

Giuliano

I bang on the window as my mother lies dying. "Mom, I'm here. Hold on."

Her head slumps as I begin to try to break down the door. "I'm here, Mom. Don't go, wait for me."

I watch on helplessly as her guards come running. "Angelina," one cries. "Call an ambulance."

I bang frantically on the door, I've never known a panic like this.

A scream wakes me and I sit up in a rush, I look around the dark silent room as my heart hammers hard in my chest. Who was screaming?

I was.

It was my screams that woke me.

Fuck.

I sit up and swing my legs out of the bed, I'm wet with perspiration, with my elbows resting on my knees I sit in the darkness. What the fuck is going on with me?

I'm losing it.

Ferrara

I feel Lorenzo walk into the office. "You're quiet today," he says as he puts his two hands on my shoulders from behind.

"That's because he's worn out," Val teases. "Lucky prick."

I exhale heavily. "Shut up."

I'm not in the mood for this fucking shit today.

"Who is she?" Lorenzo smiles as he sits down at my desk.

"Nobody." I sigh as I open my email folder.

"Bullshit," Carlo snaps. "Tell me she tasted as good as she looked?"

I drag my hand through my hair. "Can you two just get out and let me do some work?"

Everyone saunters out of the office and I try to focus on my computer screen, but I can't. My brain is fried and I feel so unstable that it's ridiculous.

Nothing should affect me this badly.

Alex walks back into my office and puts his hands onto my shoulders from behind. "You, okay?" he asks.

"Uh-huh." I keep staring at my screen.

"You're worrying me."

"I'm fine." I dismiss him.

"It's been six weeks since you saw her."

"I said I'm fine," I snap angrily. "Get the fuck out."

"Take a week off, you're burned out. You had one day off when your mother died. You need to cut yourself some slack, Giuliano. I know you forget this, but you're only human. You've been through a lot this last few months."

I get a lump in my throat as I stare at my computer. "Lombardi...."

"Fuck Lombardi, I'll take care of Lombardi. So, he killed another three men, they weren't ours. Who fucking cares?"

"He's getting out of control."

"Which is why I need you well and rested." He slaps me on the back and then spins my chair toward him and leans his hands on the armrests as his eyes hold mine. "Go home to Lake Como, take the time you need. Come back when you're feeling better, whenever that may be. I have it under control, Carlo and Val are here, we're all on deck and prepared for anything."

Forever the faithful friend.

I inhale deeply, a few days off does sound good.

"Okay," I concede.

He reaches over me and switches my computer off. "Go now." I stand and pack my laptop into my briefcase and head for the door, I turn back. "Thanks, hey."

He gives me a sad smile. "Do whatever it takes to relax. We need you."

"I will."

I let out a deep exhale as I unlock the front door to my mother's house, I'm met with the full force of an image of my parents. The life-size painting, the perfect family.

The man and his mistress.

I stare at his face, strong, handsome and wise.... Or, so I thought.

I never even knew him.

I walk up to the painting and run my finger over his face and I pull it away as if burned.

We stand face-to-face, the dead and the living.

The truth and the lie.

An overwhelming sadness falls over me and the painting blurs through tears.

"I hate you for a lot of reasons," I whisper angrily. "But I will never ever fucking forgive you for taking her from me."

Francesca

I sip my coffee as I stare at the plans, maybe I need to add an extra wall in there. That could then work as another foyer for the space, hmmm.... I really need extra space in this area.

There's a buzz in the air, everyone is busy and happily talking.

I'm in my one happy place at the moment, my office.

I can't be working from home at the moment, I'm already on the edge of sanity. I know how close the cliff is and I'm not walking near it. So, for the moment, the office it is. I don't care about the interruptions, bring them on. Interruptions are better than crying alone on my couch.

Knock, knock, sounds at the door.

"Come in," I call without looking up. The door opens and then closes behind it and when nobody says anything, I glance up to be shocked to silence.

Giuliano.

Emotion overwhelms me and without hesitation I stand.

His eyes search mine, "I just...." He shrugs as if lost for words.

We stare at each other and dear God, *I miss him.*

I open my mouth to speak and he holds his hand up, instantly silencing me.

"I just have to say something." He inhales deeply as if steeling himself. "I know...that you're back with Marso."

"Marcel," I correct him.

"Whatever the fuck his name is," he snaps. "And I know

you're happy, and that's great. I want you to be happy. You deserve the best."

My eyes hold his.

"But I just wanted you to know something. And I don't know why I feel like I need you to know this but I just know that I do."

My brow furrows.

"I'm not going to marry, I'm not going to fall in love with someone. There is no family on my horizon," he says softly.

"Why not?"

"Because I don't want the second prize. I don't want to pretend to love someone else. I don't want to look back on my life and have lived my whole life as a lie like my father did."

My eyes search his.

"I know you're getting married and I'm happy for you, I really am."

"Giuliano."

He throws his hand up as if defeated, "What I'm trying to say, Chesk, is...I love you. I have loved you for every single day since I was nineteen years old. And I will love you until the day I die...which will hopefully be soon, because I don't want to live a life without you in it."

13

Francesca

My breath catches as I stare at him. He looks so lost and broken, his eyes are wild.

"I'm not marrying Marcel."

He frowns.

I step toward him, crossing my moral compass line once more. "I don't want the second prize either."

We stare at each other, "But…you're back with him."

"No. I'm not."

"Antonio told me."

"He got it wrong," I say, sterner, I take his two hands in mine. "Why did you come to France?"

"I had to see you."

"To tell me that you loved me?"

His words are pretty and damn it I just want to jump into his arms, but does he know what weight they carry?

"Yes."

"In a perfect world, Giuliano, where would your declaration of love lead us?"

His brow furrows as he contemplates his answer.

"How could this possibly work?" I prompt him, he's a womanizer, a heartbreaker. I wouldn't survive him betraying me.

"If...." He pauses. "If you felt the same, I would ask you to move to Milan and...." His voice trails off.

"And what?"

"And start a relationship with me."

"In secret?"

"Yes." His eyes hold mine.

"How would we do that?"

He bites his bottom lip and I get the feeling that he already knows the answer to my question. He's thought about this.

"I own the apartment underneath yours in Milan. If you moved in there, and I moved into mine. We could move between the two apartments unseen. The guards don't come up to the top floors. We could be together without anyone knowing."

I stare at him as an unfamiliar emotion runs through me.

Hope.

"And where would we stand?"

"What do you mean?" He frowns.

"Well, if nobody knows about us."

"There would be no one else if that's what you mean. I stopped seeing Amber, I can't lie anymore and pretend to want someone I don't." He cups my face in his hand as he looks down at me. "This isn't something I am throwing about on a whim, I've thought long and hard about it. I want this, you are it for me, Chesk." He kisses me softly. "I would take you as my wife.

Perhaps it wouldn't be legal.... But, in my eyes...." He shrugs as if lost for words.

My eyes well with tears as I stare up at my beautiful man. *What about children?*

"Do you want me to beg...because I will, I'll get down on my hands and knees right here," he stammers. "I'll do anything, whatever it takes."

And this is it, the moment where I choose between my morals and my heart. Both can't survive this. It's one or the other.

"What took you so long?" I whisper as I kiss him.

He frowns against me and his hands snake around my waist. "What are you saying?"

"I love you."

He smiles as his lips take mine, his tongue slowly slides over my lips and someone goes to open the door and he reaches over and slams it shut. "Come back later," he calls.

My eyes widen, he did not just do that.

"Let's go," he says.

"No."

He pulls back to look at my face. "What?"

"Our guards are outside. If you want this to legitimately work and for us to go undetected, you are going to go home to Milan today. We can't be seen together, there can be no sign that we are a couple. Move into the apartment and get things ready and in place."

His eyes search mine.

"I'll come on Friday."

"You'll move on Friday? This Friday," he confirms.

"Yes." It's perfect timing actually, I already have permission to work from home.

He kisses me again, this time with more urgency, he glances over to the door.

"There's no lock." I smirk, reading his mind.

"Who cares?"

"I do." I pull out of his arms before I completely lose my head. "Go home to Milan and get ready for me. Set the wheels in motion, get everything in order and ready."

He grabs my hands and we stand and stare at each other.

"I love you," I whisper.

"I love you." He gives me a breathtaking smile. "You won't regret this, Chesk. We're going to be happy. I promise."

My eyes cloud over again. "I know."

We kiss tenderly, so much love is between us. Like a tangible force I can feel it.

"Friday." He smiles against my lips as he holds my face in his hands.

"Friday."

He turns and without looking back leaves my office and I smile goofily at the back of the door. Filled with hope and love and so much relief.

I don't care anymore. As long as we're together, that's all that matters.

To hell with the world.

I struggle through the front door of my apartment; these bags are heavy.

Anna's eyes widen. "Holy hell? Did you buy the whole damn shops?"

"Maybe." I wince.

I've been shopping up a storm, I need sexy supplies for my secret date weekend with Giuliano.

I put the bags down and run to the bathroom. "How was your day?" I call as I go.

"Good," she calls. "Holy shit! Who is this lingerie for?"

My eyes widen, oh shit. She's gone through my purchases.

"Um." I zip up my pants and wash my hands, what the hell do I say? "I have a date this weekend," I lie, well not technically a lie, there is a little truth to it. I walk around the corner to see the black leather and lace lingerie spread all over the dining table.

"Who with?" Anna scoffs. "And good God, there's enough lingerie here for ten dates."

I pick up a lace teddy and hold it up over my body. "You think he'll like it?"

Her eyes widen. "I think he'll love it, but who *is* he?"

"Well...." I try to think on my feet. "A guy I met through work in Milan has asked me out."

"Who?"

"Umm...he's a diplomat."

She frowns.

"We've had this chemistry thing for years and now he knows that I'm single he asked me out."

"He's in Milan?"

"Yes."

"I'm going home this weekend too." She smiles. "Maybe we could go on a double date with Carlo and him."

Oh hell.

"No," I snap way too fast. "I mean...he broke up with someone for me, so...we have to keep it super-secret for a while."

Her eyes widen. "He ended a relationship for you?"

"Well...." Oh fuck, why did I say that? Now I sound like a home wrecker. "They were on the way out already, this just sped things up a little."

"Oh." She listens intently. "Carlo asked me to move home to Milan."

I frown. "In with him?"

"No, but...he wants to start a relationship and I live in another country."

Shit.

I go to the fridge and pour us both a glass of wine while I contemplate my next sentence. I need to tell her.

"What does that mean?" she says.

"What?"

"The no answer."

I pass her glass of wine over, this has been on my mind for a long time but I didn't know how to approach the subject. "How much do you know about Carlo, Anna?"

"What do you mean?"

"Do you trust him?"

"Of course."

"Do you know what he does at Ferrara?"

"Not specifics." She shrugs. "But I'm sure...."

"I'm pretty sure he's a hit man," I just blurt out. "He's one of Giuliano's personal security team, I know for a fact that Giuliano would only have him there if he was capable and willing."

She stares at me, shocked to her core.

"Look, I'm not saying he's a bad person."

"What *are* you saying then, Francesca?" she snaps, annoyed.

"I'm saying that he's like my family, he's like Giuliano. He *is* one of them. And if dating one of them is okay with you, then go for it. But you can't let yourself get two years down the track and then realize that it's too late."

She drops to the chair at the dining table and sits down, shocked to silence.

I sit down beside her. "Look, I'm not saying don't move to Milan to be with him, or don't pursue this. I just want you to be aware of the entire picture. He's a powerful man and I want you to know exactly who you're getting involved with. It's not going to be all honey and roses. There's a dark side to his life too."

She nods sadly and thinks for a moment. "Would you get involved with a man like him?"

"Yes." I reply without hesitation. "If I loved him, then yes, I would. Nothing would stop me from pursuing love."

I'm in love with his boss.

She nods as she weighs up my words. "You know, I really wish you and Giuliano weren't related."

My eyes shoot up to her, did I say that out loud? "Why do you say that?"

"Because you guys were so great together, seeing him in Ibiza must have been bittersweet for you? Did it bring back any memories?"

I want to blurt out and tell her everything...I don't want to keep this from her, but I know that I can't. I can't risk anybody knowing about us at all.

Not now, not ever.

"He's just a good friend, that's all. We have a history and I did enjoy his company in Ibiza, it was great to see him again," I reply.

She smiles and takes my hand in hers. "Thanks for hanging around with him while I got to know Carlo, the fact that you were prepared to do that for me means a lot."

Guilt fills me. *I'm a terrible person.*

I smile sadly. "What are friends for if not to be the awkward wingman."

She glances over at me as if surprised. "Was it really that awkward?"

I shrug. "Maybe it's time for me to move home to Milan too." I sigh.

"So, you can secretly date your diplomat and I can openly date a hitman?"

I giggle. "That sounds very...." I frown as I try to find the right words.

"Ridiculous?" she offers.

"Yeah, that's it. Ridiculous."

"Hey, maybe if you're not going out with your diplomat on Saturday night you could come out with Carlo and me, we could get Giuliano to come. Carlo mentioned inviting Valentino and his girlfriend too."

A smile nearly creeps onto my face. "Yeah maybe." I act casual. "Hopefully I'll be on a date though."

"What's his name?"

"Who?"

"The diplomat."

Oh crap, that's right, what *is* his name? "Massimo."

She raises her eyebrow, her interest piqued. "Hot name."

I smirk, for a fake guy I guess it is.

I lie in the darkness under the covers, phone in hand, he'll call me soon to say good night.

He has every night this week and it's been the highlight of my day, it brings back memories of when we met all those years ago, secret phone calls and stolen kisses.

Young and forbidden love, when we thought we could have it all.

We didn't just think it, we knew it, or at least thought we did.

I go home to Milan on Friday and I should be having second thoughts and doubting my life choices, but the truth is I can't wait.

I need to see him so badly.

My phone vibrates in my hand, and I quickly swipe it open. "Hello."

"Hi, Chesk," his deep voice whispers, Emotion overwhelms me. How can hearing someone's voice mean so much?

"Hi." I smile. "You're late tonight?"

He exhales heavily. "I had a meeting on, I ended up leaving early so I could call you."

I smile into the darkness; I like that he left early.

"Two days," he whispers.

Excitement swirls in my stomach like never before. "I can't wait," I murmur.

"What's the first thing you're going to do when you see me?" he asks.

"Hug you."

"Oh." He acts disappointed.

"Why, what were you hoping I would do?"

"I don't know, drop to your knees and suck my dick or something."

I laugh. "Dream on."

I totally will.

"Is it just me or has this week gone incredibly slow?"

"So slow." I remember something, "Oh Anna asked me if I wanted to go out with her and Carlo on Saturday night, they were going to ask you and Valentino and his girlfriend."

"Val won't go."

"Why not?"

"Because he's furious that Anna is with Carlo."

"What? Why?"

"He's always had a thing for her, went ballistic about Carlo sleeping with her in Ibiza."

My mouth falls open in shock. "What?"

"Was raving on that he's not in her league."

"But doesn't he have a girlfriend?"

"That's what I said to him."

"Well, what did he say to that?"

"Just that he had her reserved and I knew it and I should never have given Anna to him."

I screw up my face in disbelief.

"He was seriously fucking ropeable, didn't speak to me for three days."

"Jeez." I think for a moment. "He mustn't be in love with his girlfriend then."

"That's the stupid thing, he is. He'll marry her for sure."

"So, what you're saying is that he wanted to keep Anna on ice in case he was ever single."

Fucking men.

Giuliano chuckles. "Who knows? Let's talk about you being on your knees again."

"How come our late-night calls always end up as phone sex?"

"Because it's you, and I haven't had sex in a very long time. Not to mention that you have the sexiest voice of all time."

I smile into the darkness, I like that answer.

"Just so you know, we aren't getting out of bed on the weekend," he adds.

Bring it....

"Ugh, sounds terrible."

Friday, Milan.

The car pulls into the underground parking lot of my building and the cars behind us park. The guards retrieve my luggage from the trunk and the bellboy loads it onto a trolley. It's Friday afternoon and after the longest week in history, today, I get to see him.

"I'll take it from here," Antonio says.

While the other three men stand around, Antonio gets into the elevator with me with the trolley of luggage. I scan my key; the elevator doors close and we begin to travel up. He's the only one who ever comes into my homes, I don't like anyone else to see my private living quarters.

The elevator doors open and we arrive at my private foyer, I scan my fingerprint and the door releases with a click. This place has so much security that it's like a spy movie.

"Thank you, just put the bags here by the door."

"You don't want me to carry them up to your room?" he asks.

"No. That's fine." I smile. "I have washing to do, thanks anyway."

He unloads my suitcases from the luggage trolley. "Is there anything else I can get you, Miss Ferrara?"

"No thanks," I reply as I look around. "I won't be leaving again tonight, you can retire."

"There will be the usual men downstairs if you need anything," he replies.

"Thank you, have a nice night."

"See you tomorrow," he says as the elevator doors close behind him.

I turn and look around my penthouse, I love this place.

Secluded and private.

The guards are able to wait downstairs, they don't need to be so close that I can see them. I forget they are even around when I'm here.

This was the first piece of property that Giuliano signed over to me after my father died. I guess you could say that it has sentimental value, it was such a shock when he broke tradition and gave it to me. Little did we know at the time, it was to be the first of many properties that he signed over to me and my brothers over the next few months.

There are floor-to-ceiling windows looking over the city, and because it's the rooftop and I'm the only apartment up here, I have a huge deck and entertaining area, complete with a pool and cabana. Beautiful gardens are planted outside, I even have a lawn with trees.

Green grass in an apartment, who knew?

I open the heavy slider door and walk out into my garden, strategically positioned spotlights shine up onto the plants and the sound of the water feature trickles in the distance.

I sit down on one of the deckchairs, and text Giuliano.

I'm here

ox

Now.... I wait. I'm excited and nervous and terrified that I'm doing the wrong thing all at once.

But...there's no going back now. I'm here and I'm ready to take the chance.

Because he's worth it, that I know for sure.

I lie back and look up at the sky, I'm in Italy. Maybe for forever this time.

A warm and fuzzy feeling filters through my bloodstream.
It's good to be home.

Giuliano

I glance at the time on the top of my computer screen, I'm on the countdown until I can leave work. After Francesca's text to tell me she's here over two hours ago, I'm like a cat on a hot tin roof. I just want to get out of here, playing it cool is not as easy as I thought it was going to be.

I'm always the last to leave and I'm not acting any different, I can't risk anything being picked up.

Lorenzo knocks twice on the door. "I'm going home."

"Okay. Have a good night."

He lingers, causing me to glance up at him.

"I hear you went to Paris earlier in the week...you visited Francesca."

I sit back in my chair, annoyed. "Keeping tabs on me now, are you?"

"Not at all, just...." He hesitates.

"Just what?"

"It does make me wonder why you would take the trouble to go to another country to see her."

Fuck off already.

"I picked up a computer from France from a new contact, I wanted to meet him in person and seeing I was already there I called in to visit Francesca for ten minutes at her office. I hadn't seen her since my mother's funeral and I wanted to thank her for coming. This may come as a surprise, Lorenzo, but I don't run everything by you."

His eyes hold mine.

"Is that all?" I snap.

We stare at each other; an unspoken warning runs between us.

Stay out of my fucking way.

He nods once, clearly annoyed. "Have a nice night."

"You too."

He disappears down the hall and I sit back in my chair and exhale heavily, and so it begins.

An hour later I pull my Ferrari into the underground parking lot, the two cars pull in behind me and park, I get out and walk toward the guards' cars. "I'm not leaving tonight so you can retire."

"How long will you be staying here, Mr. Ferrara?"

I shrug. "As long as the renovations on my other place take," I reply casually.

I had to speed-plan a whole remodel of my other apartment so that it doesn't look suspicious that I'm suddenly staying here. "This building is safe, you can leave."

"The cars will be out the front if you need us."

"Thank you." I take the lift up with my heart beating hard in my chest, with every floor that I rise it brings me closer to her.

I get to my apartment and throw my briefcase down and race to the bathroom, I undress at lightning speed and get into the shower.

My heart is racing as I anticipate the night I'm about to have.

She's here.

I let the hot water run over my head as I put my head into my hands to try to calm myself down. Don't fuck this up.

She's here.

. . .

Fifteen minutes later I walk out of my apartment and enter the fire stairs, I can't risk someone seeing the light on the elevator go from my apartment up to hers. I take the stairs two at a time and arrive at her floor, I open the door slightly and peer out. I don't know why I'm doing this, I already know that nobody can get up to her floor. With my heart in my throat, I press her doorbell and I hear it echo inside. My palms are sweating, my heart is hammering and damn it, why does she affect me so much.

The door opens in a rush and there stands my beautiful angel. Her long dark hair is out and her big welcoming smile instantly dissipates all my fears.

Calm falls over me and I take her into my arms, her body melts against mine and we hold each other close.

"Thank God you're here," she whispers into my neck, I hug her tighter.

Damn it, it's been too long.

We kiss, and it's as if the entire earth spins on its axis. This is all that matters, me and her. As long as we're together is all that matters.

We kiss again and again, the urgency building between us. She goes to drop to her knees and I hold her up to keep her close. "I need to kiss you."

She smiles against my lips. "Are you knocking me back?"

I chuckle. "For the moment." I lead her into the apartment and sit down on the couch and pull her down onto my lap.

I'm lost, lost in a sea of perfect kisses, to the power this woman has over me.

"I love you," she whispers as her eyes search mine.

Emotion overwhelms me, the erection tents my pants and she spreads her legs over mine, searching for a deeper connection. For a long time, we kiss, tender and loving and my hands are on her hips guiding her body over mine.

She shudders and I know she's close, damn it...not yet, I want to kiss her like this forever.

I need to be inside her, I slide her panties off and pull my cock out, she goes up onto her knees and I guide myself into her. I swipe the tip of my cock through her wet lips, she's dripping wet and I'm rock hard.

The ultimate combination.

We stare at each other as I slowly slide into the hilt, we both moan in pleasure.

Fuck.

A perfect intimacy runs between us as she slowly rocks on my cock. Her tight body rippling around mine.

Finally.

"I love you." I whisper up at her in awe. "So, so much."

Francesca

The light peeks through the sides of the drapes and I inhale deeply with a stretch, I'm relaxed and so sleepy. What time is it? I drag my eyes open and am met by big brown ones. Giuliano is lying on his side, propped up on his elbow watching me, he reaches over and pushes my hair back from my forehead with a soft smile. "Hi.

I smile shyly and lean over and kiss his big beautiful lips. "Hi." He puts his arm around me and pulls me to his chest and we lie sated in each other's arms.

"What a night." I feel him smile above me.

I giggle as his lips rest on my temple and it's the weirdest thing, it's like we're sharing the one body. Nothing between us, our hearts beating as one. We made love all night, whispered sweet nothings under the covers until the wee hours.

Intoxicated by the sheer happiness of being together. And this is it, the epitome of love. How it should be.

I've never felt so close to anyone and I know I never will, he's the one.

The man I was born to love.

"What are we doing today?" I beam over at my handsome man.

"We...." His eyebrows flick up as if surprised. "There's a word I...." His voice trails off.

"You haven't heard before?"

He smiles above me. "I kind of like it."

I sit up to look at him as I fake horror. "Well, you better."

He chuckles and rolls me over onto my back and holds my hands over my head. "Or what?"

"Or you're going to get it," I tease. "That's what."

"And *you're* going to give it to me?" He widens his eyes in jest as he spreads my legs with his knee. "Go on then, tough guy." He kisses me. "Do it now."

I struggle to break free as I laugh out loud and he stares down at me, we fall serious.

"What's that look?" I whisper.

"You look...." He frowns as if searching for the right words.

I smile hopefully, I like this game.

"Disgusting."

"What?" I burst out laughing. "Disgusting?" I gasp.

He rolls us over so that I am on top of him. "Disgustingly fuckable."

I sit up as I straddle his body, his hand reaches up and cups my breast, his thumb brushes back and forth over my nipple.

We fall silent as we stare at each other, the magic swirling between us.

"It's you who's disgusting," I say.

He smiles up at me. "I know *that* for certain." He grabs the back of my head and drags me down to him and kisses me. "We're disgustingly perfect for each other." I laugh against his lips, he's right, to hell with the world.

We are.

I turn and look at my behind in the mirror, my tight black dress fits in all the right places. "Are you getting ready or not?" I call.

"Not," Giuliano replies flatly from the living room. "You go, I'll wait here for you."

I walk out to see him lying on the couch, totally uninterested, and I put my hands on my hips. "Why don't you want to go to dinner with Anna and Carlo?"

He rolls his eyes. "Because I don't." He exhales heavily and turns the television off then throws the remote onto the ottoman.

"Why not?"

"It pisses me off that I can't touch you and they get to fawn all over each other after knowing each other for all of five fucking minutes."

I sit down on his lap. "I know, but don't you want to go out?" I kiss him and brush the hair back from his forehead. "We can't just stay in this apartment and have sex all the time."

He raises an eyebrow. "Works for me."

"Giuliano, we need to get used to acting as friends."

His unimpressed eyes hold mine.

"I mean...we have to do it for a lifetime."

He pushes me off his lap and stands in a rush, he goes to the window and stares out over the view. He's not okay with this arrangement, I can tell already.

I shouldn't have said that.

"Hey." I hug him from behind. "As long as we're together, right?" I kiss his shoulder. "Nobody said this was going to be easy, we knew it was going to be like this."

He keeps staring out the window in silence and if the truth be told, he's struggling with this secret a lot more than I am. It isn't in his nature to lie. Giuliano is used to being exactly who he is.

I, however, have been lying about our relationship since the day we met.

"Look, I promised Anna I would come, I can't back out now."

He nods, seemingly deep in thought.

I wait for a moment, this really *is* bothering him, maybe I should give him some room to get his head around it, pressuring him to do something that he's uncomfortable with isn't going to help. "It's okay," I agree. "You don't have to come, I'll only be a few hours. We were going in separate cars anyway."

I kiss his shoulder once more and retrieve my bag. "I'll see you in a few hours?"

"Okay," he murmurs softly, he's completely distracted.

I hesitate and turn back to him as I get to the front door. "You really won't come?"

"You go, babe, have fun." He turns and comes and kisses me. "I'm sorry...I just don't want to ruin a perfect day." He sighs.

My heart sinks and I smile sadly. "Okay."

He kisses me once more. "You look beautiful, by the way."

"Thanks." I take the elevator down to the ground floor, is this how it's going to be?

Separate lives, only being together in private?

You know it is.

The doors open on the ground floor and I step out confidently. "Good evening, Miss Ferrara," Bruno says.

"Good evening." I fake a smile as I walk past them, but I don't feel happy. I feel a sense of dread.

I left my heart upstairs.

Anna

I sit at the table and stare into the big brown eyes of Valentino. His girlfriend is in the bathroom of the restaurant and I'm here with Carlo.

This is the first time we've seen each other while with other people.

It feels weird.

Carlo's phone rings and he glances at the screen, "I have to take this, back in a minute." He marches off toward the front doors.

I rearrange the napkin on my lap, feeling uncomfortable.

"How are you?" He asks in his deep sexy voice.

"Okay." I force a smile.

His dark eyes hold mine, "You look good."

The air swirls between us and it's there again, this cosmic attraction to each other.

In slow motion, he lifts his wine glass to his lips and takes a sip, "Real good."

"Val." I whisper, "Cut it out."

"I don't like you with him."

"You have a girlfriend." I whisper angrily as I look around.

"I'm not coming onto you, I'm just saying I don't like you with him."

"You don't have a choice."

"You won't be happy with him." He snaps.

"I'm not asking for your opinion." I whisper infuriated.

Valentino's girlfriend comes back to the table and sits down, she's so nice and friendly. She smiles warmly over at me, "It's so lovely to meet you."

"You too." I fake a smile. I take a big gulp of my wine, hurry up and get here Francesca.

Francesca

The restaurant is a hive of activity and I smile as I make my way through to the table. Milan...is there a more vibrant city in the world? No, there isn't. I know that for certain.

I see Anna and Carlo sitting at the table with another couple and I smile and wave, my stomach drops a little. Great, a double date...and me.

Damn it, why didn't he come?

"Hello." I smile as I arrive, Anna stands and kisses my cheek. "Hey, thank God you're here, I thought you were going to bail on us?"

I really wish I did.

"No." I smile.

Anna turns to the others. "You remember Carlo, and this is Val and his girlfriend, Giovanna."

My eyes flick around the table. "Hello." They all smile.

I awkwardly sit down into my seat.

Damn, Valentino turned into one hot man. I remembered that he was good looking as a teenager, but now he's....

"It's so lovely to meet you," Giovanna says from her seat beside me. "Anna tells me you're an interior designer?" She fills my glass with wine and passes it to me, with long dark hair and a figure to die for, she's super glamorous.

"The best in Italy," Anna interrupts, she holds her wineglass up in a toast symbol.

I roll my eyes. "Hardly, do you work?" I ask her.

"Yes, I'm a doctor, I work at the Memorial Hospital in pediatrics."

"Wow." I smile, impressed.

"How could someone this beautiful have brains as well?" Anna teases.

"I know," I agree.

The girls and I continue to talk and from my peripheral vision I see that Valentino texts someone and Carlo takes out his phone and does too.

"Didn't you say that Giuliano was coming?" Anna asks.

"He couldn't make it." Valentino says as his eyes find mine across the table, he subtly raises his eyebrow.

He knows.

Shit.

I pick up my glass and take a huge gulp.

Carlo is sitting back in his chair, his arm casually draped across the back of Anna's, his fingers dust across her skin as he talks. He's completely smitten with her, it's as clear as day. Anna is glowing, I watch as they exchange looks and laugh and chat. It makes me nervous, I mean, I'm happy that she's happy and that he seems happy...but I do worry about her. Up until now she has been completely shielded from the kind of man that Carlo is.

I know his type, I've lived his type through my father and grandfather...perhaps even Giuliano, I worry that by the time she realizes that this isn't the life she wants, she will already be in love with him and it will be too late to escape. That's if it isn't already.

I want her to run far, far away while she still can. Before she ends up messed up like me.

"Francesca," Carlo says across the table. "Tell us, what did you do today?"

It's like he's goading me.

I sucked your best friend's dick.

"Not much." I fake a smile. "Shopping, boring things."

Val clinks his wineglass with mine. "Thank God you saved the day by coming out with us then."

"I know." Anna laughs. "Let's get some cocktails."

I walk into my apartment just on twelve, while I wanted to rush home to Giuliano, I also wanted to stay out to give him time to be alone and think.

Perhaps he's having second thoughts about us already?

I walk through the darkened apartment, lit up only by the lamps.

Is he still here?

I put my purse down and take the stairs up to my bedroom as a sense of urgency runs through me. Please still be here.

I open the bedroom door to find him fast asleep and my shoulders slump in relief.

Thank God.

I watch him in the moonlight for a while, a moment in time of perfect stillness.

Uninterrupted viewing of the man I love so desperately.

To everyone he's a killer, a drug lord...my brother.

To me, he's the world, the love of my life.

He's lying on his back; his broad chest rises and falls as he breathes. His dark hair falls messily over his forehead. The white blanket pools over his groin covering his most private parts.

It's not often I get to see him like this, completely relaxed and calm.

Vulnerable.

I know why he couldn't go tonight, I get it.

I take my makeup off and shower and then I climb in under the covers and cuddle his back, he stirs. "Hmm," he whispers sleepily as he turns and kisses my arm. "What time is it?"

"Midnight," I whisper.

"Hmm." His eyes stay closed, his regulated breathing tells me he's drifted back off to sleep and I smile against his back.

Coming home to him will never get old. "I love you," I whisper as I kiss the back of his shoulder.

He sleeps on and I smile.

I love this.

I wake to the feeling of my back arching off the bed as I shudder.

What the hell?

I feel a tongue between my legs, and strong hands spreading my thighs wide apart.

"Oh...." I blink as I try to focus my eyes and I pull back the blankets to find Giuliano in all his glory between my legs.

"Morning," he whispers darkly, his lips glisten with my arousal.

I smile broadly. "Why yes...yes, it is."

14

Giuliano

I stare at the spreadsheets on my computer screen, these figures aren't adding up, Lorenzo and I have been working on them all morning. There's a few hundred thousand dollars missing. "There has to be a miscalculation somewhere."

Lorenzo lets out a deep sigh. "Fuck knows, it can't be out by that much."

"It's okay, I'll find it. You go do what you have to," I say.

Alex puts his head around the door. "I'm going to get some lunch, you coming?"

"No. I'm good."

"What are you having?" Lorenzo asks.

"Apollo's."

"Yeah, I'll come. I'm out of the office this afternoon, I'll catch you tomorrow."

My eyes stay glued to the screen. "Bye."

Lorenzo stands and they disappear out through reception together.

Mario walks past my office. "Hey." He stops at my door.

"Hi."

"I saw a photograph of your old man last night."

I glance up from what I'm doing. "Really, where at?"

"At the public library."

"Yeah?"

"My son had a school art show and they had an archived photograph section from past years' donated art."

"Hmm." I nod as I turn back to my computer. "What was the photo of?"

"Him and your mother."

I smile.

"I noticed it because his wife, Bianca, was also in the photo, she was pregnant."

I look up from what I'm doing. "What?" I frown. "What do you mean his wife was in the photo? My mother would never go somewhere with him and his wife."

"That's what made me notice it, I thought it was weird too."

I stare at him, confused. "You say his wife was pregnant and my mother was there?"

"Uh-huh." He nods. "Lorenzo was in the photo too."

I spin my chair toward him, my interest piqued. "Lorenzo?"

"Yeah."

"Our Lorenzo?'

"Uh-huh."

My mind begins to race. "Where was the photo?"

"It was on a display board as you walked into the room at the art display."

"You sure it was them?"

"Positive. Your dad had his arm around your mother's waist."

What?

With his pregnant wife there?

"Milan library?" I confirm.

"Yes."

I fake a smile. "Thanks for letting me know. I'll check it out next time I'm there."

"No worries." He walks casually down the hall and I turn back to my computer.

What the fuck?

My mother and Bianca at a function together, it doesn't make any sense.

His two women hated each other...didn't they?

I grab my keys and head for the door, I need to see this fucking photo.

Francesca

My phone vibrates on the table and I pick it up to see the name *Dominic* light up the screen, "Hello, Dominic."

"Hi, Francesca. I was wondering when you'll be in Milan next?"

I frown, does he already know that I'm here? "I'm actually already in Milan."

"Good, I have some things I need to go over with you. I've been going through the plans and the tile choice for the bathrooms on level four is off."

"What's wrong with them?"

"I'm not happy with the way they correlate with the other floors."

"Oh." Shit. "Let me try and reshuffle my appointments for this afternoon and I'll try and fit you in for a meeting."

"Thank you, that would be appreciated."

"Where are your offices here in Milan?"

"Ahh...." He hesitates. "My office is being repainted at the moment, let's meet in the restaurant where we usually meet."

"Okay." I pause as I pretend to reschedule appointments. "How's one p.m.?"

"Good. I'll meet you there."

"Great." I hang up and instantly open my computer in a panic, what tiles did I pick for level four?

I walk into the restaurant right on one o'clock, Dominic stands and smiles.

"Hello, I hope you haven't been waiting long?" I apologize as I shake his hand.

"Not at all." He pulls out my chair for me.

"Thank you." I smile as I push it in.

"I took the liberty of ordering us a bottle of wine, may as well make our meetings enjoyable." He fills two wineglasses with the wine.

"Thanks." I fake a smile, why does he always order alcohol as if it's a date?

Stop it.

I open my large folder and flip through to the appropriate floor divider. "Okay, so let's talk about these tiles."

He stays silent and when he doesn't answer me I glance up at him.

"Are they your guards by the door?"

I frown and glance over to the door to see Nico and Sergio.

How does he know I have guards?

"No." I smile calmly. "What makes you think I would have guards?"

His eyes hold mine and I know that he knows that I thought that was an odd question.

"Well, I just assumed that being a Ferrara you would have guards." He sips his wine as if fascinated.

"Really?" I reply, "Why is that?"

"You hear stories...." His voice trails off.

I sit back, annoyed. "I thought we were here to discuss tiles not idle gossip."

"Oh, we are." He laughs. "Calm down, it was just a question." He sips his wine. "Just wanted to know how many guards I will have to fight off to ask you out."

"Only my brother."

He raises an eyebrow as his eyes hold mine. "Where do you stay when in Milan, Francesca?"

The alarm bells sound again, what is it about this guy?

"With family," I reply. "Oh, I keep forgetting, my boss wants a business card of yours to put on file."

"Yes of course." He takes out his wallet and looks through it. "It seems I don't have one on me. I must have run out." He smiles calmly. "Next time."

Something feels off here.

"What is it about the tiles that you don't like?" I ask.

"I don't think the colors are right."

"Why not, it was the color scheme we agreed on, you signed off on it."

"I know, but since then I've been thinking that they are too gaudy. I don't like the color combination with the furnishings.

Perhaps if we went with the same tile as level seven, the Coco in chocolate."

I stare at him as I try to reconcile what he's saying, he really does have an issue with the tiles.

Giuliano has made me completely paranoid.

"Okay." I flip through my folder. "I could contact the supplier, I have already ordered the tiles but perhaps it's not too late to change that floor."

"Good." He studies my vision board pictures and points to the Coco tiles in chocolate. "I definitely prefer these ones, don't you?"

"No. I like the first choice, but the decision lies ultimately with you." I concentrate on the pictures and then glance up to see him looking over toward my guards again. I watch his eyes scan them and then look out to the footpath to the two others waiting outside.

He's counting them.

Fuck.

Who is he?

"I need to go to the restroom; will you excuse me for a moment?" I smile.

"Of course."

I walk into the ladies' bathroom and into the cubicle and close the door behind me.

I quickly take out my phone and text Sergio.

> **There is something off with the man I am with.**
> **I want you to wait out of sight.**
> **He knows you're my guards**
> **How?**

Ferrara

My heart races as I wait for his reply.

Get to the car.

I reply.

Okay.

Fuck.

I wash my hands and stare at my reflection in the mirror. I'm probably being completely paranoid.

Giuliano's words come back to me. *"Do you have any idea how much a female Ferrara scalp is worth?"*

Double fuck.

I drop my shoulders as I steel myself and I walk calmly back out into the restaurant.

Dominic smiles warmly. "Where were we?"

I slide my folder over toward me and I close it. "I've got all the details I need, I'll be in touch."

"You're leaving?"

"Yes, as mentioned I'm booked solid. My next appointment is waiting."

"But...."

I stand and fake a smile. "Goodbye, Dominic."

"I'll walk you out." He stands.

"No need." I turn and with my folder under my arm I march out of the restaurant as fast as I can. The car is waiting, double-parked, and Nico is standing holding the door open for me, I practically dive into the back seat and in moments we pull out at speed. I turn to look back just as Dominic appears out the front doors.

My heart hammers hard in my chest.

"Who is he?" Sergio asks.

"He works for the hotel that I'm refurbishing, he's one of the bosses and I'm probably being paranoid, but I don't know...he knew that I had guards."

Sergio and Nico exchange looks.

"How would he know that?" I ask.

"Perhaps he just assumed," Nico offers. "Could be a coincidence."

"Do you think it is?"

Sergio turns and looks over his shoulder. "No. No, I don't."

Giuliano

I walk up the stairs into the Milan library and I smile as I take a trip down memory lane. I haven't been here since I used to sneak in to see Francesca when we were kids.

My phone vibrates in my pocket and I take it out to see the name *Sergio* light up the screen. I'll call him back later, I stuff my phone back in my pocket.

"Can I help you?" the librarian asks, she's small and petite with gray hair, I would say she's in her sixties or seventies and very sweet and demure.

"Yes, my friend was here last night at an art show," I reply.

She smiles. "Yes, that was in the grand ballroom."

"Apparently there was a photo display board or something?"

"There were many."

"It was like a past year's donation or something?" I shrug. "My late parents were apparently in one of the photos, I was hoping to see it."

"Oh." She nods. "Yes, it was near the door. This way." She

toddles off and I follow her, we walk out through the gardens and into an adjoining ballroom. She gestures to the wall and the numerous photo boards on display. "Here they are."

"Thanks." I put my hands into my suit pockets and begin to look over the boards. "How far back do these photos date to?" I ask.

"Since the library opened."

"How long ago was that?"

"Eighty years."

"Wow." I keep looking at the boards, it's like walking into a time machine, some photos are in black and white, some are modern. All centered around art donations. I look and look and look. Mario must have been mistaken, there isn't a photo here. "Bettina," someone calls.

"Yes," the sweet little old lady calls.

"Can you help me for a minute?"

"Will you be okay here for a minute, dear?"

"Of course."

She toddles off and my eyes roam back over the boards, I walk to the next one and the next one. My eyes scan the boards and then I stop dead on the spot.

And there is it, just as Mario said.

A photo of my father with his arm around my mother. Bianca is standing to the side of them, beside her is Lorenzo.

I step back, shocked to silence.

I rub my fingers through my stubble as I stare at it, I would have been twelve months old when this photo was taken.

Bianca was heavily pregnant...*what?*

My eyes flick out toward the door and I unpin the photo from the board and slip it into the inside pocket of my suit jacket. I put my hands casually back into my pants pockets and walk away from the scene of the crime.

"How did you go, dear?" the lady asks as she returns.

"I can't find anything, it must have been a mistake. Thanks anyway."

She smiles sympathetically. "I'm sorry."

"Yeah." I nod. "Me too." I walk out the front and my black Lamborghini unlocks automatically as I approach it. I give a wave to my four security guards as they wait close by and I get into the car and pull out into the traffic. "Call Lorenzo," I tell my car.

Ring, ring, ring, ring.

"What's up?" Lorenzo asks.

"Can you meet me at the office?"

"I wasn't coming back there this afternoon."

"Change your plans." I hang up and with my mind running at a million miles per minute, I grip the steering wheel and turn a sharp corner, I want some fucking answers.

Half an hour later I sit at my desk with the photo in my hand, staring hard at the image. I'm trying my best to work out what it could possibly mean.

Lorenzo walks in. "Hey."

"Close the door."

He frowns before turning and closing the door, I point to the seat with my pen. "Sit."

He sits down, and I stare at him for a moment as I try to choose the right words.

There are no right words for this question so I'll just say it as it is.

"Are you Francesca's father?

His face falls. "What?"

"You heard me, are you Francesca's biological father?"

"Why would you think that?"

"Answer the fucking question," I bark.

I slide the photograph across my desk to him. He frowns and stares at the image, eventually he opens his mouth to say something and I cut him off.

"Lie to me and I'll fucking kill you."

15

Giuliano

He twists his lips. "Where did you get this?"

"None of your business." I glare at him. "Answer. The. Fucking. Question."

"No."

"No what?"

"I'm not her father."

"Who is?"

"Giuliano Ferrara. *Your* father."

I clench my jaw and snatch the photograph from him, I hold it up. "Explain this to me."

He stares at it for a moment and remains silent, finally he answers. "Bianca and I were friends, she had broken up with your father and he had moved in with Angelina, one Sunday she asked me to take her to an art show." He rolls his lips as he remembers. "You can imagine her horror when we arrived to find that your father and Angelina were at the same function together."

I listen.

"This photo was snapped by a photographer about two minutes before all hell broke loose."

"Bullshit. My father has his arm around my mother, he wouldn't be so inconsiderate to Bianca, he wasn't a monster."

He shrugs. "By this time, he and Bianca were well and truly over."

"She was pregnant with his child," I snap, outraged.

"That didn't seem to bother him."

"At exactly what point did you start dating my father's wife?" I fume.

Hs smirks, amused by my venom. "I cleaned up his mess and fell in love with the woman he broke, Francesca was around three." He stands. "Don't blame me for your father's shortcomings." He walks toward the door and then turns back toward me. "The day I stood in that library with a heavily pregnant Bianca and watched her heart break as her husband paraded his lover in public as if she was nothing," he pauses, "I was ashamed to be his friend." His eyes hold mine for an extended beat and then he turns and walks out of the office as I stare after him.

Fuck.

I slump back in my chair...not half as ashamed as I am.

I fucking hate him.

Francesca

I smile as I stir dinner, I've got a romantic night planned. We fucked like animals all weekend, but tonight will be different.

I feel him before I see him, and I glance over to see Giuliano leaning on the doorjamb. "How long have you been standing there?" I smirk as I keep stirring.

He steps forward, closing the distance between us, and takes me into his arms. "I could stare at you all day." He kisses me softly. "Dinner smells amazing."

"Cooking for people that I love is my most favorite thing to do."

His dark eyes hold mine as he slowly undoes his tie. "Is that so?"

"Uh-huh." I whisper, distracted by his tie as he slowly slides it all the way off and holds it in his hands.

"You know what my favorite thing is?" he asks as he holds the tie between his fingers.

"What?"

"Fucking."

I swallow the lump in my throat as we stare at each other. "Don't look at me like that."

He smiles. "Like what?"

"Like you're going to eat me, I want a proper date where we aren't fucking like animals."

He raises an eyebrow. "You should have probably thought about that before you got dressed into that outfit...or should I say, undressed into that outfit." He taps his lap.

"No." I smile.

"*Now*," he demands, for some reason my body instantly obeys him. He has this sexual dominance that oozes out of him, my need to please him is something I've never experienced before. I walk over to him and he puts my wrists together and wraps his tie around them, I watch on as he does it up with a tight knot.

Effectively bringing me at his mercy and completely under his control.

He slowly pulls the ribbon sash on my robe and it falls undone, my naked body is instantly on display and he gives me a satisfied smile as his eyes roam over my naked flesh. Raising his hand, he cups my breast and dusts his thumb back and forth over my nipple, it hardens for him and he lets out a low hum. "I love how your body is so responsive to mine," he murmurs, distracted. He bends and takes it into his mouth and goose bumps instantly scatter over my skin.

Every time he touches me…it's like the first time.

How did I live without this?

He bares his teeth as his dark eyes hold mine and he bites my nipple, hard enough to hurt but just before pain. "Oww," I whimper.

"E doloroso, piccola?" (Translation: "Does that hurt, baby?) he whispers.

A thrill runs through me, he's never spoken to me in Italian before, this is new.

I nod.

He bites me harder. "Bene." (Translation: Good.)

"Oww." I go to step back and he holds the tie that is wrapped around my wrists. "Non andrai da nessuna parte." (Translation: You're not going anywhere.) I glance down to see the large erection in his suit pants.

I stare at him as my arousal hits fever pitch.

Gone is my childhood sweetheart. The king of Italy is here.

He's here as the man he is now, an animal, so virile, primal.

Holding me by my tied hands, he leads me over to my couch and stands me at the end of it. "Solleva le Braccia." (Translation: Arms up.)

"Huh?"

He pulls my arms up by the tie and bends me over the end of the couch, my arms are tied above my head as I lean onto my elbows. Then he lifts my robe so that my bare behind is sticking up into the air. "Cosi va meglio," (Translation: Better.) he murmurs darkly as he rubs my skin in a slow circular motion. He then lifts my right leg and leans it up against the back of the couch, effectively spreading me right out.

I smirk into the couch. *Fucking deviant.*

"Ecco un panorama mozzafiato," (Translation: This is a much better view.) he replies.

I giggle and then he spreads my behind cheeks apart with his two hands and I fall instantly silent.

What's he doing?

He traces his fingertip over my back entrance.

"Jules."

"Sshh, don't make me gag you, baby girl. You may not like the taste of my socks."

English, he's back with me.

I smile, relieved, into the couch and then I feel his tongue there.

Oh....

I hold my breath as he licks me again, I've never....

Oh fuck....

He licks me again and I can feel his stubble, goose bumps scatter all over.

"You know I'm going to fuck you here, don't you?" he growls as he really begins to lick me harder, his hands pulling my cheeks apart, opening me completely up for him.

My sex throbs for attention as she searches for more.

In the position he's got me in, legs spread wide with my hands tied above my head, I couldn't move, even if I wanted to.

He unzips his suit pants and my heart is hammering hard in my chest.

This is what he does to me, sets me on fire.

Every.

Single.

Time.

He pulls his pants down a little, revealing his rock-hard erection, he's swollen and engorged with a thick vein running down his length. Pre-ejaculate drips, as his body searches for more too.

His hands become almost violent as he spreads me apart, his tongue in places where it shouldn't be.

I shudder and he slaps me hard on the behind. "Non osarevenire, cazzo." (Translation: Don't you dare fucking come.) he growls.

What?

Like I can help it?

He rubs saliva into the lips of my sex and then, holding himself at his base, positions himself at my entrance and in one hard pump he's into the hilt.

My mouth falls open as my body quivers around him, there is no air left in my lungs at all.

Fuck...he's big.

No matter how many times we do it, I still have to get used to him.

He rolls his hips one way and then the other to try to loosen me up for him.

"Accoglimi dentro di te, piccola," (Translation: Let me in, baby.) he murmurs.

"Fammi sentire quanto sei eccitata." (Translation: Give me some of that cream.)

Filthy bastard.

I smile into the couch at the delicious feeling…God, that feels good.

He inhales with a deep moan and grabs my hipbones in his hands and then pulls out and slams in hard.

Oh…. Fuck.

He pulls out and does it again and again and then we are hard at it.

This is when Giuliano Ferrara is at his best.

When he's fucking for the sheer joy of it, overtaking a woman's body for his pleasure.

With no fucks to give about anything.

His hand comes to between my shoulder blades and he pushes my chest down to the couch, changing my position. "Careful," I whimper, I'm completely at his mercy like this.

He slows, as if realizing it himself, before letting out a deep guttural moan. "Sei cos incredibile, cazzo." (Translation: You feel so fucking good.) He pumps me. "You feel that, take every fucking inch." He pumps me harder and then slides his thumb deep into my ass.

My eyes begin to roll back in my head…*oh fuck.*

So much for my slow romantic date.

The position I'm in, his thumb where it is and the way he is fucking me at piston pace, I don't have a chance in hell at holding this.

I cry out as I see stars, my body clenching hard around his as it comes in a rush.

"*Fuck,*" he cries, he holds himself deep and I feel the telling jerk of his cock as he comes deep inside me. He pumps me harder, long deep strokes as he empties his body completely inside of mine.

He falls over the top of my back and we both pant as we

struggle for air, my face buried into the couch, his face against my back.

After a while he pulls out and kisses my butt cheek. "Brava ragazza." (Translation: Good girl.) He kisses my other cheek and I smile against the cushion.

"I wanted tonight to be romantic."

He chuckles as he pulls me to my feet. "That *was* me being romantic." He pulls my face to his and holds it in his two hands and kisses me, it's deep and tender, erotically slow.

Perfection.

The hotplate hisses and we both turn toward it as the vegetables boil over.

"Oh shit. I just burned dinner."

He chuckles as he kisses me again. "Not the first thing you burned tonight."

It's late, after a long hot bath, Giuliano and I are sitting on the couch watching television.

"I found something today," he says softly.

"What?" I smile.

"Well...." He sips his wine and hesitates as if choosing his words carefully. "One of my men was at their child's art show last night at the library."

"Okay," I reply, where is this going?

"Anyway." He pauses again and if I'm not mistaken, seems a little nervous.

"What is it?"

He goes to his suit jacket that's still sprawled over the couch and retrieves something from the inside pocket, he passes it to me and I frown.

It's a photograph of my mother and father...and Angelina.

Dad has his arm around Angelina, but my mother is heavily pregnant, Lorenzo is there too.

Huh?

My eyes rise to his. "When is this from?"

"The date is on the back of it."

I turn the photo over and see the date. "It's the year I was born." I frown and turn the photo over to study it again. "Since when...." I screw up my face in confusion. "My mother is pregnant, but Angelina is there, his arm is around her? I don't understand this photo, it doesn't make any sense."

"I know."

"And what's Lorenzo doing there?"

"Precisely."

"Hmm." I stare at it. "What do you make of it?"

"I mean." He sighs heavily. "From a first glance, if I didn't know better, it looks like a double date. My father and mother and your mother and Lorenzo."

I put the photo down onto the counter and stare at it as I bite my thumbnail. "You're right, it does."

"And we know that Lorenzo and your mother started dating when you were young."

"But Angelina and my mother hated each other."

"But did they?" He gestures to the image, "Does it look like they hated each other? They are both smiling in that photo."

My eyes rise to his. "What are you saying?"

"It's possible that Lorenzo and your mother were in love earlier than we were led to believe."

I blink in surprise.

"Is it possible that Lorenzo and your mother had my father's blessing to be together well before you were conceived?"

I put my hand over my mouth in horror and my eyes rise to meet his. "You think Lorenzo could be my biological father?"

He shrugs. "Would explain a lot of things."

"Like what?"

"Like why your mother got pregnant to a man who had declared his love for another woman and had given her a child only a year before."

My eyes search his. "Could this be real?"

"Does it make me a bad person if I hope it is?"

I put my head in my hands.

"Chesk, do you know what this means?" he says as he grabs my hand in his. "It would mean we are not biologically related."

My saucer-sized eyes hold his.

"We could be together. Properly together."

"But why would they lie?"

"Can you imagine the public uproar if one of my father's men got his wife pregnant? He would be immediately killed by my father's men for being a traitor, your mother too for that matter. Think about it Chesk, your very protection comes from you being a Ferrara, if you are not a Ferrara, in the eyes of his men, you are the child of a traitor and would be disposed of."

I hold my temples with my fingertips.

"Think about it, he left your mother for Angelina and had a baby with her. We know that he cared for your mother as a friend and that he wanted her happy. It would have been the perfect scenario for her to secretly date his closest friend, someone he could trust in his home with his children. He gets to live with the love of his life and his beloved wife is happy and safe in the arms of another man."

"But...she fell pregnant," I whisper.

"So, they had to lie...or all of them would have lost face."

The pieces of the puzzle all fall into place and my eyes rise to meet his. "Jules."

"I know." He smiles hopefully.

"If this is true...."

"We can get married, Chesk." He picks up my hand and kisses it. "We can have children, we can be fucking normal."

My face falls. "But...what if it's not?" I whisper.

"It is, I know it is. I can't love someone as much as I love you and not be able to celebrate it. No life could be that cruel."

Oh...my heart.

My eyes well with tears and I wipe them away with a nod. "True." I think for a moment. "I'll go and see my mother."

"Do you want me to come?"

"No, it's okay. I've got to do this alone."

We smile at each other and for the first time in a long time, something different buzzes in the air between us.

Hope.

———

I walk into my mother's house at just on eight a.m., I couldn't wait a moment longer.

"Hi, Mom."

She frowns. "Hello, darling." She kisses my cheek. "You're up early today, I didn't even know you were in Milan." She's dressed in her workout gear and looks like she's been up for hours.

"Work. Work meetings, all the work meetings," I splutter. "Very busy working."

Shut up, you're wrecking it. Why am I such a terrible liar?

"Would you like a cup of coffee?" she asks.

"Yes, please."

I follow her out to the kitchen and sit down at the counter and she gets to making coffee.

My heart is pumping, and I feel sick, a lot depends on this meeting.

My entire future.

She makes us both a cup of coffee and sits down opposite me. "So? What's up?"

"Why do you think something is up?"

"Because you never get here at eight a.m. unannounced. I'm your mother, Francesca, I know you better than you know yourself."

"Mom." My eyes search hers. "I'm going to ask you a question and I need you to promise me that you'll tell me the truth."

She frowns.

"Because there is no right or wrong answer to this question."

"What are you talking about?"

"And there is no judgement, the past is the past and we are all happy and love each other." I wring my hands together on my lap nervously.

"Francesca," she snaps. "What is it?"

"Is Lorenzo my father?"

Her face falls. "What?"

"Did you start dating Lorenzo before I was conceived? It's okay if you did, I completely understand." I smile hopefully. "Dad was a cad, I get it. I completely get it."

"Honey...." She sighs.

I pass the photo over to her. "I found this and I know that it doesn't marry up with what I've been told and I love Lorenzo. So...."

She stares at the photo and puts it down onto the counter. "No."

"No what?"

"Lorenzo is not your father."

My nostrils flare as I try to hold in the tears. "What do you mean? How could this photo...." Words fail me.

"This was taken at the public library; your father and I had split up for good and I was friends with Lorenzo. Not wanting to go alone, I asked Lorenzo to take me to an art show, when we got there we ran into Giuliano and Angelina."

My heart drops as I stare at her.

"I saw them, not a second later a photographer asked us to stand together and smile, not wanting to cause a scene we did."

"But...." My eyes well with tears.

"Sweetheart." She cups my face in her hand. "Is this to do with Giuliano junior?"

I drop my head in sadness.

"You're in love with him?"

My eyes rise to meet hers.

"I see the way you look at each other, I can feel the love between you. I know that you fell in love with each other before you knew who his father was. Why do you think that Enrico was so determined to keep you apart?"

I get a lump in my throat as I remember him going crazy when he found us together in the library all those years ago. "He knew?"

"Yes, he knew." She nods. "I'm so sorry, darling. The truth is, your father was a womanizer and I loved him. Time and time again I fell for his charm and into his bed. I was pregnant with his child when he left me for her. Lorenzo is a dear man who picked up the pieces and saved me. Trust me, more than anything, I wish you *were* Lorenzo's daughter. He doesn't have any children of his own, he gave up that privilege to be with me. If I could have given him that gift it would have made my life complete."

Her silhouette blurs as I stare at her.

She takes my hands in hers. "You cannot love Giuliano, sweetheart. He is your brother. You have to let him go."

The tears break the dam and roll down my face. "I wanted it to be true," I whisper.

She smiles sadly and wipes my tears. "Me too. I wish I could give you this."

"But ...I love him." I whisper.

"I know. But there isn't enough love in the world that can fix this problem. You need to let him go."

―――――

I sit in my old bedroom of my mother's house and cry and cry and cry.

All my hopes and dreams are shattered and I need to get it out before I face the guards...and him.

I imagine Giuliano's face when I tell him and I cry harder.

He deserves a happy ending and damn it, I wanted to be the one who gave it to him.

But Mother's right.

There is no easy way around this.

We can play pretend in each other's arms all we want, but it will never fix this problem.

If I want him to be happy, really happy. He needs to have children of his own to carry on the Ferrara name, and I know that...I need to let him go, he needs to move on and meet someone that can give him a family life, the one that he deserves.

I get into the shower in my bathroom and slide down the tiles to sit on the floor under the hot water.

Once I pull myself together, I'll go home and pull my world apart.

Again.

Three hours later, I open the door to my apartment and I can immediately feel that Giuliano is here.

His presence is overwhelming and as I turn the corner he rushes me. "What did she say?"

I put my keys onto the side table and turn toward him. "You were wrong." I shrug, "It was...." I pause. "It happened just as Lorenzo explained."

"Bullshit."

I throw my hands up in defeat. "I'm sorry, okay?"

"You're sorry?" He frowns. "What does that mean?"

"It means I know how much you want this to be true."

"Don't you?"

"Yes...and no."

"No?" he snaps. "Why, no?"

"Unlike you, Giuliano, I loved my father, the thought that I wasn't his...." My voice trails off.

"Wasn't what?" he barks. "Worth it?"

I brush past him and walk into the kitchen, he follows me like the Hulk.

"What did she say?" he demands.

"That Lorenzo and she were friends and she went to the art gallery with him and Dad was there with your mother and throwing it in her face."

He narrows his eyes. "And you believed her?"

"My mother wouldn't lie to me," I snap.

"She was not angry in that photo, I saw it with my own eyes and she lied to you your whole fucking life, Francesca," he yells. "Did you know about me?" He hits his chest. "Did you know that Daddy dearest was giving it to another woman every day?

Did you know he had another family? Did you know he was a murdering fucking prick?"

"Stop it," I cry.

"Your mother *is* lying. I don't believe a thing that comes out of her fucking mouth. She was there with Lorenzo, I know it. He was keeping her warm whenever my father wasn't home."

I begin to hear my angry heartbeat in my ears, I'm sick of her being painted the villain, she's a good woman who was in love with a player. "Do not dare disrespect my mother, Giuliano. Ever! Drop it."

"Drop it?" He frowns. "Drop it? Our whole fucking future together depends on this and you tell me to fucking drop it?"

I put my hands onto my hips.

"Go to hell, Francesca."

"What does that mean?" I yell.

"It means I'm not sleeping with my fucking sister anymore. I can't do it. I won't."

Wow.

And there it is, the cold hard facts.

Suddenly I'm angry, at this fucked situation, the world, my father...but inexplicably, most of all him. "Fine." I storm up the hall. "Don't then."

I was supposed to be letting him down easy, not getting dumped myself.

"You go back over there and demand the fucking truth," he yells.

I walk into my bedroom. "Get out." I pick up a perfume bottle and turn and hurl it at him.

He ducks as it flies past his head. "You get over there and demand the truth."

"I got the truth, you idiot, and I'm sorry." I throw my hands up in defeat. "I'm sorry that I'm not the person you want me to be. I'm sorry I'm not Lorenzo's daughter."

He's so angry that veins in his neck are sticking out, his chest rises and falls as he struggles to control his anger.

"And don't worry, you don't have to sleep with your sister anymore."

"What does that mean?"

"It means we're done. Get the fuck out."

"You don't get to end it with me."

"I just did. Get out." I push him out of my bedroom, slam the door and flick the lock.

"Francesca. Open this fucking door," he yells as he bangs on it.

"Go away."

The door bangs hard, nearly coming off its hinges, I jump. He's punched it. "I hope you broke your hand, you idiot."

"You get out here right now!"

"Or what?" I cry through the door, "You'll get your gun out and shoot me? I'm not scared of you, Giuliano."

The door bangs hard again.

I roll my eyes, this is a fucking disaster if ever I saw one.

I get my suitcase out and put it onto the bed, I begin to throw my clothes into it at double speed, I'm getting the fuck out of here.

This is toxic.

With him yelling on the other side of the door, I pack my things and zip up my suitcase, I open the door and march past him down the hall wheeling my suitcase.

"Where are you going?" he demands as he follows me hot on my heels.

"Home." I open the front door in a rush.

"This *is* your home!" His eyes are about to bulge from their sockets.

"No, Giuliano." I get into the elevator. "You've made it quite clear where we stand. I won't darken your door anymore. Don't worry, I won't interrupt you ever again. Fuck whoever you want." I hit the elevator button. "Just stay the hell away from me."

"Where are you going?" he yells.

"Paris…. Where I belong."

Seven days. Seven nights. A million broken dreams.

I'm in a fetal position on the couch, under my blanket, my trusty laptop and phone by my side.

How can only one week in Milan with him feel like it's ended my world?

Seven days…and look at me, I'm a mess.

A knock sounds at the door and I frown, that's weird, nobody can get up to my floor.

I get up and it knocks again, harder this time, more urgent.

I peek through the peephole and see two men, who are they?

Shit.

"Francesca, open the door," a familiar voice calls.

Huh?

I'm trying to see who exactly is out there through the tiny peephole, why don't they make these fucking things bigger?

"It's me, Dr. Miracash."

"Oh." What? It's my family doctor from home. "What's going on?" I call through the door.

"Open the door and I'll explain."

I think for a moment and then shrug, if I can't trust my family doctor, who can I trust? I tentatively open the door. "Hello." I frown.

He smiles warmly. "Hello." He gestures to the other man, "This is Dr. Ormond."

My eyes flick between the two of them. "What's going on?"

"We've been sent here to do some testing."

"What kind of testing?"

"A paternity test, Mr. Ferrara sent us."

16

Francesca

"Oh," I say, although I can't say I'm surprised, Giuliano will never believe a word my mother says and after thinking on it for a few days, I have to admit it, there *are* holes in her story. Enough for me to cast doubt too, after all she's lied to me about so many things up until now in regard to my father, what makes this any different. My mother hasn't contacted me once since I went to her...which is odd.

Does she have a guilty conscience? I do wonder.

Truth be told, I am relieved that he hasn't given up on us.

I step back and hold my arm out. "Please, do come in." They walk in and Dr. Miracash puts his bag onto the table, I watch on as he takes out a swab and a test tube. "This isn't an invasive test, you just need to rub this swab around on the inside of your cheek and we will send it off for analysis."

"That's it?" I frown.

"Yes, this will give us enough DNA to see if further testing is required."

"Have you...." My voice trails off, I don't want to say it out loud.

"Mr. Ferrara has already done his test."

"Oh." I fake a smile, there's my answer. "Sure."

I watch on as he takes the swab out and passes it to me and I swipe it around the inside of my cheek and then the other side. I dig it in until I swear I nearly draw blood.

I want answers too.

I pass it back over to him and then he puts it into the test tube and bags it up.

Dr. Ormond then takes out another swab and passes it over, I frown in question.

"Mr. Ferrara wants two tests carried and sent to separate labs to be sure."

Of course he does, I roll my lips to hide my smile and take the test from him and repeat the process.

"I'll need you to fill this paperwork out," Dr. Ormond asks as he passes me a clipboard with a permission slip attached. I do as I'm asked, fill it out and pass it back.

"How long until the results are back?" I ask.

"Mr. Ferrara has expressed the urgency of this matter, so hopefully within a few days."

My heart swells, he wants to see me urgently. That makes two of us, this last week without him has felt like an eternity in hell.

"Okay," I smile as we walk toward the door. "Are you flying home now?"

"Yes, we came on the Ferrara jet, returning tonight."

A thought comes to my mind. I've only ever seen Dr. Miracash when he came to our home. "Do you have your own practice in Milan?" I ask, it's never even crossed my mind to ask this before.

"No, I'm a general practitioner, also a surgeon. I work full time for Ferrara industries," Dr. Miracash replies.

"Oh...." I stare at him as I wonder how many of the Ferrara men he has put back together over the years. "I see." A surgeon...wow, that would be so they could go untraced by the hospital system. "Well, thank you for coming." I open the door. "So you will call me?" I ask.

"Mr. Ferrara has requested that the test results go to him first, he will instruct us from there."

"Okay." I nod in understanding. That's code for, if it's good news Giuliano wants to tell me himself, if it's bad news, which I think it is, the doctor will call me. "Goodbye."

I watch the two men walk down the hall and get into the elevator, the doors close and they disappear out of sight.

I stare at the closed doors for a moment, I never thought that my future life would depend on the results of a stick covered in saliva. I exhale heavily and close the door, don't get your hopes up.

The rain pours down as I push out through the heavy glass doors at my office. I worked on-site today and just as my boss predicted, I was interrupted almost every ten minutes and achieved next to nothing. I definitely will be working from home for the next few weeks, there's no way I'm going to make all my deadlines with today's productivity.

As I walk out I see my black Mercedes and another man

standing with the door open, he's in the customary black suit and is holding an umbrella over his head. I haven't seen him before, who is he?

Shit.

I dart back into the building and check my messages. There's one from Lorenzo that came through an hour ago, I haven't seen it yet.

Hi Cheska,
You have a new driver today.
His name is Davidoff.
Lorenzo
Xox

What?

I instantly dial Lorenzo's number and he answers first ring as if expecting my call. "Hello, darling."

"Hi." I force myself to use my manners. "Where's Antonio?"

"He's been moved back to Italy," Lorenzo replies calmly.

"Why?" I snap, although I already know the answer, it's because he told Giuliano that I'm back with Marcel.

"Giuliano wants him in Rome for the time being."

"Rome?" My eyes bulge from their sockets. "It's not safe in Rome, why would he send him to Rome?"

Lorenzo lets out a deep exhale. "It is not for us to decide where Giuliano stations his staff, Francesca, Davidoff will now be looking after you."

"Davidoff?" I gasp, annoyed, I peer through the glass windows to see the burly man.

He's huge, mid to late forties, and hardened.

Nobody is messing with Davidoff.

"He's been with the company for many years and is one of Giuliano's most trusted guards," Lorenzo replies.

"One of Giuliano's most trusted guards is code for hit men.... I'm not stupid, Lorenzo. No, that won't do," I announce. "I want Antonio back. Thank you." I try to sound dismissive.

"You have no say in the matter, my darling," Lorenzo replies calmly. "When are you coming home, your mother and I miss you."

I frown, that tone.... The one he uses with me. I've never noticed it before but it's fatherly. "Soon."

"Good, I look forward to it."

The rain really comes down, it's torrential outside. "Can you hear that rain?" I ask him.

"Is that what that is? My God, I thought it was a bad line. Go, get out of the weather."

"Okay." I smile and I go to say what I always say when we finish our calls and I stop myself.

Why do I tell Lorenzo that I love him?

It's something that we've always done to each other. In fact, I probably tell Lorenzo that I love him more than I tell my mother. It's always been him who has been my nurturer...not her.

Weird.

"I love you, my darling," he says.

"You too," I reply softly as my feelings for him become real and apparent.

"Go. Get home and out of the weather, Davidoff is a good man, you will grow to like him."

I roll my eyes, unimpressed. "Goodbye." I hang up and make a run for the car, Davidoff smiles and holds the umbrella over me. "Good afternoon, Miss Ferrara."

"Hello." I force a smile and get into the car, he closes the door behind me and gets behind the wheel, as we pull out into the traffic I exhale heavily.

Where are you, Antonio?

I'm sorry.

———

I open my email, check it again for the tenth time and exhale in exasperation. Damn it, why isn't he replying?

Dominic is missing in action, I can change the tiles but not to the ones he wanted, they are currently out of stock and won't fit with the timeline schedule we have with the tilers. He did give me a second option but I would like to clear it with him first. I've called him, I've emailed him...no answer.

Maybe he's on vacation?

Giuliano

My pointer finger steeples at my temple as I stare aimlessly at the dance floor in front of me. The air is smoky, the music tantric and while the men at my table chatter and laugh, the gorgeous woman on stage does a seductive striptease.

Carlo smirks up at the stage like a predator. "She's fucking hot, man," he mutters under his breath.

I nod, acting impressed.

This is the bachelor life, the one I am accustomed to.

The one I no longer want.

My thoughts are not here, or my surroundings, or the naked women and certainly not with the company I keep.

They are with her...*they are always with her.*

And damn it, where are these fucking results?

It's been five days since Francesca took that paternity test, how long can it take? What are they doing, growing a fucking clone from her DNA?

I turn my phone over and glance at the screen.

No missed calls

Val and Alex appear through the crowd and give me a smile and nod as they walk toward our table.

I smile, excited for the first time tonight. The two best friends a man could ever asked for. They've been with me since childhood, we grew up together and then I found out who I really was, a Ferrara. They showed their true loyalty, instead of judgement and fear, they stood beside me and showed up for the challenge to become my two right-hand men.

Risking everything for me.

They could have walked away. Turned their backs. Instead, let their hopes and dreams of a normal life trickle down the drain along with mine.

They are loyal, the best of the best.

While Alex has stayed exactly the same and more interested in the running of the staff, Valentino has become a darker version of himself.

Running the logistics of our assets. There are things that he, Carlo and I don't share with Alex, simply because he just couldn't handle it, but that's okay, we can.

We protect him where we can, he doesn't need to know everything. He is here by default, by being our friend and we respect that.

Me.... I'm different.

I often wonder if I was always this dark. Was it simmering inside me, waiting to come out? If my life hadn't turned out as it has, would I still have ended up working in organized crime?

Maybe...it feels very natural to be here, but perhaps that's because it's in my blood. The men before me have been living like this for decades.

I'm fucked in the head; I already know that. Any man who sleeps with his own sister is. I cannot deny it, I have no regrets.

I am what I am, fuck everyone else.

I truly believe that Valentino would have always had this life, he thrives on the power, the adrenaline, the women, the money, chasing the kill.

He was made for this role in life, the cocaine king of Italy.

With Carlo running the brawn and Valentino running the blow, we can't lose.

Carlo shuffles over and Valentino and Alex fall into the seat beside me, Val takes out a cigar and puts it between his teeth, he smiles darkly up at the naked woman on stage as he lights it up. "Is she new?" he asks before blowing a thin stream of smoke in the air.

I shrug as my gaze turns toward her, she has long blond hair and a body to die for. Curvy and fuckable. "No idea." I raise my finger and the scantily dressed waitress appears. "Another round, please."

"Of course, sir." She smiles with a nod before disappearing.

We're in the Viper club, we own this establishment. A bar with live shows and exotic guests, high-end girls are entertaining men upstairs and the place is filled with Ferrara men. This is our turf.

We are safe here, *protected.*

Val answers his phone, he listens and then frowns. "What do you mean?" He inhales his cigar as he listens and then narrows his eyes. "Since when?" His eyes flick to me and he gives a subtle shake of his head. "Send out a chopper." He listens again. "And what happened?" He exhales heavily. "Keep me informed." He hangs up and leans into me, I put my ear to his mouth. "The yacht is missing."

My eyes meet his, "What time was it due in?"

"Two p.m. this afternoon. They've made no contact and their tracking device has just been switched off."

I glance at my watch, Ten p.m.

Fuck.

I tip my head back and drain my scotch.

Val glares at me as he inhales his cigar, he leans over and whispers the same thing to Carlo and he clenches his jaw before muttering the words, "Someone's going to fucking die."

Early morning and the office is abuzz with drama.

Our yacht filled with the blow is missing, there's been no contact since one p.m. yesterday when it was on track to land at our port. The satellite tracking was turned off about an hour from port yesterday and since then the chopper was unable to trace it. The only explanation could be that the tracking device was switched to another vessel, which traveled the course to throw us off the scent.

It could be fucking anywhere.

A twenty-million-dollar superyacht doesn't go missing by itself and it could mean only one of two things.

The crew are dead and someone else has our eighty million worth of blow...and our yacht. Or the crew are the ones who stole it and are prepared to live with a death wish.

Either way it's a fucking nightmare and something we've never encountered before.

Val is staring at the satellite-tracking map to see where and when this could have happened.

Lorenzo is sending men to all of the crew's homes and family to put them under surveillance, check for any inconsistencies. If the crew have revolted and do have it, someone will return home for their girl, they always do.

My phone rings.

Nicolai

"Here we go." I click my fingers to get Val's attention and he jumps up and closes the office door. I put the phone on speaker and answer, "Nicolai."

"Giuliano. How are you my friend?"

I lean back and swing on my chair, speaking with the chief of police is always a pleasure. "Good, good. What have you got for me?"

"The word is that one of your men is on Lombardi's payroll."

My eyes meet Carlo's and he narrows his eyes in contempt.

"Who?" I ask.

"I don't know, there's talk they're about to come into some serious blow. Big time from what I hear."

"Interesting," I reply.

Carlo and I glare at each other.

My phone lights up as another call comes in and I immediately hit decline.

"Where are they getting this...blow?" I ask.

"I believe a yacht was hijacked two days ago as it left Columbia. The tracking device was put into a dummy ship which stayed on course to throw them off the scent."

"I see."

He has information, he's fishing for funds.

Val scribbles a note on the paper to tell me what to offer.

Ten million for whereabouts of yacht: Ten million for traitor's name.

I screw up my face and shake my head, "Too much," I mouth.

He scribbles on the paper again.

If we don't get a name,
We're fucked!!

I swing on my chair as I contemplate my offer, fuck.

Val is right, we need answers.

This is a problem that won't go away until it's taken care of. If we have a traitor, we need to take care of it now.

"Find my yacht and we'll deliver ten million," I say.

"Nice," Nicolai replies.

"Give me a name and you'll receive another ten."

"Done," Nicolai replies. "I'll need some time."

"Make it quick." I hang up.

Val screws up the paper in his hands and throws it at the wall with force. "I'm going to fucking kill someone."

Carlo walks in. "We've got surveillance on everyone involved, I have the chopper going up and down the coast. We'll find it, don't worry. And when we do, they will fucking pay."

He and Alex start to discuss their conspiracy theories and I click through my phone to the missed call, I don't know that number.

I dial the number and wait as it rings. "Dr. Miracash," the voice answers.

Shit.

My eyes flick to the boys and I stand and walk out of the office as my heart hammers in my chest. "Hello, this is Giuliano Ferrara, returning your call."

"Yes, Giuliano. The results are back."

"And?"

"Negative."

My face falls in disappointment.

"There is no way the two of you are genetically related."

"What?" I stop still in the corridor as the earth moves beneath me. "Are you sure?"

"We ran the tests three times at both pathologies. One hundred percent that there's no match."

I smile, euphoria runs through me. "Thank you."

"Do you want us to deliver the results to Francesca?"

"No...I'll do it."

"Okay."

"Thanks again." I hang up and put my head into my hands.

Thank God.

"Everything alright?" Alex asks as he walks down the hall.

"Yep." I grab him and kiss his forehead, unable to hide my delight.

He frowns. "Haven't you got a yacht missing or something."

"Yep." I smile, like I could care about missing cocaine.

No DNA matches.

I catch sight of Lorenzo in the foyer and I step toward him, my first instinct to knock him out.

No.

Francesca needs to be the first to know.

She needs to be the one to tell them that she knows. It's not my place.

I march back into my office. "I'm going to France," I announce to Val and Carlo.

"What?" They look up. "When?"

"I'll be back tomorrow."

"What? Today? No. You're needed here." Val snaps.

They watch me in horror as I gather my things.

"How the fuck can you even think about her when this shit is going on?" Val snaps.

I smile broadly and want to jump and punch the air.

How can I not?

They frown at me as if I'm going crazy.... And maybe I am.

"My dear Valentino." I laugh and kiss his forehead. "See you tomorrow, my friend." I grab my keys and briefcase.

"Are you fucking kidding me right now?" I hear Val call from my office as I march toward reception. "Giuliano," he cries. "You're fucked," I hear him cry.

I laugh and get into the elevator.

No DNA match.

The car travels through the peak hour traffic in Paris and I stare out the window smiling like a Cheshire cat.

I can hardly contain my excitement.

I imagine Francesca's door opening and then telling her, she jumps into my arms and we live happily ever after, but I know it won't go like that.

How could it possibly?

While this is the best news I've ever received, Francesca is about to lose the only identity she's ever known. It's going to be messy and complicated and will take time to work through the legalities of the situation. She's going to be devastated.

The car pulls to a stop out the front of her apartment and I take a moment to steel myself.

Please let this go well.

Five minutes later, I stand at her door. *Knock, knock.*

I turn and look back up the corridor, this place is so different to anywhere else she stays. Modest, dated. If I didn't know better, I could never have imagined her living somewhere like this.

The door opens in a rush and she lets out an audible gasp as she sees me.

Her eyes search mine, the air swirling between us. "Tell me something good," she whispers.

I try to hold my smile and fail miserably. "There's no DNA match."

Her eyes well with tears. "You mean...."

I nod as I get a lump in my throat.

"We're not...."

"No."

She throws herself into my arms and we hold each other tight. For a long time, we hug. Standing in the hallway.

A million emotions passing between us, relief, despair...

anger from my side for all the years of pain we've been put through, and for what?

But mostly, all I can feel is excited. Because for the first time in forever, I have hope of a future with the only woman I've ever loved.

My beloved Francesca.

She takes my hand and pulls me into her apartment, and once the door shuts behind us, I take her into my arms abruptly and kiss her, she smiles against my lips.

Our kiss is long, slow and intimate as if we have all the time in the world.

And now we do.

I run my hand down over her back and feel that she's lost more weight. "Are you okay?"

She nods with a forced smile and pulls out of my arms, her eyes search mine for answers. "She lied."

I remain silent, what is there to say?

"All this time, she knew...."

"In Bianca's defense, it wouldn't have been an easy thing to own up to." I shrug. "I can see why she wouldn't want it out there."

"How can you defend her?" She frowns.

"You know...." I roll my lips as I try to articulate my thoughts properly. "I've thought about this and how things were run back then. It would have been scandalous for one of our father's—"

"Your father." She cuts me off.

My heart sinks, and so it begins. "It would be scandalous for one of his men to even date his wife, let alone get her pregnant. Can you imagine the drama it would have caused within the ranks of Ferrara? There would have been an uprising."

Her eyes hold mine as she listens.

"Having a mistress back then was normal...hell, it still is in some parts. But your wife, is *your* wife. She is off limits to any other man, regardless of who you are fucking on the side. My father was protecting not only Bianca, but Lorenzo too. He wanted your mother happy and looked after, he cared for them both and I have no doubt that he knew that one day the truth would come out, but at the time, the three of them did the best that they could. You can't begrudge them for that."

Francesca's eyes well with tears.

"Hey." I pull her in close and hug her. "He loved you, you are always going to be his daughter," I whisper into her hair.

"But what does this mean?" she murmurs sadly. "How do we...even?"

"Just don't worry about it for the time being. We know, that's all that matters at this point." I kiss her softly. "We can be together and that's all that fucking matters. Take your time to get your head around this, there's no rush to make any huge announcement or anything." I put my finger under her chin and bring her face up to mine. "When you feel ready, talk to your mother." I wipe her tears with my thumbs.

"I love you," she whispers.

I smile against her. "And I love you."

"You're too thoughtful to be a bad guy."

I chuckle as I hold her. "I'm a prick."

"When?" She smiles up at me.

"In a minute when I drag you to bed and make up for ten years of missed sex."

She smirks and pushes the hair back from my forehead. "Jules...it's not a good time of the month for me."

What?

My face falls. "Don't even...."

She smirks up at me. "Uh-huh."

"Seriously?" My shoulders slump in defeat.

"Yep."

"Well...how long does that take?"

"A week."

My eyes widen in horror. "A week?" I gasp.

"Uh-huh." She walks into the kitchen.

This is uncharted territory, everything between the two of us has always been so sexual. We've never just hung out. Like ever.

And on a night like tonight...fuck's sake.

"Well, what are we going to do all night?" I gasp.

"You're going to lie on my couch and google how to be a normal boyfriend and I'm going to cook us dinner."

I stare at her, horrified.

"And then, if you're a good boy, you can rub my feet."

"Or you could rub my dick?" I offer.

"No," she replies sharply, "That's not happening, you're waiting for me."

"Seven days?"

"Uh-huh."

I flop into the couch in disgust and she begins to fuss around in the kitchen.

I don't know what I was expecting but it sure wasn't this. Not the hot and heavy makeup sex I was hoping for, that's for sure. I watch her as she fusses around in the kitchen for a long time and after a while, I smile to myself.

Maybe this is even better than hot and heavy.

The truth is, this is what I always craved with her. Normalcy, an ordinary life with the girl of my dreams.

I know it will take me a while to get used to, but I'm up to the challenge.

Maybe I *will* google how to be a normal boyfriend.

Domestic bliss.

An hour later we are just finishing our dinner, Francesca has been quiet and there's one more issue I have to bring up. I know she's got a lot going through her head but there's no way around it.

"Babe," I say softly as I take her hand over the table. "I need you to move back to Milan and in with me."

She frowns.

"I can't...I can't do this long-distance thing. I've been loving you from a distance for ten years and it's been like living in fucking hell. I know that means leaving a job that you love and I know that's a big ask. But I can't...." I hesitate. "I can't move, it's not even an option. If I could I would."

She stares at me for a moment. "Okay."

I frown, surely it isn't going to be that easy.

"When do we leave?"

I smile over at my beautiful girl. "I have to be back tomorrow. We can come back in a week or two and pack up your things, but right now I have things going on that I have to get back for and I can't...I can't leave you here again. Don't ask me to."

She gets up from her seat and comes around and sits on my lap, she puts her arms around my neck and kisses me softly. "Okay."

I smile against her lips as our kiss deepens. "I'll do something for you now."

"Like what?"

I chuckle. "Well, I like getting my dick sucked in the shower."

"That's for you, you idiot." She laughs as she stands and, taking my hand, pulls me to my feet. "Then let's take a shower." She leads me to the bathroom and turns the hot water on and pulls my shirt off over my head. I stare at her as I try to contain myself, don't push for it.

She said no sex.

Her lips take mine as she unzips my pants and slides her hand down the front of my pants, she cups my balls and my eyes flutter closed.

What she makes me feel.

Everything.

She strokes me as we kiss and I am literally at her mercy.

I would do anything she wants; I *will* do anything she wants.

I put my hand around hers and clench it closed hard, I jerk myself harder, so she knows what I need.

Hard.

So fucking hard.

She whimpers into my mouth as we kiss frantically and dear God.

I love this woman…so much.

My new life starts right here, right now.

Francesca

Five days.

Five perfect, loved-up days.

Giuliano and I have officially been together for only five days but it feels like it's been coming for a lifetime. Let me rephrase that, it *has* been coming for a lifetime.

I have loved this man with all of my heart since I was seventeen years old and we have been through hell by being kept from each other...but now, every moment together is a gift that we both treasure.

We kiss and laugh and catch each other staring...we talk for hours in the darkness at the late of night.

I love him more than ever.... More than I ever thought possible.

He is my soul mate, I know it for certain and I don't have one reservation.

Anything to be with him.

He's moved into my apartment and because we can't tell anyone that we're even together, we've done a million sneaky trips up and down the internal lift with his personal belongings. I sometimes find myself staring in awe at his suits in my wardrobe hanging next to my clothes.

Our things together...like our hearts have always been.

I stare at myself in the mirror and smile. I have music playing with a glass of champagne, I'm wearing a black lace-up corset and thigh-high suspender belt with all the trimmings.

We are going out tonight, to a charity ball of all places.

And I know it's not out in public yet, but it's really our first official date. We've never got dressed up and gone out together alone before, I'm excited and nervous and slightly terrified.

What if we don't work out?

What if we love each other just too much and it works against us?

This is a love that I would never recover from.

I'm not sure if it's normal to be this besotted with a partner. I've never had it before, and I have to keep reminding myself that Giuliano has never even been in a serious relationship. He is in a much bigger adjustment phase than I am. I need to give him time and space to let him find his feet.

He's at the office, working on a Saturday. Apparently, there's something he needed to attend to, he should be home soon though.

I finish reapplying my makeup and I feel him before I see him, I turn to see Giuliano leaning on the doorjamb, his hungry eyes slide down my body and back up before he lets out a low whistle. "And there she is," he murmurs almost to himself.

Excitement bubbles in my stomach and I put my hands on my hips and give him a sexy sashay of my hips.

My monthly is finally gone…tonight, I'm all his.

Then he's on me, his lips on my neck, his hands on my ass. His large erection up against my stomach. "Ho bisogno di scoparti," (Translation: I need to fuck you.) he growls against my skin, goose bumps scatter up my arms.

Italian.

He's here.

His teeth graze my jawline as he loses control. "Ora." (Translation: Now.) He pushes me over to the bed and turns me to face it and pushes me down onto my knees, he stands behind me and slowly rubs his hand over my ass as he hisses in approval.

I watch him in the mirror, this is how I love him. When he can't filter his needs, running purely on instinct to fuck.

He runs his hand over my G-string and then with two fingers he pulls it to the side and lets out a low whistle as he stares at my sex. "Sei perfetta." (Translation: Perfection.)

I wiggle my hips as an enticement. "Tonight, baby."

"Adesso." (Translation: Now.) He bends and kisses me there. "I need you now."

We do have time now but I want some delayed gratification. "We don't have time now, you need to get ready."

He licks me again, a low hum rumbling through the lips of my sex, and I know if I let him do that it's all over. "Jules," I say to snap him out of his instinctive trance.

He rolls me onto my back and lies over me, his strong arms holding his body off of mine. "I need you," he whispers.

"You have me." I smile up at him.

"Ne ho bisogno" (Translation: I need this.) His fingers rub over my sex through my panties. "Ti desidero da impazzire." (Translation: I'm so fucking hungry for you.)

"Tonight." I kiss him. "You need to get ready."

His brow furrows and then he gets up and stands over me, his hands clench at his sides.

I smile up at him and point to the bathroom. "Shower," I mouth.

"Fucking," he mouths back.

I giggle and he bends and holds my hands above my head and kisses me deeply, his tongue taking no prisoners.

Oh.... The way he kisses me.

Seriously...fuck the date. Who cares about going out anyway?

No.

"Jules," I remind him.

He lets out a disgusted growl, drags himself up and walks into the bathroom. I lie on my back smiling goofily up at the ceiling.

Life is good.

The ballroom is grand, there are waiters walking around with cocktails and champagne on silver trays. The crowd is dressed to the nines in their very best black-tie and everyone who is everyone is here.

Giuliano and I walk in and over to the seating board, I can hear people letting out soft gasps as they see the two of us together.

The protected princess daughter with the black sheep of the family. This mistress's son, the darkness that nobody talks about.

I look over at my beautiful man, so handsome in his black tie. I have never been prouder to arrive on somebody's arm as I am his.

The fact that he came is another testament to our commitment to each other.

"This way." I gesture over to our table and he glances over and inhales sharply.

I smile and lead him over to our table and smile sweetly at my family.

"Hello everyone." I smile, Giuliano raises an unimpressed eyebrow before pulling out my chair, I sit down and he sits down beside me.

My mother's face falls, Lorenzo looks like he's swallowed a fly and my two brothers' eyes are wide.

"What are you doing?" my mother whispers in horror as she looks around to see who's watching.

I smile triumphantly. "I think it's time that Giuliano takes his place in society with the rest of the Ferrara's...don't you?"

Giuliano's eyes meet mine and he gives me the best come-fuck-me look I have ever seen.

"Francesca," she whispers angrily. "What the hell do you think you are doing?"

I pick up my glass of champagne and hold it up to her. "Celebrating."

"Celebrating what?"

I smile and clink my glass with Giuliano. "Our paternity tests came back...Mother." I sneer.

The blood drains from her face.

"You have twenty-eight days to confess...or I will." I turn to Giuliano. "Do you want to dance, darling?"

Giuliano gives me a sexy wink. "You bet I do."

17

Francesca

THE DANCE FLOOR is packed and Giuliano makes sure to keep a respectable distance and holds me at arm's length. Well aware that to everyone in the ballroom he is technically still my brother. "What are you doing?" he asks as his eyes roam over the crowd.

"It's time."

"For what?"

"For you to come out of the shadows and step into the light."

A frown flashes across his face and then disappears just as quickly as it came.

"Maybe I don't want to be in the light," he replies casually as we sway to the music.

"You were kept a secret for a reason, Giuliano."

"And we both know why that is, don't we?"

"This was never about having a secret love child, there's

more to it than that," I say softly. "He raised you to take over Ferrara. To lead."

His eyes hold mine as he listens.

"He has two other sons, Giuliano, and yet, it is you who he chose. When the time was right, he wanted you to come out of the shadows and shine." I smile up at him. "And look at you," I whisper. "He would be so proud of the man you have become."

His nostrils flare and I know that I've just hit a nerve.

"You are more than shining, my love. Just as he always knew that you would."

"And what about us?" he asks.

I frown in question.

"If your mother won't admit the truth, where does that leave us? I'm not hiding forever, I'm happy to expose her right now."

"We have to wait until the shock of this dies down." I roll my lips as I try to think of the right thing to say. "She'll come around and when she gets to know how wonderful you are, she will accept us and announce who I really am."

"To everyone in this room, Francesca, I'm your older brother. The crime boss who everyone fears. She will never accept us."

"Well, she wanted her own sons to lead Ferrara, and you did kick her out of her house when you took over and you made it very clear how much you hated her. Do you really think she's going to welcome you with open arms?"

He winces. "In hindsight, not my smartest move."

I smile up at my handsome man. "I really want to kiss you right now."

He chuckles. "I dare you to."

"Can you try to be nice to her tonight...for me?" I smile sweetly up at him.

He rolls his eyes.

"I'm not cutting my mother out of my life, Giuliano, you and she have to find a way to get along. She is my mother, I only have one."

He exhales heavily.

"Please?"

"Fine."

The song finishes. "Let's get back to the table."

"Let's not," he mutters dryly.

I widen my eyes. "You promised to try."

"Fuck's sake," he mutters under his breath. "Fine."

We make our way back to the table and find nobody sitting down, hmm where are they? Giuliano and I take a seat and Matteo comes back and sits down.

"Where's Mom and Lorenzo?" I ask him.

"They left," he replies as he takes a sip of his drink.

"What?" I snap. *She fucking left?*

"Said she's not lowering herself to sit here with you two." He shrugs. "I have to agree with her that it is kind of weird that you arrived together. Since when are you two friends?"

I begin to perspire.

"We've always been friends." I fake a smile and look over at Giuliano, "Haven't we?" I let out an awkward laugh.

"It's weird that you two are friends, seeing how he's treated your mother," Matteo replies dryly.

I swallow the lump in my throat.

Oh, fucking hell...this is spiraling.

Straight down.

Giuliano drains his glass of scotch and crunches on the ice, his cold eyes hold Matteo's.

My eyes flick between them, shit. I have to defuse the situation. "Can you get me a drink, please, Giuliano."

He keeps glaring at my brother, animosity swirls in the air and it feels like they are seconds off having a full-on world war.

"Jules." I tap him on the leg to try to snap him out of it. "Please?"

He lifts his chin in defiance as he stares at Matteo, and I know that if I wasn't here he would have knocked him clean out by now.

"Giuliano," I snap. "Go to the bar." I hit his leg once more. "Now."

Giuliano's cold eyes hold Matteo's. "Stay out of my way," he sneers.

"Or what?" Matteo replies.

Giuliano smiles darkly. "You'll see."

"Is that a threat?" Matteo spits.

"That's a fucking promise." He stands and walks to the bar.

My heart hammers in my chest, fuck.

I admit it, he can be scary when he wants to be.

"What the fuck are you doing?" Matteo whispers. "He's fucked up. Did you hear that? Stay out of his way or he's going to kill me."

"He never said he was going to kill you," I snap. "I might. If you don't be nice to him."

"You know, I tolerated him for a long time. But if he thinks you and he are going to be besties, I'm drawing the line. Do you really expect Mother to sit here and play happy families after the way he's treated her? No way in hell are you hanging around with him, he's fucking bad news, Francesca. Why the fuck would you even think that bringing him here was a good idea?"

Oh God, *this is a disaster.*

"She has treated him just as bad," I fire back.

"How? For not accepting her husband's affair and his love child with a mistress?"

I blink, surprised.

"When you get married, Francesca, tell me how you'll feel when your husband gets another woman pregnant, and then that child grows up and throws you out of your own house after he steals the company from your own two sons after your eldest son dies."

"He stole nothing, the company was left to him, Dad wanted him in charge," I snap. "I'm not even…." I cut myself off. I can't tell him about my paternity, this isn't the time or place. "You know what." I hold my hands up. "This was a bad idea."

"Yeah, it was."

"If you just got to know him."

"I don't want to fucking know him."

"He's a good guy."

"For a drug dealer," he huffs.

"Oh please, where do you think all your money comes from. Don't sit there and pretend to be all high and mighty, he has signed millions of dollars of property over to you. How dare you treat him with such disrespect."

"I don't want you hanging around with him."

Something snaps deep inside. Something wrong and sinister and spiteful.

"I'm doing more than hanging around with him, Matteo, I'm sleeping with him."

"What?" he explodes.

"We're not even genetically related," I whisper angrily. "So next time you defend your angelic mother, ask her who fathered her daughter, because it wasn't her fucking husband." I grab my purse, stand and march over to Giuliano at the bar. "We're leaving."

"Hallelujah."

The car ride home is long, and silent. Giuliano stares out the window, he too is lost in his own thoughts.

For some stupid reason, I thought that being sat at a table with my family for the night would force an outcome, we would talk about what happened in a safe place where nobody could run, shout or scream. Lorenzo and my mother would own up and my brothers could get their heads around it. We would come up with a solution and Giuliano and I could move forward...together.

But no.

That would be too easy, and if I've learned anything over the last ten years it's that Giuliano and I never get the easy road.

The scenery flies past and I let out a deep exhale, Giuliano glances over at me and then his eyes go back to the front, emotionless and cold, his jaw ticking as he clenches it.

He's angry, like a silent bomb ticking away about to explode at any moment.

And I can't say that I blame him, my mother didn't even have the decency to sit with him for more than two minutes.

Not even for me.

Damn it.... I should have told Giuliano that my family were going to be at the ball tonight.

What on earth was I thinking? This plan was perfect on paper.

The car turns into the underground parking lot and the heavy garage doors slowly go up, we drive through and the two black cars following us do the same.

Always the convoy, and now...the secrets.

We can't even have a fight in public because nobody can

even know that we are together. To the whole world we are still brother and sister and if my mother won't admit the truth, how do we get around this?

How do we move forward?

She showed tonight just how anti-Giuliano she really is. She hates him with such a passion and she doesn't even know him. She will never give us her blessing, no matter who my father is. She will give me an ultimatum, him or her, I know she will.

I get a lump in my throat just thinking about it.

Davidoff opens the car door and Giuliano climbs out and then turns and takes my hand and helps me out. "Thank you."

Without a word he turns and walks into the waiting elevator and I follow him in.

He hits the button and the doors close, we travel to the top floor in silence.

The mood is somber and sad…angry from his side.

Reality's a bitch…and then some.

The doors open at my floor and we both step out, I unlock the door and we walk in. Giuliano empties his wallet and keys from his pockets, puts them on the side table and walks toward the bedroom.

"Are you alright?" I ask.

"Yep." He keeps walking up the hall and disappears out of sight, I hear the shower turn on and my heart drops. Not the first date I was hoping for, I throw my purse onto the table in disgust.

I walk into the bathroom to find Giuliano soaping himself up, he glances up and then turns his back on me.

My eyes roam up over his broad back and his bare behind.

Such a beautiful man.

"Are you angry with me?" I ask.

"Why would I be angry at you?" He keeps washing himself.

"You're acting angry with me."

His eyes flick up and I see a glimmer of his temper. "If you think this is angry, you're fucking kidding yourself, Francesca," he snaps.

I throw my hands up in surrender. "And there it is."

"Just leave it," he barks.

I roll my lips as I try to think of the right thing to say. "I'll talk to her tomorrow."

"Don't bother." He turns the shower off and brushes past me, he grabs a towel, wraps it around his waist and marches out of the bathroom.

"What's that supposed to mean?" I call after him.

Silence.

Fuck's sake, I walk into the bedroom to see him drying himself with vigor, he's rubbing his skin so hard it's a wonder he's not drawing blood. "I don't need her approval," he snaps.

But you want it.

"I know." I slink down to sit on the bed, he brushes his teeth and then turns the light off. "Good night." He flicks the blankets over himself angrily and turns his back to me.

I sit in the darkness and look at him lying there, he's hurt.

And suddenly I'm angry.

Furious.

Nobody gets to hurt him, he's a good man.

Fuck them.

How is this going to work out?

If they won't admit that I'm Lorenzo's daughter...how do Giuliano and I ever come out as a couple? If my mother doesn't come forward with the truth people will naturally assume the paternity results have been faked. I need her to show a united front with us. We can't do this alone.

Ferrara

So close and yet, so far.

For a long time, I sit alone in the darkness and even though Giuliano is here with me, I am all alone.

He's lost in his own head, with no fucks to give about mine.

Eventually I take a long hot shower and get into bed behind Giuliano, I cuddle his back and kiss his shoulder. "I love you," I whisper into the darkness.

Silence.

"Baby?"

"I love you too," he says softly.

I kiss his back again, he loves me.

That's all that matters.

The sound of a text coming in wakes me from my sleep and I vaguely hear Giuliano roll over and check his phone. He sits up and texts someone and gets out of bed.

He walks into the bathroom and I hear the shower turn on, I glance at the clock, Eight a.m.

What's he doing?

Two minutes later the shower turns off and he walks back into the bedroom wrapped in a towel and walks into the wardrobe. "What are you doing?" I call.

"I have to go into work."

"What?" I sit up onto my elbows. "It's Sunday."

"I know." He reappears and I watch on as he buttons up his business shirt. "There are...." He pauses. "Things going on."

"What things?"

"We have a mole working for Ferrara."

"What?" Panic runs through me. "Well, is this dangerous?"

"Not for me." He leans over and kisses me and lays me back

down. "Go back to sleep, angel." He pushes my hair back behind my ears as he stares down at me.

"I'm sorry about last night." I whisper.

"Don't be." He cups my face in his hand. "Your mother and I are never going to get along. This will never be the big happy family that you want, you need to get your head around it."

"I just...."

He kisses me softly, cutting me off. "Go back to sleep."

"Well, what am I going to do all day?" I ask.

He shrugs as he stands. "Go see Anna."

"She's away with Carlo."

"He's on his way back now, she'll be around."

"Oh." I smile, feeling a little bit better that her weekend plans got interrupted too.

"Jules." I just want to wash last night from our memory. "I love you."

"I know." He kisses my forehead and then without another word turns and leaves.

I flop back onto my pillow in disgust, no *I love you too*.

How annoying.

Ugh...he can try to hide it all he wants but I know he's disappointed at how last night went too, and he didn't even hear what my brother had to say.

I get a vision of Giuliano threatening Matteo to stay out of his way and my stomach drops.

This is just one big fucking disaster.

Giuliano

The elevator opens at the top floor of the Ferrara building and I step out with purpose.

Nicolai has intel, he texted me this morning and wants

me to meet him at the dock at one p.m., he knows who the mole is. And as soon as I know, that person will be meeting his maker. It's one thing to be stolen from, but to find out it's an inside job and that one of my own men is to blame…is a betrayal that I can't accept.

He's a dead man.

I walk through reception and down the corridor and catch sight of Lorenzo, he smiles. "Hello, son."

"Fuck off." I walk past him and into my office, I sit down at my desk and turn my computer on.

He appears at my door. "Have you got a moment?"

"Nope."

He exhales heavily and walks in and closes the door behind him. "We need to talk about last night."

"I've got nothing to say to you."

He drops into the chair at my desk anyway. "Francesca is not my daughter."

My eyes shoot up to his and I glare at him.

"I mean…." He shrugs as if searching for words. "Francesca is not my daughter, so whatever you were implying last night…. Whatever you think you know, it isn't correct."

I stare at him, my mind a clusterfuck of confusion. "I don't understand."

"Well, that makes two of us, because I want some fucking answers too."

"Are you saying that you weren't sleeping with her before she fell pregnant?"

"We were in love, most definitely, and there were one or two times but the dates were way off, trust me. I wish more than anything Francesca was my daughter."

I roll my eyes. "I don't have time for this shit today."

"I left last night because I wanted answers."

"You left?"

"Yes, I walked out and Bianca followed me. She swears that she didn't sleep with anyone else."

"You don't believe her?"

He rolls his lips. "She was a beautiful woman. Back then who knows what she was capable of."

"You think she was sleeping with more men on the side than just you?"

"Between you and me." He pauses. "And this doesn't leave this room, do you understand me?"

"Of course."

"I've always had my suspicions about Antonio and Bianca."

"Antonio?" I frown. "Francesca's guard, Antonio?"

"Yes, he was her guard around that time."

"He would have been only young."

"He was. Early twenties, but he was besotted with her. She was this glamorous older woman who had needs and a womanizing absent husband."

"But if she was in love with you...." My voice trails off as I try to put the pieces together.

"We had a few accidents, but I had decided that I wouldn't sleep with her again until I had your father's approval. He was my best friend and I wasn't comfortable betraying him. She wasn't happy about it, we fought often."

"You think Antonio?"

"I don't know." He shrugs. "I'm trying to find a logical explanation and it's the only thing I can come up with. I absolutely lost my shit with her last night after we left the wedding. Biggest fight we've ever had."

"What did she say?"

"She denied it, swears there was nobody else but me."

"You don't believe her?"

"Who fucking knows?" He sighs sadly. "I'm gutted. It was bad enough knowing that the woman I loved fell pregnant to another man. But to find out there was someone else, a third person...and that he got to give her the child that I desperately wanted."

"Fucking hell." I sit back in my chair and let out a deep exhale, we both fall silent, this is one fucked-up situation. "She hates me."

"She really does." Lorenzo smiles.

I smirk, for some reason amused.

"She's a good person, Giuliano. Regardless of what you think you know of her. She is a good woman who was put in a bad situation." His eyes hold mine. "And if you hurt my beloved Francesca, I *will* kill you with my bare hands."

I give him a sad smile. "I'm sorry she's not your daughter."

"Not as sorry as I am."

12:30 p.m.

"I don't like this," Alex splutters as he swings on his chair. "Can't he just tell you over the phone?"

"Nicolai's message said that I have to meet him at the town market at the fruit store at one p.m., he knows who the mole is and to come alone."

Carlo fusses around loading my gun and Val walks into the office and throws me a bulletproof vest. "Put this on."

"I don't need that shit." I roll my eyes. "I'm meeting him at a public market."

"Yeah, you fucking do. We don't know who's going to be

there. This could be a setup, you could be walking straight into a fucking trap."

I roll my eyes and put the vest on underneath my shirt. "It'll be fine. I've met with Nicolai plenty of times before, there's no issue. Stop being drama queens."

Carlo hands me my gun and I tuck it into the holder under my arm and then I put my suit coat over the top, I hold my two hands out. "Happy?"

"Better." Carlo nods. "We have six men on the ground already and we'll be around the corner, text us the name straight away so we can order the hit."

"I want him dead before I get back to my car. You got that?" I reply.

"He will be, don't worry."

I pat down my pockets to make sure I have everything. "Let's do this."

The market is busy and bustling and I head toward my destination, the fruit store. I glance around at the people surrounding me, busily shopping for their produce on an average Saturday afternoon.

I walk into the fruit store and see Nicolai from behind, he's putting apples into a plastic bag as he pretends to shop. I pick up a basket and walk over to the apples as I pretend to do the same. He glances up as he sees me and gives me a subtle nod.

"What have you got for me, dear friend?" I ask.

His eyes flick around and it's obvious that he's nervous. "Lombardi has your yacht."

That fucker.

I clench my jaw as I put the apples in the bag. "How did

he know about my fucking yacht?" I mutter under my breath.

A loud whistle rings out.

A woman's scream in the distance.

Nicolai stumbles back and clutches his chest, he reaches for me as he falls to the ground. Blood is pooling in his shirt.

He's been shot.

Fuck.

I fall to the ground on my knee beside him. "Nicolai." I grab his hand. "Stay here, stay with me. It's okay." People are screaming, running for cover, and my eyes flick around at the surroundings. "Who did this?"

He's bleeding out, I can see life slipping away from him as the blood pools around. I put my hands over the bullet hole on his chest to try to stop the bleeding. "Call an ambulance," I scream as the blood begins to squirt up onto me. "Nicolai," I stammer. "Come on. Hold on, don't go."

"Fran...France...."

"Who?" I ask in a panic.

"Francesca," he whispers in pain.

I frown as the earth beneath me moves. "My sister?"

He nods.

No.

"What about her?"

His eyes close. "Trust.... I...."

"What about Francesca?" I cry, adrenaline is pumping hard through my veins. "Nicolai, don't die," I beg. "Tell me."

His head drops, his eyes go blank as they stare into space.

He's gone.

I sit back onto my heels, covered in blood. My heart banging hard against my chest.

What the hell was he going to say?

18

Francesca

I DIAL Anna's number and wait as it rings.

"Hi, babe, I was just about to call you," she answers.

"What are you up to?"

"We're on our way back from Tuscany now."

I smile broadly. "You went to Tuscany, that sounds romantic?"

"You have no idea." She laughs. "Do you want to meet up for a late lunch?"

"Sounds good."

"Okay, I'll come over around two o'clock? I have so much to tell you."

"Like what?" I hear Carlo say in the background. "What do you have to tell her?"

I imagine him driving as he listens to our conversation.

"How crap you are in bed," she replies.

"You wish," his voice growls.

I hear her laugh out loud and I know that he's just pinched her on the leg or something.

I smile as I listen to them play, I love that she sounds so happy.

My door buzzer sounds and I frown, who would that be?

"Someone is at the door, I have to go."

"Okay, see you soon."

I hang up and answer the door, my mother walks straight past me and into the apartment.

Great.

"Hi, Mom."

"Hello, darling."

She's wearing a camel-color fitted dress and sky-high heels, her hair is styled to perfection and as usual she looks like she just stepped off a designer photo shoot.

"How was church?" I ask.

"Good. I prayed for you." She puts her handbag down on the kitchen counter and walks to my coffee machine.

"You don't need to pray for me, Mom."

"Yes, I do. After last night's little brain snap on your behalf somebody has to." She gets to making a cup of coffee. "Do you want one?"

"No thanks." I cross my arms, annoyed. "Did you come here to fight with me? Because you needn't bother, I'm already kind of pissed off with you about leaving last night without saying goodbye."

She exhales heavily. "That was Lorenzo being dramatic. He walked out and I had to follow him."

I frown as I stare at her. "Why would *he* walk out?"

"Because he's not your father, Francesca. If he was, I would have told you long ago. How do you think that made him feel having that information slung at me across the table in front of him?"

"You were married to another man when he was sleeping with you, how should he fucking feel?" I snap, outraged.

"Listen to me." She sips her coffee casually as if she has this conversation every day. "I know that you think that you know everything, but I can assure you. You have this wrong."

"So, you never slept with Lorenzo before I was conceived?" I ask.

"I did. I admit it, I did."

I roll my eyes in disgust. "Why are we even having this conversation?"

"Because the dates were way out. There is no way you are Lorenzo's daughter and I would have dearly loved you to have been, he doesn't have any children and loves you like you are his own. To give you to him would have been the ultimate gift of love."

"So, you can tell me with one hundred percent certainty that I am not Lorenzo's?"

She shrugs. "If you are."

"So...there is an if?" I scoff.

"I'm just saying, if you were Lorenzo's, that would mean that you were born at forty-two weeks' gestation. You didn't look like an overdue baby."

I throw my hands up in disgust, "That's your argument? I didn't look like an overdue baby?" I shake my head. "Can you hear yourself right now? Give me a break."

"It's a fact."

"No, Mom, this is the facts. You were sleeping with two men at the same time and I have just had a paternity test that proves I am not who you assumed I was."

She tilts her chin upward in defiance. "Regardless, he is not the man for you."

"I love him."

"I don't care. You cannot."

"It's a little too late for that, Mom. We fell in love long before Enrico died, long before we knew anything about Giuliano being related."

"I know." She holds her hands up in defeat. "Enrico predicted this mess when he caught the two of you in the library."

"You knew about us that long ago?"

"Yes, and in hindsight I should have told you back then."

I shake my head in disbelief. "You're too late, we're already in love and living together."

Her face falls. "You can't love a man like him, sweetheart."

"Why not?"

"Because I loved a man just like him. His twin, in fact. And look how my life turned out."

"Dad?"

She nods sadly and takes my hand in hers. "I know this doesn't make sense to you now, darling, but I promise you from the bottom of my heart that I am telling the truth. Powerful men who look and love like Giuliano Ferrara will never be satisfied by one woman."

For the first time I see my mother for what she really is...*broken.*

She really did love him.

"Everybody thinks that he and Angelina had this grand love story...and they did, there's no denying it, he couldn't stay away from her no matter how much he wanted to," she says softly. "But there were other women too."

"What?" I frown.

"He would tell me that he was working and tell Angelina that he was with me, but he would be out in clubs. Living the life of a crime boss, there were strippers, party girls, gambling and casinos. Gang bangs, orgies...you name it, he did it. And he did it well, every woman in Italy wanted him."

I get a vision of that porno with Giuliano and those two girls and my heart sinks.

He loved it, he was in his glory in that threesome.

"And you can't blame Giuliano for having those things...it comes with the territory. His men look up to him and I have no doubt that he loves you, my darling." She smiles sadly as she runs her hand down my hair to try to soften her hurtful words. "But in time...he *will* stray. I can guarantee my life on it. And you will have his children and have no choice but to turn a blind eye to it, because the thought of living without him will kill you."

I stare at her.

God.

"He will tell you he loves you and you will believe him. It is a long-drawn-out death of your own self-respect."

"But I love him..." I whisper.

"I know. Men like him are easy to love." I drop to sit on the couch and she sits beside me. "I'm sorry. I wish I could change the way things are."

My eyes hold hers. "How did you do it, Mom? How did you love a man who constantly slept with other women?"

"Through tears," she whispers.

I get a lump in my throat as I stare at her. "He's different," I whisper. "Giuliano is different." Am I trying to convince her or myself?

Maybe a bit of both.

She presses her lips together and forces a sad smile, realizing her words are falling on deaf ears.

Only they aren't.

I can hear her warning loud and clear.

It's terrifying.

She straightens her back and stands, her steely armor slipping firmly back into place. "I will let you go." Her high heels click as she walks to the front door and I follow behind her, lost in my own depressing thoughts.

She turns toward me. "Goodbye, darling."

"How do Giuliano and I come out, Mom? How do we announce to the world that we aren't related and are together?"

"Take your time with this decision, Francesca. Your happiness for the rest of your life depends on it. This is not something you want to rush."

My eyes hold hers.

"If you do decide that this is the life you want, we will deal with it together." She tucks a piece of my hair behind my ear. "You have my word."

"Okay."

She smiles and kisses my cheek. "I love you."

I nod through tears. "I love you too."

Anna and I walk into the restaurant around four p.m., I haven't heard from Giuliano all day.

I have no idea what could be so important that he has to work on a Sunday.

The waiter shows us to our seats and pulls out our chairs for us. "Thank you."

"Why are there so many guards today?" Anna whispers.

"What?"

"We had four cars on us as we drove here, didn't you notice?"

I glance out the window to see Davidoff and three men standing on the sidewalk. "No, I didn't." I frown. "Probably Jules being overprotective again."

She smiles. "What's going on with you two?"

I stare at my loyal friend and I want to tell her everything, but my mother's words are weighing heavily on my chest.

I feel confused and lost and I just want Giuliano to come home, he's the only one who can make me feel better. I'll wait another few days before I tell Anna about us not being related.

Mom is right, there is no rush.

"Nothing new, we are just friends," I lie.

"Have you seen him since you got back?"

"No." I roll my lips to change the subject, another lie.

I'm a shitty friend.

"So...tell me about Carlo?" I say to change the subject.

"Oh, Chesk." She smiles dreamily. "He's perfect. He took me to Tuscany and we laughed and made love and...." She gives me a subtle shake of her head. "I'm falling hard for him."

I want to give her the same warning lecture that my mother gave me, but then I remember that I am in a worse off position than she is. "That's great."

"You know, we haven't spent a night apart since I came home."

I fake a smile as I listen to her.

"He's just so...and the sex, God. I have been missing out all this time," she gushes.

I giggle, I can sure relate to that one.

Her phone rings and the name Carlo flashes up on the

screen. "Speak of the devil." She answers. "Hi." She smiles sexily. "Are your ears burning?"

She giggles as she listens to him speak, I can vaguely hear him. "Oh." Her face falls. "Okay." She listens again and smiles. "I'll see what I can do."

I discreetly get my phone out of my bag and glance at it.

No missed calls.

I listen to the two of them flirt for a few minutes. "Okay, see you later then."

She giggles and I know he's said something playful and sexy. "I look forward to it, bye." She hangs up and sips her wine.

"Where is he?" I ask, secretly wanting to know where the hell Giuliano is and why the fuck hasn't he called me?

"They're at a strip club or some bullshit."

I blink, surprised. "What? He's at a strip club?"

"Yeah, that's what he said."

"That doesn't bother you?"

"No." She shrugs as she fills my wineglass. "It's obviously innocent or he wouldn't have told me."

I frown as I stare at her.

"It's when they don't tell you that you have to worry. If he was keeping secrets, I would know he's up to something."

"Who's he with?" I casually ask.

"Giuliano, Alex and Valentino. He said all his work friends, so whoever they are."

My mother's warning sets off alarm bells in my psyche.

I tip my head back and gulp my wine.

Giuliano left me at home alone on a Sunday to go to a strip club with the boys.

Wow.

And so it begins.

. . .

The clock ticks over to eleven p.m. as I stare at it, my apartment is deathly silent.

And while I lie here in bed alone, he's at a strip club. I get a vision of what it would be like, him sitting around laughing with the boys, beautiful naked women all throwing themselves at him.

It would be easier for him to walk away, to follow lust and a hot piece of ass.

Loving me is hard work.

I get a vision of him with those two women in the porno, the look on his face as he went between them. The carefree lust in his eyes and I die a little inside.

That's something I can never give him.

Maybe my mother is right, powerful men who look like him can have any woman they want. Why would he want a complicated relationship with his supposed sister when...?

My eyes well with tears and the lump in my throat begins to hurt.

I've never been insecure before, maybe I never loved anyone enough to have a fear of losing them.

What will my life be like without him?

I have to be a realist, maybe we really won't work out, perhaps this is another life lesson. Maybe his attraction to me is simply that he couldn't have me?

And now that he does....

I inhale on a shaky breath and think back to how I felt when Carlo called Anna, they've been dating for only weeks. And yet somehow, he is more dedicated to her.

I wonder do the strippers have sex with the customers...of course they do.

I angrily wipe my tears away.

Fuck this.

I feel like such a fool.

I hear the front door and I quickly wipe my eyes, I don't want to deal with him tonight while I'm feeling weak and vulnerable.

I'm not giving him that satisfaction.

The bedroom door opens and he walks in and stands over me for a moment as he watches me, the smell of cigar smoke and alcohol permeate off him.

Asshole.

My eyes stay closed tight as I pretend to be asleep, I hear the shower turn on.

Is he washing another woman off of his skin?

Surely...he wouldn't...would he?

My eyes well with tears again.

Fuck.

I can't hold it, I lose control and I begin to cry into my pillow. Hard sobs where my shoulders shake.

"Hey," he whispers as he sits down beside me, he puts his hand on the back of my head. "What's wrong, sweetheart?"

Damn it, I thought he was in the shower. I push my face harder into the pillow, now I'm ashamed of being a cry baby too.

He rolls me onto my back so he can see my face. "Francesca, what's wrong?"

I screw up my face in tears and stare at him.

"What's happened?" His face is panicked.

"Were they nice?"

"Was what nice?"

"Don't insult my intelligence, Giuliano," I cry as I fly out of bed, I need some distance between us. "Is this how it's always going to be?"

He frowns as if confused. "What the fuck are you talking about?"

"If you think I want their sloppy seconds you're wrong!" I march out of the room and down the hallway like a firecracker.

"What the fuck are you talking about?" he yells as he storms after me.

I throw my hands up in the air. "Deny it. Go on. I dare you."

He stares at me as if I've grown two heads…and maybe I have, he's never seen my temper before. Hell, I didn't even know I could be this dramatic.

"You make me fucking crazy!" I yell.

"Obviously."

Suddenly I'm embarrassed, because I know I'm carrying on like a lunatic and I can't stop myself. I screw up my face in tears and sob out loud.

"Baby…." His voice softens.

"How do you think it makes me feel, Giuliano?" I sob.

He stares at me, completely lost.

I hold my hands out wide. "Am I not enough for you?"

"What?"

"Will I ever be enough for you?"

"Francesca," he demands. "Speak English because I don't know what the fuck is going on here?"

"Do they make you hard?" I whisper.

"Huh?"

"Do you tip them? Take them upstairs? How many?"

His face falls. "You can't be serious?"

His silhouette blurs as the tears flood my eyes.

"You think I…." He gives a subtle shake of his head in disbelief. "You think I would go to a stripper instead of coming home to you."

"I don't think it, I know it. That's exactly what you did tonight, Giuliano."

"I was working."

"Working! Ha," I huff. "Stop lying," I yell. "You don't need to lie to me. I'm a big girl, I can take it."

"You have got to be fucking joking," he yells as he loses his temper. "I have loved you every fucking day since I was nineteen years old. Do you honestly fucking believe I would sleep around on you now that I finally have you?"

I screw up my face, unable to even try to act cool.

His face fills with empathy. "Chesk." He wraps his arms around me and holds me tight. "I love you, how could you even think that I would...."

"Why did you go there then?" I blurt out.

"We own the club, it's a place where I meet my men. I don't even look at the girls when I'm there."

Oh God, it gets worse, they are on his fucking payroll. I mean, somewhere in the back of my mind I always knew this but hearing it in this moment doesn't make me feel any better.

"I was waiting for you," I whisper. "And to think of you there...getting hard over them. It makes me fucking crazy. I will not live the life of my mother Giuliano. I can't do it. Let me go if you want to be like my father. Just let me go."

"I know," he says softly as he kisses me. "I will never treat you like that. You have my word. I'm sorry, I didn't even think." He kisses me again as he takes my face into his hands. "I won't go there anymore if you don't want me to."

"I don't."

"Okay." His lips take mine and I can taste my salty tears.

He holds me in his arms for a long time and I don't know what the hell I'm even thinking right now.

Only that he makes it better.

"I love you, Chesk, you're everything to me. How could you even think such a thing? Do you really think I would risk what we have...for sleazy sex?" he says softly. "You know what we have." He kisses my temple. "How could you even think? Look at your eyes, how long have you been crying?"

I screw up my face against his, I feel like I've just had a full-on mental breakdown or something. "I was freaking out," I sob.

"Sweetheart," he whispers as he tries to calm me. "It's okay, I'm home now."

I put my head into the crook of his neck and he holds me tight, we stay in each other's arms for a long time, I feel my heartbeat begin to slow back down. "Come on, baby. Shower."

He takes my hand and leads me back to the bedroom; the shower is still running and the bedroom is now filled with steam. He lifts my nightgown over my head and I stand before him, naked. His thumb dusts over my nipple as he stares down at me, his eyes roaming over my skin. "I missed my girl today," he murmurs.

I stare up at him, and suddenly I'm desperate to be closer. It's as if my fragile heart can only be eased with sex.

I need this, I need him.

My lips take his as our kiss deepens.

I undo the buttons on his shirt and take it off over his shoulders, then I slide down his zipper and take his pants off.

He stares at me with his big brown eyes, so honest and empathetic, filled with love.

"I can't stand the thought of...."

He cuts me off with a kiss. "It's not going to happen." He wraps my hand around his thick erection and strokes himself. "I'm yours." He kisses me. "Only yours." His grip around my hand tightens and I know he needs it hard tonight. I can feel the need oozing out of him, I smile softly against his lips. "I've only ever been yours, Chesk," he whispers. "It's always been you."

Oh...*my heart.*

Our kiss turns desperate and we fall into the shower, naked and overwrought with emotion.

Close to the edge of insanity. Everything about us is fucked up.

He pins me to the wall and lifts my legs around his body, with our lips locked he slides deep inside my body.

The air crackles between us, my body rippling around his.

The feeling between us is so magical.

"I love you," I whisper.

"I love you." He kisses me. "So much that I need you to do something for me."

"Anything," I murmur.

His eyes search mine. "Marry me."

19

Francesca

WHAT?

Did I just hear that right?

I stare at him, shocked to my core.

"I mean...this isn't how I...I know we haven't been together long and I.... Fuck. World's worst proposal." He's tripping over his words. "I fucked it, I was supposed to wait. I told myself I had to wait."

He's actually thought about this?

I love that it just came out without a heap of grand planning.

It came from his heart.

I smile down at my beautiful man, his body deep inside mine. "Yes."

"Yes what?"

"Yes, I'll marry you."

He squeezes me tight and we hold each other and those

damn tears are back. Streaming down my face, because I know this wasn't planned but somehow, it's perfect.

"I need you," I whisper. "Love me like you mean it."

He smiles darkly against me and without another word lifts me and brings me back down on him hard.

Oh God.

With my body pinned to the wall, my legs lifted up over his arms, he lets me have him.

All of it, every last inch. Thick, strong and at piston pace.

The burn is so fucking good and I cling to his shoulders as we stare at each other.

Our bodies feeding off each other as they scream toward climax. I bear down on him, clenching as hard as I can and I cry out as an orgasm tears me to shreds.

One, two, three thick pumps and he holds himself deep and tips his head back and groans loud.

Deep and guttural…the hottest sound on earth.

I feel the telling jerk as his cock empties itself deep within my body.

Hearts racing, chests gasping for air, we stare at each other as a sense of home swims between us.

"My wife," he whispers in awe.

I smile goofily down at him. "And I don't even have to change my last name."

He smirks, then smiles and then tips his head back and laughs out loud.

And, so do I, it's cathartic.

Insanity in its purest form.

The sound of Giuliano's gentle breathing is rhythmic.

In…out. In…out. In…out.

I lie on my side, starstruck by the god who sleeps next to me.

He's on his back, the white sheet pooling around his groin, one hand is on his dick and the other behind his head. His golden skin, showcasing the perfect muscles beneath.

Rippled and cut.

My eyes roam lower over the chiseled abs and the thick quad muscle on his leg as it hangs out of the sheet, up over his chest to the black hair sprinkled across it.

Giuliano Ferrara is a beautiful-looking man.

Virile, masculine and strong.

But it's his heart that I love, his big beautiful heart. And it belongs to me.

I always said that marriage wouldn't change me, that I would feel exactly the same.

But weirdly, it already has.

I've been engaged for all of eight hours and the feeling of closeness and trust that it has brought me is a new kind of high.

The best kind.

We made love for most of the night, soft and hard. Hard and soft.

And somehow, we hit a new level of intimacy. Which I really don't know how it's possible, because we've always been perfect together. But this...this, is something else, something higher than the both of us.

Fate.

Giuliano Ferrara was always going to be my one true love.

And he is.

He stirs and his eyes flutter open, I watch as he gets his bearings and looks around.

"Hi," I whisper.

A slow sexy smile crosses his face and he puts his hand under my pillow and drags me closer to him. "What a night."

I smile as he wraps his big arms around me.

"Did I dream it?"

"You mean, did you ask me to marry you and did I accept?" He smiles with a frown. "Yeah, that bit."

"Uh-huh." I run my fingers through his dark stubble. "There's no getting out of it now, I've locked it in. It's a date."

He chuckles and pulls me over his body and I snuggle into his chest. "I don't want to get out of it. But I wish...." He cuts himself off.

I look up at him. "You wish what?"

"I wish I did it...better.

I lean up onto my elbow. "Did what better?"

"I had this big romantic proposal planned and I...." He shrugs as if embarrassed. "Lost my head and fucked it."

Oh....

"It *was* perfect, Jules," I whisper.

He scratches his head, as if pissed with himself. "I didn't even have a fucking ring, next time it will be better. I promise." He rolls over on top of me and holds my hands above my head, he pushes his knees between my legs to spread them.

"We need to celebrate." He smiles down at me.

"What are we celebrating?"

"A lifetime of loving you."

And there is it...the reason I love this man.

How could I not?

He's the sun, the moon and the stars in the sky.

My everything.

The rain pours down as Giuliano turns the corner.

"I feel like we are so low to the ground in this car that we are almost in the puddles," I say as I watch the road.

"It's a Lamborghini." He glances over. "That's the point."

I roll my eyes. "What is it about you and this car?"

He revs it hard and she purrs loudly, he smirks and reaches over and squeezes my thigh. "Are you jealous?"

"Ha," I scoff. "Of this car?" I cross my arms, "Absolutely not."

I am a little bit but I know it's completely irrational.

"Don't worry, I like driving you better." He gives me a sexy wink.

"Oh." I widen my eyes. "I'm flattered."

The news comes onto the radio

IN BREAKING NEWS, THE CHIEF OF POLICE HAS BEEN MURDERED. HE WAS GUNNED DOWN IN A CROWDED MARKETPLACE IN WHAT IS BEING DESCRIBED AS AN ORGANISED CRIME HIT.

Giuliano hits the button and turns off the radio.

I glance over at him, that was weird. "Did you know him?"

"Yep." He turns the corner. "Three kids, two boys and a girl. All under ten. A beautiful wife. It's a tragedy."

I frown as I watch him. "You knew him well?"

He nods once, his eyes stay fixed on the road.

"Who did it?" I ask.

"Me."

"What?" I gasp, wide eyed. "You shot the chief of police?"

"No. I didn't. It's my fault he's dead, though."

"Why?"

"He had information that I needed, someone shot him before he could tell me."

"What information?"

"We have a mole working for Ferrara."

"What do you mean?"

"Our yacht with our drugs was stolen last week, it was an inside job."

I frown in horror. "Who is it?"

"He was about to tell me yesterday and then...." His voice trails off.

"You were with him yesterday?" I frown.

"He died in my arms."

"What?" I gasp. "You were with him when he was shot?"

He bites his bottom lip as he casually drives, as if he has this conversation every day.

"And you didn't think to tell me this?" I splutter.

"I was...." He shrugs. "It doesn't matter."

I stare at him, shocked to my core. His life is so different to mine that sometimes I wonder if I really know him at all. Actually, I don't wonder, I know that I don't.

But I don't want to know the other side because it scares the hell out of me.

"I spent the day in the police station answering questions and didn't get out until about nine last night, I went to see my colleagues at the club to debrief them on the way home."

My heart drops. "At the club?"

He nods.

"And you came home to my dramatics about strippers?" I put my head into my hands, feeling like the biggest asshole on earth. "Oh God, Giuliano, why didn't you tell me?"

He shrugs.

I stare at him, mortified. "And you proposed to me after the day you had?"

"I proposed to you *because* of the day that I had."

"What do you mean?"

"Life is short. Every moment counts."

I stare at him as fear swirls around me. "Don't say that. Not your life."

He keeps driving but remains silent.

"Are you in danger?"

"No," he snaps way too quickly.

I think for a moment. "Is this why there are extra guards everywhere?"

"Yes." He reaches over and grabs my thigh once more. "You're safe, babe, don't worry."

"What about you?"

"I'm a big boy, I can look after myself."

This news is a nightmare. "You can't die, Giuliano. I couldn't bear it, promise me you won't take any risks."

He smiles over at me. "What do you want for dinner?"

"Don't change the subject." I glance behind us to see three cars following us and for once I'm glad they are there.

"I've got this," he replies as he pulls into a parking lot. "Leave it."

"But...."

"End of conversation," he snaps angrily and I know the subject is now out of bounds. He probably regrets even telling me.

I stare at him as my mind races a million miles per minute.

"What do you want for dinner?"

I exhale heavily as I take off my seat belt. "Whatever."

I'm not even hungry now.

I sit on the bathroom counter and watch as Giuliano does up his tie, my eyes roam up and down my fine specimen of a man. He's wearing a perfectly fitted charcoal suit and crisp white shirt, trendy dress shoes and a chunky silver Rolex watch. His dark hair is thick and shiny and his square jaw could cut glass.

So fucking hot.

I smile goofily up at him.

He concentrates on his task of tying his tie and gives me the side eye. "What?"

"Just admiring your masculinity."

He smirks and keeps tying. "Yeah well, tonight my masculinity will dominate your femininity."

"How does that go?"

He grabs the back of my neck and drags me to him, he kisses me with just the right amount of suction, his tongue swipes through my lips and I feel it all the way to my bones.

Oh....

"Tonight," he whispers darkly.

Oh crap. "We have dinner tonight with Carlo and Anna, I just remembered."

He winces and pulls out of my grip and walks into the bedroom. "Cancel it."

I jump off the counter and follow him. "Why?"

"Why?" he scoffs. "I wonder?" He puts his suit jacket on and does up his gold cuff links. "I love going out with friends and pretending that I'm not dating my future wife while watching two people who met fucking yesterday fawn all over each other." He fakes a smile. "It's my perfect night."

"Stop going on about that." I straighten his tie. "I'm having lunch with my mother on Thursday and we're coming up with a timeline."

"Timeline?" He repeats dryly.

"Yes, now that she's got used to the idea of us together, we can make a map forward."

"Why does *our* map depend on her?"

"You said we could wait to tell everyone until it was sorted with my family." My shoulders slump. "I don't want to feel guilty about this until I've at least tried. Please, for me?"

He rolls his eyes. "Your family are fucking annoying, Francesca."

"I know." I go up onto my tiptoes and kiss him softly.

"And if your mother doesn't give me an acceptable..." he holds his fingers up to air quote the words, "—road map—"

I smirk.

"I'm running right through her stop sign with a big fucking Mack truck."

"Okay," I agree.

"Okay?" He seems surprised.

"Uh-huh," I nod. "Thursday I will have a definite date that we can come out of hiding."

He grabs me roughly on my behind and nips my bottom lip with his teeth. "That's if you make it through tonight."

Anna and I walk into the restaurant just on seven to see Giuliano and Carlo already seated at the table, they got held up at work so have met us here.

I'm wearing a fitted hot-pink dress that hangs off the shoulders with nude sky-high stilettos and clutch. My long dark hair is out and full and I have sultry makeup on with hot-pink lipstick.

"Hello, we have a booking in the name of Smithson," I say to the waiter.

"Yes, this way." He turns and walks through the restaurant and we follow, music is being piped through the space and the crowd is trendy and eclectic. The restaurant is huge with a few split levels, the bar is on the top floor, seven steps down is the main restaurant and kitchen and down another seven stairs is the bar area with high tables and stools.

I can see Giuliano and Carlo seated at a table in the back on the middle level and smile broadly.

I missed him today.

As we get closer Giuliano's eyes drop down to my feet and then back up to my face, he gives me the best come-fuck-me look I have ever seen.

He likes this dress.

An excited thrill runs through me, getting that look from him is the ultimate.

"Hi." I smile as we get to the table.

"Hello," he replies calmly.

Anna bends and kisses Carlo. "Hey there, you."

"Look at you being all hot." Carlo smiles as he holds her hand out to inspect her closer.

Giuliano's dark eyes hold mine and a trace of a smile crosses his face and now I see what he means. Having these two being able to show affection so freely *is* fucking annoying.

"Thanks for coming out with us." Anna smiles to Giuliano as she pushes in her chair. "I know this can't be easy for you two to hang out together as friends given your history. Carlo and I appreciate it, don't we, baby?"

Giuliano stares at her.

"That's okay," I blurt out before he can reply. "We're friends, aren't we Jules. Happy to hang out with our best friends."

He raises an eyebrow and sips his drink, choosing to remain silent.

He can't lie.

I never realized this before, I smile as I pick up my wine and sip it. Another vital piece of information for the intel bank.

"Who's hungry?" Carlo asks.

Giuliano's dark eyes hold mine. "Fucking starving."

I roll my lips to hide my smile as I fake-stare at the open menu.

He doesn't mean for food.

"What's everyone having?" I ask to change the subject.

"I'm feeling carnivorous." Giuliano says casually as he looks over the menu.

"Carnivorous?" Anna frowns.

"I feel like meat," he replies dryly, still reading. "All the meat."

I giggle, surprised. What the hell?

Shut up, fool.

They'll catch on to us, he is the worst fake non-boyfriend in the world. "Meat?" I reply. "Who goes to a restaurant simply for meat?"

"I do."

I widen my eyes as I pretend to read the menu, okay then.

Guess I'm getting it hard when we get home tonight.

Bring it on, baby.

"I'd like to propose a toast," Carlo says as he holds his drink up. We all hold our glasses to his.

"To friendship," he says.

I smile, I love that Anna is with him. Once Jules and I get our situation sorted the four of us are going to have so much fun together. "To friendship."

The meal was delicious and the laughter on tap.

We've had the best night and drunk way too many bottles of wine.

Giuliano's eyes have been undressing me all night. Every time he licks his lips and I catch sight of his tongue, I feel it between my legs. He's a bad man with bad things on his mind. My things.

Anna and Carlo are deep in conversation mode and hardly notice that we are here.

Giuliano's eyes hold mine and he taps his phone as it sits on the table.

Huh? I frown.

He taps it again and widens his eyes.

Oh....

I take my phone out of my purse and put it on my lap. It beeps a text.

Go the bathroom
Don't lock the door.

My eyes flick up and he raises an eyebrow.

What?

He picks up his phone as he answers a call. "Hey." He pulls his phone down from his ear. "I've got to take this, it's an important call. Back in a moment." He disappears downstairs to the bar area.

I watch him move out of sight and my eyes flick over to Anna and Carlo, they are flirting away, completely distracted.

What...now?

Does he want me to go to the bathroom now...but he's on the phone?

Umm, I think for a moment. Oh, screw it, why not?

"I'm going to the bathroom," I say as I push my chair out.

"Okay," Anna replies, her eyes are fixed on her date.

I walk down the long corridor and I look left and then right and slink into the bathroom. I automatically go to lock the door and then I stop myself and unlock it.

I turn to the mirror and fluff up my hair, I have no idea why I can't lock the....

The door opens, interrupting my thoughts, and Giuliano walks in and flicks the lock.

My heart races at his close proximity. "Hi."

He grabs my face and licks my open lips. "Sai cosa succede alle ragazze cattive che si prendono gioco me durante la cena," (Translation: You know what happens to bad girls who prick tease me during dinner.) he whispers darkly. He licks my open lips again and my insides flutter. "What?" I breathe.

His grip on my face is near painful. "Sono punite." (Translation: They get punished.) He bites my bottom lip and I wince at his domination as a wave of arousal floods me below.

Oh...this man.

He turns me away from him aggressively so that I face the mirror, my back to his front and his lips go to my neck, his eyes close as he licks me there, he's totally lost in the moment and I can feel his huge erection as it digs into my back.

I watch us in the mirror, having a man like him want me with such a passion is out of this world.

With his lips seductively sucking on my neck, his eyes locked on mine, he slides my dress up over my hips. His lips drop to the clavicle in my neck and his fingers pull my G-string panties to the side, his fingers slide through the lips of my sex. "Come sta la mia dolce fica?" (Translation: How's my sweet pussy?) His eyes flicker with arousal as he feels me, his fingers slide through my arousal. "Fradicia." (Translation: Dripping wet.) He bites me hard and goose bumps scatter all over.

I can hear people walking up and down the corridor just outside. Oh my God, is someone waiting to use this bathroom?

This is wrong.

My heart is hammering as I watch him, waiting for his next move.

He grabs the back of my neck and pushes my head down, presenting my ass just for him.

I hear his suit pants zipper go down and then I feel the tip of his cock nudge my opening as he pulls my panties to the side.

I feel a sharp snap and then I see my torn panties fall to the floor.

Oh hell.

Guess they were in his way.

He puts his two hands on my shoulders for leverage and without warning, slides deeply into my body. He lets out a deep guttural moan.

"Fuck yeah," he hisses.

My mouth falls open at his ownership...oh...the stretch. No matter how many times we have sex, I'll never get used to his size. Not that I'm complaining.

Then he's riding me hard, so hard. His hands on my shoulders slamming my body back onto his with such force I can hardly catch my breath.

His soft moans are driving me wild and the handle on the door sounds as someone tries to come in.

He keeps pumping me, no fucks to give about anyone else.

The sound of our skin slapping hard echoes around us off the tiles, magnifying everything. But there's no stopping him, he's focused on feeding his body what it needs.

"Torna dopo," (Translation: Come back later.) he growls without missing a beat, he lifts one of my legs and I shudder hard.

He gives a satisfied smile and tips his head back. "Questa fica e cosi deliziosa cazzo," (Translation: This pussy is so fucking good.) he growls. "Wet and tight, just how I fucking want it."

Hearing his filthy words send me spiraling hard and I grip the sink to hold myself up and he slaps me hard on the behind as he rides me. "Fuck me," he whispers. "Harder." He really lets me have it.

The door handle sounds again.

"Fuck off!" he yells.

Oh, Christ on a cracker...this is so messed up.

This is not what nice girls do...especially with their life partners.

He slams in and holds himself deep, his body jerks aggressively deep inside mine and I see stars and whimper as I come.

My legs are jelly. My lungs have no air. I'm grappling for control of my body functions.

Hell....

He pulls out and zips up his pants. "Hurry up and get back to the table." He leaves without another word and I pant as I stare at the door he just disappeared through.

Oh my God, what the fuck was that?

I quickly flick the lock and stare at my disheveled reflection. I'm flushed, gasping for air, my hair is all over the place, I have bite marks on my neck.

But it's the glow that I can see. An all-consuming, well-fucked glow, I smile at my reflection.

Just fucked looks good on me.

I clean myself up and get myself together and straighten my dress as I try to calm myself down and then I open the door and walk back to the table casually.

I sit down and a trace of a smile crosses Giuliano's face.

Dirty bastard.

"What took you so long?" Anna scoffs.

"Oh." I look around guiltily. "There was a long line."

Anna looks through the menu. "Who's having dessert?" she asks.

I pretend to read the menu. "I'm full," I reply, still completely disheveled.

"You got that right," Giuliano murmurs under his breath.

Full of come.

I smirk into my menu, that's my fiancé.

The pussy punisher.

Giuliano

"Can I get you anything else to drink?" the waitress asks.

"Yes." Lorenzo swallows his food. "We'll have two more Blue Label scotches, please."

"Yes, sir." She disappears out the back and we both continue to eat in silence.

Lorenzo and I have snuck away from the office for lunch, it's rare that we are alone where we can talk privately.

"You still fighting with Bianca?" I ask.

He pushes his pasta around on his plate with his fork. "I don't know. She's saying one thing; all evidence points to another."

"And it's bothering you?"

"How could it not?"

I chew my food as I stare at him, it's obvious he's upset. "You know, it was twenty-eight years ago…maybe you should just let it go."

"I know. I keep telling myself to drop it."

I nod as I look across the crowded restaurant.

"How are you and Francesca going?"

"She's incredible." I beam proudly, to think that she's going to be my wife. I can't wait until we can tell people. I'm going to shout it from the fucking rooftops.

My dream girl, Francesca Ferrara, is going to marry me.

Un fucking believable.

A broad smile crosses his face as he watches me. "That she is."

"Giuliano." A deep voice sounds from behind me, we both turn to see Lombardi standing over us.

The sound of our cutlery hitting the plates echoes around us as we both reach inside our suit jackets for our guns.

"Relax." He holds his hands up. "I come in peace." He sits down at the table.

"What do you want?" I snap.

"We need to talk."

I glare at him. "Where's my yacht?"

His eyes flick to Lorenzo. "I need to speak to Giuliano alone."

"I'm not going anywhere," Lorenzo growls.

Lombardi smiles, clearly amused. "Then you won't hear what I have to say." He goes to stand and I hold my hand up, I want to hear what he has to say. "Leave us," I say to Lorenzo.

"I don't...."

"Now." I cut him off.

Lorenzo stands and walks over to the wall, his eyes not leaving us for a second, his hand on his gun inside his jacket.

Lombardi and I glare at each other, I hate this man with every fiber of my being.

He killed my father...and my grandfather. Enrico.

"We've never met in person," he says calmly, his voice deep, husky.

"Cut the shit. What the fuck do you want?"

He leans his elbow on the table and steeples his finger up along his temple as he stares at me. "I'm dying, Giuliano."

I frown, that's the last thing I was expecting him to say.

"Inoperable cancer, I don't have long to live."

"Good." I smile. "I hope it's slow and painful."

"How much do you know about me?" he asks.

"I don't care about you, tell me where my fucking yacht is?" I growl. "You have five minutes before I shoot you dead."

"I was your mother's bodyguard."

What?

"It was me who looked after her when her husband went back to his wife."

Our eyes are locked.

He smiles darkly. "In more ways than one."

I begin to hear my heartbeat in my ears.

"It's time to come home, son."

"What the fuck does that mean?"

"I'm your father."

20

Giuliano

"Liar."

"Am I?" he replies calmly. "Are you positive of that?"

I glare at him as animosity begins to pump through my veins.

He slides an envelope across the table to me. "My DNA profile is at this lab. If you don't believe me, believe science. This will give you the proof that you need."

I stare at the envelope in front of me, he has proof.

What the fuck?

"I only have weeks to live, I need you to take over the Lombardi operations. You are the only person capable of running the company at the level I do. To take us into the next generation."

"Go to hell," I sneer. "I wouldn't touch your infected company if my life depended on it."

"Perhaps it does." He smiles as if predicting my reaction.

"You would prefer to run a company that doesn't belong to you? You are not a Ferrara; you will never be a Ferrara. And one day, they will find out and you will be outed as a traitor, a Lombardi to the bone. And where will you be then? Do you think they will stand by you? He didn't even give you his last name until after he died, he was ashamed of you. Tell me, Giuliano, will they reward all of your hard work? We both know the answer to that, don't we?"

The sky turns red.

"I'm going to kill you," I whisper.

"This is what I respect. I tell you that you're not a Ferrara and yet all you can think about is killing me." He smirks. "I like that in you...you think like me."

I pick up the steak knife from the table and I hold it in my hand.

"What are you going to do?" He gestures around the room. "Stab me to death in a crowded restaurant for all to see? You don't have the police commissioner's protection anymore, Giuliano. Remember?"

"You took care of that," I reply.

"Nicolai was getting in my way." He shrugs. "I did what had to be done."

Something sinister snaps inside of me.

I pick up my knife and drive it through the back of his hand as it rests, pinning it to the table.

He winces as I twist the knife farther through his flesh.

"And I will do what has to be done." I sneer as I glare at him, relishing his pain. "I will kill you and it *will* hurt."

"Don't be a fool, Giuliano," he whispers in pain. "Listen to me."

I twist the knife again, pressing my point. "Stay the fuck away from me." I stand, grab the envelope and without looking back I leave the restaurant in a rush. I storm through the front door and up the street to my Lamborghini, I dive in and pull out onto the street in a rush. My men scramble as they run to their cars behind me to catch up.

I grip my steering wheel with white-knuckle force as I floor it.

My world...spinning on its axis.

No.

I pull into my underground parking lot and take the elevator up to my floor. I couldn't be at work, and I don't want to...I can't even be with Francesca.

I need to be alone.

The elevator stops at my floor and I walk into my apartment, I haven't stepped foot inside here since Francesca and I moved my things out two weeks ago.

With a shaky hand I pour myself a glass of scotch and drain it, I refill it so fast that it sloshes over the sides and I drain it again.

It burns all the way down, a happy distraction from the way my heart is hurting.

My mother slept with him.

Another man.

Lombardi.

When all this time I resented him, had my father as the villain...*he's not even my father.*

I screw up my face in tears and I fill my glass again and I drain it down.

My entire life is a lie, brought up as Linden, told I was a Ferrara and now...my stomach twists at the reality of how fucked-up this situation really is.

I get a vision of my mother and father kissing, so besotted with each other.

She declared her undying love. *She slept with someone else.*

My stomach rolls with nausea.

Who am I?

I don't even know who.

I run my two hands through my hair and as the perspiration beads on my forehead, I begin to pace.

Francesca

My procession of cars pulls into the underground parking lot just on six p.m., I just did a spin class with Anna.

I see Giuliano's black Lamborghini parked in his parking bay and I get a little thrill.

Coming home to him will never get old.

I take the elevator to the top floor and open the door to silence. "Babe?" I call.

Where is he?

I walk through the apartment. "Jules," I call. "Where are you?" I keep looking around and go out onto the terrace. "Jules?"

Hmm, that's weird.

Maybe he didn't take his car today? I can't remember if it was there when I left this morning. I call Davidoff.

"Hello, Miss Ferrara."

"Is Giuliano at home?" I ask as I try to sound casual.

"Yes, I believe so. He arrived home around lunchtime."

"Oh." He must be down in his apartment. "Thank you, I'll call him." I hang up.

I've been home all afternoon and haven't seen him.

Weird.

I get into the elevator and go down to his floor, the door to his apartment isn't locked and the hairs on the back of my neck stand to attention.

Fuck.

What's going on?

I slowly push it open and walk in, the apartment is in shadows as night creeps in.

"Jules," I call into the silence.

I catch sight of his foot, he's sitting on the floor up against the wall in the darkness.

His haunted eyes meet mine, and my heart drops.

"What's wrong?" I rush to him and I drop to the floor beside him.

He stares at me, devastation written all over his face. "One of us is a Ferrara and one of us isn't." He smells of scotch and cigars.

I frown, huh?

"But it's not the way we thought."

"What do you mean?"

"I'm not the Ferrara," he whispers sadly.

"What?"

He holds up a crinkled envelope.

I snatch it off him and tear it open, it's DNA analysis. "I don't understand."

"I thought she loved him," he whispers.

Oh....

I take him into my arms and hold him tight, he screws up his face into my neck as emotion overwhelms him.

"It's okay, sweetheart. It will be okay." I try to calm him. "It changes nothing."

"Don't you see, Francesca," he murmurs. "It changes everything."

Giuliano

"Can I get you something, baby?" Francesca asks me.

"No."

She's been hovering and fussing around me, trying to make me feel better.

If only she could.

The destructive thoughts are so noisy in my head that I just want to escape to somewhere. But where would I go?

The truth would follow.

The doorbell sounds.

"Who's that?" Francesca asks.

"I'm not home," I sigh.

"It's probably Anna, I'll get rid of her." She answers the door. "Mom," she gasps.

Fuck.

"Hello, darling."

I pinch the bridge of my nose, I can't deal with her now.

"Now is not a good time," I hear Francesca tell her.

"I'm not here to see you, I'm here to see Giuliano."

"No, Mom."

"Don't be ridiculous."

"I said not now," Francesca calls but it's obvious Bianca has barged past her.

Bianca comes into view as she stands at the door. "Hello, Giuliano," she says softly.

I get a lump in my throat, she's here to gloat.

My haunted eyes hold hers, everything she ever thought of me...is true.

"Francesca, leave us alone, please," she says.

"No. Now is not the time and you are not upsetting him further. Do you hear me!"

"I need to speak to Giuliano...alone."

"No." Francesca begins to get irate. "I want you to leave. Now!"

May as well get this over with.

"It's okay," I reply, I don't want her to have to hear this conversation. The last thing I want is her upset even more. "It's fine, Chesk. Go for a walk."

She frowns.

"It's okay, go." I give her a soft smile and she walks over and kisses my forehead. "I'll be back in ten minutes," she warns her mother, I hear the front door click as she leaves through it.

Bianca stays standing by the door and I stay seated on the couch.

Silence hangs between us.

She walks into the room and sits down on the ottoman opposite me.

I can't even look at her.

"I'm here on your mother's behalf."

I roll my lips as my vision clouds. I've never been more disappointed in another human being than I am with my mother.

"Giuliano," she says softly. "Look at me."

I drag my eyes to meet hers and she does the most unexpected thing, taking my two hands in hers. "Darling, I know this is hard for you to comprehend."

I stare at her, distant from the conversation but at the same time my heart tearing right open.

Empathy from this woman is the last thing I ever wanted.

"You mother, Giuliano. She had a hard time, she was desperately in love with a married man."

The lump in my throat threatens to block my breathing.

"Your father.... Despite what you've been told, and what you always believed, loved his wife. And it *is* true that if he had a choice, he would have married your mother instead of me. She was his one true love, his soul mate. He told me that hurtful knowledge many times over the years."

She squeezes my hands in hers.

"But your father wouldn't end his marriage and sometimes he and your mother would fight about it...for weeks at a time."

I roll my lips.

"You must understand, Giuliano, she was left in that big old house alone, for weeks at a time. No family, minimal friends. Her guards were the only people she could trust."

"You're defending her?" I spit.

"I understand her...better than anyone, I understand her." She smiles sadly. "I lived your mother's life from a different angle. And she is not the only Ferrara woman who got too close to her bodyguard. We both loved him, we both missed him when he was with the other, we all suffered. Your father...too."

"He's not my father," I reply flatly.

She squeezes my hands in hers, bringing my attention back to her face.

"Yes. He is. He loved you so, so much, Giuliano. You were the child he desperately wanted. He was so proud of you and you gave him so much happiness."

My eyes well with tears and I know what I must do. "I'll pass everything at work on to Andrea, Lorenzo can help him."

"You will do no such thing," she snaps.

I frown.

"You were born to lead Ferrara, Giuliano. This was your

calling. You are brave and loyal, intelligent and you have a harder edge that your father never had. From what I hear, our best leader yet." She smiles softly. "Perhaps you got that from your biological father." She pushes the hair back from my forehead as she stares up at me. "Tomorrow, I will announce to the world that Francesca is Lorenzo's daughter. The two of you have my blessing to marry. Nobody will ever know your true paternity. I will take it to my grave."

What?

"Why would you do that?" I whisper.

"For your father...and your mother. And all that I stole from them." Her eyes search mine. "This is what they would want. This is what is right. I'm not a fool, Giuliano. I have my own selfish reasons, I know that my own sons will get themselves killed within a week if they take over. I'm protecting them, if you do this...you will be protecting us all, including Francesca. We are all safe as long as you're in charge. The minute you step down the Ferrara empire will fall to our enemies. Your father, your mother and I, have not sacrificed our lives for nothing."

Her silhouette blurs.

"I will accept you into my family with open arms and love you like my own son, but I have one condition," she says.

"What's that?"

"If you break my daughter's heart, know that I *will* kill you."

She's serious.

I frown and for the first time I see her for who she really is. The backbone.

He *did* love her.

"Her heart is safe," I whisper. "I love her more than life itself."

She smiles. "Then we have a deal?"

I stare at her, shocked to my core. "You want me to pretend that I'm a Ferrara?"

"No pretending." She cups my face in her hand. "You *are* a Ferrara in every way that matters, make us proud."

21

Francesca

I STAND OUTSIDE the front door of my apartment.

Fuck.

I shouldn't have told her what happened, but in my defense, I needed to talk to someone and I couldn't tell anyone else. I had no idea that she was going to come rushing over here. This is the last thing my poor Giuliano needs, a drilling from my mother.

With my heartbeat hammering hard and fast, I begin to pace in the hallway.

What's happening in there?

What does she want to say to him that she doesn't want me to hear?

Does she know something?

Maybe she does...but what?

I put my ear to the door to see if I can hear them.

Silence.

At least there's no screaming, I guess.

I begin to pace again and then rush back and put my ear to the door again.

What if they have a huge fight and irreversible damage between them is done? Up until now, both of them have remained relatively civil to each other for my sake.

I listen again...silence.

Fucking hell, what do I do?

Oh, screw this, I'm going back in. I put my code into the keypad and the door releases. I quietly sneak in.

I can hear my mother's voice, she's talking softly, but what's she saying? I stand still on the spot to try to listen but I can't quite make out the conversation.

The voices are hushed.

I tiptoe up the hall farther toward them and stop still again.

"I will accept you into my family with open arms and love you like my own son, but I have one condition," she says.

"What's that?" he replies.

"If you break my daughter's heart, know that I *will* kill you."

What the hell? Mom, you're a fucking psycho.

"Her heart is safe," Giuliano replies. "I love her more than life itself."

My eyes well. *And I love you, baby.*

"You want me to pretend that I'm a Ferrara?" Giuliano replies.

What? I frown, wait...did I hear that right?

Okay, what the actual hell is going on here?

"No pretending. You *are* a Ferrara in every way that matters, make us proud."

My eyes widen as I try to make out what this means.

With my heart in my throat, I listen for his reply.

"No."

I put my hands over my mouth, oh no.

"I am who I am. I'm not spending my life pretending to be someone that I'm not. Give me a fucking break, Bianca."

My heart swells, of course he would say that. He's too honorable to lie.

"What are you doing here?" he asks her.

"What do you mean?"

"You hate me," he snaps and I can hear an edge of anger to his voice that wasn't there before.

"I don't hate you, Giuliano."

"Why would you want me to stay at the helm if I'm not a Ferrara? This doesn't make sense; this whole fucking scenario is off," he snaps. "The more I think about it, the more fucked up this is. Did you put Lombardi up to this?"

"What?" She gasps. "Don't be ridiculous."

"Something is off here," he yells. "It doesn't add up."

"I know and I agree, there *is* something off here. I don't trust Lombardi for a second," she snaps back and I know her temper is being tested too. "But what if you *are* his son, Giuliano? What then? Where the hell do we go from there?"

"I'm not," he snaps.

"You might be."

"I know my mother," he says softly. "And I know how much she loved him. She wouldn't have done this. There is no way, it goes against everything I knew about her."

"But what if she did?" she demands. "Are you really going to turn your back on the family who raised you?"

"You didn't raise me," he scoffs. "You fucking hated me."

"I never hated you, I hated what you represented, which was my husband's love for another woman."

My heart sinks...poor Mom, I hate that she went through that marriage.

"Look, I'm sorry that my father was an adultering fucking prick. But that doesn't change where we are now."

"Do not speak badly of him," she snaps. "I will not have him disrespected in such a manner. He would be rolling in his grave right now at the language you are using to me."

"I'll say what I fucking like," he growls in response. "And fuck him, it's all his fault I'm in this fucking mess.

I smile to myself as I listen.

"To be completely honest," my mother sighs, "I don't think you are Lombardi's son, you are too much like your father and Enrico. But we *have* to have a backup plan," she says.

"Why?"

"Because I cannot have my daughter be with the head of Lombardi Industries. He murdered her brother, her father and grandfather. I will not stand by and let you defect to his side. She would follow you to hell and back."

"I'm not fucking defecting, are you listening to me at all, Bianca," he barks. "I hate him more than you do, but spending my entire life living a lie, pretending to be someone I'm not and looking over my shoulder, is not an option for me."

"Do not be a fool and let pride cloud your judgement on this," she says, her voice rising. "In the event that you are a Lombardi, we keep it quiet. What does it matter if you are a Ferrara by blood or by marriage? Either way, if you marry Francesca you *will* be a Ferrara in the eyes of the law. You keep running the business as you are. Nobody will ever know. You do not tell a soul about your meeting with Lombardi, do you hear me?"

I close my eyes as hope blooms in my chest. *Take the offer, baby.*

Silence.

I listen and I know he's thinking about it.

More silence.

What's happening out there?

"And how will we ever know?" Giuliano says. "Do you really think I'm going to trust a piece of fucking paper about Lombardi's DNA?"

"I agree."

"I can't ask him to meet me at a lab because it will probably be a trap. Who knows what that piece of shit is planning?" he says.

"Agreed."

More silence.

"Hello, Matteo." I hear my mother's voice. I frown, what's she doing? She's calling my brother?

"I need you and Andrea to come home today," she says before listening for a moment. "Your brother needs you." She listens again. "Giuliano. Yes, you heard me right. Come home now." She hangs up. "We will do a DNA test for the four of you together and know the truth once and for all."

Shit.

I tiptoe back up the hall and open the front door and close it loudly, then I walk out into the living room as if I've just arrived back.

Giuliano is staring out the window, his back to us, deep in thought.

"What's going on?" I ask.

"Your mother was just leaving," Giuliano says as he turns back toward us.

"No. I'm not." My mother smiles calmly, "Make me a cup of coffee, darling, we haven't had our visit yet."

Giuliano rolls his eyes and I smile and hug my mother. "I love you," I whisper as I hold her tight.

"I love you too, darling," she whispers back.

She's trying to fix this...and maybe, just maybe.
She can.

Giuliano turns the hot water tap off and slides back in under the hot water, the deep bath sloshes over the side.

The bathroom is hot and steamy and Giuliano and I are lying top and tail in a deep bubble-filled bath. His legs are spread cradling my body and my legs are tucked under his arms.

We've been in here for over an hour, we lie until the water cools, let some water out and then refill it with hot once more.

Giuliano seems more relaxed since my mother's visit this afternoon, it's as if his mind has switched over from despair to something more positive.

Although, I'm not quite sure exactly what that is.

I've stayed silent, pretending that I don't know what my mother has offered him.

He'll tell me when he's ready.

I hope.

Giuliano's large hands slide up and down my legs as he lies deep in thought. Up on the insides of my thighs and I get tingles every time his fingers nearly skim the lips of my sex.

Nearly.

Then he runs them down on the outsides and repeats the delicious process.

I'm in bubble bath heaven.

"What did Mom say this afternoon?" I ask as I act casual.

He shrugs, his fingers gently skimming my sex this time, and I smile over at my beautiful man.

That's it.

He shrugs. "Not much."

I roll my lips to hold my tongue, tell me, damn it. I close my eyes as I act uninterested.

"She...." He pauses.

I purposely keep my eyes closed.

"She wants me to keep the Lombardi thing on the down low."

"What do you mean?" I ask as I play along.

His hands slide up my inner thighs and he parts the lips of my sex and I inhale sharply.

Yes...right there.

"If it turns out that I am Lombardi's son, she wants me to keep it a secret."

"How?"

"Not tell anyone, act as if I'm still a Ferrara."

My eyes open and meet his, I spread my legs a little wider, hoping to invite him in. "What did you say?" I ask.

"No."

"Why?"

"I'm not spending my life with your mother blackmailing me to do whatever she wants. There's no fucking way."

What?

"Why do you think that everything she does is sinister? Did it ever occur to you that maybe she is protecting me?"

He shrugs, his fingers sliding through me, I clench on the up stroke.

"Did it ever occur to you that there is something seriously off with this?" he says.

"What do you mean?"

"Lombardi turns up one day and tells me that he's my father and wants me to take over his company?"

I stare at him as I listen.

"What if your mother is working with Lombardi to get rid of me? What if this is some elaborate plan to bring me down from the inside. Don't you think it's weird that she's done a complete 180 on our relationship?"

I frown. "You need to trust her."

"Trust is earned, Francesca," he says as he sits forward in a rush, bringing himself closer.

"I trust her," I say. "My mother is a lot of things, Giuliano, but I know her. She will always do what's best for Ferrara. She's sacrificed everything for the family."

He slides his finger into my sex. "Do you trust me?" he murmurs as his dark eyes hold mine.

I nod, my legs spread a little farther open and he adds another finger, his jaw clenches as he begins to work me. The room is steamy and hot, our eyes are locked.

Arousal is bouncing between us like electricity and, as if unable to wait a second longer, he grabs himself at his base and holds his dick up, it sticks out of the water like a tent pole.

"Get on it."

Giuliano pulls his car into the car park and turns the engine off. He puffs air into his cheeks and stares straight ahead, he's been quiet all morning.

I hate seeing him like this.

I reach over and rub his thigh, his strong quad muscle making its presence known beneath his jeans. "It will be over soon," I say softly to try to make everything better. "Ten minutes and it will all be done and dusted."

We've just arrived at the doctor's to perform the DNA tests, we're meeting the rest of my family here.

"Or ten minutes and life as I know it will be done and dusted," he replies.

I nod, trying so hard not to say the wrong thing. I stay silent for a moment as I think.

"Either way." I reach over and kiss his cheek. "We get to be together. I know this is…shitty." I pull his face around so that he has to look me in the eye. "But I like this scenario a whole lot better than us being brother and sister and never being able to be together."

"You're right." He nods. "Sorry, I just…."

"Hey, don't apologize. It's perfectly normal to be pissed about this situation, both of us may have been deceived by our mothers. It's a tough reality to face."

He rests his forehead against mine.

"Anyway." I smile hopefully. "You said your gut feeling was that the Lombardi story was wrong."

"It is."

"So?" I smile hopefully. "Trust your gut…it's never wrong."

He nods with a deep exhale, then his eyes meet mine. "What if it is?"

I watch him.

"What if my whole life is a lie? Where do I go from that?"

I pick up his hand and kiss his fingertips. "We go forward, Giuliano…together. Because no matter what this testing today takes from us, it can't take away our love for each other."

"You're right." He kisses me softly. "How did I get so lucky to have you?"

"I don't know." I shrug. "I often wonder myself."

He chuckles and I giggle and we fall silent and stare at each other for a moment.

I know this is it, the moment where our life and future will be determined. "You ready?" I ask.

"As ready as I'll ever be, I guess." He opens the car door. "Let's get this over with."

I walk down the aisle of the grocery store with my list, Davidoff is pushing my cart a couple of steps behind me. We get to the herb and spices section and I smile as I look over the choices.

I'm on a mission.

I've been restocking my pantry for two days now, cooking for Giuliano is my new favorite thing. I peruse the shelf and Davidoff stands silently to the side, if Antonio was here he would be reading out the list to me and helping me find things, I miss him. "Have you spoken to Antonio?" I ask.

"No, I haven't." He shrugs. "Why?"

"No reason," I reply. "Just wondering how he is."

"I'm assuming well, I haven't heard any different."

"Hmm." I think for a moment, I'm going to ask Giuliano to bring him back from Rome, I don't like him being there. That place is too dangerous for my sweet Antonio.

My phone rings and I dig it out to see a private number caller ID. I wonder who this is? "Hello."

"Hello, is that Francesca?" a male voice replies.

"Yes."

"This is Benedict Marias, I've just taken over from Dominic."

"Oh." I frown. "He left?"

"Yes, unfortunately he received some bad news about a death in the family and left very suddenly, we were hoping he would return but it doesn't look likely. My apologies that your emails were not responded to earlier."

Someone died...oh no.

"That's okay," I reply. "I had wondered what was going on. I hadn't been able to reach him at all."

"I'll take over now, I'm reading through all the notes and getting acquainted with the job. There is so much to catch up on with the scale of things in the works."

"Okay, great."

"Let's meet and discuss, say Tuesday?" he says casually.

"Sure, where will we meet?" I wince.

"At the hotel, say ballroom, nine o'clock?"

I scrunch my face, oh crap.

Rome.

Shit, I can't get out of this without resigning from my position, and although I have been thinking of doing it anyway, I can't just do it like this without notice. I really need to bring everyone involved up to speed to do a proper handover.

"That sounds great," I lie.

That doesn't sound great at all, that sounds like one big fucking disaster, Giuliano is going to go batshit fucking crazy.

"See you then." He hangs up.

Fuck.

I stuff my phone back into my handbag, this is all so weird, first he goes missing and now someone else wants to meet me. Ugh, and it has to be in Rome, doesn't it?

Can't wait to have a domestic with Giuliano over this one. Oh well, I'll think about that on Monday, I'm not ruining my weekend away by bringing it up with him now.

We're going to Lake Como for the weekend, Giuliano's aunt in London has asked for some photographs of Angelina and her when they were young, apparently, they are in Angelina's attic. Giuliano has been putting off going through his mother's things, my suspicion is that he thinks that once he sorts out her things, then it's final that she's never coming back. It breaks my heart, I wish she was here to help us with this mess, doesn't seem fair that at a time of his life when he really needs some answers, nobody is alive to give them to him.

Giuliano has a house on the lake, not far from Enrico's house. My heart sinks, I wish I was going to see my brother this weekend, I miss him so much.

So much death....

Ferrara blood is a sport.

Giuliano's words come back to haunt me and I look around my surroundings in the supermarket.

Do you know how much a Ferrara woman's scalp is worth?

God....

Is someone watching us right now?

I get a vision of men in suits jumping out and shooting the both of us dead, I glance to the front of the store, are our other guards safe outside?

"What's wrong?" Davidoff asks, sensing my fear.

"Nothing," I reply way too fast, suddenly I just want to get out of here. I glance into the shopping cart. "I think that will do us for today."

A frown flashes across Davidoff's face. "Do you still want to go to the fruit market after here?"

"No. I just want to go home."

"Is something...."

"Nope." I take the cart from him and begin to push it toward the cash registers at speed. "Come on, hurry."

The drive to Lake Como is made in relative silence.

Giuliano is driving and deep in thought, miles away. I wonder what he's thinking about. I go to pull my hand off his thigh and he stops me by grabbing my hand, he glances over. "Don't."

"I thought I must have been annoying you."

"No." He frowns. "As if touching me would ever be annoying."

"Well, you haven't said a word for over an hour."

"Sorry." He rolls his lips. "I've got a lot on my mind."

"Such as?"

He gives a subtle shake of his head. "Nothing for you to worry about."

"Jules." I squeeze his thigh. "I know you are used to doing everything alone, but one of the main benefits of having a partner is like having your very own sounding board."

He glances over.

"If you are worried about something, it makes it easier if you talk it through with someone."

He smirks and keeps his eyes on the road, he lifts my hand to his lips and kisses my fingertips. "Really?"

"Yes." I smile hopefully over at my man. "So...what are you worried about?"

He twists his lips as if contemplating telling me. "Well...." He cuts himself off.

"Well, what?" I wait for his reply with bated breath.

"I'm worried about how my cock is going to fit into your ass."

I burst out laughing in surprise. "What?"

His eyes flick over and he raises an eyebrow. "True story."

"No need to worry about that, you fool, because it's not happening." I giggle, this man kills me.

"We'll see." He smiles as he watches the road. "Give me time."

I know that's not what he was worried about but it was his way of deflecting a serious subject.

Giuliano pulls into the driveway of his mother's house and we both fall silent.

I can feel the weight of his grief as it falls over him.

"When were you last here?" I ask.

"The funeral."

I frown. "You haven't been back?"

"Only in my nightmares."

Oh....

Suddenly I feel every bit of his anxiety, it overwhelms me as I take on his pain.

He turns the car off and we sit in silence and stare at the darkened house, the headlights from the cars behind us turn in off the road too.

"You know what we should do?" I say.

"Go home?"

I smile. "No, we should go straight in and do the photo thing tonight, that way we can get it over with and enjoy the rest of the weekend without a sense of dread."

"Yeah, maybe." He sighs.

"Come on." I open my car door. "If you be good, I'll let you fuck me in your old bed."

He chuckles. "It's so cute how you say you'll let me...like you have a choice."

We walk up to the front door and he fusses around with the keys and the door finally opens. He flicks the lights on and a huge, larger than life painting of my father and the young boy that he loved so much, hits me square in the face.

My heart constricts as I stare at it.

Giuliano is right, he has so much to lose.

. . .

It's just gone midnight.

The house is eerily silent, we are in the attic going through boxes and boxes of photographs. The lights are dim, along with my love's mood.

The photographs are bringing up a lot of memories for both him and me, the good, the bad and the ugly.

I made us dinner, we drank a bottle of wine and although Giuliano would have preferred to have sex in his childhood bed and gone to sleep, I wanted to do it now.

I hate the looming anxiety, better to get it over with. But, now we are in the here and now, I'm not sure I want to be doing this either.

All these photos of his mother and my father, so in love... makes me so sad for my mother and the life she has lived.

I imagine the embarrassment she must have felt in front of the guards every time he returned to her from this house. They were with him every step of the way, they knew everything. When he left Angelina's bed and returned to hers...they all knew.

How did she cope with the shame?

If he were my husband, I'm quite sure I would have cut off his dick in his sleep with a pair of scissors.

Bastard.

I dig through the box I'm unpacking, we are putting the photographs into piles to be put in separate albums one day. A family pile, a friend pile and a random pile.

I pick up a photograph and stare at it for a moment, it's of a man lying on the couch. The couch is different but I can tell that it's downstairs here.

He's good looking, his dark hair is tousled and he's muscular, wearing only a pair of boardshorts.

Hmm....

I pick up another photo and it's of the same man, this time in a suit. I smile, he's so handsome, this must be her brother. I keep looking and find another image of the same man again, this time, he's lying on a bed in boxer shorts.

I stare at it and smile, he looks naughty...and familiar. I must have seen a previous photograph of him or something.

"What are you smiling at?" Giuliano asks.

"Is this your mom's brother?"

"Who?" He takes the photo from me and then his face falls as he stares at it.

"What?"

"This isn't my uncle." His haunted eyes rise to meet mine. "This is Luciano Lombardi."

My eyes widen.

Fuck.

22

Francesca

Giuliano sits back onto his knees as he stares at the image in his hand.

Why would a photo of a young Luciano Lombardi be in his mother's attic?

Unless....

He stays silent and so do I, because holy crap, we both know that this means that the Lombardi story could actually be true.

Shit.

He throws the stack of photos onto the pile, stands and rushes from the attic, I hear the panic in his footsteps as he takes the stairs two at a time.

With my heart racing, I pick up the photographs and flick through them again. I get to another photo, it's of Luciano and Giuliano senior, they are both dressed in suits and are standing with another two men that I haven't seen before.

"Angelina...what did you do?" I whisper angrily. "What did you fucking do?"

"Francesca," Giuliano calls in a rush. "We're leaving."

I screw up my face, huh?

I want him to face this fear head on, running home isn't going to change it.

"What do you mean?" I call back.

"I said. We're leaving," he demands.

I walk to the top of the stairs and look down at him as he stands at the bottom. "I thought we were staying here tonight."

"No." He puts his hands on his hips, annoyed by me questioning him. "Change of plans, I want to go home. Now."

"I want to sort the photos out." I gesture upstairs. "We can't leave them like this."

"I'll tell you how to sort those photos," he yells. "Pour petrol over the top and burn the motherfuckers. Get in the car," he barks before marching out the front door, it slams shut behind him with a loud bang.

What the hell?

Is he even getting our overnight bags from the bedroom?

This is all such a mess.

I look over to the photos strewn all over the floor, I can't leave them like this and I'm not just throwing everything back into the boxes and wasting the two hours of sorting that we've just done. I kneel down onto the floor and begin to put the piles of photos into large manila envelopes.

As I scramble to restore some sort of order I hear the front door bang open downstairs and Giuliano come barreling up the stairs. "I said now!" he growls.

I look up, shocked by his venom and to be honest, a little pissed. "Have some patience Giuliano," I snap. "Like I already told you, I'm putting these photographs away before I go anywhere. You do not snap your fingers and expect me to jump."

His eyes bulge from their sockets. "Now!" he yells, he marches over and grabs my hand and pulls me to my feet. "We need to get out of here, right fucking now." He pulls me out of the room and down the stairs and out the front door, he slams it shut behind us and hurries me to his car and he opens the door in a rush. "Get in."

I raise my eyebrow, unimpressed with his dramatics.

"Now!" The veins are sticking out of his forehead and he looks like he's about to explode.

I fall into the car, exasperated. In this instance, I'll humor him, I'm quite sure that he's having some kind of mental breakdown of some sort right now.

He gets into the car and slams the door hard, he takes off at one hundred miles per hour and the tires screech in disapproval. I grip the dashboard. "What are you doing, you maniac? Slow down."

He glares through the windshield as his eyes stay fixed on the road. He changes the gears at speed.

My eyes flick between him and the road as it comes barreling toward us. "It's okay."

He punches the steering wheel with force causing me to jump. "Nothing about this is fucking okay, Francesca!" he yells as he loses all control. "I am the child of a mistress and her affair with her bodyguard. I'm the result of a montage of lie after lie, I have no identity at all." His eyes well with tears as he grips the steering wheel at white-knuckle force.

Oh....

I watch him, unsure what to say. "We don't know that," I whisper softly.

"Don't we?" he screams like a madman. "What the fuck was

that photo?" He punches the steering wheel again as he takes a corner at speed.

I grip the dash to hold on. "Will you slow down?" I cry. "Killing us is not going to make this situation better."

He clenches his jaw and with a defiant tilt of his chin a cold demeanor falls over him as if having an epiphany. "But I know what will," he mutters.

My eyes flick between him and the road. "What's that?"

He stays silent, the hairs on the back of my neck stand to attention.

"What are you going to do?" I stammer.

He stays silent, eyes on the road.

"Giuliano. Answer me, what are you going to do?"

He changes the gears at speed. "What needs to be done."

Panic runs through me. "Killing Lombardi is not going to fix this, Giuliano. Don't be a fool, you don't need an all-out war."

"This one isn't for me."

"Who's it for?"

"Your father."

Giuliano

I do up my tie as I stand at the end of the bed, Francesca is naked and sleepy still under the covers. "You are not to leave the apartment today," I tell her.

Her eyes find mine.

"Do you understand me?"

She doesn't answer.

"Francesca, do you understand me," I snap, making myself clear.

"Yes." She sighs, her eyes follow me around the room as I

put on my watch and shoes. "What time will you be home tonight?"

"I'm not sure."

"We have church tomorrow with my mother, remember?"

"I won't be going to church."

Her face falls. "Faith means a lot to me; I want you to convert to Catholic."

"That won't be happening."

She sits up, annoyed. "Why wouldn't you want to go to church?"

"Because I'm not a fucking hypocrite like the rest of the Ferrara men were. I'm pretty sure they don't sell blow in heaven, Francesca." I put on my cuff links.

"Do you think you're going to catch on fire the minute you walk into the church or something?" she snaps.

I smirk, an image comes to my mind of exactly that. "To see your mother's face."

She twists the blankets between her fingers as she thinks. "If you're not a Catholic, we can't get married in a church."

"You told me you always wanted to get married in the snow."

"I do." Her eyes search mine. "But...."

I watch her for a moment, her face is filled with sadness, empathy wins and I crawl over her. "I'll make a deal with you."

"What's that?" she whispers up at me.

"If I *am* a Ferrara, I will become a Catholic...*for you*."

The truth is that we both know that's not happening.

She smiles softly as her eyes fill with tears, I kiss her big beautiful lips. "Promise me that you won't leave the apartment today."

"Why?"

"Because I have a lot on my mind and I don't want to be worrying about you."

"Okay." She puts her arms around my neck and holds me down to her. "What are you doing today?"

"Working."

"Don't get yourself killed."

"I haven't yet."

She hugs me tighter. "But you have more to lose now, we have a wedding to plan."

I smile into her neck, she's right, I do.

"I love you." I spread her legs with my knee as I kiss her once more. "See you tonight."

I take the elevator down to the ground floor and walk out to see Bruno.

"Giuliano." He smiles. "Good morning."

"I want extra staff with you. As many as you need, Francesca is not to leave the building until further notice, do you understand?"

"Is something going on?"

"Yes." I roll my lips as I consider if I should tell him my next move. Fuck it, he needs to know. "Lombardi is going to die in the foreseeable future, I know for a fact that she will be their retaliation target."

His face falls.

"She is the one person...." My voice trails off.

If they want to hurt me, they will hurt her.

"I will guard her with my life. You have my word."

"Thank you."

I think for a moment, there *is* one person who I know that will give his life to guard her. "I'll organize for Antonio to return from Rome to assist you."

He nods. "Good idea."

I go to walk off.

"Giuliano," he calls.

I turn back toward him.

"Are you sure about this?" he asks.

"It's time."

He nods. "Yes, sir."

I take the elevator down to my car, get into my Ferrari and pull out of the parking lot, I dial Valentino's number as my eyes flick up to the rearview mirror and the three cars following me.

"Hey," he answers.

"Find me Lombardi's whereabouts."

"Why is that?"

"I'm going to kill him."

Silence.

"Did you hear me?"

"I'll have someone else do it."

"No," I snap. "This kill is mine."

Francesca

I lie on the couch and stare at the television, ugh, this day is long. I've exercised, I've baked a cake, I had a swim and now what?

I hear a bang outside my front door and I sit up, startled.

What's that?

I walk over and put my ears to the double doors, is someone out there? I look out the peephole, can't see anyone. I flick on the iPad next to the door and hit the camera.

The foyer is empty.

My shoulders slump in relief, I'm imagining things now.

I open the door and look around, my eyes widen. The door to the fire stairs is open. It's never open.

I slam my door shut and lock it, my heart hammers in my chest.

It's just a coincidence, I tell myself. It's just a coincidence.

I dial Bruno's number.

"Hello, Miss Ferrara," he answers.

"Can you check the fire stairs please?"

"Why, what's wrong?"

"The door on my level is open."

"I'll be right up."

It's just on six when I hear the door and I smile broadly. *He's home.*

Giuliano comes into view, he's wearing a charcoal suit and crisp white shirt. His dark hair is messed to perfection and he gives me a slow sexy smile before taking me into his arms. "Hey you," he whispers, his voice is soft and cajoling, the one he saves just for me.

We kiss, slow and tender, and he brushes the hair back from my face as he stares down at me. "How was my girl's day?"

"Long without you."

He sits down onto the dining chair and pulls me onto his lap and holds me tight.

We hug, as if we haven't seen each other in years.

The warmth from each other slowly defrosting the cold.

How is it possible to miss someone so much when they were only gone for eight hours?

"What happened with the fire stairs?" he asks.

"I don't know, I heard a bang."

He frowns as he listens. "What kind of bang?"

"It sounded like a door or...." I shrug. "When I checked the cameras, the room was empty so I went out there."

"Rule number one, Francesca," he says sternly. "Never unlock a fucking door, not for anyone other than me."

"But the cameras...."

"Can be manipulated."

"Anyway, it was a false alarm. The serviceman was changing the lightbulbs in the staircase, they must have left it open."

His eyes hold mine as he runs his hand up my thigh. "The staircase is now under surveillance."

I nod, relieved. "Why do I feel like everything is coming to a head?" I ask.

"Because it is." He kisses me softly. "The paternity tests will be back, we can soon be publicly together and...."

"And what?"

"And other things...are being taken care of."

"Lombardi?" I ask.

"You don't need to worry about Lombardi."

"He's dying anyway, Giuliano. Let him go naturally without starting the war," I whisper. "Don't bring any danger to us that isn't necessary."

He gives me a stifled smile as he kisses my nose. "You do not need to worry about my work, sweetheart."

I stare at him, so lost in his light, so, so in love with this beautiful man.

"If something happened to you."

"It won't."

"Promise me that you won't die."

"If you promise to marry me."

"I already did that."

He gives me his best cheeky smile. "That's right, you did."

He stands, holding me in his arms like a bride, and begins to walk to our bedroom. "It's shower time."

"I already showered."

"That doesn't count."

"Why not?"

"Because you're about to get dirty again."

I listen to the grand organ play its hymns and I stare into space.

The priest is delivering his sermon, and we, his faithful disciples, listen in awe.

I wasn't joking when I said I want Giuliano to convert to Catholic.

Religion means something to me, it means a lot. To have our marriage accepted in the eyes of the Lord is important.

I look around at my surroundings, my mother, Lorenzo and my brothers are sitting in the church pews beside me, I'm sitting on the end near the aisle. The church is grand and eccentric, hundreds of years old. A place where Ferraras have always worshiped.

"Is this seat taken?" I hear a familiar voice.

I glance up and my face falls. Giuliano is standing in the aisle, navy suit, white shirt and a confident twinkle in his eyes.

My eyebrows rise by themselves in question and he gives me a sexy wink as he sits down beside me. The tests must have come back, and he's here in a church...for me.

My mother gasps from her place beside me and my eyes well with tears.

He's a Ferrara.

23

Francesca

THE PROCESSION of cars pulls into my mother's place and this may very well be the last time I have to ride in a different car to my love.

I'm in Lorenzo and Mother's car, my brothers behind us and Giuliano behind them, she wanted us all to come back to her house after the church service to discuss the paternity test results. I don't know what's going on, but if Giuliano was in church that means he is a Ferrara. I have no idea what that means for me. Who am I? The answer has created a million questions. I know that for our life to stay the same, it was best for Giuliano to be the Ferrara...but I can't help feeling a little...I don't even know what I'm feeling.

Jaded.

"Did you get an email?" my mother asks Giuliano as we walk through the front door.

"Yes. You got one too."

She nods. "Go into the garden for refreshments, everyone, I'll get my computer and be right out."

She disappears into the office while the rest of us are ushered out the back to the lush gardens and we all sit around the large table.

The mood is heavy, and Lorenzo is somber as we wait for her return.

She reappears and sits down with her laptop and opens it up and we all watch on in silence. As she reads, her eyes well with tears.

"What is it?" Andrea asks.

"Giuliano is a Ferrara," she whispers, her eyes rise to mine and she smiles through tears. "Lorenzo is your biological father, Francesca."

Lorenzo gasps as my eyes widen.

He takes the computer from her as if not believing it, he reads the email and tears begin to roll down his cheeks. "Thank you, my God," he whispers. "Thank you."

He stands in a rush and takes me into his arms, he openly weeps.

"I prayed for this day, my darling daughter. I prayed for this. Thank you, God." He sobs into my neck. "Thank you."

The drive home from my mother's house is strange, yet surreal.

Giuliano is driving and, with my hand on his thigh, we are both silent, lost deep in our own thoughts.

"Have you heard from Antonio?" he asks me.

"No, why?"

"We can't reach him."

"Why, where is he?" I frown.

"He took a few days off to go home and hasn't returned."

"That's strange."

He shrugs. "He'll be around. Maybe they got his return date wrong."

"Probably." We fall deep back into thought once more.

This afternoon, my mother is announcing to the world that Lorenzo is my biological father.

In doing that, Giuliano and I are finally free.

"I have a surprise for you," Giuliano says as his eyes flick over to me.

"Haven't we had enough surprises lately?"

"This is a good one."

I smile over at him.

"But we have to go away to get it."

I frown, puzzled. "Well, that's probably a good idea anyway. I don't want to be around for the circus that's about to erupt."

He picks up my hand and kisses my fingertips. "I love you."

My heart swells and I smile through tears, and there it is.

My reason.

"And I love you, my darling," I whisper. "So much."

"After all we've been through to be together." He smiles softly. "Our new life starts today, baby."

Hope runs through my veins, everything is finally falling into place. We won't have to hide anymore. "I know."

Six hours later we drive into the night, and Giuliano shuffles around in his pocket and pulls out an eye mask. "Put this on."

I frown. "What?"

"Put this on, I told you it was a surprise."

I giggle. "Now?" I look around at our surroundings. "We're on the freeway, my surprise is on the freeway?"

"Don't ask questions, just do it." He smiles and raises his eyebrow, I can tell he's excited to give me whatever this is.

"Okay. Okay." I slip the mask on and am brought into darkness. "Now what?"

"Now you reach over and take my dick in your hand...."

I burst out laughing. "*This* is my surprise?"

He laughs too. "This is *my* surprise."

"Because I can't see your dick?"

"Precisely."

We laugh and he brings my fingers to his lips and kisses them tenderly, this isn't about his dick at all.

Oh...I love this man.

We drive in silence and I hear the car phone ring, Bruno from the car behind us answers. "Hey, boss."

"Hi, when we get there you all stay out on the road, please."

"Okay. Got you." He hangs up.

I put my hands up and feel the mask over my eyes. "Do they know about us?"

"They have their suspicions."

"How do you know?"

"Because the rumor mill has been circulating for weeks."

I frown, shit. I didn't even realize.

"Don't worry, in about two hours they're about to find out that we're not brother and sister. That you are Lorenzo's daughter."

"How do you think that's going to go down?"

"A lot better than if I wasn't a Ferrara, that's for sure."

I smile goofily under my mask and feel the car turn off the road. "Where are we?" I ask as we seem to drive down a second road

"Somewhere I hope that you like."

"What happens if I don't?" I tease.

"Then this was a really fucking expensive mistake."

I giggle, excitement bubbles in my stomach and I bounce in my seat. "Hurry up."

We keep driving and driving and then finally he stops the car. "Stay there."

"Hurry," I gasp. "The suspense is killing me."

He comes around and opens my door and helps me out of the car, he turns me away from him and I hear him let out a deep breath as if nervous.

What is this?

"Okay, you can take the mask off."

I slowly slide the mask off and frown, we are at a house. Scratch that, a mansion. There's a huge red bow on the door and I frown as I look around. The house is huge with large sandstone steps leading up to the double front doors. It looks like a library or something stately. Perfectly manicured gardens, huge trees lit up with fairy lights, my eyes roam around the surroundings and then meet Giuliano's.

"Where are we?" I ask.

"Do you remember when we were kids, you used to tell me all about the pink house that you loved."

I frown as I look around.

"Well, it's not pink anymore."

My eyes widen. "*This* is the pink house?"

He gives me a breathtaking broad smile.

"You bought the pink house?" I gasp as my hands fly over my mouth.

This can't be happening?'

The pink house was near Enrico's on Lake Como, it's incredible and Anna and I used to dream about coming here one day.

"I bought *you* the pink house." He takes me into his arms. "Welcome to our new home, baby."

I squeal in excitement. "You can't be serious?"

He laughs out loud, excited by my reaction, and holds me tight as my feet dangle off the ground. "Do you know how much I love this house?" I cry.

"I do. That's why I paid a ridiculous amount of money for it." He laughs.

"Oh my God. Oh my God...oh my fucking God," I cry.

He leads me up the front steps and I look around in wonder, it's the most luxurious place I've ever seen, which is saying something because I am well used to luxury.

He opens the front door with a key while I bounce behind him. "Hurry up, hurry up."

He opens the door and steps back. "Ladies first."

I walk in and my jaw hits the floor, the living room is dark but lit with hundreds of candles, there are flowers everywhere. "What the...." I turn back to Giuliano to see him down on one knee, holding a ring box open.

"Marry me." He smiles hopefully up at me.

I smile through tears and drop to my knees beside him, I take his beautiful face in my hands. "Yes, yes, a thousand times yes."

We giggle as we kiss and this is perfect.

He takes the ring out, it's a single solitaire diamond. Huge, so beautiful, and my mouth drops open in awe as he slides it onto my finger.

It's heavy on my finger.

"Now there's no getting out of it." He smiles. "I've locked it in."

I hold my hand out and stare at my finger, is this real?

My eyes shoot up and look around the romantic candles and flowers. "But how did you..."

"Anna and Giovanna helped."

My eyes widen. "They know about us?"

"They do now." He smiles.

"Oh." Panic runs through me; I should have told Anna. "I have to call them."

"Why don't you just go see them?" He gestures to the back of the house.

I frown.

He takes my hand and leads me to the glass doors that lead out into the back garden.

Down on the water's edge on the wharf I can see that there is a large dining table adorned with candles, fairy lights hang overhead. I can see people are sitting there and I can hear laughter but I can't really make out who as it's far away. "They're here?" I gasp.

"I thought you'd want to celebrate with Anna."

Oh my God, this man is the living end. I jump into Giuliano's arms once more. "And I do, I do."

He opens the door and I go running out, I run down across the grass as everyone laughs and cheers, there is Carlo and Anna, Valentino and Giovanna and Alex. Anna stands and I nearly knock her off her feet as we hug.

"Anna," I half laugh and half cry.

"There is a God after all." She hugs me tight. "Everything is how it should be."

"I know." I squeeze her tighter.

"Congratulations, baby."

"I'm sorry I didn't tell you," I whisper.

"I've known all along," she whispers. "You're a terrible liar."

I laugh and Giuliano arrives down at the dock, his friends all stand and shake his hand and kiss me. "Congratulations."

Alex fills glasses of champagne and passes them to everyone. "A toast," he announces.

We all smile as we wait for his toast, this is such a happy time.

He holds his glass in the air. "To my best friend, and the love of his life."

My eyes well with tears.

"To the next generation of Ferraras," he shouts.

Everyone laughs at his dramatics. "The Ferraras."

Giuliano kisses me and they all laugh and cheer.

This is the best night in all of history...and he's mine.

Forever.

I feel fingertips run up my arm and warm big lips softly kiss my temple.

I smile, my eyes still closed. "Good morning."

"Good morning," Giuliano's husky morning voice replies, his hand slides up my leg as he leans up onto his elbow.

I hold my hand up to look at my ring.

"It's still there." He smirks.

"Just making sure I didn't dream last night." I smile shyly.

"No." He leans and kisses me softly. "Very real."

"I mean, I know we were getting married before but now that I have a ring and our friends all know about us, it just seems so real, you know?"

He smiles and kisses me, and then pulls me down onto his chest, his fingers idly run through my hair. "Thank fuck I'm marrying an interior designer," he mutters.

I giggle as I look around the main bedroom.

"Who in their right mind paints a bedroom canary fucking yellow?"

I laugh again. "I love this house." I crawl up over him.

"Thank you so much for buying it for us, this has always been my dream."

"You're *my* dream."

My heart swells as I stare down at my beautiful man. "Last night was...incredible. So romantic."

He smiles and pulls me back down onto his chest. "Only the best for my girl."

Giuliano

I pull out of the underground parking lot on a mission, it's Monday morning and after the best weekend of all time.

It's back to reality.

They found our yacht, it's one hundred kilometers off the coast. And soon ... I know who took it ... he will pay.

An eeriness falls over the water, a deserted vessel drifts unguided.

My superyacht.

Once lost, now found...but what did it cost me, I'm about to find out.

The sun is just setting, casting a red glow over the ocean below, and as we get closer, we all grip our guns with white-knuckle force. With no idea what we are about to be met with, we are on high alert.

Shit's about to go down.

We pull up beside it and the sound of the water lapping on our yacht echoes.

Carlo, Val and I exchange looks, what the fuck is going on here?

"Hello," Val calls.

Silence.

"Is anyone there?" he calls again.

Bruno throws a rope over their mast to bring us closer and we slowly come to a halt.

"I don't fucking like this," Carlo whispers.

"That was too easy," Val mutters. "This is a trap." He holds his hand up in a stop symbol. "You all stay here." They all load onto the vessel.

"Fuck that," I snap and with my gun drawn, I step over onto the yacht. "Surrender and you will live," I call as I creep up the deck.

Carlo twirls his hand in the air to signal for us to spread out. We sneak along the sides of the deck and I can hear music playing in the distance. It sounds like traditional Italian accordion music.

What the fuck is going on here?

"Hello," I call.

Val's eyes hold mine. "Trap," he mouths.

I nod, something is off here. I peer through the window into the cabin, it's empty.

"Check the engine room," I whisper.

Carlo walks past me and disappears up the stairs, Val crouches and skulks up the front. I look around as I try to work out what the fuck is going on here?

The engine is off, the yacht is just drifting along.

Is the anchor down?

There are drinks and cheese and biscuits out on the table as if people were just sitting out here on deck.

Where are they now?

I slowly walk inside the cabin and my heart drops.

Antonio is on the floor, a bullet through his head.

Dead.

I squeeze my gun harder, who the fuck did this?

"Clear," I hear Carlo call from upstairs.

"It's empty," Val calls, "There's nobody on here."

"There is somebody," I call back.

Carlo and Val come down and stop when they see it. "What the fuck is he doing here?" Carlo whispers.

Val bends down onto his knees and looks him over. "I think we found our traitor."

24

Six weeks later.

Giuliano

THE BLOOD RUSHES to my cock as I watch the hot ass in the tight white dress and I sip my drink to hide my smile.

Francesca.

No matter how long I watch her dance, I'm always in awe.

The hottest woman in the world...is marrying me. All my Christmases have come at once.

Life is good, fucking great actually.

Francesca wanted to move into our Lake Como house while she plans the remodel, and I have to agree with her, it's been a great decision. I've found a happiness in that house that I never knew existed. It doesn't matter how dated it is, it's our home. The one we are creating together.

Now that we're out of the shadows, we can socialize. The

seven of us are going out to restaurants and clubs every weekend, we even went away to Ibiza last weekend.

I never thought I would have this, a friend group where my wife would be an integral part of it. My social life has always been so male orientated, it's different now, the dynamics have changed....and for the better.

Francesca and Anna have become close with Giovanna, Val's girl. They even hang out through the week sometimes without us boys with them.

Slowly but surely, my family...is becoming her family.

Her family though.... I mean, her mother still fucking pisses me off, some things will never change.

"Another round?" Val asks.

"Yep." I sip my scotch and he disappears to the bar.

Carlo's phone vibrates on the table in front of him and he answers, unable to hear, he puts his hand over his ear. "What?" he says as he screws up his face. "Say that again?"

He listens and then his eyes find mine, he smiles broadly. "Are you sure?" He laughs. "Excellent, thanks." He hangs up and clinks his glass with mine.

"What?" I smirk, he seems very happy with himself.

"Lombardi's dead."

"What?" I sit up, suddenly interested. "Are you sure?"

"He died today."

"Fuck it, I wanted it to be at my hands," I snap, infuriated.

"That's why we haven't been able to find the fucker, he's been in hospital dying from cancer. The audacity of the fucker."

"Are you one hundred percent sure?"

"Lombardi Industry have a week of mourning starting tomorrow. All their brothels are closing as a mark of respect."

I think for a moment, "So...he *did* actually have cancer?"

He shrugs. "Must have."

Val returns carrying a tray of drinks. "What?" he says as he sees my face.

"Lombardi's dead."

"What?" He falls into the chair. "Who?"

"Cancer."

"Fuck...." He says shocked.

Carlo holds his glass in the air to symbolize a toast. "To us."

Val and I chuckle, typical Carlo, everything comes back to him.

"To us."

Francesca

Giuliano lies on the couch watching television and I sit on the chair with my pen and pad in my hand. My mind is in overdrive. "What about if we put a huge arch window in the far wall next to the entry?" I talk to myself out loud.

"Aren't you supposed to be finalizing the hotel plans not thinking of more ways for us to demolish this house?" he murmurs, distracted.

"Yes, I'm nearly done with the hotel, thank goodness they let me do everything remotely."

"Well, you weren't going back to Rome, that was for sure."

I go back to my topic. "What do you think about the arch window? A really huge one with the metal gable."

He glances over. "That wall?"

"Yeah."

"Why would you want to put a window in that wall?"

"So that when we put our Christmas tree up you can see it from the front."

He smirks as his eyes stay fixed on the television. "Why are you so obsessed with Christmas?"

"Because it's my favorite time of the year."

"You're like a big baby."

I smile broadly. "I was thinking for Christmas Day, we could go to church and then my mother's for breakfast but then come back here for the rest of the day. What do you think?"

He looks over at me, "Or...."

"Or what?"

"Or we could go to Switzerland and get married."

My eyes widen. "That's a choice?"

"Why not?" He shrugs casually. "You always said you wanted to get married in the snow." He stands and goes to retrieve something from his office, he returns and passes it to me. It's a brochure from a resort in Switzerland, there's a glass atrium chapel in the side of the mountain, nestled in the snow. It's incredible and looks like a fairy tale.

"Oh my God...," I whisper in awe as I study the brochure.

"We could get married on Christmas Eve night, that way your favorite time of the year would be mine too."

My wide eyes rise to meet his. "But...everyone."

"Is on board, ready and waiting to come with us."

"They can come too?"

"Of course, I already asked them."

I stare at him as my mind begins to race a million miles per minute, "That's only a month away, I have so much to...." I stand and begin to pace. "I need a dress and then there's the...." I put my hands in my hair. "Jules, I don't think I can pull this off in only a month."

He stands and takes me into his arms, he puts his hand under my jaw and brings my face up to meet his. "Francesca."

"What?"

"I want you as my wife."

I smile goofily up at my handsome man. "I want that too, more than anything."

"Do you want to marry me in Switzerland on Christmas Eve or not?"

"Yes." Excitement bubbles in my stomach. "I do."

"Then." He kisses me softly. "We will make it work."

We.

I smile goofily up at him. "What exactly are *you* going to do?"

Who is he kidding? I run our whole lives.

"Fuck you until you're calm each night," he replies casually.

I burst out laughing. "That's what you're going to do to plan our wedding, fuck me until I'm calm?"

He holds his hands out wide as if offended. "It's very helpful to keep calm, Francesca."

My mouth falls open as I fake horror.

"It's a full-time fucking job keeping you sexually sated."

He picks me up and throws me over his shoulder and begins to walk to the stairs. "Speaking of which."

I laugh out loud. "I don't have time for sex, Giuliano," I tease as I rest my hands on his lower back. "I have a wedding to plan."

He slaps me hard on the behind. "You're going to suck my cock first." He slaps me again. "And you're swallowing."

I laugh out loud again. "Wives don't do those sorts of dirty things."

He slaps me again. "Mine does."

The plane touches down on the runway and I can hardly keep the beaming smile from my face. Giuliano smiles as he kisses my hand. "Are you ready, my love?"

Switzerland.

The place of our upcoming nuptials, in just three days I am marrying the love of my life. Everyone who is important to us is on this plane.

My mother, Lorenzo, Andrea and Matteo, my brothers. Anna and Giovanna, Valentino, Carlo and Alex.

The intimate wedding party that I never imagined would be so perfect.

Our guards unload our luggage and we get off the plane and walk down the stairs, snow is falling and already this feels uber romantic.

"I'm so excited," I yell and everyone laughs.

Giuliano smiles and kisses me softly, and I know that he's just as excited as me. This is such a happy time.

We load into our cars and Giuliano takes my hand in his as we sit in the back seat.

"You still want to do this?" He smiles over at me.

"Try and stop me."

An hour later we pull into the resort. "This place is incredible," I whisper in awe as I look around. We make our way to reception. "Party for Jones," Giuliano says to the receptionist.

"Yes." She smiles. "You're the wedding party?" She turns her attention to me, "Are you the bride to be?"

Excitement runs through me, "Uh-huh."

She laughs at my over-the-top excitement. "We have you all staying in the summit wing. Ten rooms in total."

"Okay." Giuliano smiles.

"And…." She types into her computer. "Francesca…is it?"

"Yes."

"We have your pre-wedding schedule planned. Tomorrow at one p.m., you have a meeting with our wedding planner."

"Okay."

"And the day after that you have a wedding rehearsal in the atrium at five p.m."

Giuliano smiles broadly as he puts his arm around me.

Oh my God, can you die from excitement?

Because I just might.

She slides the keys over the counter to us. "The conditions are perfect today, get out on the slopes before dark if you can. The powder coverage is just incredible."

I nearly bounce on the spot. I love skiing so much, it's all I can do not to scream.

"Thanks, I will."

We return to the others who are all waiting patiently and Giuliano hands out the keys. "Who wants to come for a ski?" I ask them.

"Today?" Giuliano frowns.

"Just a quick one."

"Not me," says Anna. "Don't feel like breaking my neck today."

Giuliano screws up his face. "I fancied a scotch by the fire in the bar to be honest."

"You do that, I'll meet you there. I'll be an hour tops." I smile.

His eyes hold mine as he contemplates his choice.

"I'll come," Giovanna replies.

"Me too," Carlo chips in.

"Great. So, I'll meet you both back here in half an hour?" I ask them.

"Sounds good," Giovanna says.

"I guess I'll meet the rest of you in the bar around the same time?" Giuliano asks everyone.

"Yes, sounds good."

The ski chairlift rises high in the sky as it takes us up the mountain.

"Look." Giovanna points. "Is that your atrium?"

I peer down below and see a glass chapel nestled into the side of the mountain, I can see an open fire flickering inside. "Yes."

We both squeal in excitement and I turn back to Carlo and Bruno who are in the chairlift behind us. "That's the atrium."

They both look down. "Looks good." Carlo laughs.

We all watch it fly by underneath as we pass over and Bruno gives me the thumbs-up.

Giovanna takes my hand in hers. "Can you believe that you are getting married in this heavenly place?"

"No." I laugh.

She fiddles with her boot as we ride up. "Anna may have been on to something, I may break my neck too, I haven't skied for three years."

"It's like riding a bike, you never forget." I fiddle with my gloves to try to pull my fingers in properly.

"As long as you don't break anything," she teases. "Plaster isn't the white you want to be wearing."

I laugh out loud. "Don't hex me."

Giuliano

I sit by the open fire with Alex and Val, scotch in hand.

After the crazy week we've had to prepare for coming away, I'm finally beginning to unwind. I look out the window and the snow coming down. "This place is incredible, isn't it?"

"I'll say." Val smiles as he stares out over the view.

My phone beeps a text, it's from Francesca.

> It's our chapel baby
> Can't wait to marry you.
> xoxox

It's a pic of the mountain and the glass atrium below, I smile broadly. "Check this out." I hold my phone out and the boys smile as they look at it.

We keep chatting and about fifteen minutes later another text from Francesca bounces in.

> Look who I just ran into
> It's my boss.

I stare at the photo and my eyes widen.

Fuck.

I slam my drink down on the table with a thud.

The picture is of Francesca in the snow, a man has his arm around her as they pose for the photograph.

It's Lombardi.

25

Francesca

WE RIDE the ski lift to the top of the mountain and ski off. "Let's go down into the next valley," I say to the others.

"Okay." Giovanna smiles, she's pretty good. I can tell already.

"Let go this way." Carlo gestures to a run that isn't the usual one.

"Okay." We ski down and over another hill and on for a while and we see a man standing under a tree. As we get closer I realize that I know him, that's Mr. Carballo, the boss from the hotels. "What in the world are you doing here?" I laugh as I approach him.

"Ahh, Francesca." He smiles. "What a pleasant surprise."

"Fancy seeing you up here?" I laugh.

"Take a quick photo?" he asks. "I will send it to the office, they won't believe the coincidence. Fancy running into you of all people all the way in Switzerland."

"Okay." I laugh. "It is pretty weird, isn't it?"

"Let me." Carlo holds his hand out for my phone. "Open it," he says.

I swipe my phone open and hand it over to him, I put my arm around Mr. Carballo, smile as we pose, and Carlo takes the photo.

"Do you come here often?" I ask him.

"First time."

I see Carlo typing something into my phone and I hold my hand out for it.

"You won't be needing your phone, Francesca," Mr. Carballo says.

I turn my attention back to him to see he is pointing a gun at me and Giovanna. "What are you doing?" I frown.

"We haven't been properly introduced." He smiles and dips his head. "I'm Luciano Lombardi. Pleased to make your acquaintance"

What?

I take a step back in fear. "What are you doing?" I whisper as I take Giovanna's hand in mine, we take another shuffle back. Bruno holds his hands up as his eyes flick to meet mine. My heart hammers in my chest and something catches my eye to the left, I turn to see five men, all with guns pointed at us. Where did they come from?

Fuck.

He smiles calmly. "You have something I want."

"What's that?" I whisper.

"His name is Giuliano Ferrara," he announces loudly, he looks at his watch. "And he'll be here in about... five minutes."

A trap.

"No." I shake my head. "I'm not calling him."

What the hell? I've been working with him all this time.

"You already did," he replies calmly.

"Huh?" I look around in a panic, what does he mean. "Mr. Lombardi, please...don't do this," I whisper in a panic. "Your war is with his father, not him. He's not your enemy."

"Run," Giovanna screams, she makes a run for it and a gunshot rings out, she falls to the ground and blood splatters all over the snow.

I turn and see Carlo holding the gun that just shot her, my eyes widen in horror.

What the fuck?

"What are you doing?" I cry.

Bruno dives for him and in lightning speed, he points the gun at Bruno and without hesitation pulls the trigger, Bruno drops to the snow and blood runs out from underneath his body.

Carlo points the gun at me.

"Carlo," I scream. "No. What are you doing?"

"What needs to be done." He gestures up the hill with his gun. "Go."

"Carlo!" I cry. "We trusted you."

"Dumb move."

I stare at him as my mind tries to catch up...what the fuck?

His eyes are cold and he's completely detached...as if he doesn't know me at all.

My God.

Bang, bang, bang goes my heart.

I look around frantically, I have to get out of here, I need to warn Giuliano. I slowly click my skis off and look around.

"Don't even think about it, princess," Carlo snarls. "Happy to shoot you too."

What the fuck is happening right now?

"Now go." He pushes me up the hill and I stumble and fall, he drags me up by the arm and pulls me along.

"What are you doing?" I cry. "You don't want to do this. It's not too late."

"Shut the fuck up," he cries as he loses control.

We walk over the top of the hill and a helicopter comes into view. Suddenly the plan becomes crystal clear. They're going to take me somewhere secluded so they can kill me too.

No.

I stumble backward. "No," I cry, I fight to get out of his arms, Carlo holds me tight as he struggles to control me and in desperation hits me with the barrel of the gun.

Sharp pain steals my sight and I drop to my knees, I feel the hot blood run down my face and see it drip onto the snow in front of me. I look over and see Giovanna and Bruno dead in the snow, the blood running out from their bodies creating a sea of red.

Oh my God.

I'm gasping to catch my breath and Carlo grabs me by the hair and drags me back up to my feet. "Get into the chopper," he demands.

"Go to fucking hell, you traitor," I spit, I slap him hard across the face and he smiles sarcastically.

"It's going to be fun killing you." He hits me again with the gun and I fall backward. I hit my head on a rock.

Fear, pain...darkness.

Giuliano

"Oh my God," I cry as I run for the door, Valentino and Alex are hot on my heels. "What's happening?" Val cries from behind me.

"Lombardi has Francesca at the top of the mountain."

Our guards run from everywhere and we pull people off the ski lift to take their seats.

My hands are in my hair as panic runs through me.

The chairlift rises at a snail's pace and I look around frantically to search for a quicker route.

No...no...no...no.

Please don't hurt her, please don't hurt her.

As we get closer, I see panic as people scream as they come down the mountain.

What's happened up there?

No.

A loud sound echoes and we all look around and then we see a chopper rise from over the back of the mountain.

"Ahhhh," I scream as I lose all control.

Valentino holds his gun up to shoot at it and I grab his arm. "She might be on there," I yell. "Don't shoot, she might be on there."

The ski lift gets to the end and we jump off and run to the top of the hill and over it to try to find where the chopper left from. We are slipping and falling in the snow and finally we get to a clearing and we see Giovanna and Bruno lying in the snow, blood everywhere.

"Nooooooo," Valentino cries, he holds his gun in the sky and shoots off three rounds as he screams. He drops to the snow beside Giovanna and takes her as he rocks her in his arms. "Hold on. Hold on. Somebody call an ambulance. Please," he yells. "Hurry, please. Don't you leave me, baby!" he cries through tears. "Hold on."

She stares straight through him. It's too late.

She's gone.

Bruno's dead too.

I frantically dig my phone out to call someone to track the chopper.

No reception.

"Fuck it," I scream. "Who has reception?"

Everyone is scrambling to call for backup.

No reception.

"Ahhhhhhhhhhh," I scream, it echoes into the valley and I hold my gun up and shoot it into the sky. "He's got Francesca," I cry. "He's fucking got her."

"No sign of Carlo," someone yells from behind me. "They've taken him too."

I stare up into the sky as the chopper disappears out of sight.

Dear God.

Francesca

The dull ache throbs through my skull and I frown as the distinct smell of cigars fills my nose.

My head drops forward, waking me up, and it's then that I realize my hands are tied. I'm sitting on a chair, my feet tied to the chair legs.

Where am I?

The walls are timber, I can see through the window, it's dark and snow is falling outside. I can hear men talking in the next room, what the hell happened?

"She's awake," I hear someone call.

Lombardi comes into view with Carlo behind him.

My heart hurts as my eyes search his.

We trusted you.

Lombardi leans his behind on the table and crosses his feet at the ankles, he watches me as he takes a deep drag of his cigar.

"And now we wait...to watch him rise from the dead." He smiles darkly and inhales deeply again.

My eyes fill with tears, please no.... "He's...." I screw up my face, I can't even say it out loud in case it makes it happen for real. "Your war is not with Giuliano, he doesn't deserve this."

"I'm not after Giuliano."

I frown, confused. "Who are you waiting to rise from the dead?"

Lombardi takes another deep drag, he blows the smoke up in a thin stream as his cold eyes hold mine."

"Your brother...Enrico Ferrara."

26

Francesca

"WHAT ARE YOU TALKING ABOUT?" I spit. "Enrico is dead."

He throws his head back and laughs out loud. "You poor deluded child. Enrico Ferrara is alive and well, living comfortably on an island somewhere in the Caribbean."

What?

My heart begins to sound in my ears.

Can't be...he's alive?

"It is time for retribution!" Lombardi cries out loud. "An eye for an eye."

I stare at him horrified; he's gone completely mad.

"He killed my only son. Stole my ancestry line, something I can never get back," he yells in a dramatic fashion. "Cut me so deep that I've never recovered." He takes a slow drag of his cigar as he seemingly contemplates his next sentence. "And now *I* am going to kill him," he says calmly and then looks over at me and waves his cigar toward me. "And you."

I'm crippled with fear, my eyes well with tears.

"He will be here." He looks at his watch. "In approximately twelve hours."

What?

How does he know that?

I look over to Carlo who is sitting in the corner, a cigar in his hand and his eyes fixed on me. "How could you?" I whisper through tears. "You were our friend."

He raises an eyebrow and inhales and then, as if thinking, he rolls the cigar in the ashtray.

"A deal's a deal," Lombardi says to Carlo. "You have kept your side of the bargain and delivered her to me and now I will deliver what was promised to you. I give you my blood."

Huh?

He walks over to Carlo and picks up a knife from the table and cuts the palm of his hand. Blood runs down his hand.

What the fuck is happening right now?

Carlo stands, he takes the knife and cuts his hand the same way.

I wince, the brutality of this is too much.

They shake hands, palm to palm. Blood to blood.

Lombardi pulls Carlo into a hug. "Lead wisely, my son." He kisses his cheek.

"Yes sir, I will," Carlo replies. "You have my word."

My eyes widen in horror...what?

Lombardi turns to the other guards in the room. "Meet your new leader." He holds his hand out. "Carlo Bernetti. Our next generation."

They all bow their head in a mark of respect.

What the fuck?

Carlo takes out his phone and dials a number, he waits while it rings. "It is done."

Who's he talking to?

"I want a team sent down." He listens again. "Snipers."

What?

"We are at the second location."

Wait...what was the first?

"Enrico Ferrara is Lombardi's kill, do you hear me? Nobody is to take that from him," he continues.

He listens again with a cool detachment, and it all becomes crystal clear.

Carlo has already been running Lombardi Industries from afar.

For how long?

Dear God.

He listens again. "Have the chopper ready."

Lombardi coughs, it's loud and rumbly, deep from his chest. Carlo's eyes rise to him and he walks over and gently hits Lombardi on the back to help him get his breath. An intimate act that depicts their closeness.

Lombardi *is* dying.

He keeps coughing, struggling to regain control, and Carlo takes the cigar from him and puts it down in the ashtray as he talks on the phone.

"Have a nurse on the chopper," he says calmly, he pats Lombardi's pockets and pulls out a bottle of pills, he takes two and passes them to Lombardi who swallows them whole.

Fuck.

Lombardi really doesn't have long.

He has nothing to lose, that makes him more dangerous than ever.

"I'll be going ahead with stage three." He smiles darkly as he listens. "I will, don't worry." He listens again. "I'll call you when it's done." He hangs up.

Stage three? What's stage three?

I watch him, I've never felt so betrayed.

Anna.

Dear God, Anna.

The gorgeous man who Anna loves…is pure evil.

Carlo kisses Lombardi on both cheeks. "You are in safe hands; another team will be here soon. I'll be back when it is done."

"When what is done?" I ask as my eyes flick between them.

Carlo's cold eyes meet mine and he smiles darkly. "My first task as the Lombardi leader."

What's that?

My eyes search his.

He walks up close, leans down, puts his mouth to my ear and whispers, "I'm going to kill your beloved Giuliano." He grabs my face and licks it. "Now, while he trusts me."

Oh no….

Giuliano *does* trust him.

I struggle in my chair to get away but I'm tied in place. "No," I cry. "You can't. Please. Don't touch him."

He gives a nod to the other men and then walks toward the door.

"What about Anna?" I cry. "She loves you. How could you do this to her?" His step falters and I know I just hit a nerve.

Maybe the only nerve of decency that he has left. Still facing the door, he says, "I'll be back for Anna."

His silhouette blurs.

"I look after mine," he replies coldly before walking out the door, it slams behind him with a bang.

Giuliano

I look around the mountaintop, searching for an answer.

"What the fuck is going on?" Alex cries as he looks around in horror. "Bruno." He drops to his knees to check for a pulse.

Our other guards walk around, guns drawn as they search.

The snow is coming down and while Valentino weeps over the body of his girl, I know I don't have much time to work out what went on here. Falling snow is about to cover everything. My eyes skim over the surface of the mountain in search of clues.

Footprints.

There are a group, they were standing here.

I look over to where Bruno and Giovanna lie, this is where they stood when they shot them. There is a large dent in the snow with blood, as if someone was hit and knocked over. I study the size and shape of the hole in the snow.

Francesca.

From there, I can see there was a struggle, she put up a fight as she was dragged up the hill. I survey the whole area, six sets of footprints in total.

I look out over the snow-covered mountain and then follow the footsteps up and over the mountain. There I find the chopper rail marks, there is no snow on the trees around here, the chopper blades have blown it all off. I get a vision of the horror that went down here.

Francesca.

I run back to Valentino. "We have to find phone service."

"I'm not leaving her here," he cries. "This is all my fault."

My heart breaks for him. "You stay with her. I'll send someone." I turn to the guards. "Stay here with him."

"But you...."

"He needs you more. They're gone. I'm safe," I yell, I turn and begin to run down the mountain.

I slip and slide and somersault and fuck me...I hate fucking snow.

I roll my ankle and near knock myself out. I have to zigzag down the mountain, it's too slippery to go the quickest route.

Why the fuck didn't I go skiing with her?

My hands are burning from the ice...and why the fuck aren't I wearing gloves?

I slip again and fall hard and flat on my ass. I try to get up and fall again, I try again and fall even harder.

Fuck!

I pant as I lie in the ice.

What the hell are these stupid fucking shoes I'm wearing?

On my hands and knees, I crawl down the mountain, every second longer I take I know that Francesca is more at risk.

I hear screaming and I look up to see Alex trying to follow me and being absolutely smashed as he somersaults out of control down the mountain. He crashes at high speed into a tree.

This can't be fucking happening.

I finally get to the bottom and run into the hotel to see Lorenzo in the foyer, his face falls when he sees me. "What's happened?" he cries.

I'm panting, gasping for air, and I point to the top of the mountain. "Call for backup. We...need...."

"What's happened?" he cries again.

"Lombardi has Francesca." I put my hands on my hips to try to catch my breath, I can't even speak. "And Carlo…took them in a chopper."

I put my hands on my knees, fuck, I'm about to have a heart attack.

"Where's Val and Alex?"

I point up the hill. "Giovanna is dead and Bruno too," I pant. "And probably Alex has now fallen to his death in the snow on the way down as well."

"Oh, dear God," he cries, he takes out his phone and dials. "We need help. Shit's gone down."

Far, far away on a Caribbean Island.

Enrico

I sit on the deck and watch my family.

Olivia and our five children are walking along the beach with our dog.

We've been here on our island in paradise for ten years now, it's been the happiest time of my life.

I've given my children something that I never had. Something that I never knew I was missing.

My undivided attention.

We have two sons and three daughters, and Olivia is my queen.

I never knew that love could be like this, not until I met her. I wanted to give her more from life than being in a Mafia family in Italy. She deserved more.

My phone beeps, notifying me of a text, and I get up to check, it's from Lorenzo.

> Francesca has been kidnapped

I pick up the phone and dial his number.
"Hello."
"What's going on?"
"Lombardi has Francesca."
"How?"
"We are in Switzerland, she and Giuliano were getting married on Christmas Eve. She was skiing and a chopper landed and killed her guard and Valentino's girl."

I close my eyes, the horrific scene playing out in my head. "Fuck."

"I have to go, I'll keep you posted." He hangs up and I walk into my office and turn my computer on. I drop into my seat and with my heart hammering in my chest I do something I have never done before.

I click on the program and hit,

Activate Satellite

I wait, the program zooms out and a map of the world comes up.

"Please work." I close my eyes and say a prayer.

When our father died, I put a microchip in a diamond necklace and gave it to Francesca in the instance that something like this ever happened.

"Please still be wearing it." I close my eyes, if this doesn't work.... "Please, please, please."

A red light comes up with a beep that sounds like a heartbeat. I watch it flash as it comes to life.

I zoom in on the picture and lean into my computer screen as I concentrate.

Switzerland

"Bingo." I sit back in my chair. "Got her."

27

Enrico

"No," Olivia snaps. "You're not going."

I glance up from the suitcase that I'm packing. "I wasn't asking for your permission." I walk into the bathroom and retrieve and then throw my toiletries bag into the suitcase as it lies open on the bed. "I'll be gone three days…tops."

"You left that life behind for a reason," she snaps. "What are you going to do?" She throws her hands up in the air in disgust. "They have a million fucking guards at Ferrara, Enrico. If they couldn't keep her safe, what in the hell makes you think that you can?"

I throw my shoes into the suitcase with force. "Don't."

"Don't?" she cries. "Don't?" She puts her hands on her hips. "Don't you dare don't me!"

I grab her by the arms. "Listen to me. Francesca is my baby sister and I left her there unguarded."

"She has guards," she spits.

"None that can watch her like I do," I growl.

"So...you're going to put yourself in danger to try and save her?"

"I have to try."

"What about *your* children, Rico. Who will guard *them* if you die?" Her voice cracks, betraying her hurt. "I have not lived here hidden away for ten years for you to risk your life at the first thing that goes wrong back home."

I throw a stack of shirts into the suitcase.

"She is my sister."

"They have a leader, Giuliano. Let him do his job." She begins to pace, her hand on her forehead as she processes what I'm about to do.

"He is too close to her to be of any use."

Her eyes nearly bulge from their sockets. "And you're not?" she screams.

"I'm just going to Milan to help strategize." I throw in a pile of pants, I go to my drawer and grab a stack of boxers and socks, I throw them in too. "I'm not going to do anything stupid."

"Going home is stupid!" she cries. "I don't want you to go. You're not going!"

I zip up my suitcase. "You have no choice."

Her eyes well with tears as she stares at me. "Please," she whispers. "Don't do this."

I pull my suitcase off the bed and stand it up. "I have to."

Her face screws up in tears and she turns her back to me, she crosses her arms, she walks over to the window and looks out and watches the children as they play downstairs in the yard.

I walk up behind her and put my hand on her shoulder and she flicks it off.

"I love you..." I whisper as I stand behind her.

Silence.

"Olivia...."

Silence.

I get a lump in my throat, what if this is our last goodbye?

"Are you going to say anything at all?" I ask.

"If you die, I will never forgive you," she whispers as she stares straight ahead.

Her words cut like a knife and I close my eyes.

I wheel my suitcase to the door and turn back to look at her. "I love you," I tell her again.

Silence.

Tell me you love me, God damn it.

I wait, but she doesn't turn.

With a heavy heart I walk down the stairs and out onto the deck, my car is waiting out the front.

"Come give Papa a hug," I call to the children. "I have to go away for a few days." They come bouncing up and I take them into my arms and hug them one by one. "I love you," I tell each of them. "Look after Mama."

I glance up to see Oliva watching us through the bedroom window.

I smile softly and wave up at her and she turns her back and walks away.

Ouch.

I get into the car and wave to my beloved family, the thing is, deep down I know that Olivia is right...but I can't not go.

It's Francesca.

I'll never forgive myself if she is killed and I didn't at least try to save her.

With the children laughing and squealing as they and the dog chase the car up the driveway, my heart is in my throat.

What if...don't.

It will be okay...it has to be.

Twenty minutes later we arrive at the airport, my private plane is waiting, along with my three guards. I retrieve my luggage from the trunk and walk up the stairs.

"Good afternoon, Mr. Ferrara." The captain nods.

"Hello."

"Departing for Milan in ten minutes, sir." He smiles.

I sit down in my chair. "Change of plans," I reply flatly as I stare out the window. "Take us directly to Switzerland."

Giuliano

The red lights from the police cars flash their reflection onto the snow, the ski slopes are empty.

The snow is coming down and after hours of questioning by the police, they are finally bringing the bodies down the mountain.

The ambulances are lined up waiting and every fucking moment I stand wasting time here, Francesca is in their hands.

We watch on as the Snowmobiles come slowly down the mountain, pulling a trailer behind them, on each a body bag.

An eerie silence has fallen over us.

An incomprehensible dread.

My girl missing, Valentino's girl dead.

Bruno, their guard...my heart sinks. How did this happen on my watch?

He was there all the time, she worked for him. She trusted him.

I didn't protect her.

The Snowmobiles pull up and the paramedics lift the first of the body bags into the back of the ambulance.

Valentino watches on with a calm detachment, I've never seen him like this.

Broken.

He loved her.

He walks over and talks to the paramedic and then runs his hand over where the head would be in the body bag.

My eyes well with tears.

The paramedics count to three and then lift her into the back of the ambulance and close the doors; Val watches on in silence as it drives away.

He takes out his phone. "I have to call her parents."

I close my eyes in regret, it doesn't get any worse than this.

Alex and I wait beside him in silence as he holds the phone to his ear. "Hello, Mrs. Morelli?"

He listens for a moment.

"This is Valentino."

He drops his head.

How do you tell someone that their daughter has just been murdered?

"There's been an accident...."

1 a.m., Valbella Forest, Switzerland.

Enrico

We drive in darkness, creeping along at a snail's pace.

The snow is coming down hard and the conditions are treacherous. Fog appears from our mouths as we breathe.

It's fucking freezing.

I watch my phone like a hawk, the little red heartbeat is close. "Stop here." I say. "We'll walk in. Park the car out of sight."

"It's too far. We'll freeze to death."

"If we drive in, we're dead anyway," I mutter.

Henry pulls the car into a slipway off the road and we get out and drag branches over the back of it so that it can't be seen from the road.

We are in full white snow gear, camouflaged to perfection. I pull my white beanie down over my head and pull the white gloves on. "It must be fucking minus twenty."

"And the rest," someone mutters.

We fill our backpacks with ammunition and put the silencers onto the guns. Henry passes us the night goggles and we pull them on.

"Let's do this." I point over the hill. "It's about seven kilometers in."

"Fucking hell. Seven kilometers in these conditions?" He looks back at me, "We have better chances of survival driving in."

"Go," I snap.

We begin walking, the night goggles lighting our path. Our snow boots grip to the earth beneath us. Our guns held tightly in our hands.

I'm coming, Francesca, hold on.

Two hours later, we lie in the bushes as we survey the cabin in the distance up ahead. It's lit up, smoke billowing from its chimney, and I stare at the beating red heart on my app.

"She's in there."

"What now?" Henry whispers.

"We spread out." I grip my gun. "Shoot to kill."

My men nod, the mission crystal clear.

"Keep the silencers on, they can't know what's going on out here."

I see a flicker of a light and realize someone is up ahead, lighting his cigarette as he makes his patrols.

"Mine," I whisper as I take aim.

I line him up in the scope and hold steady as I pull the trigger, he drops to the ground in silence.

"One down," I whisper.

My three men all get low to the ground and commando crawl to spread out.

I crawl to the man I've just shot and I fire again at close range, I drag his body out of the way to hide it. The longer we go undiscovered the better off we are.

We all lie waiting, guns aimed.

Now, it's a waiting game, we tick them off...one at a time.

Five of their men are dead.

As far as I can see we have three more to go, they just need to get out here and walk around so I can get a clear shot.

Another man comes out, I see him look around and then call out a name.

I put my eye to the scope and feel the sharp sting of a blade to my neck.

My head is pulled back by the hair and a razor-sharp knife is held to my throat from behind.

Fuck.

"Well, well, well...look what the cat dragged in." He digs the knife into my throat. "We've been waiting for you."

Giuliano

I pace in my bedroom, back and forth.

Intel are trying to track the phones from the tower, but no word yet.

We're searching for Lombardi's phone number. If he took her alive,

he wants something.

Happy to exchange my life for hers.

We've just got to find her.

Please be alive.

My phone rings and the name *Carlo* lights up the screen, I scramble to answer it.

"Carlo."

"Giuliano, help me," he moans.

"Where are you?" I snap.

"I just woke up, I'm in the snow." His teeth are chattering. "I must have been knocked out. I have no idea where I am." His teeth chatter harder. "I'm freezing to death. Help, help me."

"Look around you," I stammer. "What do you see? I need a landmark."

"I'm at the top of a hill." He sounds disorientated. "There's a ski lift to the left, and a...." His voice trails off.

"And a what?"

"I can see the resort down below." He goes silent. "Where's Francesca?"

"He's near where they were today," I yell. "Go, go."

Everyone runs from the room, and I do too. "Hold on,

Carlo, we're coming." We run to the elevator and all pile in. "Hold on, we're coming."

We get to the ground floor where we have skimobiles on standby, Alex and Marko climb on one and Val and I get onto the back of the other. "To the top of the hill."

We take off at speed, going straight up. It seems to take forever and when we get up there, I look down at the hotel to try to get my bearings to his directions. "Carlo," I call as I jump off the skimobile.

"Carlo."

"Carlo." Our voices echo across the canyon.

We all listen as the wind howls around us.

Silence.

"Carlo."

We run left and we run right.

"Over here," someone calls.

We all run to see Marko hunched over a figure on the ground and I run up and drop my knees.

Carlo's eyes flutter open and he smiles in relief. "Thank God, you found me."

I press my gun to his temple. "Where the fuck is she?"

28

Francesca

I STRUGGLE with the ties on my hands, I have to get out of here and warn Giuliano about Carlo. Panic is running through my veins and I know that I don't have long.

What if he's already back there?

I get a lump in my throat as I imagine my Giuliano being shot in cold blood by his best friend.

No.

I struggle harder, I need to break free.

Now!

As Lombardi talks to the two other men in the room, he keeps breaking into a deep cough, barely able to speak at times. Wheezing and gasping as if there is no air in his lungs.

I wish there wasn't.

I look around the room, what do I do? How can I get out of here?

A gunshot rings out, the room falls silent.

Lombardi holds his hand out toward me. "Gag her."

Another shot is fired.

Someone's out there.

"I'm in here," I yell.

Suddenly I feel duct tape go around the circumference of my head and over my mouth. I struggle to try to stop them. "Help. Help," I cry in a muffled voice as I fight, I rock the chair as I try to get away. "I'm in here."

Another round of bullets rings out, a man screams, and my eyes widen.

Someone's been shot.

Lombardi calmly plays with my hair, completely unfazed. "I told you he would come."

A text pings on a phone that sits on the table, Lombardi picks it up and then after reading it, smiles and his eyes rise to meet mine. "Carlo has succeeded. Giuliano Ferrara is no more." He rubs his hand over my hair. "I would offer my condolences, Miss Ferrara...if I cared."

No.

The earth shatters beneath, my vision blurs.

No.

He can't be dead.... He can't leave me here alone.

I get a vision of his beautiful face, us laughing and rolling around together in bed.

That can't be it.

This can't be where our love story ends.

It's not finished yet.

I stare into space through tears as a million memories run through my mind. I see us kissing in the library when we were kids. Dancing in the kitchen, loving in the dark.

The tenderness, the passion.

The way he loves me with his whole heart.

Loved.

The air leaves my lungs.

"I have to say." Lombardi smirks. "That was easier than I anticipated." He shrugs. "Weak. Carlo will make a much better leader."

No.

This can't be happening.

Automatic guns sound from outside and the windows smash, everyone dives to the floor. A piece of the broken glass flies at speed and hits my upper arm and my chair is knocked over to its side, I fall heavily onto the floor.

"Oww." I screw up my face in pain. To the sound of crazed gunfire, I feel something warm under my face and drag my eyes open to see that it's a puddle of blood. The cut in my arm is deep...I feel the pulse in my shoulder as I bleed.

Giuliano's beautiful face comes into my mind and my heart hurts.

He can't be gone...no, I can't do this. I can't live in a world without him.

Did he suffer?

Tears roll down my face and drip to the floor, heartbreak and blood blend together to make a red river of devastation.

I hope I die.

Would they bury us together?

The guns fall silent, and in the distance, I hear a man cry, "He's down."

Giuliano

His face falls. "What are you doing?"

I click the trigger as I pull it back. "Where the fuck is she?" I growl.

"I don't know, I just woke up. I swear," he stammers. "It's me...Giuliano."

"What are you doing?" Alex snaps. "Giuliano, stop it."

"Take his guns and his phone," I demand.

Valentino leans down and takes his gun from his pocket.

"And the other ones," I say.

He pats him down and finds another gun strapped to his shin, along with a large knife.

Val's brow furrows and his eyes meet mine.

"Get him up," I demand as I snatch his phone from Val. "Take him down to the car." I begin to walk off.

"What are you doing?" Carlo cries. "I don't know what's happening, one minute I'm skiing, the next I wake up on a mountain."

Something snaps deep inside of me, and I march back and grab Carlo by the throat. "One person was dragged to that helicopter. One," I cry as I stare at his lying face. My nostrils flare as I struggle for control, I've never wanted to kill someone so bad in all my life. "And the person who dragged her there had a size fourteen foot."

His face drops and I know that I'm right.

"It was you!"

"It wasn't...I swear."

"Liar," I scream in his face. "They had inside information, what country we were in, what ski lodge we were at, what mountain she was on." I step back from him, disgust filling my every cell.

"You've got the wrong man."

"Tie him up and put him in the trunk of my car."

"This wasn't me!" he cries. "Come on, Giuliano. You're my best friend."

"She'd better be alive...." I turn and march off.

"Or what?" he calls from behind me.

I turn, adrenaline surging through my bloodstream,

Val puts his hand over my chest to hold me back, knowing I'm about to lose my living shit and kill him right here, right now.

"Or...your death is not only imminent...I'm going to cut you up alive."

Our eyes are locked.

"Tie him up." I reach into my jacket and pass over a bag of cable ties.

I've come prepared.

Val takes them and ties his hands and feet together and they load him onto the back of the skimobile, we drive down the mountain in silence.

We haven't had a close friend betray us before. This is new territory, another level of fucked up.

"Take him to the main road on the ski, Val and I will pick him up in the car. We can't transfer him here, someone will see."

They keep driving down the hill and Val and I go up to the room and grab the keys to the car and go down into the basement parking lot, Val gets into the driver seat and we pull out, it's snowing again.

We drive in silence.

"Are you sure about this?" he mutters.

"Yep."

His eyes flick over to me. "What if you've got it wrong?"

"I haven't." I dig Carlo's phone out of my pocket and turn it on, I punch in his passcode.

Val frowns as he watches. "You know his code?"

"I'm with him every day, of course I see what his passcode is."

"Do you know mine?"

"Eleven sixty- five."

Val smirks. "Not bad."

I go through his messages until I get to the last one sent.

Bring the chopper,
she'll be on top of the mountain in thirty minutes.
Three guards tops

I close my eyes, the blinding betrayal hurting more than it should.

Val's eyes flick between me and the road. "What does it say?"

I read it out. "Bring the chopper, she'll be on top of the mountain in thirty minutes. Three guards tops."

"Fuck." Val runs his hand through his hair and then snaps and punches the steering wheel with force.

We see the skimobile on the side of the road and we pull over, I pop the trunk and they throw him in. Val goes behind the car and I hear him connect some punches as he loses control.

He gets back in the car and I pull out in silence, Val open and closes his hand as he tries to get some feeling back into it.

We drive in silence for a few minutes. "What now?" Val sighs.

"I'm going through the call register now." I go through

the calls made and incoming and one number keeps coming up.

I call my men who are already trying to track Francesca's phone from the tower.

"Hey, boss. Her phone is still not showing up anywhere."

"Run this number for me."

"Okay."

I read out the number.

"Give me ten."

"Okay." I hang up and look over to Val.

"Now what?"

"We wait." I pull the car over to the side of the road in a parking bay and we sit in silence.

The snow floats down onto the car.

"You alright?" I ask.

"It's my fault she's dead."

I roll my lips, choosing to remain silent.

"I told her she was safe with me."

"We thought she was."

His nostrils flare as if grappling for control. "Her mother when I told her...."

Hell.

My phone rings and I answer, "Yes."

"We've got a match; the phone is sixty kilometers from where you are now. I'll send the coordinates."

Thank fuck.

Adrenaline surges through me; Francesca's life depends on us getting this right. "Thanks." I hear a text arrive with a ping.

"Giuliano..." he says, "Good luck, hey."

I immediately call Leon. "We've got an address, bring the guards and ammunition."

"On our way." I hang up and look over to Val. "We can't fuck this up."

"We won't." He pulls out onto the road and a bang sounds from the trunk as Carlo tries to kick himself free.

"I will be fucking him up, though," he mutters dryly.

"Get in line."

29

Francesca

I LISTEN...SILENCE.

Lombardi coughs as he lies on the floor and struggles to get his pills from his pocket and suddenly I'm furious.

How dare he do this to us?

More silence.

What's happening out there?

The door bangs open and although my view is distorted, I see someone being dragged inside by two men.

"Get your fucking hands off me," he growls as he struggles. "Francesca. Get her up," he cries. "She's injured."

I know that voice, I've missed that voice.

Enrico.

He *is* alive....

"Let her go," he yells. "It's me that you want. Let her fucking go."

Whack! I see a boot connect at full force to his stomach as somebody kicks him.

I hear the air knocked from his lungs as he moans.

No.

Has he really been bought back from the dead so that I can witness his murder all over again?

Help. Help.

Somebody...help him.

I lift my head to see that he's been shot in the leg, they drag him up and prop him against the wall while they tie his hands.

What do I do?

His eyes meet mine and he gives me a soft smile and my heart breaks.

No...not you too.

Giuliano

We pull off the main road while we wait for the others, I dial Leon's number. "Where are you?"

"Just driving in now."

"Okay." My heart races and this is it. The pivotal moment where I find out if my forward planning was worth it.

"I've got the house in view," he says.

I close my eyes.

"Something's already gone down here," he says.

"What do you mean?"

"There are bodies everywhere. I'll put you on speaker."

Val's and my eyes meet as my heart hammers hard in my chest, I hold my breath as I listen.

Are we too late?

The car door slams and I hear Leon walking. "Is she still alive?" he says. "What the hell has gone on here?"

"We just bagged Enrico," a man's voice replies.

My eyes widen.... *Enrico?*

What the fuck? I start the car.

No word if she's alive.

"Pop the trunk," Val growls.

"Not now."

"Pop the fucking trunk," he cries furiously and I know that he needs to do this now...while he still can.

I pop the trunk, he gets out and goes to the back, I hear two gunshots through the silencer.

He gets back into the car and slams the door hard.

"Now," Leon whispers through the phone. "Get here now."

Francesca

"Get her up," Lombardi says.

Two men sit my chair up and the horrific scene comes into full view.

Enrico is disheveled and bleeding from a gunshot wound to his thigh, he's been fighting, his hair is wild, his face banged up. He's propped up against the wall with his hands tied in front of him.

"Time to pay," Lombardi says.

Enrico glares at him, emotionless.

"You killed Lucky, my son. You wrote your own fate." Lombardi paces back and forth as if he's practiced this sermon many a time in his head. "And what would cause you the most pain, Enrico?" He runs his fingers through his stubble as if thinking. "Killing you quickly is not an option...you need to suffer the pain like I have."

Enrico glares at him, remaining silent.

He gestures to me. "Watching your beloved sister be tortured to death...now, that would be something though." He smiles. "Wouldn't it?"

Dear God.

Enrico's eyes meet mine and for the first time, I see fear. "Kill me. Take my life, she is a good person, she doesn't deserve to die. I do."

"No deal," Lombardi growls.

The door opens and we all turn, startled.

"Leon." Lombardi frowns. "What are you doing here?"

"Carlo sent me. There's a car of men, three kilometers down the track. He wanted me to warn you."

Lombardi's eyes widen and he turns to the other three men in the cabin. "Go check it out."

The men all leave and two minutes later, automatic gunfire rings out.

"What's happening?" Lombardi whispers.

Leon puts a gun to Lombardi's head and clicks the trigger back.

"What are you doing?" he cries.

The door bangs open and Giuliano appears, his eyes are dark and wild.

He's here.

"Stop underestimating me."

Lombardi's face falls as he connects the dots.

"You're not the only one who thought ahead. Do you really think I wouldn't have a mole close to you?" Giuliano smiles as he raises his gun. "Your time has come."

I close my eyes and a gunshot rings out, Lombardi falls to the floor. I open them to see Giuliano standing over him, he pulls the trigger again and again, and I screw up my face to block out the horror; I know that it was his life or mine but it's so brutal and way too real.

Then I feel myself being untied and Giuliano takes his shirt off and ties it around my arm, he lifts me into his big strong arms. "Are you alright, baby?" he says softly.

I really don't think I am but I nod through tears.

He's alive.

"Come on, let's get you to the hospital." He begins to carry me to the door.

"What about me?" Enrico says.

Giuliano stops and glares at him. "You can rot in hell for all I care."

Enrico's eyes search his.

"Get him to the car," Valentino growls, he wraps a cloth around his leg to act as a bandage to stop the bleeding.

Leon and Val lift Enrico and Giuliano carries me out to the waiting car and his step falters, what's wrong? I glance up to see the trunk is open.

"Where is he?" Val snaps as he looks out into the forest. "He was fucking dead, I made sure of it."

Giuliano looks around at the surrounding forest. "I don't know."

My face falls, there are bodies everywhere. The forest is eerily still and deathly quiet.

Giuliano carefully places me in and climbs into the back seat alongside of me. "Worry about him later, just get us to a hospital."

The boys lift Enrico into the front seat and he winces. Giuliano reaches over and punches him in the back of the shoulder. "What the fuck where you thinking going in there alone? I should kill you myself for being so fucking stupid."

Val starts it with an urgent rev of the engine and takes off fast. "Let's get the fuck out of here."

We drive up the track at speed and I can feel the panic coming out of Valentino as he looks around in the darkness.

"Where the fuck is he?" he cries as he punches the steering wheel.

"Calm down. He's injured, he's going to be in hiding," Giuliano says as he wraps his coat around my shoulders. He leans in and kisses my temple. "Thank God," he whispers as he holds me tight. "I thought I lost you." He screws up his face in tears as he holds me. "Thank you. Thank you." He kisses my face all over. "We'll get you to the hospital. Hold on baby," he whispers. "It's okay now, I'm here."

"There's no blood," Val mutters under his breath as if thinking out loud.

"What do you mean?" Giuliano asks.

"There's no fucking blood in the trunk," he cries.

"Where did you shoot him?"

My eyes widen, dear God. Valentino shot Carlo and he didn't die.

Where *is* he?

Now the panic is making sense, I begin to look around at the forest as it flies by too.

What if he's coming back?

"In the chest."

"Fuck," Giuliano mutters. "He was wearing a vest. Why wouldn't you check that?"

Valentino punches the steering wheel again and again as he completely loses his shit. "This is just the fucking beginning," he cries. "He will come back again and again."

"Just drive the fucking car," Giuliano screams. He takes out his phone and dials a number. "We've got her."

"They've got her," I hear Lorenzo scream, I hear cheers in the background.

"We've got Enrico too. He's shot, we're on our way to hospital. Listen to me and listen carefully," he says in a rush. "Carlo is the new head of Lombardi."

"What?"

I can hear every word they are saying.

"Just as you heard me. Carlo is the mole. Carlo is the one who organized this. You need to get on the computer and change every fucking password. He has had access to everything for a long, long time."

"Dear God," I hear Lorenzo whisper. "Carlo?"

The car takes the corner at speed and we slide to the left. "Ahhhh," I cry.

"Slow the fuck down," Enrico growls as he grips the dashboard.

"What's happening?" I hear Anna say. "Is Carlo alright?"

Giuliano's and my eyes meet and my heart constricts.

Poor Anna.

"Change the security codes to every Ferrara building and put a public ten-million- dollar bounty on his head."

Enrico looks over to the back seat. "Twenty million."

"Twenty million," Giuliano snaps. "Did you hear me? Twenty-million-dollar bounty to whoever kills him, Lombardi's men and all."

"Yes, yes," Lorenzo stammers. "Is Francesca alright?"

I take the phone from him. "Dad?"

"Oh, dear God." He sobs.

I get a lump in my throat, hearing his voice brings me to my knees, I thought I was never going to hear it again. I didn't realize how much I loved him until I thought it was too late.

"Francesca...are you alright, my darling?" Lorenzo asks.

"I am." I smile up at my beautiful protector as he stares down at me. "Giuliano saved me."

"What about me?" Enrico says from the front, half joking.

Giuliano reaches forward and punches his shoulder again. "You got shot, you dumb fuck."

Val begins to feel under the dash as he drives.

"What are you doing?" Enrico barks as his eyes flick between him and the track. "Concentrate on the road."

Val keeps going and then reaches over and feels some more. "Son of a fucking bitch," he cries as he pulls something out and holds it in his hands. It's black and small.

The car falls deathly silent.

"What is it?" I stammer as I look between them. "What's wrong?"

Valentino holds it to his mouth. "You listen here, Carlo Bernetti," he growls. "I'm going to tear you limb from fucking limb!" he screams. "Do you hear me!" he's completely losing control.

My eyes widen.

A bug.

Valentino opens the car window and hurls the bug out into the snow.

Giuliano puffs air into his cheeks, he's completely rattled.

"What's happening?" Lorenzo's voice snaps through the phone.

"There was a bug in the car," Giuliano snarls through gritted teeth. "Sweep everything, he's listening to every fucking thing we say."

"Dear God," I hear Lorenzo whisper again. "But how...."

"Trust nobody!" Giuliano screams. "There are bugs...probably in every fucking office we own. We have no idea who is on his payroll."

Ferrara

"Fuck..." Enrico mutters under his breath in the front seat.

Val drags his hand through his hair in frustration.

God...this isn't over.

We arrive out on to the main road, Val slows and then pulls out. The road is tar here and the car falls silent.

Giuliano wraps his jacket around me and holds me close, he kisses my temple as he stares out the window.

But he's not here in the moment with me.

He's plotting Carlo's death.

———

Giuliano sits at the side of my hospital bed, holding my hand in his, he's quiet and pensive, he hasn't left my side for even a moment.

I've been kept in overnight for a concussion from when I hit my head on the rock and was knocked unconscious.

I drag open my heavy eyelids and he smiles softly as he brushes the hair back from my forehead. "There she is," he whispers.

I frown, was that all a nightmare?

A collage of horror images filling my memory bank. "Giovanna?"

He leans down and kisses my forehead softly.

"Where is she?"

He gives a subtle shake of his head. "I'm sorry, baby."

What?

"She's...." My voice cracks.

"Yes."

Then I remember who's responsible and I go to sit up onto my elbows. "Where's Anna?" I stammer as I look around. "He said he was going to come back for her."

"In a safe place." He kisses my forehead.

"But...."

"But nothing." He lays me down and brushes the hair back from my forehead. "Anna has returned home to Milan with Val last night after we got you safely to the hospital. Valentino had to get Giovanna's body home to her parents. Bruno home to his family too."

I get a vision of Giovanna and Bruno being loaded onto the plane in coffins and my eyes well with tears.

"It's okay, you're safe now," he says.

I glance out the window in the door and see men standing guard in the corridor.

"Where's Enrico?" I ask.

"He had surgery last night and is recovering downstairs in the orthopedic ward."

"So...he's okay?"

"For now." He raises his eyebrow as if unimpressed.

"What does that mean?" I frown.

"I haven't had a chance to kill him yet," he mutters dryly.

"Oh." I smile softly. "Remember when he threw you down the stairs at the library?"

"How could I ever forget?"

I run my fingers through his stubble. "I love you, thank you for saving me."

He smiles as he leans over me and we stare at each other, there's just so much love between us. It's a palpable energy in the room.

Knock, knock sounds on the door and a doctor appears, he's in his fifties with gray hair, and kind looking. "Miss Ferrara." He smiles. "I'm Dr. Schwartz."

"Hello."

Giuliano stands back. "Hello." He nods politely.

"You've had quite the dramatic night," he says as he looks into my eyes with a torch.

"Yes."

He takes my vitals. "Good news. You are a very lucky young lady, Francesca. Everything is progressing just as it should be and the concussion can be managed from home from here on in. The stitches in your arm are looking good. You are free to go home."

I smile. "Thanks."

"I want you to check in with your doctor in a few days to have your scans assessed and the stitches will need to come out in two to three weeks, depending on how well it's healing."

"Okay." I smile, acting brave. From deep inside a frisson of fear runs through me.

What if Carlo is there waiting for us?

Stop it.

What if more of our men have defected and are waiting for the first opportunity to strike?

I feel so unsure of everything and everyone with no idea who to longer trust.

This is exactly what Carlo would want.

Stop it.

As if reading my mind, Giuliano gives me a reassuring smile and takes my hand in his and I know that he's right.

We can't let them win. Our fear is their victory.

"Thank you," I tell the doctor, determined to get on with it. "Can I leave now?"

"Yes." He smiles. "Of course."

"My brother...."

"Enrico is down on level three, his operation was successful and he is recovering well, he will be in hospital here for a while longer though. You may visit him before you leave if you want."

"Thank you."

The doctor heads toward the door and Giuliano takes my hand and begins to help me up. "Francesca," the doctor says.

I look up to him.

"Be careful out there, hey?"

I nod. "I will."

Giuliano's and my eyes meet, shivers run down my spine, the doctor thinks we are still in danger too.

"Let's go home, baby," Giuliano says, his voice is soft and cajoling, the one he saves only for me. He pulls me up and helps me dress in the clothes he's brought for me.

He opens my panties up and, with my hands on his shoulders, I step into them and he carefully pulls them up. He pulls my pants on and then my sweater over my head and gently straightens it out. Then he takes the hairbrush. "Turn around." I turn away from him and he takes his time as he gently brushes my hair.

My heart constricts and my eyes fill with tears. "Thank you."

"For what?"

"For loving me the way you do."

He turns me in his arms and kisses me tenderly. "Promise me you'll never leave me."

I nod, emotion stealing my words, and he pulls me into his arms and we hold each other tightly. Just how close we came to never seeing each other again has traumatized the both of us.

"Promise me you won't die," he murmurs into my hair. "That we will die together."

I smile up at my beautiful man. "We're not dying, Jules."

His eyes hold mine and I realize that it's him who needs reassuring, I can't imagine how traumatic this has been for him.

"I want a baby."

He frowns in surprise. "What?"

"When I was in that cabin, all I could think about was that we didn't get our baby yet. That there was more to our story than just the two of us."

"Francesca." He sighs as he pulls away from me. "That is the very last thing on my mind right now."

"Why?"

"I just want to focus on keeping you safe, that's all. We are nowhere near starting a family. I'm not even discussing this until things have died down."

"Oh...." Disappointment runs through me and I shrug, feeling embarrassed that we are on totally different pages.

"Hey." He puts his finger under my chin and lifts my face to his. "Just because now isn't the time, doesn't mean that I don't want that too."

If he dies, I'll never get his baby. If I die, he'll never get mine.

I get a lump in my throat as I stare up at him.

"It's okay," he whispers. "We have time."

"Do we, though?"

He smiles softly. "We do. And besides, we have to get married first. Let's just get through that first, hey?"

I roll my eyes. "Who cares about a piece of paper?"

"I do." He kisses me softly; his lips linger over mine. "You are the love of my life, Francesca. I need you as my wife." He kisses me again. "Anything after that is just a bonus."

My heart swells.

And there it is, the reason. He makes complicated things simple.

I smile up at him, without a doubt I know my place in the world. I am the most important thing in his life.

I just love the way he loves me...and it makes me love him that bit harder.

Giuliano

We walk down the corridor on level three, we get to Enrico's room. "I'll just wait outside."

Francesca's face falls. "What? You don't want to see him?"

Not really.

"You have to come and visit, he saved my life."

I raise my eyebrow.

"Well...he didn't actually save my life, you saved our lives," she corrects herself. "But he did risk his for me. I think you at least owe him civility." She takes my hand in hers. "He's my brother, Giuliano. Please...for me?"

I exhale, she's right. "Yeah, okay."

She knocks quietly.

"Come in," he calls.

She opens the door and peers in, his leg is all bandaged and he is sitting up in bed. He smiles broadly and holds his arms out for her and she rushes to him as she half laughs and half cries.

They hug each other in a long-lost greeting and it's all I can do not to roll my eyes as I hang back.

"You're alive." She smiles down at him.

"I am." He holds her hands in his. "Look how beautiful you turned out to be." He pulls her close and hugs her again. "I've missed you so much."

"And Olivia?" she asks.

"Is alive and well, we have five children."

"Five." She gasps. "Oh my gosh, you must be so busy." She laughs as she sits on the bed beside him.

What else is there to do on an island but reproduce?

I bite my bottom lip to hold my snarky tongue.

Enrico's eyes find mine at the bottom of the bed and he gives me the first genuine smile I've ever seen from him. "Giuliano."

I nod.

"Thank you."

I nod again, I get a vision of myself walking over and punching him until I knock the fucker clean out.

Knock, knock sounds at the door.

"Come in," he calls.

Bianca puts her head around the corner. "Room for one more?" She smiles.

No actually…there isn't.

Fuck off.

Great, this is the visit from hell.

Stop it.

This is Francesca's family. Be nice…for her. Hold your tongue and get the fuck out of here.

Bianca goos and gushes. "My two children together again." She kisses them both. "I've been so terrified. I could have lost you both."

I clench my jaw. Fuck, I hate this woman.

She turns to me. "Giuliano."

I stare at her blankly.

"Thank you, my dear boy, you saved them both."

Francesca raises her eyebrow as a warning and I fake a smile. "Glad things worked out."

A nurse comes into the room. "Francesca?"

"Yes," she replies.

"You didn't sign the discharge forms, can you come down to the office now and do it."

"Oh sure."

"I'll come," I offer.

"No, no." Francesca smiles. "You stay here, I'll be right back."

I poke my head out the door to the guards. "Go with her, please."

"Sure thing." They follow Francesca and the nurse down the corridor and I go back into the room.

Great.

Enrico and Bianca both smile over at me.

I roll my eyes. "Oh please, fuck off, you two. You can cut the act now, she's gone."

"Whatever do you mean?" Bianca acts shocked.

"Stop pretending to like me, you only wanted me to run the company so that darling little Enrico didn't have to come out of hiding."

Enrico chuckles, clearly amused.

"And don't you laugh, prick, you're a fucking coward. Thanks very much for leaving a nineteen-year-old kid to take over the company and clean up your mess. If I knew you were still alive I would have found you and killed you myself."

"I didn't run."

"Yes, you fucking did," I snap. "You're a coward."

"Olivia was pregnant, I wasn't going to risk her and our child's life for a company I didn't even want."

"So, you risked Francesca's instead. Nice brother you are."

"When Francesca falls pregnant, you will understand why I did what I did."

I already understand. Not that I'll ever admit it.

"I admire you, Giuliano." Bianca smiles. "You stand by

your beliefs and I meant what I said. You are the best person for this job."

I roll my eyes. "Let's get this straight, Bianca, I tolerate you for Francesca's sake only. You piss me off and we are not friends."

She smiles. "Not yet."

I turn to Enrico. "Move your family home, you're not going anywhere until Carlo is caught."

He frowns. "I don't want a part of this business."

"Oh, don't worry, you're not fucking getting it."

"Then what do you need me for?" he snaps.

"Protect your sister for me. I can't do it all. When I get Carlo you can go, until then I'm not giving you a choice."

"And if I choose to leave?"

"Then I will kill you myself."

"Giuliano," Bianca gasps. "You wouldn't."

"Try me."

Enrico smiles, seemingly impressed.

We stare at each other while he contemplates his answer.

"Last chance," I snap.

"Alright, I'll stay. But only until he is caught."

The door opens back up and Francesca appears, she smiles broadly at me and my heart somersaults in my chest. "Ready to go?" I ask her.

Her eyes flick to Enrico.

"I'll see you back in Milan?" he asks her.

"You're staying?" She gasps.

He nods. "Olivia and the children will be coming home too."

"Oh," Francesca cries in excitement as she pulls him into a hug. "I can't wait to see Olivia and meet the children. It's a dream come true."

Oh please....

I roll my eyes and Bianca flicks me on the leg. "Stop it," she whispers.

I flick her back. "You stop it."

She smiles over at me and I nearly smile back.

Nearly.

Francesca

We sit in the airport private lounge waiting to board our plane.

My mother and Lorenzo and our guards are with us, they are sitting by the bar.

Lorenzo is on his laptop and he stands and walks over. "Look at this."

He passes his laptop to Giuliano and we both concentrate to try to make out the footage.

"It's security footage from an airport in Belgium." he says.

We watch as a man in a black cap boards a plane alone.

"Got him," Giuliano whispers darkly.

I look harder to see that it's Carlo. "Where is he going?"

"New York."

Giuliano frowns. "New York?" He thinks for a moment. "Get a team to New York immediately."

"On it." Lorenzo walks back over to the bar and my mind is racing a million miles per minute. I really need to speak to Anna.

"I'm just going to call Anna," I say.

Giuliano nods. "Do you want a drink?"

"Yes, please."

He gets up and walks to the bar and I dial Anna's number.

"Chesk," she answers, I can tell she's been crying. "Are you okay?"

My heart sinks hearing how sad she sounds. "I am. Are you?"

"Did he really do this?" she whispers.

My eyes well with tears. "Yes," I whisper sadly.

"I don't understand how…how is this possible? Carlo is a good man, I know he is. I just…." She cuts herself off before she says anything else.

"Babe." I sigh sadly. "Carlo is gone, he was spotted in a Belgium airport leaving for the United States."

"What?"

"Honey…I wish this wasn't true, but Carlo is…."

"He's what?" She cuts me off.

"He's bad, Anna. He isn't who we thought he was at all. You need to forget that you ever met him."

She sniffs loudly and I know that she's crying. She's been betrayed more than anyone, she loved him.

The stewardess announces our plane is ready for boarding.

"We're boarding our plane; I'll call you tomorrow?"

"Thank God you're okay, that was the most horrific twenty-four hours of my life," she stammers through tears.

"I know, mine too."

"I love you," she whispers.

"I love you too."

I stand back as Giuliano opens the door to my apartment, it's late at night and after the longest day in history and the never-ending flight, we can't even go to our home in Lake Como until it is combed for bugs and security risks. Carlo was at the property just last week and who knows what he planted.

Giuliano pushes the door open and stands back and I peer inside and hesitate.

"It's okay, sweetheart," Giuliano murmurs as he puts his arm around me and pulls me close. "Everything has been triple-checked."

I nod, feeling silly. "I'm just...."

"I know." He kisses my temple. "You've been through a lot, you have good reason to be unsettled."

"Are you unsettled?" I ask.

"No."

My eyes search his. "Are you telling me the truth?"

He takes my hand and leads me into the apartment. "Now that I know what we're up against, I'm honestly not." He puts our bags down and leads me up the hall.

"Why is that?"

"Because...." He pauses as if choosing his words correctly. "I know I can take Carlo."

I frown, "What makes you so sure?"

"He has his weaknesses, and...." He shrugs as we walk into our bedroom as if not wanting to elaborate.

"Like what?"

He turns me toward him. "I am not talking about Carlo anymore. It is over, he is on the run...and in a matter of days his time will be up. It is he who is running scared now. He knows what's coming for him. His grand plan failed." He walks into the bathroom and turns the shower on and then lifts my shirt over my head. "Shower and bed, you look exhausted." He undoes my jeans and slides them down, he sees a dark bruise on my thigh and he frowns, he traces it with his finger. "What happened here?"

I stare down at the dark black bruise. "I don't know." I

shrug. "It must have been when I fell and hit my head and blacked out."

"How long were you unconscious?" His eyes roam up and down my body as he searches for more injuries.

"I don't know. When I woke up I was in the cabin."

His eyes rise to meet mine. "Was there any sign you were... tampered with?"

"You mean...sexually? No. God no, it was nothing like that. I would know if something had happened, definitely not."

He exhales as if relieved. "Good."

My God, does he really think that could have happened?

He undoes my bra and slides down my panties. "In the shower, babe."

"You getting in with me?"

He frowns as if conflicted. "I'll just wash you from out here."

"Why won't you get in with me?"

"I'm just—" he pauses, "—feeling overemotional and...." He cuts himself off. "You are not up to it and if I get in it will start and I just want you to rest."

He thinks I'm not up to sex.

I smile at my beautiful man and push him backward into the shower clothes and all. "Get in the fucking shower." I lean up onto my toes and kiss him, my tongue slides through his open lips. "I need you."

He frowns against my lips. "Chesk...."

I run my hand over his crotch and feel him harden under my touch. "I'm fine."

Our kiss deepens and suddenly I'm desperate to have him, I tear his shirt over his shoulders and pull his pants down, his thick hard cock springs free.

"Scopami." (Translation: Fuck me.)

His dark eyes hold mine and he slowly slides his hand down my body and in between my legs. "Vuoi questo uccello?" (Translation: You want this cock?)

"Si." (translation: Yes.)

He slides his fingers through my flesh, I'm dripping wet.

I need this more than anything, I want to feel normal. Us having rough sex is exactly what I need to bring me back down to earth...and he knows it.

He needs it too.

With our eyes locked he parts my lips and rubs over my clitoris softly; I shudder in approval and he smirks. "Si, cosi, Tesoro. Brva regazza." (Translation: That's it, baby. Good girl.) He slides three thick fingers deep into my body.

"Oh..." I moan into his mouth.

He pulls back to watch me, his fingers slowly fucking me hard. "Sei cosi bagnata, cazzo." (Translation: You are so fucking creamy.)

He jerks his hand hard and I grip his forearm as I ride his thick fingers, I can feel the muscles contract in his arm as he uses them with force.

Suddenly we're desperate for it, our kisses are hard and passionate. His fingers fucking me at piston pace, deep and hard.

Just how I need it.

He lifts my leg and rests my knee up against his chest, completely opening me up for him.

His fingers hit that spot deep inside that only he has ever found. "Oh..." I moan, my eyes roll back in my head.

Fuck he's so good at this.

"Mi prosciugherai fino all' ultima goccia, piccola?" (Translation: You going to milk my cock, baby?) His teeth take my neck, and he bites down, goose bumps scatter all over and I know that he's close to the edge of control.

So am I.

Damn it, I love him when he's overemotional.

"Si." I smile against his lips. "Ne ho un bisogno disperato, cazzo. Aiutami a dimenticare." (Translation: I need it so fucking hard. Make me forget.)

Without another word he lifts me and wraps my legs around his waist, his thick cock slides in deep and we both stare at each other in awe.

"Siamo perfetti insieme," (Translation: The perfect fit.) I whisper.

"Il nostro amore e perfetto," (Translation: The perfect love.) he whispers back.

"Ti amo." (Translation: I love you.)

"Per sempre." (Translation: Forever.)

One month later.

The limousine pulls up out the front of the Milan Cathedral.

"This is it." Lorenzo smiles over at me and I grip his hand with excitement.

It's my wedding day.

Today I become his wife…in a church.

Anna and Olivia, my bridesmaids, are ushered out of their car in front and walk back to help me out of mine.

My dress is white, a tight bodice with a full skirt. My long dark hair is swept up underneath my full-length veil.

I wanted the fairy tale…and I got it.

Dress and all.

Lorenzo holds his arm out and I link mine through it, with

my nerves thumping hard in my chest, we take the steps and wait in the reception area of the church.

The traditional bridal song begins and Anna kisses my cheek with a big smile. "Ready to get married?"

I giggle. "Uh-huh."

She walks through the double doors and now it's Olivia's turn. She turns to me. "You look so beautiful, Chesk."

"Thanks."

She kisses my cheek and disappears too.

The double doors open, and I look up the aisle to see Giuliano standing at the end waiting for me.

He's wearing a black dinner suit and a white vest and cravat. His dark hair is just messed perfection.

He's breathtakingly handsome, Valentino and Alex, his groomsmen are by his side.

He turns toward me and our eyes meet, he gives me a slow sexy smile.

My world stops.

His eyes well with tears and with my love about to explode in my chest I want to run down the aisle to him as fast as I can.

This is it, the moment in time where we become one.

We walk down to the beat and with every step closer to him, I feel braver.

More myself.

Lorenzo kisses my cheek and turns and shakes Giuliano's hand and then places my hands in his.

"Thank you," Giuliano whispers.

Lorenzo breaks tradition and leans in and kisses him on each cheek too, the crowd give a little chuckle.

Giuliano turns and smiles over at me, the look in his eye could start a fire.

I know that look...*I live for that look.*

"We are gathered here today." The priest begins his sermon.

Giuliano's eyes darken.

I can hardly hear the words, they all sound jumbled. I'm too enamored with the beautiful man in front of me. Wearing his black suit and looking like he's about to bend me over the church pew in front of everyone.

"Repeat after me," the priest says.

Giuliano slides the gold band onto my finger. "With this ring, I thee wed."

I slide the gold band onto Giuliano's finger.

"Do you take this woman, to have and to hold, for richer, for poorer, in sickness and in health for as long as you both shall live?"

"I do." His eyes hold mine and he raises an eyebrow playfully.

I giggle.

"Do you take this man, to have and to hold, for richer, for poorer, in sickness and in health for as long as you both shall live?"

"I do."

A million memories from over the last ten years flash before my eyes. But most of all, the beautiful love between us.

I'd climb any mountain, fight any battle, do it all over again in an instant.

To get to this precise moment in time.

"I now pronounce you man and wife, you may kiss your bride."

Giuliano takes my face in his two hands and kisses me tenderly, his eyes close and he's completely lost in the moment as if we have all the time in the world.

And now we do.

THE END

Read on for an excerpt of *Valentino* and also for the first chapter of another amazing TL Swan book; *Play Along*

EXCERPT - VALENTINO

Anna

The rain pours down and I peer through the glass door at my office block.

I can see out on the road my car is waiting, along with the two bodyguards that accompany me everywhere now.

Francesca and Giuliano are on their honeymoon aboard a luxury superyacht. They've been gone for four weeks and boy, do I miss them.

My phone beeps a text and I frown when I see the name light up the screen.

Carlo

Can you talk?

Good God.

My heart speeds up, it's been eight weeks since everything

happened and I haven't heard from him once. I want to hear what he has to say.

Without hesitation, I walk back into my office and take the elevator back up to my floor and text back.

Yes

I'm alone.

My phone rings and with my heart in my throat I answer, "Hello."

"Anna," he whispers.

Emotion overwhelms me at the sound of his voice and I screw up my face in tears.

"What do you want?" I whisper.

"Don't cry."

Damn it, I hate that he can tell that he's upset me. I get a lump in my throat as I try to stay silent.

"I miss you." His voice is deep and hushed.

"Don't lie," I stammer.

"I'm telling you the truth. By the time we fell in love I was already too far in, I had to go through with it."

"No. You didn't," I cry as I lose control. "You should have walked away...for me. How could you kill Giovanna? How could you?"

"I didn't kill Giovanna," he snaps.

"Yes. you did."

"No. I didn't. I didn't kill anyone, I promise you. I held my gun up at them but someone else shot them from afar. I swear to you it wasn't me."

We fall silent.

"I never meant to hurt you."

"Well you did," I sob.

Excerpt - Valentino

So fucking much.

"I do the same job as Giuliano, he's no angel, Anna. Don't be fooled into thinking I'm the only bad guy in this picture. Trust me, if you knew what he was capable of."

I stay silent.

"You accept him, but you won't accept me?"

"You betrayed us," I cry.

"I never betrayed you. I love you."

I screw up my face, pain searing through my heart, I so badly want to believe him.

"Where are you?" I ask.

He stays silent this time.

"Are you hurt?"

"I'm okay."

"They're going to find you, Carlo. What then?"

"It was worth the risk.... I had to hear your voice."

I close my eyes, my attachment to him runs way deeper than I thought.

"I miss you," he whispers.

"Don't."

"Come with me."

"What?"

"I'll send for you."

"Come where, Carlo?" I whisper angrily. "To a life on the run? I have to go."

"Don't go," he stammers, almost panicked.

"Carlo."

"Anna...what happened with Giuliano is business. It has nothing to do with the way I feel about you."

"I can't...." I cut myself off.

"I'll call you tonight?" he says softly.

I stay silent, unable to push the word *no* past my lips.

Excerpt - Valentino

"Carlo, if they find out where you are...." I throw my hands up in despair. "You need to tell them that you didn't kill anyone. They think you shot Giovanna."

"I would never kill a woman, you know that."

"I'm going."

"I'll call you tonight."

I don't answer.

"I love you."

"Don't." I hang up, disgusted with myself for even taking the call.

I stare at my phone in my hands, what the fuck?

I take the elevator down to the ground floor and walk out and get into the waiting car.

The car pulls out into the rain and I stare out at the passing scenery in shock.

Did that just happen?

Fuck.

Why did I answer?

I should tell Giuliano...but then....

Twenty minutes later the car pulls up to my apartment. "Thank you." I fake a smile as I get out. I practically run into my building and take the elevator up to my apartment and I open the door in a rush and slam it behind me.

Fuck.

Fuck.

Fuck.

I pour myself a glass of wine so fast that it sloshes over the sides and I stand at the sink and drink it down.

They're going to kill him.

I fill my glass again and drain it once more.

A hard knock sounds at the door, my eyes widen.

Oh no...*is that him?*

Excerpt - Valentino

This day is a living nightmare.

I sneak to the door and peek through the peephole.

Valentino.

What's he doing here? I really don't have time for him right now, I'm in the middle of a freak-out. I open the door in a rush. "Hi."

"Hello."

I get the distinct feeling he has an agenda.

"What's wrong?"

His dark eyes hold mine. "Have you heard from Carlo?"

He knows.

"No."

"Don't lie to me, Anna."

Adrenaline surges through my system. "Are you spying on me?"

"Protecting you."

"Go to hell, Valentino. I don't need your protection." I go to slam the door in his face and he stops it with his hand and holds it open.

"I'm moving in."

"What?" I explode. "That's ridiculous."

His cold eyes hold mine. "If he wants you...he's got to get through me first."

Valentino
Coming soon.

EXCERPT - PLAY ALONG

Roshelle

In a world full of deceit and lies, who do you trust?

I stand alone in the corner of the nightclub, watching him take her in his arms before he kisses her.

The air evaporates from my lungs. I can't breathe.

Despair is pumping through my bloodstream, but for some sick self-destructive reason, I can't bring myself to look away. I have to see this—see what he is capable of and exactly how far this has gone.

The signs were there, I saw them. But like a fool I ignored them for as long as my gut instinct would allow.

I believed that he loved me. I believed that she loved me.

As I stand there and watch my boyfriend of two years kissing my best friend and roommate of five years, I realize I have never felt so betrayed on so many levels. I can't even begin to comprehend what I am witnessing.

The hairs on the back of my neck stand to attention. I feel

like I am having an out of body experience watching the horrific nightmare unfold.

This can't be happening.

My first inkling was two weeks ago. Melissa, my roommate, had a date with a guy she has been seeing for a few weeks and when he arrived to pick her up, Todd, my boyfriend, was really nasty to him. I watched him glare at her as she left, and I saw her practically run from the apartment just to get Todd away from that man.

Why?

Why wasn't he happy that she was dating? They had become friends and hell, had spent many nights alone in my apartment as he waited for me to get home from my nightshift. A sick thought had crossed my mind that night... was he jealous?

No, he couldn't be.

So, I thought I would test the theory. Over the following week I was overly affectionate towards Todd in front of Melissa, and every single time she went to bed early, acting happy even though I knew she was fuming inside. The catalyst came on Thursday night when I decided to call in sick for work and Todd and Melissa were both openly annoyed that I wasn't going in.

I had obviously ruined their plans of having sex, and that's when the deep sickening truth slayed me. Did they have sex in her bed or mine?

How often did my roommate satisfy my lover?

Unable to help myself, I put a tracking device app on Melissa's phone. I knew her password. Of course, I did. We shared everything.

Even a cock, it seemed.

On Friday she announced that she was going away for the

Excerpt - Play Along

weekend and Todd announced that he had a night away planned to somewhere else for work.

Coincidence? I didn't think so.

I knew they were meeting up and probably going to be fucking in a hotel room somewhere.

I took my time. I waited.

And now it's 11 p.m. on Saturday night and I'm in a different town, in a nightclub where I know nobody, witnessing my worst nightmare.

He can go. A leopard never changes his sickening spots... but why the fuck did he have to take her from me?

I watch them through unshed tears as my heart tries to escape my chest.

My best friend—the only constant in my life since my mother passed away five years ago. My father, an abusing control freak, left when I was a kid, and then when Mom died, I moved here for college and met Melissa. My life changed that day. Mel was happy, confident, and attractive.

More than I was... than I am.

I watch her grind herself against him while he looks down on her seductively as she dances. His hands are on her behind. He's smiling as he says something and then they laugh together, and I feel myself die a little inside.

They are not just fucking.

They have feelings for each other.

He kisses her again and his hands go to the back of her head to hold her exactly how he wants her. Their kiss is long, deep, and erotic.

Through blurred vision, I try to make myself look away. No.

I can't look away because I know when I leave this nightclub two of the most important people in my life will no longer

Excerpt - Play Along

be a part of it. The floor sways beneath me. How is this possible?

What have I done to deserve this betrayal?

I can't move.

He kisses her again and they fall back against a wall where he pins her and then they start to really go for it.

No. Stop it!

The tears burst the dam and I start to stride toward them as the adrenaline hits its crescendo. I need to stop them, stop everything.

Stop kissing her, you fucking asshole! Please, stop it!

But then I pause mid-step.

Don't do this. Don't lower yourself. Go home and move out. Don't give them a chance to deny or defend it.

I am better than this.

I stand for a moment and stare at the square pattern on the carpet beneath my feet. I'm dizzy and disorientated. I stay there for a while longer with my eyes firmly on the dirty treasons. He kisses her and lifts her thigh up to wrap around his, a move he always pulls on me.

Does he like to do her from behind, too?

That last thought snaps something deep inside. I don't remember getting over to them, but I push him in the back as he pins her to the wall, he falls forward and then looks around, his expression drops in horror. Before I know what I'm doing, I've punched him in the face.

Melissa's hands fly to her mouth. "Oh my God!" she gasps. "T-this isn't what it looks like," she stammers.

"You slut!" I scream, unable to control myself. I grab a drink from a man walking past and throw it in her face, following it up with a hard slap across her cheek. She staggers back in shock, her hand flying up to her smarting face.

Excerpt - Play Along

"Roshelle," Todd cries as he grabs my arm to try and control me. "Calm down." He pulls me away from Melissa, clearly scared that I am going to hit her again.

"I will not fucking calm down." I push out as the tears fall. I turn to him, and a myriad of emotions fill me, but it is his betrayal that steals my voice. I have so many things I want to say, so many things that have escaped my brain. My eyes search his and he tries to grab my hand.

"Don't touch me!" I yell as I whip my hand away from him. "Never again."

I turn to Melissa. "Get your things and get out of my house." I sneer.

"Roshelle," she whispers. "I'm so sorry." She shakes her head in disbelief. Suddenly the walls start closing in, and I know I have got to get out of here.

I have got to get away from this hurt.

I see an exit sign and make a beeline for it without looking back. I push out into the cold night air, the door slamming behind me.

"Shut the fuck up before I blow your fucking head off!" a man's voice yells.

"You don't have the fucking guts," someone else sneers in reply.

Huh?

I try to focus, despite my tears, and I angrily swipe them from my eyes. It's dark and there are people out here. I try to focus on the shadows in front of me, then I turn back and try to open the door I just came out of. It's locked and there is no handle on this side. It's clearly a fire door.

What? Where am I?

The tears are streaming down my face.

Excerpt - Play Along

A gunshot rings out and a man drops in front of me clutching his stomach. My eyes widen in horror as I grasp the situation I have just unknowingly stumbled upon.

What?

Suddenly, I'm surrounded by five men on all sides. I've interrupted some kind of deal.

Oh no.

"Who the fuck is she?" one man calls out.

I shake my head in a panic. "I didn't see anything, I swear." I push through the group of men and one of them grabs me by the arm. "I need me some clean ass tonight."

I try to rip my arm from his clutches, but he hits me hard across the face with his gun, the pain ringing through my head like a lightning bolt before I fall to the ground.

"Bring her with us," someone yells.

"No, we don't need that baggage. Leave her, she said she didn't see anything."

They continue arguing.

"Yeah, well, my cock needs new pussy. "Bring her." The shooter growls.

I feel my body being lifted and then thrown into the tight space of a car trunk. "No," I whisper. "No." My handbag falls to the ground and I see someone pick it up and throw it in the car.

The trunk lid slams with a thud.

I taste blood in my mouth as I lie in a semi-conscious state in the dark.

The pain from my head throbs. What has just happened?

I put my hands up in the darkness and feel the cold metal that encases me.

The reality of the situation rings true as the car starts to drive, and I hear them talking to each other in the backseats behind me. Everything is foggy and my head, it hurts so much. I

Excerpt - Play Along

feel something hot run through my hair. What is it? I put my hand up and feel a deep gash in my head, the dripping blood hot and sticky. What the fuck? Oh no. They will kill me.

With renewed purpose and splayed hands, I start to hit the roof in a panic.

They just killed someone. I need some new pussy.

His words run through my head. Oh my God, they are going to rape me before they kill me, all five of them.

I start to run my hands frantically over the metal that encases me. How do you get out of a car trunk? Is there a latch? "Help!" I scream. "Help me," I call out as I slam my open

hands on the roof. The car slows down. Shit! My eyes widen.

Is this it? I pant as I listen to their movements, and I hear the whirl of the traffic lights walk indicator. Now! I need to scream now. We are static, stuck in traffic.

I start to bang on the roof with force. "Help me!" I scream. I lift my legs and try to push the lid open, but fuck, it's so cramped in here. I bang frantically on the ceiling, and I feel around underneath me, grabbing the corner of the carpet. Tools. There will be tools under here. I half roll over and tear back the carpet and grab a metal toolbox. "Help me. I'm in the trunk. I'm being kidnapped. Heeeeeeelp!" I scream.

"Shut the fuck up or I'll come back there and shut you up,"
a male voice growls from inside the car.

My eyes widen. Oh, he sounds scary. I really begin to freak out. I have to get out of here. Now.

I struggle to open the toolbox in front of me in the dark, but eventually it flies open in a rush and a tire iron flings back, hitting me straight in the nose.

"Ah, fuck!" I scream.

Ouch, that fucking hurt. The impact brings tears to my eyes,

Excerpt - Play Along

and I clutch my face. Oh, crap, I think I broke my own nose. I grab the tire iron and hit it on the roof with all of my strength. The impact makes it ricochet back and hits me straight in the eyebrow.

"Ahh!" I scream again. I feel a hot trickle run down the side of my face. If they don't kill me, I am doing a good job of it myself here.

I keep banging the tire iron on the roof. This has got to be

gaining some kind of attention. "Help me," I yell. "Someone... call the police. Help."

The car speeds up and I am flung to the back of the trunk. The lights change, the car flies around the corner, and I go flying, sending the tools scattering throughout the trunk so they hit me. The driver turns a right like a maniac, and I slide and hit my head against the side.

"Fucking assholes," I scream, and I hear them all laugh inside the car. Then the vehicle flies around a left corner and I go sliding again. I can hear the tires screeching as the car races down the street.

I'm going to die. Oh God, I'm going to die. I try to grip onto the metal roof to stop myself from hitting the edge, but I can't, and as the car flies around the corner I crumple into the hard metal end of the trunk. The tools are flying around and hitting me. Shit. I feel around frantically for the tire iron again. I may need it, but I can't find it, and my hand feels around the carpeted floor.

Where are you? Where are you?

I bend and feel along the other end of the trunk and finally feel the cold hard metal. My heart is racing as the car races out of control. I need a plan, but what is the damn plan?

Think.

Excerpt - Play Along

I clutch the tire iron in my hand with white-knuckle force as I try to stop myself from flying around. Whoever opens the trunk is getting knocked out with this fucker. My thoughts cross to Oprah and her sound advice to never go to the second location. I don't remember much from Oprah, but I do know that she said never go to the second location if being kidnapped—fight like hell to escape because they are going to kill you as soon as you get there.

Oh God, this is great.

I'm already in the fucking car on the way to the second location. I begin to get mad, like, furious mad. How dare they? I've had a really fucking bad night and I'm not in the mood for this shit. After about twenty minutes and sixty attack plans, the car slows down and goes over speed bumps.

Where are we?

Adrenaline starts to pump through my blood.

Speed bumps are in parking lots... So that must mean we are in a deserted parking lot.

The car stops and the men go silent. I close my eyes, knowing this is it.

Holy shit.

My heart is hammering, and I grip the tire iron in one hand and the car jack in the other. If I'm going to die tonight, someone is coming with me. I wriggle around so my feet are facing the opening, and I pull them back towards my chest. I can hardly breathe, I'm so scared. I hold my weapons in my hand and wait. The car doors open and the whole car lifts as the men get out.

Where are we?

I hear them begin to talk as if I have been totally forgotten about and another sickening thought crosses my mind. What if they just leave me in here?

Excerpt - Play Along

What if I just die a slow death in the car from no water or food? Oh my God.

What do I do? What do I do?

I stay quiet for five minutes as I try to think until I can't stand it any longer.

Screw this. I am not dying alone in the trunk of a car in a deserted parking lot. I put my tire iron down next to me on the floor and I bang on the trunk lid. "Help me. Let me out," I call.

The men go silent.

"Just get her out and let her go," someone says.

"I will be having some fun first," another answers.

I can't understand what is said next, but they all laugh out loud and I grip the tire iron in my hand.

Assholes.

I pull my legs back, and as the trunk is opened, I kick out with all my might and connect my feet with a man's face, knocking him to the ground. I jump out of the trunk and one man comes at me. I swing the tire iron as violently as I can and hit him hard in the head, watching as he falls away. The other men all laugh at their two friends on the ground. Another man comes at me, and I swing the car jack as hard as I can and cut his face open.

Then I run.

As fast as I can, I run across the cement. It's dark and we are in a parking lot that seems to be near the ocean. I can smell the sea and hear the seagulls. I run with two men chasing after me. I have no defense in these damn high-heeled shoes. They catch up with me easily and tackle me to the ground.

"Get off me," I scream as I fight and kick. One man hits me across the face, and they struggle to contain me as I wrestle to get out of their grip. They are too strong.

They drag me up from the ground, one on each arm, as I

Excerpt - Play Along

kick my legs out and wrestle to try and get away. They fight with me through the darkness, guiding me back to the car.

One man has his T-shirt off and is holding it up against his face to try and stop the bleeding from my car jack attack and the other two men watch.

One man is leaning on the car watching me intently. I glare at him, and he smirks back.

"Let me go!" I yell as I try to break the gorilla grip the two men have on me. I bend down and they struggle. I kick out again and connect with the man on my left, hitting his balls and he cries out and doubles over. The distraction lets me rip from the other man's grip and I punch him hard in the face. The man who I hit with the tire jack comes to their aid and helps them hold me down.

"You're coming with us, bitch."

"She's going to be fun to break in." The man on my left laughs.

"Fuck you!" I scream as I kick him in the balls again.

He doubles over in pain and the man leaning against the car laughs out loud.

My eyes glance over to him. He's tall, scary looking, and the other men all seem to be looking to him for guidance. He's calm and controlled, not like them. He's clearly the alpha of the group.

Their leader.

He smirks as he watches me and lights a cigarette as if thinking and shakes his head.

"I don't have time for this shit." He sighs.

I kick out and connect with the other man's shin, he cries out. "I'm going to fucking bash you in a minute, bitch." He growls. "What are we fucking doing with her?" he yells at the man leaning on the car. "She's out of fucking control."

Excerpt - Play Along

The tall man takes a drag of his cigarette, his eyes dropping to my feet before rising back up. He smirks darkly. "Bring her."

I shake my head and start to fight. "Like fuck you will," I scream as I kick out.

His eyes hold mine, and he smiles darkly and takes another drag of his cigarette. He licks his lips as his eyes drop to my breasts.

Fear runs through me. I start to go animalistic and fight like hell.

"Get the cloth," he says to the two the other man standing next to him. The guy disappears to the car and shuffles around as I fight and kick the two men on either side of me. He reappears with a black cloth and holds it over my face as I struggle with the two men who are holding me down.

"No." I scream as I try to move my head out of their reach. I can't get away from the black cloth that smells like chemicals.

I struggle.

I fight.

I feel faint.

I lose consciousness.

I wake as a wave of nausea rolls through my stomach, and I go to wipe the perspiration from my forehead. I can't move my arm.

Huh? I pull my arm, but it won't move, and I glance over my head to see it is tied to a post.

I struggle and look down at my body. Horror dawns on me. Oh my God.

I'm naked and tied to a bed by my hands.

Excerpt - Play Along

My eyes flicker nervously around the room as I try to focus. I see the tall man leaning up against a dresser in the corner, completely shirtless. He is looking through my wallet from my handbag.

What the fuck?

I start to struggle frantically. I have got to get out of here. I jiggle my whole body to try and loosen the ties. "What do you want?" I cry.

He ignores me and pulls my licence from my wallet. He holds it up and reads it.

"Roshelle Meyers," he murmurs. "Get out of my things," I snap.

He glances up and smirks, walking towards me before he kneels next to me on the bed. "I have already been in your..." He hesitates and runs his fingers through my open sex and then puts them into his mouth. "Things," he replies dryly, arching his brow.

My eyes close. Oh God. I don't remember.

Shame fills me.

"Let me go," I whisper as tears escape and roll down my cheeks.

His hand travels slowly up my torso. He cups my full breast and then bends and takes it in his mouth. "I like these," he whispers into my breast.

I screw up my face and shake my head. "Please... stop it. Please," I beg. "What do you want? Let me go. You have had your fun."

He bites my nipple hard, and I gasp in pain.

"I haven't started to have fun yet," he whispers coldly.

"Untie me. Please, untie me," I beg.

He shakes his head as he runs his fingers back toward my

Excerpt - Play Along

sex and slides them through my lubricated flesh. I'm wet. Have I had sex? "Did you...?" I hesitate.

His dark eyes dance with delight. "My tongue did."

My eyes widen in horror.

He bends and kisses my sex and I buck off the bed to try and get him off me.

"I couldn't help myself," he whispers. "A sweet-smelling pussy tied open for my gaze is something that I can't resist. You enjoyed it, by the way." He lies next to me on the bed and rests up on his elbow. He looks down at me as his hand slides back up my body to cup my breast. "Let's get one thing straight." He sneers.

I turn my head away so I don't have to look at him and he grabs my face and drags my eyes to meet his.

"I'm the boss here."

I glare at him.

"You do what I want, when I want." "Like fuck I do," I whisper angrily.

He smiles an evil smile. "If what I want is my cock splitting your virginal ass in two... then that's my call. Not fucking yours."

I swallow the fear in my throat as his cold eyes hold mine.

"Go to Hell," I whisper.

"I'm the gate keeper of Hell, baby. Welcome home."

532

Made in the USA
Columbia, SC
28 November 2022